"十三五"国家重点图书规划项目

天津市重点出版扶持项目

中国文化外译:典范化传播实践与研究

总主编　谢天振

再造的镜像

——阿瑟·韦利的中国古诗翻译

郑培凯　鄢秀　编著

南开大学出版社

天　津

图书在版编目(CIP)数据

再造的镜像：阿瑟·韦利的中国古诗翻译：汉英对照 / 郑培凯，鄢秀编著. —天津：南开大学出版社，2021.9

（中国文化外译：典范化传播实践与研究 / 谢天振总主编）

ISBN 978-7-310-06138-9

Ⅰ.①再… Ⅱ.①郑… ②鄢… Ⅲ.①古典诗歌－文学翻译－研究－中国－汉、英 Ⅳ.①I207.22②I046

中国版本图书馆 CIP 数据核字(2021)第 186732 号

再造的镜像——阿瑟·韦利的中国古诗翻译
ZAIZAO DE JINGXIANG—ASE WEILI DE ZHONGGUO GUSHI FANYI

南开大学出版社出版发行
出版人：陈　敬

地址：天津市南开区卫津路 94 号　　邮政编码：300071
营销部电话：(022)23508339　营销部传真：(022)23508542
https://nkup.nankai.edu.cn

天津市蓟县宏图印务有限公司印刷　全国各地新华书店经销
2021 年 9 月第 1 版　　2021 年 9 月第 1 次印刷
230×170 毫米　16 开本　36.75 印张　2 插页　665 千字
定价：182.00 元

如遇图书印装质量问题，请与本社营销部联系调换，电话：(022)23508339

总序

谢天振

一

中国文学、文化如何才能切实有效地走出去？随着中国经济实力的增强和国际地位的提升，这个问题被越来越多的人所关注，从国家领导人到普通百姓大众。追溯起来，中国人通过自己亲力亲为的翻译活动让中国文学、文化走出去的努力早已有之。不追溯得太远的话，可以举出被称为"东学西渐第一人"的陈季同，他在1884年出版的《中国人自画像》一书中即把我国唐代诗人李白、杜甫、孟浩然、白居易等人的诗翻译成了法文，他同年出版的另一本书《中国故事》则把《聊斋志异》中的一些故事译介给了法语读者。至于辜鸿铭在其所著的《春秋大义》中把儒家经典的一些片段翻译成英文，敬隐渔把《阿Q正传》翻译成法文，林语堂把中国文化译介给英语世界，等等，都为中国文学、文化走出去做出了各自的贡献。

当然，有意识、有组织、有规模地向世界译介中国文学和文化，那还是1949年以后的事。1949年中华人民共和国成立以后，我们需要向世界宣传中华人民共和国的情况，而文学作品的外译是一个很合适的宣传渠道。1951年，国家有关领导部门组织了一个专门的编辑、翻译、出版队伍，还陆续聘请了不少外国专家，创办了英文版的期刊《中国文学》（*Chinese Literature*）。该期刊自1958年起改为定期出版发行，最后发展成月刊，并同时推出了法文版（季刊）。《中国文学》前后共出版了590期，介绍中国古今作家和艺术家两千多人次，在相当长的时期里，它是我们向外译介中国文学的最主要的渠道。"文化大革命"期间勉力维持，1976年10月以后进入繁荣期；20世纪90年代再度式微，国外读者越来越少，于2000年最终停刊。

创办了半个世纪之久的英文、法文版《中国文学》最终不得不黯然停刊，令人不胜唏嘘，同时也引发我们的深省。研究者郑晔博士在她的博士论文《国家机构赞助下中国文学的对外译介——以英文版〈中国文学〉（1951—2000）

为个案》中总结了其中的经验教训，将其归纳为四条：一是译介主体的问题。郑博士认为像《中国文学》这样国家机构赞助下的译介行为必然受国家主流意识形态和诗学的制约，这是由赞助机制自身决定的。译本和编译人员只能在其允许的范围内做出有限的选择。这种机制既有优点，也有缺点。优点是政府有能力为刊物和专业人员提供资金保障，并保证刊物顺利出版发行。缺点是由于过多行政干预和指令性要求，出版社和译者缺乏自主性和能动性，刊物的内容和翻译容易带有保守色彩，逐渐对读者失去吸引力。二是用对外宣传的政策来指导文学译介并不合理，也达不到外宣的目的，最终反而导致译介行为的终止。三是只在源语（输出方）环境下考察译者和译作（指在《中国文学》上发表的译文）并不能说明其真正的翻译水平，也不能说明这个团队整体的翻译水平，必须通过接受方（译入语环境）的反馈才能发现在译入语环境下哪些译者的哪些译作能够被接受。四是政府垄断翻译文学的译介并不可取，应该允许更多译者生产更多不同风格、不同形式、不同题材的译本，通过各种渠道对外译介，由市场规律去淘汰不合格的译者和译本。①

　　"文化大革命"以后，在 20 世纪的八九十年代，我们国家在向外译介中国文学方面还有过一个引人注目的行为，那就是由著名翻译家杨宪益主持编辑、组织翻译和出版的"熊猫丛书"。这套"熊猫丛书"共翻译出版了 195 部文学作品，包括小说 145 部、诗歌 24 部、民间传说 14 部、散文 8 部、寓言 3 部、戏剧 1 部。但正如研究者所指出的，这套丛书同样"并未获得预期的效果。除个别译本获得英美读者的欢迎外，大部分译本并未在他们中间产生任何反响"。因此，"熊猫丛书"最后也难以为继，于 2007 年黯然收场。

　　"熊猫丛书"未能取得预期效果的原因，研究者耿强博士在他的博士论文《文学译介与中国文学"走向世界"——熊猫丛书英译中国文学研究》中总结为五点：一是缺乏清醒的文学译介意识。他质疑："完成了'合格的译本'之后，是否就意味着它一定能获得海外读者的阅读和欢迎？"二是"审查制度"对译介选材方面的限制和干扰。三是通过国家机构对外译介的这种模式，虽然可以投入巨大的人力、物力和财力，也能生产出高质量的译本，但却无法保证其传播的顺畅。四是翻译策略。他认为"要尽量采取归化策略及'跨文化阐释'的翻译方法，使译作阅读起来流畅自然，增加译本的可接受性，避免过于生硬和陌生化的文本"。五是对跨文化译介的阶段性性质认识不足，

---

　　① 有关《中国文学》译介中国文学的详细分析，可参阅上海外国语大学郑晔的博士论文《国家机构赞助下中国文学的对外译介——以英文版〈中国文学〉（1951—2000）为个案》。该论文经作者补充修改后也收录在本丛书中。

看不到目前中国当代文学的对外译介尚处于起步阶段这种性质。①

　　另一个更发人深省甚至让人不无震撼的个案，是杨宪益、戴乃迭夫妇合作翻译的《红楼梦》在英语世界的遭遇。我们都知道，杨译《红楼梦》在国内翻译界备受推崇，享有极高声誉，可以说代表了我们国家外译文学作品的最高水平。然而研究者江帆博士远赴美国，在美国高校图书馆里潜心研读了大量第一手英语文献，最后惊讶地发现，杨译《红楼梦》与英国汉学家霍克斯的《红楼梦》英译本相比，在英语世界竟然备受冷落。江帆在其博士论文《他乡的石头记：〈红楼梦〉百年英译史研究》（后拓展为同名著作）中指出："首先，英美学术圈对霍译本的实际认同程度远远超过了杨译本：英语世界的中国或亚洲文学史、文学选集和文学概论一般都直接收录或援引霍译本片段，《朗曼世界文学选集》选择的也是霍译本片段，杨译本在类似的选集中很少露面；在相关学术论著中，作者一般都将两种译本并列为参考书目，也对杨译本表示相当的尊重，但在实际需要引用原文片段时，选用的都是霍译本，极少将杨译本作为引文来源。其次，以馆藏量为依据，以美国的伊利诺伊州（Illinois）为样本，全州65所大学的联合馆藏目录（I-Share）表明，13所大学存有霍译本，只有两所大学存有杨译本。最后，以英语世界最大的购书网站亚马逊的读者对两种译本的留言和评分为依据，我们发现，在有限的普通读者群中，霍译本获得了一致的推崇，而杨译本在同样的读者群中的评价却相当低，二者之间的分数相差悬殊，部分读者对杨译本的评论极为严苛。"②

　　杨译本之所以会在英语世界遭受"冷遇"，其原因与上述两个个案同出一辙：首先是译介者对"译入语国家的诸多操控因素"认识不足，一厢情愿地进行外译"输出"；其次是"在编审行为中强行输出本国意识形态"，造成了译介效果的干扰；最后是译介的方式需要调整，"对外译介机构应该增强与译入语国家的译者和赞助人的合作，以求从最大限度上吸纳不同层次的读者，尽可能使我们的对外译介达到较好的效果"。③

　　进入21世纪以后，我们国家有关部门又推出了一个规模宏大的、目前正进行得热火朝天的中国文化走出去"工程"，那就是汉英对照的《大中华文库》的翻译与出版。这套标举"全面系统地翻译介绍中国传统文化典籍"、旨在促进"中学西传"的丛书，规模宏大，拟译选题达200种，几乎囊括了全

---

　　① 详见上海外国语大学耿强的博士论文《文学译介与中国文学"走向世界"——熊猫丛书英译中国文学研究》。该论文经作者补充修改后也收录在本丛书中。

　　② 详见复旦大学江帆的博士论文《他乡的石头记：〈红楼梦〉百年英译史研究》。该论文经作者补充修改后也收录在本丛书中。

　　③ 详见复旦大学江帆的博士论文《他乡的石头记：〈红楼梦〉百年英译史研究》。

部中国古典文学名著和传统文化典籍。迄今为止，这套丛书已经翻译出版了一百余种选题，一百七八十册，然而除个别几个选题被国外相关出版机构看中并购买版权外，其余绝大多数已经出版的选题都局限在国内的发行圈内，似尚未真正"传出去"。

不难发现，中华人民共和国成立以来，我们国家的领导人和相关翻译出版部门在推动中国文学、文化走出去一事上倾注了极大的热情和关怀，组织了一大批国内（还有部分国外的）中译外的翻译专家，投入了大量的人力、物力、财力，但如上所述，总体而言收效甚微，实际效果并不理想。

二

2012 年底，莫言获得诺贝尔文学奖之后，又引发了国内学术界特别是翻译界围绕中国文学、文化走出去问题的讨论热情。学界和译界都想通过对莫言获得诺贝尔文学奖一事背后翻译问题的讨论，获得对中国文学、文化典籍外译的启示。我当时就撰文指出，严格来讲，莫言获奖背后的翻译问题，其实质已经超越了传统翻译和翻译研究中那种狭隘的语言文字转换层面上的认识，而是进入了跨文化交际的层面，具体而言，也就是进入了译介学的层面，这就意味着我们今天在讨论中国文学、文化外译问题时，不仅要关注如何翻译的问题，还要关注译作的传播与接受等问题。在我看来，"经过了中外翻译界一两千年的讨论，前一个问题已经基本解决，'翻译应该忠实原作'已是译界的基本常识，无须赘言；至于应该'逐字译''逐意译'，还是两相结合，等等，具有独特追求的翻译家自有其主张，也不必强求一律。倒是对后一个问题，即译作的传播与接受等问题，长期以来遭到我们的忽视甚至无视，需要我们认真对待。由于长期以来我们国家对外来的先进文化和优秀文学作品一直有一种强烈的需求，所以我们的翻译家只须关心如何把原作翻译好，而甚少甚至根本无须关心译作在我国的传播与接受问题。然而今天我们面对的却是一个新的问题：中国文学与文化的外译问题。更有甚者，在国外，尤其在西方尚未形成像我们国家这样一个对外来文化、文学有强烈需求的接受环境，这就要求我们必须考虑如何在国外，尤其是在西方国家培育中国文学和文化的受众和接受环境的问题"①。

莫言作品外译的成功让我们注意到了以往我们忽视的一些问题。一是"谁来译"的问题。莫言作品的外译者都是国外著名的汉学家、翻译家，虽然

---

① 谢天振，《莫言作品"外译"成功的启示》，《文汇读书周报》，2012 年 12 月 14 日。

单就外语水平而言，国内并不缺乏与这些国外翻译家水平相当的译者，但在对译入语国家读者细微的用语习惯、独特的文字偏好、微妙的审美趣味等方面的把握上，我们得承认，国外翻译家显示出了国内翻译家较难企及的优势。有些人对这个问题不理解，觉得这些国外翻译家在对原文的理解甚至表达方面有时候其实还比不上我们自己的翻译家，我们为何不能用自己的翻译家呢？这个问题其实只要换位思考一下就很容易解释清楚。试想一想，我国读者是通过自己翻译家的翻译作品接受外来文学、文化的呢，还是通过外国翻译家把他们的文学作品、文化典籍译介给我们的？再想一想，假设在你面前摆着两本巴尔扎克小说的译作，一本是一位精通中文的法国汉学家翻译的，一本是著名翻译家傅雷翻译的，你会选择哪一本呢？答案不言而喻。实际上可以说世界上绝大多数的国家和民族，主要都是通过自己国家和民族的翻译家来接受外国文学文化的，这是文学文化跨语言、跨国界译介的一条基本规律。

二是"作者对译者的态度"问题。莫言在对待他的作品的外译者方面表现得特别宽容和大度，给予了充分的理解和尊重。他不仅没有把译者当作自己的"奴隶"，而且还对他们明确放手："外文我不懂，我把书交给你翻译，这就是你的书了，你做主吧，想怎么弄就怎么弄。"正是由于莫言对待译者的这种宽容大度，所以他的译者才得以放开手脚，大胆地"连译带改"以适应译入语环境读者的阅读习惯和审美趣味，从而让莫言作品的外译本顺利跨越了"中西方文化心理与叙述模式差异"的"隐形门槛"，并成功地进入了西方的主流阅读语境。我们国内有的作家不懂这个道理，自以为很认真，要求国外翻译家先试译一两个章节给他看。其实这个作家本人并不懂外文，而是请他懂外文的两个朋友帮忙审阅。然而这两个朋友能审阅出什么问题来呢？无非是看看译文有无错译、漏译，文字是否顺畅而已。然而一个没有错译、漏译，文字顺畅的译文，也即我们所说的一个"合格的译本"能否保证译文在译入语环境中受到欢迎、得到广泛的传播并产生影响呢？本文前面提到的杨译《红楼梦》在英语世界的遭遇就是一个很好的例子：英国翻译家霍克斯的《红楼梦》译本因其中的某些误译、错译曾颇受我们国内翻译界的诟病，而杨宪益夫妇的《红楼梦》译本国内翻译界评价极高，被推崇备至。然而如前所述，研究者在美国高校进行实地调研后得到的大量数据表明，在英语世界是霍译本更受欢迎，而杨译本却备受冷遇。[①]这个事实应该引起我们有些作家，更应该引起我们国内翻译界的反思。

---

① 详见复旦大学江帆的博士论文《他乡的石头记：〈红楼梦〉百年英译史研究》。

三是"谁来出版"的问题。莫言作品的译作都是由国外一流的重要出版社出版，譬如他的作品法译本的出版社瑟伊（Seuil）出版社就是法国最重要的出版社之一，他的作品英译本则是由美国的拱廊出版社、纽约海鸥出版社、俄克拉荷马大学出版社以及闻名世界的企鹅出版社出版，这使得莫言作品的外译本能很快进入西方的主流发行渠道，也使得莫言的作品在西方得到了有效的传播。反之，如果莫言的译作全是由国内出版社出版的，恐怕就很难取得目前的成功。近年来国内出版社已经注意到这一问题，并开始积极开展与国外出版社的合作，很值得肯定。

四是"作品本身的可译性"。这里的可译性不是指一般意义上作品翻译时的难易程度，而是指作品在翻译过程中其原有的风格、创作特征、原作特有的"滋味"的可传递性，在翻译成外文后这些风格、这些特征、这些"滋味"能否基本保留下来并被译入语读者所理解和接受。譬如有的作品以独特的语言风格见长，其"土得掉渣"的语言让中国读者印象深刻并颇为欣赏，但是经过翻译后它的"土味"荡然无存，也就不易获得在中文语境中同样的接受效果。莫言作品翻译成外文后，"既接近西方社会的文学标准，又符合西方世界对中国文学的期待"，这就让西方读者较易接受。其实类似情况在中国文学史上也早有先例，譬如白居易、寒山的诗外译的就很多，传播也广；相比较而言，李商隐的诗的外译和传播就要少，原因就在于前两者的诗浅显、直白，易于译介。寒山诗更由于其内容中的"禅意"而在正好盛行学禅之风的 20 世纪五六十年代的日本和美国得到广泛传播，其地位甚至超过了孟浩然。作品本身的可译性问题提醒我们，在对外译介中国文学作品、文化典籍时，应当挑选具有可译性的，也就是在译入语环境里更容易接受的作品首先进行译介。

三

以上关于莫言作品外译成功原因的几点分析，其触及的几个问题其实也还是表面上的，如果我们对上述《中国文学》期刊等几个个案进行深入分析，当能发现，真正影响中国文学、文化切实有效地走出去的因素还与以下几个实质性问题有关。

首先，与我们对翻译的认识存在误区有关。

大家都知道，中国文学、文化要走出去，里面有个翻译的问题，然而却远非所有人都清楚翻译是个什么样的问题。绝大多数人都以为，翻译无非就是两种语言文字之间的转换。我们要让中国文学、文化走出去，只要把那些用中国语言文字写成的文学作品（包括典籍作品）翻译成外文就可以了。应该说，这样的翻译认识不仅仅是我们翻译界、学术界，甚至还是我们全社会的一个共识。譬如我们的权威工具书《辞海》（1980 年版）对"翻译"的释义就是："把一种语言文字的意义用另一种语言文字表达出来"。另一部权威工具书《中国大百科全书·语言文字》（1988 年版）对"翻译"的定义也与此相仿："把已说出或写出的话的意思用另一种语言表达出来的活动"。正是在这样的翻译认识或翻译思想的指导下，长期以来，我们在进行中国文学作品、文化典籍外译时，考虑的问题也就只是如何尽可能忠实、准确地进行两种语言文字的转换，或者说得更具体一些，考虑的问题就是如何交出一份"合格的译文"。然而问题是交出一份"合格的译文"后是否就意味着能够让中国文学、文化自然而然地"走出去"了呢？上述几个个案表明，事情显然并没有那么简单，因为在上述几个个案里，无论是长达半个世纪的英文、法文版《中国文学》杂志，还是杨宪益主持的"熊猫丛书"，以及目前仍然在热闹地进行着的《大中华文库》的编辑、翻译、出版，其中的大多数甚至绝大多数译文都称得上"合格"。然而一个无可回避却不免让人感到沮丧的事实是，这些"合格的译文"除了极小部分外，却并没有促成我们的中国文学、文化整体切实有效地"走出去"。

问题出在哪里？我以为就出在我们对翻译的认识失之偏颇。我们一直简单地认为翻译就只是两种语言文字之间的转换行为，却忽视了翻译的任务和目标。我们相当忠实、准确地实现了两种语言文字之间的转换，或者说我们交出了一份份"合格的译文"，然而如果这些行为和译文并不能促成两种文化之间的有效交际的话，并不能让翻译成外文的中国文学作品、中国文化典籍在译入语环境中被接受、被传播并产生影响的话，那么这样的转换（翻译行为）及其成果（译文）能够说是成功的吗？这样的译文，尽管从传统的翻译标准来看都不失为一篇篇"合格的译文"，但恐怕与一堆废纸并无实质性的差异。这个话也许说得重了些，但事实就是如此。当你看到那一本本堆放在我们各地高校图书馆里的翻译成外文的中国文学、文化典籍乏人借阅、无人问津时，你会作何感想呢？事实上，国外已经有学者从职业翻译的角度指出，"翻译质量在于交际效果，而不是表达方式和方法"[①]。

为此，我以为我们今天在定义翻译的概念时，倒是有必要重温我国唐代贾公彦在其所撰《周礼义疏》里对翻译所下的定义："译即易，谓换易言语使

---

① 达尼尔·葛岱克，《职业翻译与翻译职业》，刘和平、文韫译，北京：外语教学与研究出版社，2011年，第 6 页。

相解也。"我很欣赏一千多年前贾公彦所下的这个翻译定义，寥寥十几个字，言简意赅。这个定义首先指出"翻译就是两种语言之间的转换"（译即易），然后强调"换易言语"的目的是"使相解也"，也即要促成交际双方相互理解，达成有效的交流。我们把它与上述两个权威工具书对翻译所下的定义进行一下对照的话，可以发现，贾公彦的翻译定义并没有仅仅局限在对两种语言文字转换的描述上，而是把翻译的目的、任务也一并包含进去了。而在我看来，这才是一个比较完整的翻译定义，一个在今天仍然不失其现实意义的翻译定义。我们应该看到，两种语言文字之间的转换（包括口头的和书面的）只是翻译的表象，而翻译的目的和任务，也即是促成操不同语言的双方实现切实有效的交流、达成交际双方相互之间切实有效的理解和沟通，这才是翻译的本质。然而，一千多年来我们在谈论翻译的认识或是在进行翻译活动（尤其是笔译活动）时，恰恰是在这个翻译的本质问题上偏离了甚至迷失了方向：我们经常只顾盯着完成两种语言文字之间的转换，却忘了完成这种语言文字转换的目的是什么、任务是什么。我们的翻译研究者也把他们的研究对象局限在探讨"怎么译""怎样才能译得更好、译得更准确"等问题上，于是在相当长的历史时期内我们的翻译研究就一直停留在研究翻译技巧的层面上。这也许就是这 60 多年来尽管我们花了大量的人力、物力、财力进行中国文学、文化典籍的外译，希望以此能够推动中国文学、文化走出去，然而却未能取得预期效果的一个重要原因吧。

其次，与我们看不到译入（in-coming translation）与译出（out-going translation）这两种翻译行为之间的区别有关。

其实，上面提到的对翻译的认识存在偏颇、偏离甚至迷失了翻译的本质目标，其中一个表现也反映在对译入与译出两种翻译行为之间的区别缺乏正确的认识上。我们往往只看到译入与译出都是两种语言文字之间的转换，却看不到两者的实质性差别，以为只是翻译的方向有所不同而已。其实这里的差别涉及一个本质性问题：前者（译入）是建立在一个国家、一个民族内在的对异族他国文学、文化的强烈需求基础上的翻译行为，而后者（译出）在多数情况下则是一个国家、一个民族一厢情愿地向异族他国译介自己的文学和文化，对方对你的文学、文化不一定有强烈的主动需求。这样，由于译入行为所处的语境对外来文学、文化已经具有一种强烈的内在需求，因此译入活动的发起者和具体从事译入活动的译介者考虑的问题就只是如何把外来的文学作品、文化典籍译得忠实、准确和流畅，也就是传统译学理念中的交出一份"合格的译作"，而基本不需考虑译入语环境中制约或影响翻译行为的诸多因素。对他们而言，他们只要交出了"合格的译作"，他们的翻译行为及其翻译成果也就自然而然地能够赢得读者，赢得市场，甚至在译入语环境里产生一定影响。过去两千多年来，我们国家的翻译活动基本上就是这样一种性质的活动，即建立在以外译中为主的基础上的译入行为。无论是历史上长达千年之久的佛经翻译，还是清末民初以来这一百多年间的文学名著和社科经典翻译，莫不如此。

但是译出行为则不然。由于译出行为的译入语（或称目的语）方对你的文学、文化尚未产生强烈的内在需求，更遑论形成一个比较成熟的接受群体和接受环境，在这样的情况下，译出行为的发起者和译介者如果也像译入行为的发起者和译介者一样，只考虑译得忠实、准确、流畅，而不考虑其他许多制约和影响翻译活动成败得失的因素，包括目的语国家读者的阅读习惯、审美趣味，目的语国家的意识形态、诗学观念，以及译介者自己的译介方式、方法、策略等因素，那么这样的译介行为能否取得预期成功显然值得怀疑。

令人遗憾的是，这样一个显而易见的道理却并没有被我国发起和从事中国文学、中国文化典籍外译工作的有关领导和具体翻译工作者所理解和接受。其原因同样显而易见，这是因为在两千年来的译入翻译实践（从古代的佛经翻译到清末民初以来的文学名著、社科经典翻译）中形成的译学理念——奉"忠实原文"为翻译的唯一标准、拜"原文至上"为圭臬等——已经深深扎根在这些领导和翻译工作者的脑海之中，他们以建立在译入翻译实践基础上的这些翻译理念、标准、方法论来看待和指导今天的中国文学、文化典籍的译出行为，继续只关心语言文字转换层面的"怎么译"的问题，而甚少甚至完全不考虑翻译行为以外的诸种因素，譬如传播手段、接受环境、译出行为的目的语国家的意识形态、诗学观念，等等。由此我们也就不难明白：上述几个中国文学走出去个案之所以未能取得理想的译出效果，完全是情理之中的事了。所以我在拙著《隐身与现身——从传统译论到现代译论》中明确指出："简单地用建立在'译入'翻译实践基础上的翻译理论（更遑论经验）来指导当今的中国文学、文化'走出去'的'译出'翻译实践，那就不可能取得预期的成功。"[①]

再次，是对文学、文化的跨语言传播与交流的基本译介规律缺乏应有的认识。一般情况下，文化总是由强势文化向弱势文化译介，而且总是由弱势文化语境里的译者主动地把强势文化译入自己的文化语境。所以法国学者葛岱克教授说："当一个国家在技术、经济和文化上属于强国时，其语言和文化的译出量一定很大；而当一个国家在技术、经济和文化上属于弱国时，语言

---

① 谢天振，《隐身与现身——从传统译论到现代译论》，北京：北京大学出版社，2014年，第13页。

9

和文化的译入量一定很大。在第一种情况下，这个国家属于语言和文化的出口国，而在第二种情况下，它则变为语言和文化的进口国。"①历史上，当中华文化处于强势文化地位时，我们周边的国家就曾纷纷主动地把中华文化译入他们各自的国家即是一例，当时我国的语言和文化的译出量确实很大。然而当西方文化处于强势地位、中华文化处于弱势地位时，譬如在我国的晚清时期，我国的知识分子也是积极主动地把西方文化译介给我国读者的，于是我国的语言和文化的译入量同样变得很大。今天在整个世界文化格局中，西方文化仍然处于强势地位，与之相比，中华文化也仍然处于弱势地位，这从各自国家的翻译出版物的数量中也可见出：数年前联合国教科文组织的一份统计资料表明，翻译出版物仅占美国的全部出版物总数的百分之三，占英国的全部出版物总数的百分之五。而在我们国家，我虽然没有看到具体的数据，但粗略估计一下，说翻译出版物占我国出版物总数百分之十恐怕不会算太过吧。

与此同时，翻译出版物占一个国家总出版物数量比例的高低还从一个方面折射出这个国家对待外来文学、文化的态度和立场。翻译出版物在英美两国以及相关英语国家的总出版物中所占比例相当低，反映出英语世界发达国家对待发展中国家（包括中国）的文学、文化的那种强势文化国家的心态和立场。由此可见，要让中国文学、文化走出去（其实质首先是希望走进英语世界）实际上是一种由弱势文化向强势文化的"逆势"译介行为，这样的译介行为要取得成功，那就不能仅仅停留在把中国文学、文化典籍翻译成外文，交出一份所谓的"合格的译文"就算完事，而必须从译介学规律的高度全面审时度势并对之进行合理的调整。

最后，迄今为止我们在中国文学、文化走出去一事上未能取得预期的理想效果，还与我们未能认识到并正视在中西文化交流中存在着的两个特殊现象或称事实有关，那就是"时间差"（time gap）和"语言差"（language gap）②。

所谓时间差，指的是中国人全面、深入地认识西方、了解西方已经有一百多年的历史了，而当代西方人对中国开始有比较全面深入的了解，也就是最近二三十年的事。具体而言，从鸦片战争时期起，西方列强已经开始进入中国并带来了西方文化，从清末民初时期起，中国人更是兴起了积极主动学习西方文化的热潮。与之形成对照的是，西方国家对我们开始有比较多的认识并积极主动地来了解中国文学、文化只是最近这二三十年的事。这种时间

---

① 谢天振，《莫言作品"外译"成功的启示》，《文汇读书周报》，2012 年 12 月 14 日。

② 这两个术语的英译由史志康教授提供，我以为史译较好地传递出了我提出并使用的这两个术语"时间差"和"语言差"的语义内涵。

上的差别，使得我们拥有丰厚的西方文化的积累，我们的广大读者也都能较轻松地阅读和理解译自西方的文学作品和学术著作，而西方则不具备我们这样的条件和优势，他们更缺乏相当数量的能够轻松阅读和理解译自中国的文学作品和学术著作的读者。从某种程度上而言，当今西方各国的中国文学作品和文化典籍的普通读者，其接受水平相当于我们国家严复、林纾那个年代的阅读西方作品的中国读者。我们不妨回想一下，在严复、林纾那个年代，我们国家的西方文学、西方文化典籍的读者是怎样的接受水平：译自西方的学术著作肯定都有大幅度的删节，如严复翻译的《天演论》；译自西方的小说，其中的风景描写、心理描写等通常都会被删去，如林纾、伍光建的译作。不仅如此，有时整部小说的形式都要被改造成章回体小说的样子，还要给每一章取一个对联式的标题，在每一章的结尾处还要写上"欲知后事如何，且听下回分解"，等等。更有甚者，一些译者明确标榜："译者宜参以己见，当笔则笔，当削则削耳。"①明乎此，我们也就能够理解，为什么当今西方国家的翻译家们在翻译中国作品时，多会采取归化的手法，且对原作都会有不同程度甚至大幅度的删节。

时间差这个事实提醒我们，在积极推进中国文学、文化走出去一事时，现阶段不宜贪大求全，编译一本诸如《先秦诸子百家寓言故事选》《聊斋志异故事选》《唐宋传奇故事选》，也许比你花了大力气翻译出版一大套诸子百家的全集更受当代西方读者的欢迎。有人担心如此迁就西方读者的接受水平和阅读趣味，他们会接触不到中国文化的精华，读不到中国文学的名著。这些人是把文学交流和文化交际与开设文学史课和文化教程混为一谈了，想一想我们当初接受西方文学和文化难道都非得从荷马史诗、柏拉图、亚里士多德开始吗？

所谓语言差，指的是操汉语的中国人在学习、掌握英语等现代西方语言并理解与之相关的文化方面，比操英、法、德、西、俄等西方现代语言的西方国家的人民学习、掌握汉语要来得容易。这种语言差使得我们国家能够拥有一批精通英、法、德、西、俄等西方语言并理解相关文化的专家学者，甚至还有一大批粗通这些语言并比较了解与之相关的民族文化的普通读者，而在西方我们就不可能指望他们也拥有如此众多精通汉语并深刻理解博大精深的中国文化的专家学者，更不可能指望有一大批能够直接阅读中文作品、能够轻松理解中国文化的普通读者。

语言差这个事实告诉我们，在现阶段乃至今后相当长的一个时期里，在

---

① 谢天振，《译介学》（增订本），南京：译林出版社，2013 年，第 63 页。

西方国家，中国文学和文化典籍的读者注定还是相当有限的，能够胜任和从事中国文学和文化译介工作的当地汉学家、翻译家也将是有限的，这就要求我们在推动中国文学、文化走出去的同时，还必须关注如何在西方国家培育中国文学、文化的接受群体——近年来我们与有关国家互相举办对方国家的"文化年"即是一个相当有效的举措；还必须关注如何扩大国外汉学家、翻译家的队伍，关注如何为他们提供切实有效的帮助，包括项目资金、专家咨询、配备翻译合作者等。

文学与文化的跨语言、跨国界传播是一项牵涉面广、制约因素复杂的活动，决定文学译介的效果更是有多方面的因素，但只要我们树立正确、全面的翻译理念，理解把握译介学的规律，正视中西文化交流中存在的"语言差""时间差"等实际情况，确立正确的中国文学、文化外译的指导思想，那么中国文学和文化就一定能够切实有效地"走出去"。

2014 年 7 月

阿瑟·韦利原著第一版序（1946）

郑培凯 鄢秀 译

这本选集包括了选自《诗经》（*The Book of Songs*，1937）的译诗，以及《中国诗歌一百七十首》（*A Hundred and Seventy Chinese Poems*，1918）、《续译中国文学》（*More Translations*，1919）、《庙宇》（*The Temple*，1923）等作品里的大部分译诗。我尽可能按年代先后安排次序，所有的翻译都经过仔细的修订。

现在呈现的译诗次序，当然并不反映翻译的时间先后。我的翻译方法，在过去三十年间，也经历了不少改变，读者会发现，其中有直译如洋泾浜英语的版本，也有比较完美的作品。我很少在修辞风格上进行改动，但是我觉得《国殇》一首的原译很差，所以我做了大幅修订，现在它看起来好多了。

翻译中国五言诗，我在 1916 年到 1923 年之间，以霍普金斯（Gerard Manley Hopkins）创制的"跃动韵律"为基础，发展出一种音律，最接近英诗韵律的无韵体（素体诗）。七言诗比较难以处理，我就不曾企图使用这种音律来翻译长诗。

这就让我回到选诗的问题。我这本书不是一本系统、均衡的中国诗选，只是我译作中效果出色的作品选集，有直译的痕迹，但同时又文气充沛。当然这就排除了一些充满典故、需要大量诠释的诗作。我翻译白居易的诗，数量十倍于其他诗人的作品，并不是我认为白居易的诗比其他诗人的作品好过十倍，只是我觉得他在中国大诗人中最为出色。我并非不熟悉其他唐宋诗人的作品，其实我尝试译过李白、杜甫、苏轼，可是结果都不让我满意。

这本书主要是为了呈现一本诗集，我也就排除了传记与历史背景的文章。那些材料在《中国诗歌一百七十首》中可以找得到。

阿瑟·韦利原著平装版序（1960）

郑培凯 鄢秀 译

　　本书是《中国诗》（1946）的重印本，删去了原来的"附加注释"（Additional Notes），加进了1946年以后的一些译作——寒山诗系列与冯梦龙的一首情歌。寒山诗系列原来发表在《邂逅》（*Encounter*）杂志，冯梦龙的情歌发表在《长青评论》（*Evergreen Review*）。我这本书不是系统、均衡、有代表性的中国诗史选集，只是我特别喜欢而且翻译得好的诗作选集。这些译作的翻译时段很长，从1916年到1959年。我更正了一些早期翻译的错误，但是有两三处我没做更动，因为我发现，一旦改动，就会破坏诗的韵味。例如古诗"庭中有奇树，绿叶发华滋"，说的是绿荫丰茂，而非绿荫滋润（ooze with a fragrant moisture），可是我无法改得更让我自己满意。

古诗词出处一览表

《全唐诗》，上海：上海古籍出版社，1986年。

陈元龙，辑，《历代赋汇》，北京：北京图书馆出版社，1999年。

费振刚、胡双宝、宗明华，辑校，《全汉赋》，北京：北京大学出版社，1993年。

费振刚、仇仲谦、刘南平，校注，《全汉赋校注》，广州：广东教育出版社，2005年。

冯梦龙，撰，卢前，编，《宛转歌》，北京：商务印书馆，1941年。

顾学颉，校点，《白居易集》，北京：中华书局，1979年。

郭茂倩，撰，《乐府诗集》，北京：中华书局，1979年。

纪昀等，编，《四库全书·集部总集类》，上海：上海古籍出版社，1985年，第1434册：张玉书、汪霖等，编，《御定佩文斋咏物诗选》。

金开诚、董洪利、高路明，校注，《屈原集校注》，北京：中华书局，1996年。

孔颖达等，正义，《毛诗正义》，上海：上海古籍出版社，1990年。

龙榆生，撰，《中国韵文史》，上海：上海古籍出版社，2001年。

陆游，著，《陆放翁全集》，北京：中国书店，1986年。

逯钦立，辑校，《先秦汉魏晋南北朝诗》，北京：中华书局，1984年。

逯钦立，校注，《陶渊明集》，北京：中华书局，1979年。

罗振玉，编，《敦煌拾零》，《敦煌资料丛编三种》，北京：北京图书馆出版社，2000年。

欧阳永叔，著，《欧阳修全集》，北京：中国书店，1986年。

彭定求等，编，《全唐诗》，北京：中华书局，1960年。

瞿蜕园、朱金城，校注，《李白集校注》，上海：上海古籍出版社，1998年。

沈德潜，选，《古诗源》，北京：中华书局，1963年。

陶潜，著，龚斌，校笺，《陶渊明集校笺》，上海：上海古籍出版社，1996年。

吴孟复、蒋立甫，主编，《古文辞类纂评注》，合肥：安徽教育出版社，1995年。

吴小如、王运熙、章培恒、曹道衡、骆玉明等，《汉魏六朝诗鉴赏辞典》，上海：上海辞书出版社，1992 年。

萧涤非等，《汉魏晋南北朝隋诗鉴赏词典》，太原：山西人民出版社，1989 年。

徐陵，编，《玉台新咏》，郑州：中州古籍出版社，1991 年。

元稹，著，冀勤，点校，《元稹集》，北京：中华书局，1982 年。

袁行云、高尚贤，选注，《明诗选》，北京：春秋出版社，1988 年。

曾昭岷、曹济平、王兆鹏、刘尊明，编著，《全唐五代词》，北京：中华书局，1999 年。

钟京铎，著，《左思诗集释》，台北：学海出版社，2001 年。

朱金城，笺校，《白居易集笺校》，上海：上海古籍出版社，1988 年。

目录

引言

在中国古典文学英译这个领域，阿瑟·韦利（Arthur Waley，1889-1966）是个不世出的奇才。他原名阿瑟·戴维·施劳斯（Arthur David Schloss），祖先是德系犹太人，后迁至英国，父亲是犹太裔经济学家戴维·弗雷德里克·施劳斯（David Frederick Schloss）。在第一次世界大战爆发之前，为了避免因英国人仇视德国而遭受歧视，他随母亲家族改了姓氏，从此以阿瑟·戴维·韦利（Arthur David Waley）为名。他 1907 年进入剑桥大学国王学院（King's College），修读的专业是古典文学（Classics），主要研读古希腊罗马文学与文献，对西方文化传承有着深刻的认识，同时也学了梵文，对各类古籍经典产生了兴趣。他 1913 年进入大英博物馆的东方图籍部，担任宾永（Laurence Binyon，1869-1943）的助理，保管及整理东方书画、手稿等。宾永是著名的诗人与东方艺术学者，在日本与波斯艺术方面造诣颇深。他在指导工作与日常接触中给了韦利两方面的启发：一是对中日古典文学的兴趣，二是诗人情怀的熏陶。环境的耳濡目染与工作的需要，使韦利自学了中文、日文，以完成藏品记录、分类、编册的任务。这种特殊的经历激起了韦利的诗情想象，在大英博物馆琳琅满目的书库中，他像福尔摩斯探案一样研读神秘的异域文字，进而对古老东方文学表意与抒情的审美追求产生了浓厚兴趣。他的主要工作是整理斯坦因的敦煌资料，如此，韦利开始了翻译与介绍东方文化的毕生追求。他不会中文与日文的口语，也从来没去过东方，却对中日古典文学著作情有独钟，所做工作甚至超出了图籍管理的职责。像发愿剃度的僧人一样，他把生命的意义定位成译介中日文学，一发而不可收，终于在 1929 年完成斯坦因图录的整理之后，辞去了博物馆的职位，全心投入到文学翻译之中。

韦利在 1916 年自己印了他的第一本译著《中国诗歌》（*Chinese Poems*），这是一本只有 16 页的小册子，书名页上引了《孟子·离娄上》的一段："有孺子歌曰：'沧浪之水清兮，可以濯我缨；沧浪之水浊兮，可以濯我足。'孔子曰：'小子听之：清斯濯缨，浊斯濯足矣。'"显然是感到心有戚戚，觉得中国古典诗歌如沧浪之水，可以洗涤他的心灵，也可以洗涤他在尘世中遭遇的污染。他将此段译成英文：

> Confucius heard a boy singing:/ "When the waters of the Ts'ang-lang are clean,/ They do to wash my cap-tassels in./ When the waters of the Ts'ang-lang are muddy,/ They do to wash my feet in." (Waley, 1916: title page)

这本小册子虽然只有 16 页，却选译了 52 首诗，包括屈原的《国殇》，《诗经》选篇及曹植、王维、李白、杜甫、白居易的诗作。值得注意的是，韦利选译的诗作，除了两首之外，都是上古到唐代的古典作品，多少预示了此后他翻译中国古诗的重点选择范围，这或许与他本人的古典学训练有关。这本译诗集一共印了 50 本，被分送给朋友以及他敬重的文化圈中人，其中包括诗人叶慈（W. B. Yeats）、艾略特（T. S. Eliot）、庞德（Ezra Pound）、崔沃连（Robert C. Trevelyan），哲学家罗素（Bertrand Russell），诗人与美术史家宾永及作家伍尔夫夫妇（Leonard & Virginia Woolf）等。从他赠书的师友群，可以看到韦利交往的人物都是当时的文化精英，而且彼此之间都有相当紧密的联系。许多人都是第一次世界大战前后的青年才俊，背景都与韦利相同，在剑桥或牛津研读古典文献或哲学，酷爱诗歌写作，对东方文化与艺术有浓厚兴趣，后来还时常在伦敦聚会，成为布鲁斯伯里文会（Bloomsbury Group）的中坚。

在剑桥大学求学期间，韦利和带有社会主义色彩的费边社（Fabian Society）走得很近，又与一些精英社团的朋友交往密切。他上过摩尔（G. E. Moore，1873-1958）的哲学课，对钦慕东方文化的政治哲学家狄更生（Goldsworthy Lowes Dickinson，1862-1932）十分尊崇。摩尔是剑桥三一学院（Trinity College）的驻院学人，狄更生则是剑桥国王学院的驻院学人，两人又同是剑桥精英所组秘密学生社团"剑桥使徒社"（Cambridge Apostles）的成员。狄更生出版过一些反战的和平主义书籍，并对提倡和谐的东方文化大为赞赏，曾以中国人的口吻写过《中国佬的来信》（*Letters from John Chinaman and Other Essays*, 1901），在当时很受瞩目，接着又匿名写了《中国官员的来信：东方视角下的西方文明》（*Letters from a Chinese Official: Being an Eastern View of Western Civilization*, 1903），后来还出版了《论印度、中国与日本的文明》（*An Essay on the Civiliszations of India, China & Japan*, 1914）。韦利在大学接触的自由思想风气，交织着古希腊哲学逻辑与理性，东方文化的心灵超越，以及追求开放自由、一反维多利亚严谨诗风的现代主义文学探索。他有着远离政治的倾向，从不附和大英帝国虎视天下的霸气，更与欧洲当时剑拔弩张的政治形势相左。

韦利在大英博物馆的上司宾永，出身于牛津大学三一学院，专攻古典文学，在博物馆中负责东方图籍与绘画部的管理与运作，是指导他进入东亚文学研究与译介的领路人。宾永本人是出色的诗人，在英美现代诗的发展历史上扮演了重要角色，他介绍一些"意象诗派"（Imagists）的诗人接触东亚艺术与文学，其中就包括了当时混迹英国文坛的庞德。雷纳德·伍尔夫（Leonard Woolf）出身于剑桥大学三一学院，参加了摩尔与狄更生的"剑桥使徒社"，每个星期六晚上聚会，畅论诗文，海阔天空。当时的社员主要来自剑桥大学国王学院与三一学院，如后来成为布鲁斯伯里文会中坚分子的传记家斯特拉奇（Lytton Strachey，1880-1932，三一学院）、经济学家凯恩斯（John Maynard Keynes，1883-1946，国王学院）、哲学家摩尔及小说家福斯特（E. M. Forster，1879-1970，国王学院）。雷纳德·伍尔夫此时结识了托比·史蒂芬（Thoby Stephen），后来娶了他的妹妹弗吉尼亚·史蒂芬（Virginia Stephen），也就是著名的小说家弗吉尼亚·伍尔夫夫人。崔沃连也是剑桥大学三一学院的学生，研读古典学，一心写诗，在剑桥使徒圈中绰号"邋遢古怪诗人"（rumpled，eccentric poet）。他和韦利的关系很好，交游广阔，也扩大了韦利所能结识的师友圈，使他认识了桑塔亚纳（George Santayana，1863-1952）、贝伦森（Bernard Berenson，1865-1959）、罗素、摩尔、福斯特等人。崔沃连在 1912 年还跟狄更生与福斯特一起游历了印度，也对东方文化产生了浓厚的兴趣并以此影响了好友韦利。

韦利在 1916 年自印《中国诗歌》，可以看到他成长环境中来自师友的影响。他通过译诗触及了东方的艺术心灵，精神上得到无限满足，这使他感到可以从译诗中展示内心的诗情，以一种特殊的方式发挥诗人翱翔的想象。朋辈对他自印译诗集的赞誉与鼓励，更坚定了他的信念，自此精通古希腊文与拉丁文的韦利，转而沉浸于中国古诗的世界，继续研读中国古诗，翻译了更多作品。1917 年，他在《东方学院学报》（*Bulletin of the School of Oriental Studies*）连续发表了他翻译的唐代之前的诗歌 37 首与白居易诗 38 首，又在《小评论》（*Little Review*）与《新政治家》（*New Statesman*）接续发表了 25 首英译白居易诗。1918 年，伦敦的康斯坦布尔出版社（Constable & Co.）正式出版了他的《中国诗歌一百七十首》（*A Hundred and Seventy Chinese Poems*），售价 7 先令 6 便士，销路极佳；第二年该诗集由纽约的克诺夫出版社（A. A. Knopf）稍作调整，发行美国版，更名为《中国文学译丛》（*Translations from the Chinese*），之后风行大西洋两岸，长销一个世纪，迄今未衰，奠定了他在英译中国文学领域的崇高地位。在这本诗集中，他对以前翻译的诗作做了修订，并且有意使用"跃动韵律"的特殊自由诗体，在英语世界译介中国文学领域，建立了"韦利式"的独特风格。

韦利是诗人翻译家，也是译介中日古典文学最重要的推手，他以行云流水般的流畅英文，展现了中日古典文学的优雅风神，使得平日不会接触东方文化的英美读者，有机会感受中日文学传统的典雅，体会东方世界的思想感情。他的译文准确平实，雍容大方，带有特殊的韵律与节奏感，有如寒泉流水，清澈见底，潺潺不绝，沁人心脾。他翻译中国古典诗歌最见功力，不用传统英诗的韵律，而以霍普金斯（Gerard Manley Hopkins）提倡的"跃动韵律"一脉，讲求韵律的生动自然，展现语言的能动性。由于中英文字截然不同，中国古典诗与英诗各有其韵律传统，以英诗传统翻译中国古诗，必然受到各种桎梏与扞格，甚至可能会削足适履，丧失中国诗歌的特殊韵味。因此，韦利遵循"跃动韵律"的自由诗体，自出机杼、富有创造性地来翻译中国古诗，意在呈现中国古诗的神韵。史景迁评论韦利的翻译时曾说："韦利撷取了中国和日本文学的珠玑，静悄悄地别在胸前。之前无人这样做过，之后也无人会这样做。"

韦利译诗成为诗人，不但在布鲁斯伯里文会中受到文友的赞誉，也是近代英国诗坛的共识。著名诗人布伦登（Edmund Blunden）就称他为诗人；1936年叶慈编选《牛津现代诗选》（*The Oxford Book of Modern Verse*）时，就选入了韦利的译诗作为他的创作；英国桂冠诗人拉金（Philip Larkin）在 1973 年编选《牛津二十世纪英诗选》（*The Oxford Book of Twentieth Century English Verse*）时也收入了韦利的译诗。

1946 年韦利出版自选的《中国诗》，并不企图鸟瞰式地展现中国诗歌的全貌，更无意呈现具体而微的中国诗史，而主要是呈现令他个人感到诗意盎然的译诗。在他心目中，翻译中国诗，还是要使读者感受诗的爱抚与熏陶，不是提供中国文学史的专业知识。中国诗是令人心神荡漾的诗，他的译笔是诗人的笔，笔下不只是翻译，更重要的是诗。他在 1953 年获颁女王金奖勋章（Queen's Gold Medal of Poetry），这是他最得意的一项荣耀，因它明确表示了英国诗坛对他的尊崇。在他之前得此勋章的有 1937 年的奥登（W. H. Auden），在他之后有 1956 年的布伦登、1960 年的贝杰曼（John Betjeman）、1965 年的拉金、1968 年的格雷福斯（Robert Graves）、1971 年的斯班德（Stephen Spender）及 1974 年的泰德·休斯（Ted Hughes），这清楚地表明了他在英国诗坛的地位。他的中国诗翻译，也就不仅是英译中国诗，还是英国文学的杰作。

这本 1946 年的自选《中国诗》，在 1960 年出版了平装本，年逾古稀的韦利为此写了一篇短序，序言是这么结尾的：

我这本书不是系统、均衡、有代表性的中国诗史选集，只是我特别喜欢而且翻译得好的诗作选集。这些译作的翻译时段很长，从1916年到1959年。我更正了一些早期翻译的错误，但是有两三处我没做更动，因为我发现，一旦改动，就会破坏诗的韵味。例如古诗"庭中有奇树，绿叶发华滋"，说的是绿荫丰茂，而非绿荫滋润（ooze with a fragrant moisture），可是我无法改得更让我自己满意。

这是一段夫子自道，于此，我们可以看到韦利译诗的态度：为了让译作更像一首诗，更让自己满意，不惜牺牲原意，呈现"再创作"的作品。

本书为方便读者阅览，在体例上采取双页排英文、单页排中文的方式，以求在诗篇及其分节上做到一一对应的双语对照；鉴于英译文相较于简约凝练的汉语古诗原文，用字更多、篇幅更长，部分英译文调整为双栏排，以实现相对完整的诗节对照阅读效果。

考虑到阿瑟·韦利当年译诗所依据的中文古诗词版本已难核考，编辑在辅文中增补了"古诗词出处一览表"作为凡例，以方便读者查索核正；又因凡例中的古诗词版本信息已很齐全，正文中每首古诗词的出处附注遂应简则简，只保留书名及页码。

第一章　诗经楚辞

导言

《诗经·生民》的不同译本

《诗经》分风、雅、颂三部分，是以内容涉及的社会阶层而分，虽然说"诗三百，一言以蔽之，曰思无邪"，好像是个人性情的发抒，可是阶级性很强，反映了周朝政治结构与统治意识的影响。风，即各地方国的风谣；雅，分小雅、大雅，说的是诸侯贵族与王室的兴废；颂，则涉及祭典的颂扬，向神明陈述世间的功业。《大雅》所录的诗歌也以歌颂为主，只不过不在宗庙祭祀中宣颂，属于历史传说的陈述，其中说到周王室祖先的起源，就是《生民》这一篇。

《生民》一开头是这么说的："厥初生民、时维姜嫄。生民如何、克禋克祀、以弗无子。履帝武敏歆、攸介攸止、载震载夙、载生载育、时维后稷。"上古诗歌的遣词用字，以及语法表达方式，与现代汉语有着三千年的隔阂，现代人读起来十分艰涩，就会抱怨说不知所云。其实，并不难懂，查查古汉语词典，参考白话译文，意思就很清楚明白了。我时常说，中国人读《诗经》不难，绝对不会比阅读乔叟《坎特伯雷故事》或是托尔斯泰《战争与和平》的原文（原文！）困难，至少你对汉字还熟悉，只是不太明白上古时代的用法而已。

陈子展教授《诗经直解》的译文是："当初周民族的发生，/这是由于那个姜嫄。/周民族的发生怎样？/她能够烧香、她能够祭祀，/因而不无儿子！/踏了上帝的脚迹大拇指好欣喜，/于是在舍、于是休息。/就怀孕动胎、就严肃自己，/就生下来、就养育起。/这就是周民族的始祖后稷。"或许你会觉得译文缺少文采，生吞活剥，没有诗句的含蓄蕴藉，不如原诗在不知所云之中给人一种朦胧的铿锵雄浑。不过，也不要小看陈教授，他的译文虽然诗句有长有短，却完全符合原诗的韵脚。乾隆时期对古音韵学极有创见的经学家江永，说《生民》押韵的结构："祀、子、止、稷，上入为韵。"又说："'时维后稷'与'攸介攸止'上入遥为韵。'载震载夙''载生载育'二句，自为韵。"所以，对照陈子展白话译文与原文，就可看到，不只是准确译出原诗的意思，还亦步亦趋地押了韵。

《生民》这首诗，有 19 世纪理雅各（James Legge）的英译："The first birth of [our] people,/ Was from Jiang Yuan./ How did she give birth to [our] people?/ She had presented a pure offering and sacrificed,/ That her childlessness might be taken away./ She then trod on a toe-print made by God, and was moved,/ In the large place where she rested./ She became pregnant; she dwelt retired;/ She gave birth to, and nourished [a son],/ Who was Hou-ji." 原诗的意思译得没错，译文可真是生硬，硬邦邦的，像他老先生浆得笔挺的西装硬领，敲起来都铿然有声，而且也不押韵。

英译中国古诗，押韵不押韵，其实不是第一等大事，因为英诗与中国诗不同，有其自身的韵律节奏传统，以展现诗句的抑扬顿挫。韦利翻译此诗，用的也是自由诗体，不押韵，但却不像理雅各摆出正经八百的姿态，要跟我们传道似的，读起来流畅得多："SHE who in the beginning gave birth to the people, / This was Chiang Yüan./ How did she give birth to the people? / She sacrificed and prayed/ That she might no longer be childless./ She trod on the big toe of God's footprint, / Was accepted and got what she desired. / Then in reverence, then in awe/ She gave birth, she nurtured; / And this was Hou Chi." 对比理雅各与韦利的译文，可以发现，韦利一开头就使用"She"，让姜嫄登场，而且整段只用了一次被动式，不像理雅各连续使用被动表达方式。叙述历史传说，被动式使用过多，就缺少故事的亲和力，生动的场景与情感都变成硬邦邦的历史资料，没有传说故事引人入胜的活力了。

韦利很懂得古人如何说故事，翻译《生民》的第一段，就很吸引人。这在西方也自有渊源，是从远古以来，荷马吟唱史诗的传统。

《生民》的第二段是："诞弥厥月，先生如达。不坼不副，无菑无害，以赫厥灵。上帝不宁，不康禋祀，居然生子。"古汉语意蕴与后世不同，需要训诂学研究解说，才能明白原意，但学者经常有不同说法，也造成翻译的困难，必须做出审慎的选择。这一段诗篇有点佶屈难懂，过去的经学家有不同解释，如"诞"字、"达"字、"副"字，都与我们日常所用的词义不同，而"上帝不宁，不康禋祀"的主语宾语交错安排，更让人如堕五里雾中。陈子展的白话译文是："当她怀孕满足了那些月数，/头胎生子就像是再胎三胎。/下体不坼不裂，/临产无灾无害。因为显了这样的灵，上帝呀，她的心里就不安宁。/她因为不健康而烧香祭祀，/居然生下了这样一个儿子。"他指出，过去解释"诞"字为句首发语词，就像是说"啊""那"，并不妥善，应该是时间介词，作"当""方"来解才通顺。

"先生如达"这一句比较麻烦，因为《郑笺》解释"达"为"羊子"，就是说"生头胎如生小羊仔"那么容易。马瑞辰《毛诗传笺通释》引陶元淳的说法："凡婴儿在母腹中，皆有皮以裹之，俗所谓胞衣也。生时其衣先破，儿体手足少舒，故生之难。惟羊子之生，胞衣完具，坠地而后，母为破之，故其生易。后稷生时，盖藏于胞中，形体未露，有如羊子之生者，故言如达。"陈子展却认为，郑玄的说法太过曲折，因为《毛传》说"达，生也"，并不解释成"羊子"，而"达"为"沓"的假借字。《说文》"沓"字的段玉裁注，认为"达生即沓生"，解释此句，就是头生的后稷是顺产，有如再生三生之易，与"羊子"无关。

至于"上帝不宁"这一句也很麻烦，是上帝不安宁呢，还是姜嫄不安宁？"不康禋祀，居然生子"当然主语是姜嫄，因为上帝不会去烧香祭祀自己，也不会生下后稷，所以，上帝也不可能不安宁。为什么要说成"上帝不宁"呢？这也引出不同解释，如屈万里在《诗经释义》就说，这里"不，读为丕，下同"。也就是应该理解为："上帝丕宁，丕康禋祀，居然生子。"陈子展不赞成这种解释，认为周人叙述姜嫄生子的神话传说，是有所隐晦的，"履帝武敏歆"，类乎婚外产子。"伊因不康而禋祀，因禋祀而生子，因生子而不宁，似以倒文出之"，其中自有微词，可能是隐瞒了未婚生子的真相。

理雅各的译文是："When she had fulfilled her months, / Her first-born son (came forth) like a lamb. / There was no bursting, nor rending, / No injury, no hurt; —Showing how wonderful he would be. / Did not God give her the comfort? / Had He not accepted her pure offering and sacrifice, / So that thus easily she brought forth her son?"理雅各沿袭旧说，用了"羊子"之说，描述生产顺利。到了"上帝不宁，不康禋祀，居然生子"，主语就有点混淆，以问句方式容纳了那个"不"字，译成"难道上帝不让姜嫄安宁吗？"接着还是上帝作为主语，以问句的方式把"不康"译成"not accepted"，而非姜嫄身体不太健康。最后的"居然生子"，主语转回到姜嫄，但依然用的是问句。看来理雅各拿不准原文的词义，不知道如何置放主语是好，采用了反问的句法，稀里糊涂混过这个翻译难题。

韦利基本套用了理雅各的译文，不过全部使用主动语气，不再纠缠于"不宁""不康"所制造的麻烦，读来畅顺多了："The mother had fulfilled her months./ And her first-born came like a lamb/ With no bursting or rending,/ With no hurt or harm./ To make manifest His magic power/ God on high gave her ease./ So blessed were her sacrifice and prayer/ That easily she bore her child.""上帝不宁"译成"上帝让她安宁"，"不康禋祀"译成"她的禋祀受到祝福"，完全不管经学训诂的争论，诗句倒是明畅易读。

《生民》的第三段是："诞寘之隘巷，牛羊腓字之。诞寘之平林，会伐平林。诞寘之寒冰，鸟覆翼之。鸟乃去矣，后稷呱矣。"陈子展的白话译文是："当安置他在一条小巷里，/就有牛羊来庇护爱抚他。/当安置他在一大片林子里，/恰遇砍伐林子的人拾了他。/当安置他在一块寒冷的冰上，/就有大鸟来盖着翅膀温暖他。/大鸟然后飞去呀，/后稷叫的呱呱呀。"历来的诠释没有什么歧义，翻译起来也就少了麻烦。

理雅各的译文："He was placed in a narrow lane, / But the sheep and oxen protected him with loving care. / He was placed in a wide forest, / Where he was met with by the wood-cutters. / He was placed on the cold ice, / And a bird screened and supported him with its wings. / When the bird went away, / Hou-ji began to wail."

韦利的译文，基本遵循理雅各，但是反被动语句为主动语句，读来比较顺畅："They put it in a narrow lane;/ But oxen and sheep tenderly cherished it./ They put it in a far-off wood;/ But it chanced that woodcutters came to this wood./ They put it on the cold ice;/ But the birds covered it with their wings./ The birds at last went away,/ And Hou Chi began to wail."

特别值得注意的是，韦利遣词用字简单明了，毫不拖泥带水。如"牛羊腓字之"，牛羊的庇护爱抚，理雅各译成"protected him with loving care"，到了韦利的笔下，就是"tenderly cherished it"；"鸟覆翼之"，理雅各译成"a bird screened and supported him with its wings"，相当啰唆，韦利的译文是"the birds covered it with their wings"，简单明了，原意尽出。从译诗的修辞角度而言，理雅各是学者译诗，唯恐漏译了词义；韦利则是诗人译诗，善于利用前人成绩，还能不失原诗意蕴，点铁成金。

《诗经》联绵词的英译

汉语以单音节为主，一字一音，表达完整的意义，与欧洲语文一词多音节的现象不同。但是，汉语修辞之中也有联绵词，则是两个音节连缀成义，基本上是不能拆开的。联绵词在口语中频繁出现，应该是自古以来的语言表达习惯，而非文人的修辞创造。在古文献中也出现得很早，上古《诗经》中就层出不穷，想来是文字记载口语的修辞现象。

汉语联绵词有四种表达方式：（1）双声，两个音节的声母（子音）相同，如"仿佛"；（2）迭韵，两个音节的韵母（元音）相同，如"徘徊"；（3）迭字，两个音节重复使用同一个字，如《诗经·小雅·伐木》的"伐木丁丁，鸟鸣嘤嘤"。（4）部首相同的联绵词，与音韵无关，则是形声汉字以偏旁构成的特色，如"凤凰""鹦鹉""芙蓉""蝴蝶"。《诗经》中经常出现迭字，是歌谣传统中习见的表达手法，一直到今天还是苏州评弹的修辞特色，源远流长，可见这是民间说唱文学的历久弥新的传统。

《诗经》第一篇《周南·关雎》："关关雎鸠，在河之洲。窈窕淑女，君子好逑。"一开头就是双声加叠韵的形声迭字，"关关"，再来就有叠韵的"窈窕"。江永的《古韵标准》指出，这一章的押韵法是 AABA，到第二章转韵了："参差荇菜，左右流之。窈窕淑女，寤寐求之。求之不得，寤寐思服。悠哉悠哉，辗转反侧。"按照古韵，鸠、洲、逑，属幽部；流、求，幽部；得、服、侧，职部。值得注意的现象是，陈奂在《毛诗音》中指出，"参差双声，辗转叠韵"，完全没有放松对联绵词音韵效果的追求。其实，我们还得注意，"辗转"这两个字，是双声兼叠韵，有着音乐性的双重效果。这么复杂的音律安排，如何译成英文的诗歌形式呢？

陈子展在《诗经直解》中，尝试了白话译文，照顾到第一章 AABA 的押韵："关关地唱和的雎鸠，/正在大河的沙洲。/幽闲深居的好闺女，/是君子的好配偶！"押韵得十分准确，然而原诗的韵味却消失了。陈子展的第二章白话译文："参差不齐的荇丝菜，/或左或右漂流它。/幽闲深居的好闺女，/醒呀睡呀追求她。/追求她不得，/醒呀睡呀相思更切。/老想哟，老想哟！/翻来覆去可睡不得。"意思基本准确，但韵脚的安排就不太清楚，读起来比较像小孩子拍着手唱的儿歌，实在不像青年人的思恋情歌。

理雅各是这么译第一章的："Guan-guan go the ospreys,/ On the islet in the river./ The modest, retiring, virtuous, young lady:/ For our prince a good mate she." 古诗化成自由体，韵脚就不必管了，"关关"直译其音，也无可厚非，但是"窈窕"这个叠韵词就麻烦了，译成"modest, retiring"，虽有淑女的娴雅之意，但在声律的追求上好像缺了点什么。韦利的译文是："Guan! Guan! Cry the fish hawks/ on sandbars in the river:/ a mild-mannered good girl,/ fine match for the gentleman." 也是自由诗体，同样音译了"关关"，但是碰上"窈窕"这个叠

韵词,韦利倒是使用了英诗头韵(alliteration)的花样,译成"mild-mannered",再接着,下面"好逑"译成"fine match",一连串的"m"头韵,真是花了一番心思,给"窈窕淑女"配了"好逑"。

第二章考验英译的音律重点,在于"参差"是双声,"窈窕"是叠韵,"辗转"是双声兼叠韵。其实,麻烦还不止于此,还有汉字形声部首呈现的视觉联绵词,如"窈窕"与"寤寐"。"参差"在理雅各笔下,译成"Here long, there short, is the duckweed"。且不说"duckweed"(水生浮萍,植物学列作泽泻目、天南星科)是不是人们食用的荇菜(又名莕菜、莲叶莕菜,植物学列为龙胆目、龙胆科、莕菜属),"参差"译成"这里长那里短"(here long, there short)(令人联想到"此长彼短""家长里短"),没能顾及原词的双声效果,而且太像儿歌,不像是成人采食水生野菜所用的形容词语。"悠哉悠哉,辗转反侧",理雅各译作:"Long he thought; oh! long and anxiously;/ On his side, on his back, he turned, and back again."虽然呈现了君子睡不安稳,翻来覆去,相当传神,却完全忽略了"辗转"双声叠韵的安排。至于"寤寐"译成"waking and sleeping",以叠韵方式呈现这个联绵词,也不失为巧妙之举。

韦利译《关雎》第二章,频频使用头韵,似乎得心应手。"参差荇菜"译成"A ragged fringe is the floating-heart";"寤寐"译成"awake, asleep";"悠哉悠哉,辗转反侧"则译成"endlessly, endlessly,/ turning, tossing from side to side"。连串以叠韵收尾,可算是神来之笔。我们可以看到,韦利显然吸收了理雅各汉译的优点,摒除缺乏诗意的字句,截长补短,使译文在音韵上读起来有诗的韵味。

《国殇》的重译

1918 年版译诗集所收的第一首是屈原的《国殇》,译作"Battle",在 1916 年他自印小册子中就已经出现,也是列为第一首。经过了译诗的尝试阶段,正式出版还是列作第一首,韦利对这首诗的英译一定是郑重其事,不敢轻忽的。第一句"操吴戈兮被犀甲",译作"We grasp our battle-spears: we don our breast-plates of hide",没有明确译出"吴戈"与"犀甲"。后面有一句"带长剑兮挟秦弓",译作"Their swords lie beside them: their black bows, in their hands",也没有明确译出"秦弓"。倒是"诚既勇兮又以武",译成"They were more than brave: they were inspired with the spirit of 'Wu'",还特别别加了个注,指出"Wu"(武)就是"military genius"。既然"武"这个字可以音译,为什么前面的"吴戈"与"秦弓",不译成"Wu spears"与"Ch'in (Qin) bows",再加个注呢?至于"犀甲",韦利当然知道是"rhinoceros hide",为什么故意不用呢?

这就涉及了韦利对中诗英译的关键思考与抉择:要如何展现中国诗的情味?如何表达汉字诗歌的风韵?由于汉字与拼音文字截然不同,要让单字单音的中国诗歌译成英文之后,还有特殊的韵律与节奏,让人一读就感受到诗意,蕴藏有余不尽的东方情调,就不能率由旧章,以传统英诗的格式来表达,就必须另起炉灶,跳出固有的英诗惯用格律。既然英译中国诗歌的读者对象是英语世界的读书人,并不了解中国文化传统,翻译成英文诗句,也就不能拘泥于中国文化传统的专有名词与典故,而必须有所调整。

韦利在 1946 年出版了自选的《中国诗》(*Chinese Poems*),为一般英文读者选出他自认为满意的译诗,也可说是他觉得最有诗歌韵味,若以英诗姿态行世可列于优秀英诗之林而无愧的作品,其中选了《国殇》,却重新翻译了这首诗。诗题译作"Hymn to the Fallen",第一句"操吴戈兮被犀甲"译作:"We hold our flat shields, we wear our jerkins of hide",完全超越了早期顾及"直译"的考虑,不在乎"吴戈"与"犀甲"的问题了。"带长剑兮挟秦弓"的重新译文:"Their tall swords are at their waist, their bows are under their arms",将"长剑"的"长"明确译出,"秦弓"的"秦"则付之阙如,似乎也无关紧要了。"诚既勇兮又以武"译成:"They that fought so well—in death are warriors still","又以武"不再逐字译为"they were inspired with the spirit of 'Wu'",而译为"in death are warriors still",文字洗练不说,把意思译得更为铿锵有力,也免掉了脚注的麻烦。韦利的重译,让我们看到他对文字韵律的重视,译诗就要有英文诗的韵味。换成严复的话语,就是文章要有文气,诗要像诗,尽量做到"信、达、雅"。就韦利而言,他译中国诗,既要有中国韵味,又要是英文诗,就得在两种完全不同的诗歌传统之间,走一条令人瞠目的钢索,博得喧天价响的彩声。

第一章 诗经楚辞

古诗英汉对照

FROM THE BOOK OF SONGS

ORIGIN-LEGEND OF THE CHOU TRIBE
(*c.* 900 B.C.)

SHE who in the beginning gave birth to the people,
This was Chiang Yüan.
How did she give birth to the people?
She sacrificed and prayed
That she might no longer be childless.
She trod on the big toe of God's footprint,
Was accepted and got what she desired.
Then in reverence, then in awe
She gave birth, she nurtured;
And this was Hou Chi[①].

The mother had fulfilled her months.
And her first-born came like a lamb
With no bursting or rending,
With no hurt or harm.
To make manifest His magic power
God on high gave her ease.
So blessed were her sacrifice and prayer
That easily she bore her child.

They put it in a narrow lane;
But oxen and sheep tenderly cherished it.
They[②] put it in a far-off wood;
But it chanced that woodcutters came to this wood.
They put it on the cold ice;
But the birds covered it with their wings.
The birds at last went away,
And Hou Chi began to wail.

---

① "Lord Millet."

② The ballad does not tell us who exposed the child. According to one version it was the mother herself; according to another, the husband.

选自《诗经》

大雅·生民

厥初生民。时维姜嫄。

生民如何。克禋克祀。

以弗无子。履帝武敏歆。

攸介攸止。载震载夙。

载生载育。时维后稷。

诞弥厥月。先生如达。

不拆不副。无菑无害。

以赫厥灵。上帝不宁。

不康禋祀。居然生子。

诞寘之隘巷。牛羊腓字之。

诞寘之平林。会伐平林。

诞寘之寒冰。鸟覆翼之。

鸟乃去矣。后稷呱矣。

Truly far and wide
His voice was very loud.
Then sure enough he began to crawl;
Well he straddled, well he reared,
To reach food for his mouth.
He planted large beans;
His beans grew fat and tall.
His paddy-lines were close set,
His hemp and wheat grew thick,
His young gourds teemed.

Truly Hou Chi's husbandry
Followed the way that had been shown.[1]
He cleared away the thick grass,
He planted the yellow crop.
It failed nowhere, it grew thick,
It was heavy, it was tall,
It sprouted, it eared,
It was firm and good,
it nodded, it hung—
He made house and home in T'ai[2].

The lucky grains were sent down to us,
The black millet, the double-kernelled,
Millet pink-sprouted and white.
Far and wide the black and the double-kernelled
He reaped and acred[3];

Far and wide the millet pink and white
He carried in his arms, he bore on his back,
Brought them home, and created the sacrifice.

What are they, our sacrifices?
We pound the grain, we bale it out,
We sift, we tread,
We wash it—soak, soak;
We boil it all steamy.
Then with due care, due thought
We gather southernwood, make offering of fat,
Take lambs for the rite of expiation,
We roast, we broil,
To give a start to the coming year.

---

[1] By God.

[2] South-west of Wu-kung Hsien, west of Sianfu. Said to be where his mother came from.

[3] The yield was reckoned per acre (100 ft. square).

实覃实吁。厥声载路。

诞实匍匐。克岐克嶷。

以就口食。蓺之荏菽。

荏菽旆旆。禾役穟穟。

麻麦幪幪。瓜瓞唪唪。

诞后稷之穑。有相之道。

茀厥丰草。种之黄茂。

实方实苞。实种实褎。

实发实秀。实坚实好。

实颖实栗。即有邰家室。

诞降嘉种。维秬维秠。

维穈维芑。恒之秬秠。

是获是亩。恒之穈芑。

是任是负。以归肇祀。

诞我祀如何。或舂或揄。

或簸或蹂。释之叟叟。

烝之浮浮。载谋载惟。

取萧祭脂。取羝以軷。

载燔载烈。以兴嗣岁。

High we load the stands,

The stands of wood and of earthenware.

As soon as the smell rises

God on high is very pleased:

'What smell is this, so strong and good?'

Hou-Chi founded the sacrifices,

And without blemish or flaw

They have gone on till now.

昂盛于豆。于豆于登。
其香始升。上帝居歆。
胡臭亶时。后稷肇祀。
庶无罪悔。以迄于今。

《毛诗正义》，第 586—595 页。

SONGS OF COURTSHIP
(Seventh Century B.C.?)

(1)
OUT in the bushlands a creeper grows,
The falling dew lies thick upon it.
There was a man so lovely,
Clear brow well rounded.
By chance I came across him,
And he let me have my will.

Out in the bushlands a creeper grows,
The falling dew lies heavy on it.
There was a man so lovely,
Well rounded his clear brow.
By chance I came upon him:
'Oh, Sir, to be with you is good.'

(2)
IN the lowlands is the goat's-peach[①];
Very delicate are its boughs.
Oh, soft and tender,
Glad I am that you have no friend.

In the lowlands is the goat's-peach;
Very delicate are its flowers.
Oh, soft and tender,
Glad I am that you have no home.

In the lowlands is the goat's-peach;
Very delicate is its fruit.
Oh, soft and tender,
Glad I am that you have no house.

---

① The goat's-peach was later identified with the Chinese gooseberry, which now only grows a long way south of the Yangtze. The same names were applied to the *Actinidia Chinensis*, which grows in the north and is probably what is meant here.

郑风·野有蔓草

野有蔓草。零露漙兮。
有美一人。清扬婉兮。
邂逅相遇。适我愿兮。
野有蔓草。零露瀼瀼。
有美一人。婉如清扬。
邂逅相遇。与子偕臧。

《毛诗正义》，第181页。

桧风·隰有苌楚

隰有苌楚。猗傩其枝。
夭之沃沃。乐子之无知。
隰有苌楚。猗傩其华。
夭之沃沃。乐子之无家。
隰有苌楚。猗傩其实。
夭之沃沃。乐子之无室。

《毛诗正义》，第263—264页。

(3)

PLOP fall the plums; but there are still seven.[①]

Let those gentlemen that would court me

Come while it is lucky!

Plop fall the plums; there are still three.

Let any gentleman that would court me

Come before it is too late!

Plop fall the plums; in shallow baskets we lay them.

Any gentleman who would court me

Had better speak while there is time.

(4)

A VERY handsome gentleman

Waited for me in the lane;

I am sorry I did not go with him.

A very splendid gentleman

Waited for me in the hall;

I am sorry I did not keep company with him.

I am wearing my unlined coat, my coat all of brocade.

I am wearing my unlined skirt, my skirt all of brocade!

Oh, sir, oh my lord,

Take me with you in your coach!

I am wearing my unlined skirt, my skirt all of brocade.

And my unlined coat, my coat all of brocade.

Oh, sir, oh my lord,

Take me with you in your coach!

---

① This poem is akin to love-divinations of the type 'Loves me, loves me not' and 'This year, next year, some time, never.' Seven, as with us, is a lucky number.

召南·摽有梅

摽有梅。其实七兮。
求我庶士。迨其吉兮。
摽有梅。其实三兮。
求我庶士。迨其今兮。
摽有梅。顷筐塈之。
求我庶士。迨其谓之。

《毛诗正义》，第 61—62 页。

郑风·丰

子之丰兮。俟我乎巷兮。悔予不送兮。
子之昌兮。俟我乎堂兮。悔予不将兮。
衣锦褧衣。裳锦褧裳。
叔兮伯兮。驾予与行。
裳锦褧裳。衣锦褧衣。
叔兮伯兮。驾予与归。

《毛诗正义》，第 176—177 页。

(5)

OF fair girls the loveliest
Was to meet me at the corner of the
Wall.
But she hides and will not show
herself;
I scratch my head, pace up and
down.

Of fair girls the prettiest
Gave me a red flute.
The flush of that red flute
Is pleasure at the girl's beauty.

She has been in the pastures and
brought for me rush-wool,
Very beautiful and rare.
It is not you that are beautiful;
But you were given by a lovely girl.

(6)

I AM going to gather the dodder
To the south of Mei.[①]
Of whom do I think?
Of lovely Mêng Chiang.
She was to wait for me at Sang-
chung,
But she went all the way to Shang-
kung
And came with me to the banks of
the Ch'i.

I am going to gather goosefoot
To the north of Mei.
Of whom do I think?
Of lovely Mêng I,
She was to wait for me at Sang-
chung,
But she went all the way to Shang-
kung
And came with me to the banks of
the Ch'i.

I am going to gather charlock
To the east of Mei.
Of whom do I think?
Of lovely Mêng Yung.
She was to wait for me at Sang-
chung,
But she went all the way to Shang-
kung.
And came with me to the banks of
the Ch'i.

---

① The places mentioned in the song were all in northern Honan.

邶风·静女

静女其姝。俟我于城隅。
爱而不见。搔首踟蹰。
静女其娈。贻我彤管。
彤管有炜。说怿女美。
自牧归荑。洵美且异。
匪女之为美。美人之贻。

《毛诗正义》，第 103—104 页。

墉风·桑中

爰采唐矣。沫之乡矣。云谁之思。美孟姜矣。
期我乎桑中。要我乎上宫。送我乎淇之上矣。
爰采麦矣。沫之北矣。云谁之思。美孟弋矣。
期我乎桑中。要我乎上宫。送我乎淇之上矣。
爰采葑矣。沫之东矣。云谁之思。美孟庸矣。
期我乎桑中。要我乎上宫。送我乎淇之上矣。

《毛诗正义》，第 112—113 页。

(7)

I BEG of you, Chung Tzu,
Do not climb into our homestead,
Do not break the willows we have
planted.
Not that I mind about the willows,
But I am afraid of my father and
mother.
Chung Tzu I dearly love;
But of what my father and mother
say
Indeed I am afraid.

I beg of you, Chung Tzu,
Do not climb over our wall,
Do not break the mulberry-trees we
have planted.
Not that I mind about the mulberry-
trees,
But I am afraid of my brothers.
Chung Tzu I dearly love;
But of what my brothers say
Indeed I am afraid.

I beg of you, Chung Tzu,
Do not climb into our garden,
Do not break the hard-wood we have
planted.
Not that I mind about the hard-wood,
But I am afraid of what people will
say.
Chung Tzu I dearly love;
But of all that people will say
Indeed I am afraid.

(8)

'THE cock has crowed;
The Court by now is full.'
'It was not the cock that crowed;
It was the buzzing of those green
flies.'
'Eastward the sky is bright;
The Court must be in full swing.'
'It is not the light of dawn;
It is the moon that is going to rise.
The gnats fly drowsily;
It will be sweet to share a dream with
you.'
Soon all the Courtiers will go home;
Why get us both into this scrape?

郑风·将仲子

将仲子兮。无逾我里。
无折我树杞。岂敢爱之。
畏我父母。仲可怀也。
父母之言。亦可畏也。
将仲子兮。无逾我墙。
无折我树桑。岂敢爱之。
畏我诸兄。仲可怀也。
诸兄之言。亦可畏也。
将仲子兮。无逾我园。
无折我树檀。岂敢爱之。
畏人之多言。仲可怀也。
人之多言。亦可畏也。

《毛诗正义》，第 161 页。

齐风·鸡鸣

鸡既鸣矣。朝既盈矣。
匪鸡则鸣。苍蝇之声。
东方明矣。朝既昌矣。
匪东方则明。月出之光。
虫飞薨薨。甘与子同梦。
会且归矣。无庶予子憎。

《毛诗正义》，第 186—187 页。

(9)

SHU is away in the hunting-fields,

There is no one living in our lane.

Of course there *are* people living in our lane;

But they are not like Shu,

So beautiful, so good.

Shu has gone after game,

No one drinks wine in our lane,

Of course people *do* drink wine in our lane;

But they are not like Shu,

So beautiful, so loved.

Shu has gone to the wilds,

No one drives horses in our lane.

Of course people *do* drive horses in our lane.

But they are not like Shu,

So beautiful, so brave.

郑风·叔于田

叔于田。巷无居人。岂无居人。不如叔也。洵美且仁。
叔于狩。巷无饮酒。岂无饮酒。不如叔也。洵美且好。
叔适野。巷无服马。岂无服马。不如叔也。洵美且武。

《毛诗正义》，第 162 页。

(10)
SHU in the hunting-fields
Driving his team of four,
The reins like ribbons in his hand,
His helpers[①] leaping as in the dance!
Shu in the prairie[②].
The flames rise crackling on every side;
Bare-armed he braves a tiger
To lay at the Duke's feet.
Please, Shu, no rashness!
Take care, or it will hurt you.

Shu in the hunting-fields
Driving his team of bays.
The yoke-horses, how high they prance!
Yet the helpers keep line
Like wild-geese winging in the sky.
Shu in the prairie.
Flames leap crackling on every side.
How well he shoots, how cleverly he drives!
Now giving rein, now pulling to a halt,
Now letting fly,
Now following up his prey.

Shu in the hunting-fields,
Driving a team of greys.
The two yoke-horses with heads in line,
The two helpers obedient to his hand.
Shu in the prairie,
Huge fires crackling on every side.
His horses slow down,
Shu shoots less often.
Now he lays aside his quiver,
Now he puts his bow in its case.

---

① The two outside horses.
② That has been fired to drive the game into the open.

郑风·大叔于田

　　叔于田。乘乘马。执辔如组。两骖如舞。叔在薮。火烈具举。禧裼暴虎。献于公所。将叔无狃。戒其伤女。

　　叔于田。乘乘黄。两服上襄。两骖雁行。叔在薮。火烈具扬。叔善射忌。又良御忌。抑磬控忌。抑纵送忌。

　　叔于田。乘乘鸨。两服齐首。两骖如手。叔在薮。火烈具阜。叔马慢忌。叔发罕忌。抑释掤忌。抑鬯弓忌。

　　　　　　　　　　《毛诗正义》，第 162—163 页。

(11)
A MOON rising white
Is the beauty of my lovely one.
Ah, the tenderness, the grace!
Trouble consumes me.

A moon rising bright
Is the fairness of my lovely one.
Ah, the gentle softness!
Trouble torments me.

A moon rising in splendour
Is the beauty of my lovely one.
Ah, the delicate yielding!
Trouble confounds me.

(12)
OUTSIDE the Eastern Gate
Are girls many as the clouds;
But though they are many as clouds
There is none on whom my heart dwells.
White jacket and grey scarf
Alone could cure my woe.

Beyond the Gate Tower
Are girls lovely as rush-wool;
But though they are lovely as rush-wool
There is none with whom my heart bides.
White jacket and madder skirt
Alone could bring me joy.

陈风·月出

月出皎兮。佼人僚兮。
舒窈纠兮。劳心悄兮。
月出皓兮。佼人懰兮。
舒懮受兮。劳心慅兮。
月出照兮。佼人燎兮。
舒夭绍兮。劳心惨兮。

《毛诗正义》，第 254 页。

郑风·出其东门

出其东门。有女如云。
虽则如云。匪我思存。
缟衣綦巾。聊乐我员。
出其闉阇。有女如荼。
虽则如荼。匪我思且。
缟衣茹藘。聊可与娱。

《毛诗正义》，第 180—181 页。

(13)

LOOK at that little bay of the Ch'i,
Its kitesfoot so delicately waving.
Delicately fashioned is my lord,
As thing cut, as thing filed,
As thing chiselled, as thing polished.
Oh, the grace, the elegance!
Oh, the lustre, oh, the light!
Delicately fashioned is my lord;
Never for a moment can I forget him.

Look at that little bay of the Ch'i,
Its kitesfoot so fresh.
Delicately fashioned is my lord,
His ear-plugs are of precious stones,
His cap-gems stand out like stars.
Oh, the grace, the elegance!
Oh, the lustre, the light!
Delicately fashioned is my lord;
Never for a moment can I forget him.

Look at that little bay of the Ch'i,
Its kitesfoot in their crowds.
Delicately fashioned is my lord,
As a thing of bronze, a thing of white
metal,
As a sceptre of jade, a disc of jade.
How free, how easy
He leant over his chariot-rail!
How cleverly he chaffed and joked,
And yet was never rude!

(14)

IF along the highroad
I caught hold of your sleeve,
Do not hate me;
Old ways take time to overcome.
If along the highroad
I caught hold of your hand,
Do not be angry with me;
Friendship takes time to overcome.

卫风·淇奥

　　瞻彼淇奥。绿竹猗猗。有匪君子。如切如磋。如琢如磨。瑟兮僩兮。赫兮咺兮。有匪君子。终不可谖兮。

　　瞻彼淇奥。绿竹青青。有匪君子。充耳琇莹。会弁如星。瑟兮僩兮。赫兮咺兮。有匪君子。终不可谖兮。

　　瞻彼淇奥。绿竹如箦。有匪君子。如金如锡。如圭如璧。宽兮绰兮。猗重较兮。善戏谑兮。不为虐兮。

《毛诗正义》，第125—127页。

郑风·遵大路

　　遵大路兮。掺执子之祛兮。
　　无我恶兮。不寁故也。
　　遵大路兮。掺执子之手兮。
　　无我丑兮。不寁好也。

《毛诗正义》，第167—168页。

(15)

BY the willows of the Eastern Gate,

Whose leaves are so thick,

At dusk we were to meet;

And now the morning star is bright.

By the willows of the Eastern Gate,

Whose leaves are so close,

At dusk we were to meet;

And now the morning star is pale.

(16)

'I BROUGHT my great carriage that thunders

And a coat downy as rush-wool,

It was not that I did not love you,

But I feared that you had lost heart.

I brought my great carriage that rumbles

And a coat downy as the pink sprouts^①.

It was not that I did not love you,

But I feared that you would not elope.'

Alive, they never shared a house,

But in death they had the same grave.

'You thought I had broken faith;

I was true as the bright sun above.'

---

① Of red millet.

陈风·东门之杨

东门之杨。其叶牂牂。
昏以为期。明星煌煌。
东门之杨。其叶肺肺。
昏以为期。明星晢晢。

《毛诗正义》，第 252 页。

王风·大车

大车槛槛。毳衣如菼。
岂不尔思。畏子不敢。
大车啍啍。毳衣如璊。
岂不尔思。畏子不奔。
榖则异室。死则同穴。
谓予不信。有如皦日。

《毛诗正义》，第 152—153 页。

WEDDING SONG

MY lord is all a-glow.
In his left hand he holds the reed-pipe,
With his right he summons me to make free with him.
Oh, the joy!

My lord is care-free.
In his left hand he holds the dancing plumes,
With his right he summons me to sport with him.
Oh, the joy!

王风·君子阳阳

君子阳阳。左执簧。
右招我由房。其乐只且。
君子陶陶。左执翿。
右招我由敖。其乐只且。

《毛诗正义》，第 148 页。

WIDOW'S LAMENT

THE cloth-plant grew till it covered the thorn bush;
The bindweed spread over the wilds.
My lovely one is here no more.
With whom? No, I sit alone.

The cloth-plant grew till it covered the brambles;
The bindweed spread across the borders of the field.
My lovely one is here no more.
With whom? No, I lie down alone.

The horn pillow[①] so beautiful,
The worked coverlet so bright!
My lovely one is here no more.
With whom? No, alone I watch till dawn.

Summer days, winter nights—
Year after year of them must pass
Till I go to him where he dwells.
Winter nights, summer days—
Year after year of them must pass
Till I go to his home.

---

① A pillow of wood, inlaid with horn.

唐风·葛生

葛生蒙楚。蔹蔓于野。
予美亡此。谁与独处。
葛生蒙棘。蔹蔓于域。
予美亡此。谁与独息。
角枕粲兮。锦衾烂兮。
予美亡此。谁与独旦。
夏之日。冬之夜。
百岁之后。归于其居。
冬之夜。夏之日。
百岁之后。归于其室。

《毛诗正义》，第 226—227 页。

TWO SOLDIERS' SONGS

再
造
的
镜
像

(1)
WHAT plant is not faded?
What day do we not march?
What man is not taken
To defend the four bounds?

What plant is not wilting?
What man is not taken from his wife?
Alas for us soldiers,
Treated as though we were not fellow-men!

Are we buffaloes, are we tigers
That our home should be these desolate wilds?
Alas for us soldiers,
Neither by day nor night can we rest!

The fox bumps and drags
Through the tall, thick grass.
Inch by inch move our barrows
As we push them along the track.

小雅·鱼藻之什·何草不黄

何草不黄。何日不行。
何人不将。经营四方。
何草不玄。何人不矜。
哀我征夫。独为匪民。
匪兕匪虎。率彼旷野。
哀我征夫。朝夕不暇。
有芃者狐。率彼幽草。
有栈之车。行彼周道。

《毛诗正义》，第 526—527 页。

(2)

WE plucked the bracken, plucked the bracken
While the young shoots were springing up.
Oh, to go back, go back!
The year is ending.
We have no house, no home
Because of the Hsien-yün.
We cannot rest or bide
Because of the Hsien-yün.

We plucked the bracken, plucked the bracken
While the shoots were soft.
Oh, to go back, go back!
Our hearts are sad,
Our sad hearts burn,
We are hungry and thirsty,
But our campaign is not over.
Nor is any of us sent home with news.

We plucked the bracken, plucked the bracken;
But the shoots were hard.
Oh, to go back, go back!
The year is running out.
But the king's business never ends;
We cannot rest or bide.
Our hearts are very bitter;
We went, but do not come.

小雅·鹿鸣之什·采薇

采薇采薇。薇亦作止。
曰归曰归。岁亦莫止。
靡室靡家。猃狁之故。
不遑启居。猃狁之故。
采薇采薇。薇亦柔止。
曰归曰归。心亦忧止。
忧心烈烈。载饥载渴。
我戍未定。靡使归聘。
采薇采薇。薇亦刚止。
曰归曰归。岁亦阳止。
王事靡盬。不遑启处。
忧心孔疚。我行不来。

What splendid thing is that?
It is the flower of the cherry-tree.
What great carriage is that?
It is our lord's chariot,
His war-chariot ready yoked,
With its four steeds so eager.
How should we dare stop or tarry?
In one month we have had three alarms.

We yoke the teams of four,
Those steeds so strong,
That our lord rides behind,
That lesser men protect.
The four steeds so grand,
The ivory bow-ends, the fish-skin quiver.
Yes, we must be always on our guard;
The Hsien-yün are very swift.

Long ago, when we started,
The willows spread their shade.
Now that we turn back
The snowflakes fly.
The march before us is long,
We are thirsty and hungry,
Our hearts are stricken with sorrow,
But no one listens to our plaint.

彼尔维何。维常之华。
彼路斯何。君子之车。
戎车既驾。四牡业业。
岂敢定居。一月三捷。
驾彼四牡。四牡骙骙。
君子所依。小人所腓。
四牡翼翼。象弭鱼服。
岂不日戒。猃狁孔棘。
昔我往矣。杨柳依依。
今我来思。雨雪霏霏。
行道迟迟。载渴载饥。
我心伤悲。莫知我哀。

《毛诗正义》，第 331—333 页。

RETURN FROM BATTLE

再
造
的
镜
像

WIFE: Tall grows that pear-tree,
                  Its fruit so fair to see.[①]
                  The king's business never ends;
                  Day in, day out it claims us.

CHORUS: In spring-time, on a day so sunny—
                  Yet your heart full of grief?
                  The soldiers have leave!

WIFE: Tall grows that pear-tree,
                  Its leaves so thick.
                  The king's business never ends;
                  My heart is sick and sad.

CHORUS: Every plant and tree so leafy,
                  Yet your heart sad?
                  The soldiers are coming home!

SOLDIER: I climb that northern hill
                  To pluck the boxthorn.
                  The king's business never ends;
                  What will become of my father, of my mother?

CHORUS: Their wickered chariots drag painfully along,
                  Their horses are tired out.
                  But the soldiers have not far to go.

WIFE: If he were not expected and did not come
                  My heart would still be sad.
                  But he named a day, and that day is passed,
                  So that my torment is great indeed.

CHORUS: The tortoise and the yarrow-stalks agree;
                  Both tell glad news.
                  Your soldier is close at hand.

The tortoise and the yarrow-stalks represent two methods of divination. The first consisted in heating the carapace of a tortoise and 'reading' the cracks that appeared; the second, in shuffling stalks of the Siberian milfoil.

---

① 'The tree flowers in its season but the soldiers cannot lead a natural existence' (earliest commentator). This use of contrast was completely misunderstood by later interpreters.

小雅·鹿鸣之什·杕杜

有杕之杜。有睆其实。
王事靡盬。继嗣我日。
日月阳止。女心伤止。
征夫遑止。

有杕之杜。其叶萋萋。
王事靡盬。我心伤悲。
卉木萋止。女心悲止。
征夫归止。

陟彼北山。言采其杞。
王事靡盬。忧我父母。
檀车幝幝。四牡痯痯。
征夫不远。

匪载匪来。忧心孔疚。
期逝不至。而多为恤。
卜筮偕止。会言近止。
征夫迩止。

《毛诗正义》，第 339—340 页。

HERDSMAN'S SONG

WHO says you have no sheep?
Three hundred is the flock.
Who says you have no cattle?
Ninety are the black-lips.
Here your rams come,
Their horns thronging;
Here your cattle come,
Their ears flapping.

Some go down the slope,
Some are drinking in the pool,
Some are sleeping, some waking.
Here your herdsmen come.
In rush-cloak and bamboo-hat,
Some shouldering their dinners.
Only thirty brindled[①] beasts!
Your sacrifices will not go short.

Your herdsman comes,
Bringing faggots, bringing brushwood,
With the cock-game, with hen-game.
Your rams come,
Sturdy and sound;
None that limps, none that ails.
He beckons to them with raised arm;
All go up into the stall.

Your herdsman dreams,
Dreams of locusts and fish,
Of banners and flags.
A wise man explains the dreams:
'Locusts and fishes
Mean fat years.
Flags and banners
Mean a teeming house and home.'[②]

---

① i.e. the rest are whole-coloured and therefore suitable for sacrifice.

② This helps to explain why flag-waving plays such a prominent part in the fertility-rites of peasant Europe.

小雅·鸿雁之什·无羊

谁谓尔无羊。三百维群。
谁谓尔无牛。九十其犉。
尔羊来思。其角濈濈。
尔牛来思。其耳湿湿。
或降于阿。或饮于池。
或寝或讹。尔牧来思。
何蓑何笠。或负其餱。
三十维物。尔牲则具。
尔牧来思。以薪以蒸。
以雌以雄。尔羊来思。
矜矜兢兢。不骞不崩。
麾之以肱。毕来既升。
牧人乃梦。众维鱼矣。
旐维旟矣。大人占之。
众维鱼矣。实维丰年。
旐维旟矣。室家溱溱。

《毛诗正义》，第 387—388 页。

DYNASTIC HYMN

So they appeared before their lord the king
To get from him their emblems,
Dragon-banners blazing bright,
Tuneful bells tinkling,
Bronze-knobbed reins jangling—
The gifts shone with glorious light.
Then they showed them to their shining ancestors
Piously, making offering,
That they might be vouchsafed long life,
Everlastingly be guarded.
Oh, a mighty store of blessings!
Glorious and mighty, those former princes and lords
Who secure us with many blessings,
Through whose bright splendours
We greatly prosper.

周颂·臣工之什·载见

载见辟王。曰求厥章。
龙旂阳阳。和铃央央。
鞗革有鸧。休有烈光。
率见昭考。以孝以享。
以介眉寿。永言保之。思皇多祜。
烈文辟公。绥以多福。俾缉熙于纯嘏。

《毛诗正义》，第 734—735 页。

TWO LAMENTS

再
造
的
镜
像

(1)
GINGERLY walked the hare,
But the pheasant was caught in the snare.
At the beginning of my life
All was still quiet;
In my latter days
I have met great calamities[①].
Would that I might sleep and never stir!

Gingerly walked the hare;
But the pheasant got caught in the trap.
At the beginning of my life
The times were not yet troublous.
In my latter days
I have met great sorrows.
Would that I might sleep and wake no more!

Gingerly walked the hare;
But the pheasant got caught in the net.
At the beginning of my life
The times were still good.
In my latter days
I have met great disasters.
Would that I might sleep and hear no more!

(2)
OH, what has become of us?
Those big dish-stands that towered so high!
Today, even when we get food, there is none to spare.
Alas and alack!
We have not grown as we sprouted.

Oh, what has become of us?
Four dishes at every meal!
Today, even when we get food, there is never enough.
Alas and alack!
We have not grown as we sprouted.

---

① The fall of the western Chou dynasty?

王风·兔爰

有兔爰爰。雉离于罗。
我生之初。尚无为。
我生之后。逢此百罹。尚寐无吪。
有兔爰爰。雉离于罦。
我生之初。尚无造。
我生之后。逢此百忧。尚寐无觉。
有兔爰爰。雉离于罿。
我生之初。尚无庸。
我生之后。逢此百凶。尚寐无聪。

《毛诗正义》，第 150—151 页。

秦风·权舆

於我乎。夏屋渠渠。今也每食无余。
于嗟乎。不承权舆。
於我乎。每食四簋。今也每食不饱。
于嗟乎。不承权舆。

《毛诗正义》，第 254 页。

THE BIG CHARIOT

再
造
的
镜
像

DON'T help-on the big chariot;
You will only make yourself dusty.
Don't think about the sorrows of the world;
You will only make yourself wretched.

Don't help-on the big chariot;
You won't be able to see for dust.
Don't think about the sorrows of the world;
Or you will never escape from your despair.

Don't help-on the big chariot;
You'll be stifled with dust.
Don't think about the sorrows of the world;
You will only load yourself with care.

小雅·谷风之什·无将大车

　　无将大车。祇自尘兮。
　　无思百忧。祇自疧兮。
　　无将大车。维尘冥冥。
　　无思百忧。不出于颎。
　　无将大车。维尘雍兮。
　　无思百忧。祇自重兮。

《毛诗正义》，第 444 页。

DANCE SONG

THE unicorn's hoofs!
The duke's sons throng.
Alas for the unicorn!

The unicorn's brow!
The duke's kinsmen throng.
Alas for the unicorn!

The unicorn's horn!
The duke's clansmen throng.
Alas for the unicorn!

周南·麟之趾

麟之趾。振振公子。于嗟麟兮。
麟之定。振振公姓。于嗟麟兮。
麟之角。振振公族。于嗟麟兮。

《毛诗正义》，第 43—44 页。

HYMN TO THE FALLEN

(Fourth Century B.C.?)

再
造
的
镜
像

'WE hold our flat shields, we wear our jerkins of hide;
The axles of our chariots touch, our short swords meet.
Standards darken the sun, the foe roll on like clouds;
Arrows fall thick, the warriors press forward.
They have overrun our ranks, they have crossed our line;
The trace-horse on the left is dead, the one on the right is wounded.
The fallen horses block our wheels, our chariot is held fast;
We grasp our jade drum-sticks, we beat the rolling drums.'

Heaven decrees their fall, the dread Powers are angry;
The warriors are all dead, they lie in the open fields.
They set out, but shall not enter; they went but shall not come back.
The plains are empty and wide, the way home is long.
Their tall swords are at their waist, their bows are under their arm;
Though their heads were severed their spirit could not be subdued.
They that fought so well—in death are warriors still;
Stubborn and steadfast to the end, they could not be dishonoured.
Their bodies perished in the fight, but the magic of their souls is strong—
Captains among the ghosts, heroes among the Dead!

国殇

操吴戈兮被犀甲，车错毂兮短兵接。
旌蔽日兮敌若云，矢交坠兮士争先。
凌余阵兮躐余行，左骖殪兮右刃伤。
霾两轮兮絷四马，援玉枹兮击鸣鼓。
天时坠兮威灵怒，严杀尽兮弃原野。
出不入兮往不反，平原忽兮路超远。
带长剑兮挟秦弓，首身离兮心不惩。
诚既勇兮又以武，终刚强兮不可凌。
身既死兮神以灵，子魂魄兮为鬼雄！

《屈原集校注》（上册），第283—284页。

THE GREAT SUMMONS

Invocation to the soul of a dead or sick man.

Anon. (Third or Second Century B.C.)

GREEN Spring receiveth
The vacant earth;
The white sun shineth;
Spring wind provoketh
To burst and burgeon
Each sprout and flower.
The dark ice melts and moves; hide not, my soul!
O Soul come back again! O do not stray!

O Soul, come back again and go not east or west, or north or south!
For to the East a mighty water drowneth
Earth's other shore;
Tossed on its waves and heaving with its tides
The hornless Dragon of the Ocean rideth;
Clouds gather low and fogs enfold the sea
And gleaming ice drifts past.
O Soul go not to the East,
To the silent Valley of Sunrise!

O Soul go not to the South
Where mile on mile the earth is burnt away
And poisonous serpents slither through the flames,
Where on precipitous paths or in deep woods
Tigers and leopards prowl,
And water-scorpions wait;
Where the king-python rears his giant head.
O Soul go not to the South
Where the three-footed tortoise spits disease!

O Soul go not to the West
Where level wastes of sand stretch on and on;
And demons rage, swine-headed, hairy-skinned,
With bulging eyes;
Who in wild laughter gnash projecting fangs.
O soul go not to the West
Where many perils wait!

楚辞·大招

青春受谢，白日昭只；
春气奋发，万物遽只。
冥凌浃行，魂无逃只；
魂魄归徕！无远遥只！
魂乎归徕，无东无西，无南无北只！
东有大海，溺水浟浟只；
螭龙并流，上下悠悠只。
雾雨淫淫，白皓胶只；
魂乎无东，汤谷寂寥只。
魂乎无南！
南有炎火千里，蝮蛇蜒只；
山林险隘，虎豹蜿只；
鳙鳙短狐，王虺骞只。
魂乎无南，蜮伤躬只。
魂乎无西！
西方流沙，漭洋洋只；
豕首纵目，被发鬤只；
长爪踞牙，诶笑狂只。
魂乎无西，多害伤只。

O Soul go not to the North,

To the Lame Dragon's frozen peaks;

Where trees and grasses dare not grow;

Where the river runs too wide to cross

And too deep to plumb,

And the sky is white with snow

And the cold cuts and kills.

O Soul seek not to fill

The treacherous voids of the North!

O Soul come back to idleness and peace.

In quietude enjoy

The lands of Ching and Ch'u.

There work your will and follow your desire

Till sorrow is forgot,

And carelessness shall bring you length of days.

O Soul come back to joys beyond all telling!

Where thirty cubits high at harvest-time

The corn is stacked;

Where pies are cooked of millet and water-grain,

Guests watch the steaming bowls

And sniff the pungency of peppered herbs.

The cunning cook adds slices of bird-flesh,

Pigeon and yellow-heron and black-crane.

They taste the badger-stew.

O Soul come back to feed on foods you love!

Next are brought

Fresh turtle, and sweet chicken cooked in cheese

Pressed by the men of Ch'u.

And pickled sucking-pig

And flesh of whelps floating in liver-sauce

With salad of minced radishes in brine;

All served with that hot spice of southernwood

The land of Wu supplies.

O Soul come back to choose the meats you love!

Roasted daw, steamed mallard and grilled quail—

On every fowl they fare.

Boiled perch and sparrow broth—in each preserved

The separate flavour that is most its own.

O Soul come back to where such dainties wait!

魂乎无北！

北有寒山，逴龙赩只；

代水不可涉，深不可测只；

天白颢颢，寒凝凝只。

魂乎无往，盈北极只。

魂魄归徕，闲以静只。

自恣荆楚，安以定只。

逞志究欲，心意安只。

穷身永乐，年寿延只。

魂乎归徕，乐不可言只！

五谷六仞，设菰粱只；

鼎臑盈望，和致芳只；

内鸧鸽鹄，味豺羹只；

魂乎归徕，恣所尝只！

鲜蠵甘鸡，和楚酪只；

醢豚苦狗，脍苴蒪只；

吴酸蒿蒌，不沾薄只；

魂乎归徕，恣所择只！

炙鸹烝凫，煔鹑陈只；

煎鰿臛雀，遽爽存只；

魂乎归徕，丽以先只！

The four strong liquors are warming at the fire
So that they grate not on the drinker's throat.
How fragrant rise their fumes, how cool their taste!
Such drink is not for louts or serving-men!
And wise distillers from the land of Wu
Blend unfermented spirit with white yeast
And brew the *li* of Ch'u.
O Soul come back and let your trembling cease!

Reed-organs from the lands of Tai and Ch'in
And Wei and Chêng
Gladden the feasters, and old songs are sung:
The 'Rider's Song' that once
Fu-hsi, the ancient monarch made;
And the shrill songs of Ch'u.
Then after prelude from the pipes of Chao
The ballad-singer's voice rises alone.
O Soul come back to the hollow mulberry-tree!①

Eight and eight the dancers sway,
Weaving their steps to the poet's voice
Who speaks his odes and rhapsodies;
They tap their bells and beat their chimes
Rigidly, lest harp and flute
Should mar the measure.
Then rival singers of the Four Domains
Compete in melody, till not a tune
Is left unsung that human voice could sing.
O Soul come back and listen to their songs!

Then women enter whose red lips and dazzling teeth
Seduce the eye;
But meek and virtuous, trained in every art,
Fit sharers of play-time,
So soft their flesh and delicate their bones.
O Soul come back and let them ease your woe!

---

① The lute.

四酎并孰，不涩嗌只；
清馨冻饮，不歠役只；
吴醴白糵，和楚沥只；
魂乎归徕，不遽惕只！
代、秦、郑、卫，鸣竽张只；
伏戏《驾辩》，楚《劳商》只；
讴和《扬阿》，赵箫倡只；
魂乎归徕，定空桑只！
二八接武，投诗赋只；
叩钟调磬，娱人乱只；
四上竞气，极声变只；
魂乎归徕，听歌譔只！
朱唇皓齿，嫭以姱只；
比德好闲，习以都只；
丰肉微骨，调以娱只；
魂乎归徕，安以舒只！

Then enter other ladies with laughing
lips
And sidelong glances under moth
eyebrows,
Whose cheeks are fresh and red;
Ladies both great of heart and long
of limb,
Whose beauty by sobriety is
matched.
Well-padded cheeks and ears with
curving rim,
High-arching eyebrows, as with
compass drawn,
Great hearts and loving gestures—all
are there;
Small waists and necks as slender as
the clasp
Of courtiers' buckles.
O Soul come back to those whose
tenderness
Drives angry thoughts away!

Last enter those
Whose every action is contrived to
please;
Black-painted eyebrows and white-
powdered cheeks.
They reek with scent; with their long
sleeves they brush
The faces of the feasters whom they
pass,
Or pluck the coats of those who will
not stay.
O Soul come back to pleasures of the
night!

A summer-house with spacious
rooms
And a high hall with beams stained
red;
A little closet in the southern wing
Reached by a private stair.
And round the house a covered way
should run
Where horses might be trained.

And sometimes riding, sometimes
going afoot
You shall explore, O Soul, the parks
of spring;
Your jewelled axles gleaming in the
sun
And yoke inlaid with gold;
Or amid orchises and sandal-trees
Shall walk in the dark woods.
O Soul come back and live for these
delights!

Peacocks shall fill your gardens; you
shall rear
The rock and phoenix, and red
jungle-fowl,
Whose cry at dawn assembles river
storks
To join the play of cranes and ibises;
Where the wild-swan all day
Pursues the glint of idle kingfishers.
O Soul come back to watch the birds
in flight!

嫮目宜笑，蛾眉曼只；
容则秀雅，稚朱颜只；
魂乎归徕，静以安只！
婷修滂浩，丽以佳只；
曾颊倚耳，曲眉规只；
滂心绰态，姣丽施只；
小腰秀颈，若鲜卑只；
魂乎归徕，思怨移只！
易中利心，以动作只，
粉白黛黑，施芳泽只！
长袂拂面，善留客只；
魂乎归徕，以娱昔只！
青色直眉，美目媔只；
靥辅奇牙，宜笑嗎只；
丰肉微骨，体便娟只；
魂乎归徕，恣所便只！
夏屋广大，沙堂秀只；
南房小坛，观绝霤只；
曲屋步壛，宜扰畜只；
腾驾步游，猎春囿只；
琼毂错衡，英华假只；
菎兰桂树，郁弥路只；
魂乎归徕，恣志虑只！
孔雀盈园，畜鸾皇只；
鹍鸿群晨，杂鹙鸧只；
鸿鹄代游，曼鹔鹴只；
魂乎归徕，凤皇翔只！

He who has found such manifold delights
Shall feel his cheeks aglow
And the blood-spirit dancing through his limbs.
Stay with me, Soul, and share
The span of days that happiness will bring;
See sons and grandsons serving at the Court
Ennobled and enriched.
O Soul come back and bring prosperity
To house and stock!

The roads that lead to Ch'u
Shall teem with travellers as thick as clouds,
A thousand miles away.
For the Five Orders of Nobility
Shall summon sages to assist the King
And with godlike discrimination choose
The wise in council; by their aid to probe
The hidden discontents of humble men
And help the lonely poor.
O Soul come back and end what we began!

Fields, villages and lanes
Shall throng with happy men;
Good rule protect the people and make known
The King's benevolence to all the land;
Stern discipline prepare
Their natures for the soft caress of Art.
O Soul come back to where the good are praised!

Like the sun shining over the four seas
Shall be the reputation of our King;
His deeds, matched only in Heaven, shall repair
The wrongs endured by every tribe of men—
Northward to Yu and southward to Annam,
To the Sheep's-Gut Mountain and the Eastern Seas.
O Soul come back to where the wise are sought!

曼泽怡面，血气盛只；
永宜厥身，保寿命只；
室家盈廷，爵禄盛只；
魂乎归徕，居室定只！
接径千里，出若云只；
三圭重侯，听类神只；
察笃夭隐，孤寡存只；
魂乎归徕，正始昆只！
田邑千畛，人阜昌只；
美冒众流，德泽章只；
先威后文，善美明只；
魂乎归徕，赏罚当只！
名声若日，照四海只；
德誉配天，万民理只；
北至幽陵，南交趾只；
西薄羊肠，东穷海只；
魂乎归徕，尚贤士只！

Behold the glorious virtues of our King
Triumphant, terrible;
Behold with solemn faces in the Hall
The three Grand Ministers walk up and down—
None chosen for the post save landed-lords
Or, in default, Knights of the Nine Degrees.
Clout and pin-hole are marked, already is hung
The shooting-target, where with bow in hand
And arrows under arm
Each archer does obeisance to each,
Willing to yield his rights of precedence.
O Soul come back to where men honour still
The name of the Three Kings[①].

---

① Yü, T'ang and Wên, the three just rulers of antiquity.

发政献行，禁苛暴只；
举杰压陛，诛讥罢只；
直赢在位，近禹麾只；
豪杰执政，流泽施只；
魂乎归徕，国家为只！
雄雄赫赫，天德明只；
三公穆穆，登降堂只；
诸侯毕极，立九卿只；
昭质既设，大侯张只；
执弓挟矢，揖辞让只；
魂乎徕归，尚三王只！

《古文辞类纂评注》，第 1768—1769 页。

第二章 汉魏六朝诗

导言

跃动韵律

韦利是英译中日古典文学的巨擘，最先受人瞩目的译作，是他翻译的中国古诗。他以自由诗的形式翻译韵脚明确的古诗，译笔如行云流水，深得古诗意境的三昧。他采用不押韵的自由诗体，并非不讲究韵律，而是把重点聚焦于英文诗句的抑扬顿挫，以音步的节奏来展现音律。韦利使用的诗体韵律，基本符合霍普金斯创造的"跃动韵律"。跃动韵律的特色，是把重音放在音步的第一音节，随之以不加重音的音节，长短视情况而有所变化。霍普金斯在19世纪后半叶创造"跃动韵律"，自称源自英国古谣吟唱、莎士比亚与弥尔顿。他发现这种自然的诗歌韵律，不以音步限制为准，而以节奏的跃动为主。我们无法确定，韦利是否亦步亦趋，完全遵循霍普金斯的创意，采用这种特殊的自由诗体来翻译中国古诗。也许是韦利的古典学训练，以及他对古代英诗歌谣的关注，使他循着"跃动韵律"的脉络来译诗，特别是中国五言古诗。他不用一般英诗流行的音步与韵脚规律，而是遵循"跃动韵律"，回归英文古诗歌的风味，以之表达中国古诗诗情内敛的张力，展示辽遥夐远的诗情，效果别具一格，令人惊艳。

中国古诗常用叠字，在形式上很难用英诗形式来表达，若是完全不做翻译的应对，不以特殊形式来呈现，似乎又丧失了原作缠绵缱绻的意蕴。韦利翻译中国古诗，就利用"跃动韵律"的方式，重复叠加字词，制造特殊的文字间离效果，让读者接触诗句的疏离变化，感受东方诗歌的异国情调。最为大家传诵的就是他译的《古诗十九首》，在韦利的《中国诗》一书中则称之为《古诗十七首》。其实，汉魏期间的一批五言古诗，有些是民歌，有些是乐府歌词，也有文人的拟作，在《文选》中列为"古诗十九首"，成为历来撰著文学史的惯用称谓。昭明太子萧统组织编订的安排，只是一种权宜之计，并不能囊括汉魏期间流行的作者不明的五言古诗。韦利从中选取 17 首译成英文，也可视为他的个人别裁。

《古诗十七首》第一首《行行重行行》开头两句："行行重行行，与君生别离"，韦利译文是："On and on, always on and on/ Away from you, parted by a life-parting."不但字斟句酌，字字对应，重复使用叠字，标明了"行行重行行"，还为"生别离"创了一个英文新词"life-parting"，与"parted"作为重叠的呼应。第二首《青青河畔草》："青青河畔草，郁郁园中柳。盈盈楼上女，皎皎当窗牖。娥娥红粉妆，纤纤出素手。昔为倡家女，今为荡子妇。荡子行不归，空床难独守。"原诗前六句，都以叠字起头，韦利的译文也就特别突出千回百转的重复意象，展现了楼上怨妇内心喃喃自语的悲情：

GREEN, green, / The grass by the river-bank./ Thick, thick,/ The willow trees in the garden. / Sad, sad,/ The lady in the tower./ White, white,/ Sitting at the casement window./ Fair, fair,/ Her red-powdered face./ Small, small,/ She puts out her pale hand./ Once she was a dancing-house girl,/ Now she is a wandering man's wife./ The wandering man went, but did not return./ It is hard alone to keep an empty bed.

令人惊异的是，韦利的英译几乎逐字逐句跟随原诗，前五句连一个动词都不用，读起来依然诗意盎然。值得注意的是头韵的频繁使用，如第一句的"green""green""grass"，第二句的"thick""thick""trees"，第四句的"white""white""window"，第五句的"fair""fair""face"，以及第六句的"small""small""she"，都是有意识的安排。如此，译诗与英诗格律大相径庭，却形象鲜明，像印象派大师的作品，如行云流水一般，呈现了原诗的古雅诗情。

同样的翻译方式，在《青青陵上柏》一首开头"青青陵上柏，磊磊涧中石"，也是如此处理："GREEN, green,/ The cypress on the mound./ Firm, firm,/ The boulder in the stream."《凛凛岁云暮》的开头"凛凛岁云暮，蝼蛄夕鸣悲"，处理的方式也相同："COLD, cold the year draws to its end,/ The mole-cricket makes a doleful chirping."然而，韦利毕竟是个诗人，注重表达诗情的感受，并非机械化使用这种叠字直译的方式。如《迢迢牵牛星》一诗，开头四句都使用叠字："迢迢牵牛星，皎皎河汉女。纤纤擢素手，札札弄机杼。"韦利译文就有了变化："FAR away twinkles the Herd-boy star;/ Brightly shines the Lady of the Han River./ Slender, slender she plies her white fingers;/ Click, click go the wheels of her spinning loom." 前两句不再使用叠字法，因为要展现远方星座的闪烁亮丽，就加了 "twinkles" 与 "Brightly shines" 以体现动词的作用；后两句又回到叠字的安排，有其曲折变化，特别把札札之声，转成 "click, click"，可谓神来之笔。

以 "click, click" 来表达操弄机杼的札札之声，在他翻译的《木兰辞》中，又再度出现。有趣的是，木兰操弄织机的声音，这次是 "唧唧"："唧唧复唧唧，木兰当户织"。韦利则照着他的拟声法，一路 "click, click" 下去，非常传神地展示了织布的声音："CLICK, click, for ever click, click;/ Mulan sits at the door and weaves." "札札" 与 "唧唧" 是中文的不同拟声词，但都是形容织布的声音，到了韦利的笔下，就一视同仁，都成了 "click, click" 了。

韦利译北朝的《敕勒歌》，保留诗中的叠字，还要表达大草原苍茫的感觉，也显示了诗人的敏感。原诗是："敕勒川，阴山下。天似穹庐，笼盖四野。天苍苍，野茫茫，风吹草低见牛羊。" 他译成："TELEG River/ Lies under the Dark Mountains,/ Where the sky is like the sides of a tent/ Stretched down over the Great Steppe./ The sky is grey, grey/ And the steppe wide, wide./ Over grass that the wind has battered low/ Sheep and oxen roam." "阴山" 是地名，是专有名词，译作 "Dark Mountains" 是意译；"四野" 是普通名词，却译作 "Great Steppe"，让人想到专有名词 "戈壁"，是非常巧妙的词语转换，却指涉分明，地理概念丝毫没错。

古诗英汉对照

THE AUTUMN WIND

By Wu-ti (157-87 B.C.), sixth emperor of the Han dynasty. He came to the throne when he was only sixteen. In this poem he regrets that he is obliged to go on an official journey, leaving his mistress behind in the capital. He is seated in his state barge surrounded by his ministers.

AUTUMN wind rises; white clouds fly.
Grass and trees wither; geese go south.
Orchids, all in bloom; chrysanthemums smell sweet;
I think of my lovely lady; I never can forget.
Floating-pagoda boat crosses Fên River;
Across the mid-stream white waves rise.
Flute and drum keep time to sound of rowers' song;
Amidst revel and feasting sad thoughts come;
Youth's years how few, age how sure!

秋风辞

汉武帝

汉武帝故事曰。上行幸河东。祠后土。顾视帝京。欣然中流。与群臣饮燕。上欢甚。乃自作秋风辞曰。

秋风起兮白云飞。
草木黄落兮雁南归。
兰有秀兮菊有芳。
怀佳人兮不能忘。
泛楼船兮济汾河。
横中流兮扬素波。
箫鼓鸣兮发棹歌。
欢乐极兮哀情多。
少壮几时兮奈老何。

《先秦汉魏晋南北朝诗》（上），第 94—95 页。

LI FU-JÊN

再
造
的
镜
像

THE sound of her silk skirt has stopped.
On the marble pavement dust grows.
Her empty room is cold and still.
Fallen leaves are piled against the doors.
Longing for that lovely lady
How can I bring my aching heart to rest?

The above poem is supposed to have been written by Wu-ti when his mistrees, Li Fu-jên, died. Unable to bear his grief, he sent for wizards from all parts of China, hoping that they would be able to put him into communication with her spirit. At last one of them managed to project her shape on to a curtain. The emperor cried:

Is it or isn't it?
I stand and look.
The swish, swish of a silk skirt.
How slow she comes!

落叶哀蝉曲

罗袂兮无声。
玉墀兮尘生。
虚房冷而寂寞。
落叶依于重扃。
望彼美之女兮。
安得感余心之未宁。

《古诗源》，第 41 页。

李夫人歌

夫人卒……上思念李夫人不已，方士齐人少翁言能致鬼神。乃夜张灯烛，设帷帐，陈酒肉，而令上居他帐，遥望见好女如李夫人之貌，还幄坐而步。又不得就视。帝愈益相思悲感，为作诗，令乐府诸音家弦歌之。

是邪非邪？立而望之，偏何姗姗其来迟！

《乐府诗集》（第 4 册），第 1181 页。

LAMENT OF HSI-CHÜN

About the year 105 B.C. a Chinese lady named Hsi-chün was sent, for political reasons, to be the wife of a central Asian nomad king, K'un Mo, king of the Wu-sun. When she got there, she found her husband old and decrepit. He only saw her once or twice a year, when they drank a cup of wine together. They could not converse, as they had no language in common.

MY people have married me
In a far corner of Earth;
Sent me away to a strange land,
To the king of the Wu-sun.
A tent is my house,
Of felt are my walls;
Raw flesh my food
With mare's milk to drink.
Always thinking of my own country,
My heart sad within.
Would I were a yellow stork
And could fly to my old home!

悲愁歌

乌孙公主

吾家嫁我兮天一方，
远托异国兮乌孙王。
穹庐为室兮旃为墙，
以肉为食兮酪为浆。
居常土思兮心内伤，
愿为黄鹄兮归故乡。

《汉魏晋南北朝隋诗鉴赏词典》，第 48 页。

TO HIS WIFE

By General Su Wu (*c.* 100 B.C.)

SINCE my hair was plaited and we became man and wife
The love between us was never broken by doubt.
So let us be merry this night together,
Feasting and playing while the good time lasts.
I suddenly remember the distance that I must travel;
I spring from bed and look out to see the time.
The stars and planets are all grown dim in the sky;
Long, long is the road; I cannot stay.
I am going on service, away to the battle-ground,
And I do not know when I shall come back.
I hold your hand with only a deep sigh;
Afterwards, tears—in the days when we are parted.
With all your might enjoy the spring flowers,
But do not forget the time of our love and pride.
Know that if I live, I will come back again,
And if I die, we will go on thinking of each other.

旧题苏武诗四首（其三）

无名氏

结发为夫妻，恩爱两不疑。
欢娱在今夕，嬿婉及良时。
征夫怀远路，起视夜何其。
参辰皆已没，去去从此辞。
行役在战场，相见未有期。
握手一长叹，泪为生别滋。
努力爱春华，莫忘欢乐时。
生当复来归，死当长相思。

《汉魏六朝诗鉴赏辞典》，第 172 页。

PARTING FROM SU WU
By LI LING

THE good time will never come back **again;**
In a moment our parting will be over.
Beside the cross-road we faltered, **uneasily;**
In the open fields we paused, **hand in hand.**
The clouds above are floating **across the** sky;
Swiftly, swiftly passing; **or blending** together.
The waves in the wind **lose their fi**xed place
And are rolled away **each to a co**rner of Heaven.
From now onwards **long must** be our parting,
So let us stop again for **a little** while.
I wish I could ride on **the** wings of the morning wind
And go with you right to your journey's end.

Li Ling and Su Wu were both prisoners in the land of the Huns. After nineteen years Su Wu was released. Li Ling would not go back with him. When invited to do so, he got up and danced, singing:

I CAME ten thousand leagues
Across sandy deserts
In the service of my Prince,
To break the Hun tribes.
My way was blocked and barred,
My arrows and sword broken.
My armies had faded away,
My reputation had gone.
My old mother is long dead.
Although I want to requite my Prince
How can I return?

旧题《李少卿与苏武诗》三首（其一）

无名氏

良时不再至，离别在须臾。
屏营衢路侧，执手野踟蹰。
仰视浮云驰，奄忽互相逾。
风波一失所，各在天一隅。
长当从此别，且复立斯须。
欲因晨风发，送子以贱躯。

《汉魏六朝诗鉴赏辞典》，第 166 页。

别歌

李陵

径万里兮度沙漠，为君将兮奋匈奴。
路穷绝兮矢刃摧，士众灭兮名已隤。
老母已死，虽欲报恩将安归！

《汉魏晋南北朝隋诗鉴赏词典》，第 43 页。

POVERTY

By Yang Hsiung (52 B.C.-A.D. 18)

I, YANG TZŬ, hid from life,
Fled from the common world to a
lonely place
Where to the right a great wilderness
touched me
And on the left my neighbour was
the Hill of Sung.
Beggars whose tenements
Lie wall to wall, though they be
tattered and poor,
Rough-used, despised and scorned,
are yet in companies
And sociable clans conjoined. But I
in my despair
Called Poverty to me, saying: Long
ago
You should have been cast out,
driven far away,
Press-ganged, or pilloried as Man's
fourth curse.
Yet not in childhood only, in infancy
When laughing I would build
Castles of soil or sand, were you
My more than neighbour, for your
roof
Touched mine and our two homes
were one;
But in manhood also weighed I with
the great
Lighter because of you
Than fluff or feather; more frail my

fortunes
Than gossamer, who to the State
submitting
Great worth found small employ;
Withdrawing, heard no blame.

What prompts you, Poverty,
So long to linger, an unwanted
guest?
Others wear broidered coats; my
homespun is not whole.
Others eat millet and rice, I boil the
goosefoot seed.
No toy nor treasure is mine,
Nor aught to make me glad.
Clans gather at the feast
In great ease and gladness,
But I abroad the world
Trudge out afoot with panniers on
my back,
Sell my day-labour for a coat to
cover me.
Servant of many masters
Hand-chafed I dig, heel-blistered
hoe,
Bare-backed to the wind and rain.
And that all this befell me,
That friends and favourites forsook
me,
That up the hill of State so laboured
was my climb
Who should bear blame? Who but
you, O Poverty,
Was cause of all my woe?

逐贫赋

扬雄

扬子遁世，离俗独处，
左邻崇山，右接旷野。
邻垣乞儿，终贫且窭。
礼薄义弊，相与群聚，
惆怅失志，呼贫与语：
"汝在六极，投弃荒遐。
好为庸卒，刑戮是加。
匪惟幼稚，嬉戏土砂。
居非近邻，接屋连家。
恩轻毛羽，义薄轻罗。
进不由德，退不受呵。
久为滞客，其意谓何？
人皆文绣，余褐不完。
人皆稻粱，我独藜飧。
贫无宝玩，何以接欢。
宗室之燕，为乐不盘。
徒行负赁，出处易衣。
身服百役，手足胼胝。
或耘或耔，沾体露肌。
朋友道绝，进官凌迟，
厥咎安在，职汝为之。

I fled you high and far, but you
across the hills of heaven
Like a hawk did follow me.
I fled you among the rocks, in
caverns of stone I hid;
But you up those huge steeps
Did follow me.
I fled you to the ocean, sailed that
cypress ship
Across the storm, but you
Whether on wave-crest or in the
hollows of the sea
Did follow me.
And if I move, you too are stirring;
If I lie down you are at rest.
Have you no other friend in all the
world?
What would you seek of me?
Go, Poverty, and pester me no more.
Then said Poverty: So be it, my
master;
I am dismissed. Yet though men say
'Much chatter, little wit', listen! I too
Have a heart that is full and a tale
that must be told.

My father's father long, long ago
Was illustrious in the land, of virtue
so excellent
That by the King's throne in council
he stood
Admonishing the rulers how to make
statutes and laws.

Of earth were the stairs, roofed over
with thatch.
Not carved or hung.
But when the world in latter days
Was given over to folly, fell about in
darkness,
Then gluttons gathered together; by
ill means the covetous
Fastened upon their prey;
Despised my grand-dad, they were
so insolent and proud,
Built arbours of onyx, terraces of
jade,
And huge halls to dwell in, lapped
lakes of wine.
So that at last I left them
Suddenly as a swan that soars
And would not tread their Court.
Thrice daily I look into my heart
And find I did no wrong.
As for your home, mighty are the
blessings I brought,
Stacked high as the hills.
Your small woes you remember;
But my good deeds you have forgot.
Did I not teach you
By gradual usage, indifferent to
endure
Summer's heat and winter's cold?
(And that which neither heat nor cold
can touch—
Is it not eternal as the Gods?)

舍汝远窜，昆仑之巅。
尔复我随，翰飞戾天。
舍尔登山，岩穴隐藏。
尔复我随，陟彼高冈。
舍尔入海，泛彼柏舟。
尔复我随，载沉载浮。
我行尔动，我静尔休。
岂无他人，从我何求！
今汝去矣，勿复久留。"
贫曰："唯、唯。
主人见逐，多言益嗤。
心有所怀，愿得尽辞。
昔我乃祖，宣其明德，
克佐帝尧，誓为典则。
土阶茅茨，匪雕匪饰。
爰及世季，纵其昏惑，
饕餮之群，贪富苟得。
鄙我先人，乃傲乃骄。
瑶台琼榭，室屋崇高，
流酒为池，积肉为崤。
是用鹄逝，不践其朝。
三省吾身，谓予无訾。
处君之家，福禄如山。
忘我大德，思我小怨。
堪寒能暑，少而习焉。
寒暑不忒，等寿神仙。

'I, Poverty,

Turned from you the envy of the covetous, taught you to fear

Neither Chieh the Tyrant nor the Robber Chih.

Others, my master,

Quake behind bolt and bar, while you alone

Live open to the world.

Others by care

And pitiful apprehension are cast down,

While you are gay and free.'

Thus spoke Poverty, and when his speech was ended,

Stern of countenance and with dilated eye,

He gathered up the folds of his garment and rose from where he sat,

Passed down the stairway and left my house.

'Farewell', said Poverty, 'for now I leave you.

To that hill I take my way

Where sheltering, the Lord of Ku-chu's sons

Have learnt to ply my trade.'

Then I, Yang Tzü, left the mat where I lay

And cried: 'O Poverty, let my crooked words

Be as unspoken; forget that I have wronged you.

I have heard truth, O Poverty, and received it.

Live with me always, for of your company

I shall not weary till I die.'

Then Poverty came back and lodged with me,

Nor since has left my side.

桀跖不顾，贪类不干。
人皆重蔽，子独露居；
人皆怵惕，子独无虞。"
言辞既罄，色厉目张，
摄齐而兴，降阶下堂。
"誓将去汝，适彼首阳。
孤竹二子，与我连行。"
余乃避席，辞谢不直：
"请不贰过，闻义则服。
长与汝居，终无厌极。"
贫遂不去，与我游息。

《全汉赋》，第 211—212 页。

THE GOLDEN PALACE
Anon. (First Century A.D.?)

WE go to the Golden Palace,
We set out jade cups,
We summon the honoured guests
To enter at the Golden Gate
And go to the Golden Hall.

In the Eastern Kitchen the meat is sliced and ready,
Pounded beef and boiled pork and mutton.
The Master of the Feast hands round the wine;
The lute-players sound the High Second①.
Some play darts, some face each other at chess;
The rival pieces are marshalled rank against rank.
The fire glows and the smoke puffs and curls,
From the incense-burner rises a delicate fragrance,
The clear wine has made our cheeks red;
Round the table joy and peace prevail.
May those who shared in this day's delight
Through countless autumns enjoy like felicity.

再
造
的
镜
像

---

① Name of a mode associated with songs of unhappy love.

古歌

上金殿。著玉樽。

延贵客。入金门。

入金门。上金堂。

东厨具肴膳。椎牛烹猪羊。

主人前进酒。弹瑟为清商。

投壶对弹棋。博奕并复行。

朱火飏烟雾。博山吐微香。

清樽发朱颜。四坐乐且康。

今日乐相乐。延年寿千霜。

《先秦汉魏晋南北朝诗》（上），第 289 页。

THE ORPHAN

Anon. (First Century A.D.?)

To be an orphan,
To be fated to be an orphan,
How bitter is this lot!
When my father and mother were
alive
I used to ride in a carriage
With four fine horses.
But when they both died,
My brother and my sister-in-law
Sent me out to be a merchant.
In the south I travelled to the 'Nine
Rivers'
And in the east as far as Ch'i and Lu.
At the end of the year when I came
home
I dared not tell them what I had
suffered—
Of the lice and vermin in my head,
Of the dust in my face and eyes.
My brother told me to get ready the
dinner,
My sister-in-law told me to see after
the horses.
I was always going up into the hall
And running down again to the
parlour.
My tears fell like rain.
In the morning they sent me to draw
water,
I didn't get back till night-fall,

My hands were all sore
And I had no shoes.
I walked the cold earth
Treading on thorns and brambles.
As I stopped to pull out the thorns,
How bitter my heart was!
My tears fell and fell
And I went on sobbing and sobbing.
In winter I have no great-coat;
Nor in summer thin clothes.
It is no pleasure to be alive.
I had rather quickly leave the earth
And go beneath the Yellow Springs.
The April winds blow
And the grass is growing green.

孤儿行

孤儿生。孤子遇生。命独当苦。父母在时。乘坚车。驾驷马。父母已去。兄嫂令我行贾。南到九江。东到齐与鲁。腊月来归。不敢自言苦。头多虮虱。面目多尘。大兄言办饭。大嫂言视马。上高堂。行取殿下堂。孤儿泪下如雨。使我朝行汲。暮得水来归。手为错。足下无菲。怆怆履霜。中多蒺藜。拔断蒺藜肠月中。怆欲悲。泪下渫渫。清涕累累。冬无复襦。夏无单衣。居生不乐。不如早去。下从地下黄泉。春气动。草萌芽。

In the third month—silkworms and mulberries,
In the sixth month—the melon-harvest.
I went out with the melon-cart
And just as I was coming home
The melon-cart turned over.
The people who came to help me were few,
But the people who ate the melons were many.
'At least leave me the stalks
To take home as proof.
My brother and sister-in-law are harsh,
And will be certain to call me to account.'
When I got home, how they shouted and scolded!
I want to write a letter and send it
To my mother and father under the earth,
And tell them I can't go on any longer
Living with my brother and sister-in-law.

三月蚕桑。六月收瓜。将是瓜车。来到还家。瓜车反覆。助我者少。啖瓜者多。愿还我蒂。兄与嫂严。独且急归。当兴校计。乱曰。里中一何譊譊。愿欲寄尺书。将与地下父母。兄嫂难与久居。

《先秦汉魏晋南北朝诗》（上），第 207—271 页。

'OLD POEM'

AT fifteen I went with the army,
At fourscore I came home.
On the way I met a man from the village,
I asked him who there was at home.
'That over there is your house,
All covered over with trees and bushes.'
Rabbits had run in at the dog-hole,
Pheasants flew down from the beams of the roof.
In the courtyard was growing some wild grain;
And by the well, some wild mallows.
I'll boil the grain and make porridge,
I'll pluck the mallows and make soup.
Soup and porridge are both cooked,
But there is no one to eat them with.
I went out and looked towards the east,
While tears fell and wetted my clothes.

古诗三首（其一）·十五从军征

十五从军征。八十始得归。
道逢乡里人。家中有阿谁。
遥望是君家。松柏冢累累。
兔从狗窦入。雉从梁上飞。
中庭生旅谷。井上生旅葵。
烹谷持作饭。采葵持作羹。
羹饭一时熟。不知贻阿谁。
出门东向望。泪落沾我衣。

《先秦汉魏晋南北朝诗》（上），第 335—336 页。

MEETING IN THE ROAD

再
造
的
镜
像

IN a narrow road where there was not room to pass
My carriage met the carriage of a young man.
And while his axle was touching my axle
In the narrow road I asked him where he lived.
'The place where I live is easy enough to find,
Easy to find and difficult to forget.
The gates of my house are built of yellow gold,
The hall of my house is paved with white jade,
On the hall table flagons of wine are set,
I have summoned to serve me dancers of Han-tan[①].
In the midst of the courtyrard grows a cassia-tree—
And candles on its branches flaring away in the night.'

---

① Capital of the kingdom of Chao, where the people were famous for their beauty.

相逢行（节选）

相逢狭路间。道隘不容车。
不知何年少。夹毂问君家。
君家诚易知。易知复难忘。
黄金为君门。白玉为君堂。
堂上置樽酒。作使邯郸倡。
中庭生桂树。华灯何煌煌。

《先秦汉魏晋南北朝诗》（上），第 265 页。

FIGHTING SOUTH OF THE RAMPARTS

Anon. (First Centuty A.D.?)

THEY fought south of the ramparts,
They died north of the wall.
They died in the moors and were not buried.
Their flesh was the food of crows.
'Tell the crows we are not afraid;
We have died in the moors and cannot be buried.
Crows, how can our bodies escape you?'
The waters flowed deep
And the rushes in the pool were dark.
The riders fought and were slain;
Their horses wander neighing.
By the bridge there was a house[①].
Was it south, was it north?
The harvest was never gathered.
How can we give you your offerings?
You served your Prince faithfully,
Though all in vain.
I think of you, faithful soldiers;
Your service shall not be forgotten.
For in the morning you went out to battle
And at night you did not return.

---

① There is no trace of it left. This passage describes the havoc of war. The harvest has not been gathered: therefore corn-offerings cannot be made to the spirits of the dead.

再
造
的
镜
像

战城南

　　战城南，死郭北，野死不葬乌可食。为我谓乌，且为客豪。野死谅不葬，腐肉安能去子逃？水深激激，蒲苇冥冥。枭骑战斗死，驽马徘徊鸣。梁筑室，何以南？何以北？禾黍不获君何食？愿为忠臣安可得？思子良臣，良臣诚可思：朝行出攻，暮不夜归！

　　　　　　　　　　　　　　《汉魏六朝诗鉴赏辞典》，第 69 页。

THE EASTERN GATE

Anon. (First Century A.D.?)

A poor man determines to go out into the world and make his fortune. His wife tries to detain him.

I WENT out at the eastern gate;

I never thought to return.

But I came back to the gate with my heart full of sorrow.

There was not a peck of rice in the bin;

There was not a coat hanging on the pegs.

So I took my sword and went towards the gate.

My wife and child clutched at my coat and wept;

'Some people want to be rich and grand;

I only want to share my porridge with you.

Above, we have the blue waves of the sky;

Below, the face of this child that suckles at my breast.'

'Dear wife, I cannot stay.

Soon it will be too late.

When one is growing old

One cannot put things off.'

东门行

出东门。不顾归。来入门。怅欲悲。盎中无斗米储。还视架上无悬衣。拔剑东门去。舍中儿母牵衣啼。他家但愿富贵。贱妾与君共餔糜。上用仓浪天故。下当用此黄口儿。今非。咄。行。吾去为迟。白发时下难久居。

《先秦汉魏晋南北朝诗》（上），第 269—270 页。

OLD AND NEW

Anon. (First Century A.D.?)

SHE went up the mountain to pluck wild herbs;
She came down the mountain and met her former husband.
She knelt down and asked her former husband
'What do you find your new wife like?'
'My new wife, although her talk is clever,
Cannot charm me as my old wife could.
In beauty of face there is not much to choose,
But in usefulness they are not at all alike.
My new wife comes in from the road to meet me;
My old wife always came down from her tower.
My new wife weaves fancy silks;
My old wife was good at plain weaving.
Of fancy silk one can weave a strip a day;
Of plain weaving, more than fifty feet.
Putting her silks by the side of your weaving
I see that the new will not compare with the old.'

上山采蘼芜

上山采蘼芜。下山逢故夫。
长跪问故夫。新人复何如。
新人虽言好。未若故人姝。
颜色类相似。手爪不相如。
新人从门入。故人从阁去。
新人工织缣。故人工织素。
织缣日一匹。织素五丈余。
将缣来比素。新人不如故。

《先秦汉魏晋南北朝诗》（上），第 334 页。

SOUTH OF THE GREAT SEA

MY love is living
To the south of the Great Sea.
What shall I send to greet him?
Two pearls and a comb of tortoise-shell:
I'll send them to him bound with ropes of jade.
They tell me he is not true;
They tell me he dashed my things to the ground,
Dashed them to the ground and burnt them
And scattered the ashes to the wind.
From this day to the ends of time
I must never think of him;
Never again think of him.
The cocks are crowing,
And the dogs are barking—
My brother and his wife will soon know.
The autumn wind is blowing;
The morning wind is sighing.
In a moment the sun will rise in the east
And then it too will know.

有所思

　　有所思，乃在大海南。何用问遗君？双珠玳瑁簪，用玉绍缭之。闻君有他心，拉杂摧烧之。摧烧之，当风扬其灰。从今以往，勿复相思！相思与君绝！鸡鸣狗吠，兄嫂当知之。妃呼狶！秋风肃肃晨风飔，东方须臾高知之。

《汉魏六朝诗鉴赏辞典》，第 72 页。

THE OTHER SIDE OF THE VALLEY

I AM a prisoner in the hands of the enemy,
Enduring the shame of captivity.
My bones stick out and my strength is gone
Through not getting enough to eat.
My brother is a Mandarin
And his horses are fed on millet.
Why can't he spare a little money
To send and ransom me?

隔谷歌（节选）

兄为俘虏受困辱，骨露力疲食不足。
弟为官吏马食粟，何惜钱刀来我赎？

《汉魏晋南北朝隋诗鉴赏词典》，第 1847 页。

OATHS OF FRIENDSHIP

(1)

In the country of Yüeh when a man made friends with another they set up an altar
of earth and sacrificed upon it a dog and a cock, reciting this oath as they did so:

IF you were riding in a coach
And I were wearing a 'li'[①],
And one day we met in the road,
You would get down and bow.
If you were carrying a 'tēng'[②]
And I were riding on a horse,
And one day we met in the road
I would get down for you.

(2)

SHANG YA!
I want to be your friend
For ever and ever without break or decay.
When the hills are all flat
And the rivers are all dry,
When it lightens and thunders in winter,
When it rains and snows in summer,
When Heaven and Earth mingle—
Not till then will I part from you.

---

① A peasant's hat made of straw.
② An umbrella under which a cheap-jack sells his wares.

越谣

君乘车，我戴笠，它日相逢下车揖。
君檐簦，我跨马，它日相逢为君下。

《乐府诗集》（第 4 册），第 1222 页。

上邪

上邪，我欲与君相知，长命无绝衰。山无陵，江水为竭，冬雷震震夏雨
雪，天地合，乃敢与君绝。

《乐府诗集》（第 1 册），第 231 页。

BURIAL SONGS

(1)

'The dew on the garlic-leaf', sung at the burial of kings and princes.

HOW swiftly it dries,
The dew on the garlic-leaf,
The dew that dries so fast
Tomorrow will fall again.
But he whom we carry to the grave
Will never more return.

(2)

'The Graveyard', sung at the burial of common men.

WHAT man's land is the graveyard?
It is the crowded home of ghosts—
Wise and foolish shoulder to shoulder.
The King of the Dead claims them all;
Man's fate knows no tarrying.

薤露

薤上露。
何易晞。
露晞明朝更复落。
人死一去何时归。

蒿里

蒿里谁家地。聚敛魂魄无贤愚。
鬼伯一何相催促。人命不得少踟蹰。

《先秦汉魏晋南北朝诗》(上)，第 257 页。

再造的镜像

SEVENTEEN OLD POEMS[①]

(First and Second Centuries A. D.)

(1)

ON and on, always on and on

Away from you, parted by a life-parting[②].

Going from one another ten thousand 'li',

Each in a different corner of the World.

The way between is difficult and long,

Face to face how shall we meet again?

The Tartar horse prefers the North wind,

The bird from Yüeh nests on the Southern branch.

Since we parted the time is already long,

Daily my clothes hang looser round my waist.

Floating clouds obscure the white sun,

The wandering one has quite forgotten home.

Thinking of you has made me suddenly old,

The months and years swiftly draw to their close.

That I'm cast away and rejected I must not repine;

Better to hope that you eat your rice and thrive.

(2)

GREEN, green,

The grass by the river-bank.

Thick, thick,

The willow trees in the garden.

Sad, sad,

The lady in the tower.

White, white,

Sitting at the casement window.

Fair, fair,

Her red-powdered face.

Small, small,

She puts out her pale hand.

Once she was a dancing-house girl,

Now she is a wandering man's wife.

The wandering man went, but did not return.

It is hard alone to keep an empty bed.

---

① 阿瑟·韦利所译为《古诗十九首》中的 17 首，故英文标题与中文有差异。

② The opposite of a parting by death.

112

古诗十九首（节选）①

（一）

行行重行行。与君生别离。

相去万余里。各在天一涯。

道路阻且长。会面安可知。

胡马依北风。越鸟巢南枝。

相去日已远。衣带日已缓。

浮云蔽白日。游子不顾返。

思君令人老。岁月忽已晚。

弃捐勿复道。努力加餐饭。

（二）

青青河畔草。郁郁园中柳。

盈盈楼上女。皎皎当窗牖。

娥娥红粉妆。纤纤出素手。

昔为倡家女。今为荡子妇。

荡子行不归。空床难独守。

---

① 《古诗十九首》出自汉代文人之手，但作者姓名不详；该诗集后被收入南北朝时期文学家萧统编选的《文选》卷二十九，是汉代文人五言诗最高成就的代表。

(3)

GREEN, green,
The cypress on the mound.
Firm, firm,
The boulder in the stream.
Man's life lived within this world
Is like the sojourning of a hurried
traveller.
A cup of wine together will make us
glad,
And a little friendship is no little
matter.

Yoking my chariot I urge my
stubborn horses,
I wander about in the streets of Wan
and Lo[①].
In Lo Town how fine everything is!
The 'Caps and Belts'[②] go seeking
each other out.
The great boulevards are intersected
by lanes,
Wherein are the town-houses of
Royal Dukes.
The two palaces stare at each other
from afar,
The twin gates rise a hundred feet.
By prolonging the feast let us keep
our hearts gay,
And leave no room for sadness to
creep in.

(4)

OF this day's glorious feast and revel
The pleasure and delight are difficult
to describe.
Plucked from the lute in a swift,
tumultuous jangling
The new melodies in beauty reached
the divine.
Skilful singers intoned the high
words,
Those who knew the tune heard the
trueness of their singing.
We sat there each with the same
desire
And like thoughts by each
unexpressed:
'Man in the world lodging for a
single lifetime
Passes suddenly like dust borne on
the wind.
Then let us hurry out with high steps
And be the first to reach the
highways and fords,
Rather than stay at home wretched
and poor,
For long years plunged in sordid
grief.'

---

① Nan-yang and Lo-yang, in Honan.
② High officers.

（三）

青青陵上柏。磊磊涧中石。
人生天地间。忽如远行客。
斗酒相娱乐。聊厚不为薄。
驱车策驽马。游戏宛与洛。
洛中何郁郁。冠带自相索。
长衢罗夹巷。王侯多第宅。
两宫遥相望。双阙百余尺。
极宴娱心意。戚戚何所迫。

（四）

今日良宴会。欢乐难具陈。
弹筝奋逸响。新声妙入神。
令德唱高言。识曲听其真。
齐心同所愿。含意俱未申。
人生寄一世。奄忽若飙尘。
何不策高足。先据要路津。
无为守贫贱。轗轲长苦辛。

(5)

IN the north-west there is a high house,

Its top level with the floating clouds.

Embroidered curtains thinly screen its windows

Its storeyed tower is built on three steps.

From above there comes a noise of playing and singing,

The tune sounding, oh how sad!

Who can it be, playing so sad a tune?

Surely it must be Ch'i Liang's wife[①].

The High Second follows the wind's rising,

The middle lay lingers indecisive.

To each note, two or three sobs,

Her high will conquered by overwhelming grief.

She does not regret that she is left so sad,

But minds that so few can understand her song.

She wants to become those two wild geese

That with beating wings rise high aloft.

(6)

CROSSING the river I pluck the lotus flowers;

In the orchid-swamps are many fragrant herbs.

I gather them, but who shall I send them to?

My love is living in lands far away.

I turn and look towards my own country;

The long road stretches on for ever.

The same heart, yet a different dwelling:

Always fretting, till we are grown old!

---

① Who wailed so loud when her husband failed to return from battle that she brought down the city-wall.

（五）

西北有高楼。上与浮云齐。
交疏结绮窗。阿阁三重阶。
上有弦歌声。音响一何悲。
谁能为此曲。无乃杞梁妻。
清商随风发。中曲正徘徊。
一弹再三叹。慷慨有余哀。
不惜歌者苦。但伤知音稀。
愿为双鸿鹄。奋翅起高飞。

（六）

涉江采芙蓉。兰泽多芳草。
采之欲遗谁。所思在远道。
还顾望旧乡。长路漫浩浩。
同心而离居。忧伤以终老。

(7)

A BRIGHT moon illumines the night-prospect;

The house-cricket chirrups on the eastern wall.

The Handle of the Pole-star points to the Beginning of Winter;

The host of stars is scattered over the sky.

The white dew wets the moor-grasses—

With sudden swiftness the times and seasons change.

The autumn cicada sings among the trees,

The swallows, alas, whither are they gone?

Once I had a same-house friend,

He took flight and rose high away.

He did not remember how once we went hand in hand,

But left me like footsteps behind one in the dust.

In the South is the Winnowing-fan and the Pole-star in the North,

And a Herd-boy[①] whose ox has never borne the yoke.

A friend who is not firm as a great rock

Is of no profit and idly bears the name.

(8)

IN the courtyard there grows a strange tree,

Its green leaves ooze with a fragrant moisture.

Holding the branch I cut a flower from the tree,

Meaning to send it away to the person I love.

Its sweet smell fills my sleeves and lap.

The road is long, how shall I get it there?

Such a thing is not fine enough to send;

But it may remind him of the time that has passed since he left.[②]

---

① Name of a star. The Herd-boy, who is only figuratively speaking a herd-boy, is like the friend who is no real friend.

② i.e. (supposing he went away in the autumn) remind him that spring has come.

（七）

明月皎夜光。促织鸣东壁。
玉衡指孟冬。众星何历历。
白露沾野草。时节忽复易。
秋蝉鸣树间。玄鸟逝安适。
昔我同门友。高举振六翮。
不念携手好。弃我如遗迹。
南箕北有斗。牵牛不负轭。
良无盘石固。虚名复何益。

（八）

庭中有奇树。绿叶发华滋。
攀条折其荣。将以遗所思。
馨香盈怀袖。路远莫致之。
此物何足贵。但感别经时。

(9)

FAR away twinkles the Herd-boy star;

Brightly shines the Lady of the Han River.

Slender, slender she plies her white fingers;

Click, click go the wheels of her spinning loom.

At the end of the day she has not finished her task;

Her bitter tears fall like streaming rain.

The Han River runs shallow and clear;

Set between them, how short a space!

But the river water will not let them pass,

Gazing at each other but never able to speak.

(10)

TURNING my chariot I yoke my horses and go.

On and on down the long roads

The autumn winds shake the hundred grasses.

On every side, how desolate and bare!

The things I meet are all new things,

Their strangeness hastens the coming of old age.

Prosperity and decay each have their season;

Success is bitter when it is slow in coming.

Man's life is not metal or stone,

He cannot far prolong the days of his fate.

Suddenly he follows in the way of things that change;

Fame is the only treasure that endures.

（九）

迢迢牵牛星。皎皎河汉女。
纤纤擢素手。札札弄机杼。
终日不成章。泣涕零如雨。
河汉清且浅。相去复几许。
盈盈一水间。脉脉不得语。

（十）

回车驾言迈。悠悠涉长道。
四顾何茫茫。东风摇百草。
所遇无故物。焉得不速老。
盛衰各有时。立身苦不早。
人生非金石。岂能长寿考。
奄忽随物化。荣名以为宝。

(11)

The Eastern Wall stands high and long;

Far and wide it stretches without a break.

The whirling wind uprises and shakes the earth;

The autumn grasses grow thick and green.

The four seasons alternate without pause,

The year's end hurries swiftly on.

The Bird of the Morning Wind is stricken with sorrow;

The frail cicada suffers and is hard pressed.

Free and clear, let us loosen the bonds of our hearts.

Why should we go on always restraining and binding?

In Yen and Chao are many fair ladies,

Beautiful people with faces like jade.

Their clothes are made all of silk gauze,

They stand at the door practising shrill lays.

The echo of their singing, how sad it sounds!

By the pitch of the song one knows the stops have been tightened.

To ease their minds they arrange their shawls and belts;

Lowering their song, a little white they pause.

'I should like to be those two flying swallows

Who are carrying clay to nest in the eaves of your house.'

（十一）

东城高且长。逶迤自相属。
回风动地起。秋草萋已绿。
四时更变化。岁暮一何速。
晨风怀苦心。蟋蟀伤局促。
荡涤放情志。何为自结束。
燕赵多佳人。美者颜如玉。
被服罗裳衣。当户理清曲。
音响一何悲。弦急知柱促。
驰情整巾带。沉吟聊踯躅。
思为双飞燕。衔泥巢君屋。

(12)

I DRIVE my chariot up to the Eastern Gate;
From afar I see the graveyard north of the Wall.
The white aspens how they murmur, murmur;
Pines and cypresses flank the broad paths.
Beneath lie men who died long ago;
Black, black is the long night that holds them.
Deep down beneath the Yellow Springs,
Thousands of years they lie without waking.

In infinite succession light and darkness shift,
And years vanish like the morning dew.
Man's life is like a sojourning,
His longevity lacks the firmness of stone and metal.
For ever it has been that mourners in their turn were mourned,
Saint and Sage—all alike are trapped.
Seeking by food to obtain immortality
Many have been the dupe of strange drugs.
Better far to drink good wine
And clothe our bodies in robes of satin and silk.

(13) CONTINUATION OF (12)

The dead are gone and with them we cannot converse;
The living are here and ought to have our love.
Leaving the city gate I look ahead
And see before me only mounds and tombs.
The old graves are ploughed up into fields,
The pine and cypresses are hewn for timber.
In the white aspens sad winds sing;
Their long murmuring kills my heart with grief.
I want to go home, to ride to my village gate;
I want to go back, but there's no road back.

（十二）

驱车上东门。遥望郭北墓。
白杨何萧萧。松柏夹广路。
下有陈死人。杳杳即长暮。
潜寐黄泉下。千载永不寤。
浩浩阴阳移。年命如朝露。
人生忽如寄。寿无金石固。
万岁更相送。贤圣莫能度。
服食求神仙。多为药所误。
不如饮美酒。被服纨与素。

（十三）

去者日以疏。来者日以亲。
出郭门直视。但见丘与坟。
古墓犁为田。松柏摧为薪。
白杨多悲风。萧萧愁杀人。
思还故里闾。欲归道无因。

(14)

THE years of a lifetime do not reach a hundred,

Yet they contain a thousand years' sorrow.

When days are short and the dull nights long,

Why not take a lamp and wander forth?

If you want to be happy you must do it now,

There is no waiting till an after-time.

The fool who's loath to spend the wealth he's got

Becomes the laughing-stock of after ages.

It is true that Master Wang[①] became immortal,

But how can *we* hope to share his lot?

(15)

COLD, cold the year draws to its end,

The mole-cricket makes a doleful chirping.

The chill wind increases its violence.

My wandering love has no coat to cover him.

He gave his embroidered furs to the Lady of Lo,

But from me his bedfellow he is quite estranged.

Sleeping alone in the depth of the long night

In a dream I thought I saw the light of his face.

My dear one thought of our old joys together,

He came in his chariot and gave me the front reins.

I wanted so to prolong our play and laughter,

To hold his hand and go back with him in his coach.

But when he had come he would not stay long

Nor stop to go with me to the Inner Chamber.

Truly without the falcon's wings to carry me

How can I rival the flying wind's swiftness?

I go and lean at the gate and think of my grief,

My falling tears wet the double gates.

---

① Who ascended to Heaven on a white crane.

（十四）

生年不满百。常怀千岁忧。
昼短苦夜长。何不秉烛游。
为乐当及时。何能待来兹。
愚者爱惜费。但为后世嗤。
仙人王子乔。难可与等期。

（十五）

凛凛岁云暮。蝼蛄夕鸣悲。
凉风率已厉。游子寒无衣。
锦衾遗洛浦。同袍与我违。
独宿累长夜。梦想见容辉。
良人惟古欢。枉驾惠前绥。
愿得常巧笑。携手同车归。
既来不须臾。又不处重闱。
亮无晨风翼。焉能凌风飞。
眄睐以适意。引领遥相睎。
徙倚怀感伤。垂涕沾双扉。

(16)

AT the beginning of winter a cold spirit comes,

The North Wind blows—chill, chill.

My sorrows being many, I know the length of the nights,

Raising my head I look at the stars in their places.

On the fifteenth day the bright moon is full,

On the twentieth day the 'toad and hare' wane.[①]

A stranger came to me from a distant land

And brought me a single scroll with writing on it;

At the top of the scroll was written 'Do not forget',

At the bottom was written 'Good-bye for ever'.

I put the letter away in the folds of my dress,

For three years the writing did not fade.

How with an undivided heart I loved you

I fear that you will never know or guess.

(17)

THE bright moon, oh how white it shines,

Shines down on the gauze curtains of my bed!

Racked by sorrow I toss and cannot sleep;

Picking up my clothes, I wander up and down.

My absent love says that he is happy,

But I would rather he said he was coming back.

Out in the courtyard I stand hesitating, alone;

To whom can I tell the sad thoughts I think?

Staring before me I enter my room again;

Falling tears wet my mantle and robe.

---

① The 'toad and hare' correspond to our 'man in the moon'. The waning of the moon symbolizes the waning of the lover's affection.

（十六）

孟冬寒气至。北风何惨慄。

愁多知夜长。仰观众星列。

三五明月满。四五蟾兔缺。

客从远方来。遗我一书札。

上言长相思。下言久离别。

置书怀袖中。三岁字不灭。

一心抱区区。惧君不识察。

（十七）

明月何皎皎。照我罗床纬。

忧愁不能寐。揽衣起徘徊。

客行虽云乐。不如早旋归。

出户独彷徨。愁思当告谁。

引领还入房。泪下沾裳衣。

《先秦汉魏晋南北朝诗》（上），第 329—334 页。

SONG OF THE SNOW-WHITE HEADS
Anon. (First Century A.D.?)

OUR love was pure
As the snow on the mountains;
White as a moon
Between the clouds—
They're telling me
Your thoughts are double;
That's why I've come
To break it off.
Today we'll drink
A cup of wine.
Tomorrow we'll part
Beside the Canal:
Walking about
Beside the Canal,
Where its branches divide
East and west.
Alas and alas,
And again alas.
So must a girl
Cry when she's married,
If she find not a man
Of single heart,
Who will not leave her
Till her hair is white.

白头吟（节选）

皑如山上雪。皎若云间月。
闻君有两意。故来相决绝。
今日斗酒会。明旦沟水头。
躞蹀御沟上。沟水东西流。
凄凄复凄凄。嫁娶不须啼。
愿得一心人。白头不相离。

《先秦汉魏晋南北朝诗》（上），第 274 页。

THE SONG OF LO-FU

Anon. (First Century A.D.?)

再
造
的
镜
像

THE sun has risen on the eastern brim of the world,

Shines into the high chambers of the house of Ch'in.

In the house of Ch'in is a lovely lady dwelling,

That calls herself the Lady Lo-fu.

This lady loves her silk-worms and mulberry-trees;

She's plucking leaves at the southern corner of the walls.

With blue thread are the joints of her basket bound;

Of cassia-boughs are the loops of her basket made.

Her soft hair hangs in loose plaits;

The pearl at her ear shines like a dazzling moon.

Of yellow damask is made her skirt beneath;

Of purple damask is made her coat above.

The passer-by who looks on Lo-fu

Drops his luggage and twirls his beard and moustache.

The young men when they see Lo-fu

Doff their caps and tie their filets on their brows.

The labouring ploughman thinks no more of his plough,

The hind in the field thinks no more of his hoe.

When they come home there is temper on both sides:

'You sat all day looking at Lo-fu!'

The Lord Prefect drives his coach from the south;

His five horses suddenly show their pace.

He's sent his officer: 'Quickly bring me word

Of what house may this lovely lady be?'

'In the house of Ch'in the fair lady dwells;

She calls herself the Lady Lo-fu.'

陌上桑

　　日出东南隅。照我秦氏楼。秦氏有好女。自名为罗敷。罗敷善蚕桑。采桑城南隅。青丝为笼系。桂枝为笼钩。头上倭堕髻。耳中明月珠。缃绮为下裙。紫绮为上襦。行者见罗敷。下担捋髭须。少年见罗敷。脱帽著帩头。耕者忘其犁。锄者忘其锄。来归相怨怒。但坐观罗敷。使君从南来。五马立踟蹰。使君遣吏往。问此谁家姝。秦氏有好女。自名为罗敷。

'Oh tell me, officer, tell me how old she may be!'

'A score of years she has not yet filled;

To fifteen she has added somewhat more.'

The Lord Prefect sends to Lo-fu:

'Tell me, lady, will you ride by me or no?'

She stands before him, she gives him answer straight:

'My Lord Prefect has not ready wits.

Has he not guessed that just as he has a wife

So I too have my husband dear?

Yonder to eastward a band of horse is riding,

More than a thousand, and my love is at their head.'

'By what sign shall I your husband know?'

'His white horse is followed by a black colt,

With blue thread is tied the horse's tail;

With yellow gold is bridled that horse's head.

At his waist he wears a windlass-hilted sword

You could not buy for many pounds of gold.

At fifteen they made him the Prefect's clerk;

At twenty they made him a Captain of the Guard.

At thirty he sat at the Emperor's Council Board,

At forty they gave him a city for his very own—①

A wholesome man, fair, white and fine;

Very hairy, with a beard that is thick and long.

Proudly and proudly he walks to his palace gate;

Stately, stately he strides through his palace hall.

In that great hall thousands of followers sit,

Yet none but names him the finest man of them all.'

---

① He became Prefect of a city.

罗敷年几何。二十尚不足。十五颇有余。使君谢罗敷。宁可共载不。罗敷前致辞。使君一何愚。使君自有妇。罗敷自有夫。东方千余骑。夫婿居上头。何用识夫婿。白马从骊驹。青丝系马尾。黄金络马头。腰中鹿卢剑。可值千万余。十五府小史。二十朝大夫。三十侍中郎。四十专城居。为人洁白皙。鬑鬑颇有须。盈盈公府步。冉冉府中趋。坐中数千人。皆言夫婿殊。

《先秦汉魏晋南北朝诗》（上），第 259—260 页。

THE BONES OF CHUANG TZU[①]
By CHANG HÊNG (A.D. 78-139)

I, CHANG P'ING-Tzu, had traversed the Nine Wilds and seen their wonders,
In the eight continents beheld the ways of Man,
The Sun's procession, the orbit of the Stars,
The surging of the dragon, the soaring of the phoenix in his flight.
In the red desert to the south I sweltered,
And northward waded through the wintry burghs of Yu.
Through the Valley of Darkness to the west I wandered,
And eastward travelled to the Sun's abode,
The stooping Mulberry Tree.

So the seasons sped; weak autumn languished,
A small wind woke the cold.
And now with rearing of rein-horse,
Plunging of the tracer, round I fetched
My high-roofed chariot to westward.
Along the dykes we loitered, past many meadows,
And far away among the dunes and hills.
Suddenly I looked and by the roadside

I saw a man's bones lying in the squelchy earth,
Black rime-frost over him, and I in sorrow spoke
And asked him, saying, 'Dead man, how was it?
Fled you with your friend from famine and for the last grains
Gambled and lost? Was this earth your tomb,
Or did floods carry you from afar?
Where you mighty, were you wise,
Were you foolish and poor? A warrior, or a girl?'
Then a wonder came, for out of the silence a voice—
Thin echo only, in no substance was the Spirit seen—
Mysteriously answered, saying, 'I was a man of Sung,
Of the clan of Chuang, Chou was my name.
Beyond the climes of common thought
My reason soared, yet could I not save myself;
For at the last, when the long charter of my years was told,
I, too, for all my magic, by Age was brought
To the Black Hill of Death.
Wherefore, O Master, do you question me?'
Then I answered:
'Let me plead for you upon the Five Hill-tops,
Let me pray for you to the Gods of Heaven and the Gods of Earth,

---

① The great Taoist philosopher, see my *Three Ways of Thought Ancient China*, 1939.

髑髅赋

〔汉〕张衡

张平子将游目于九野，观化乎八方。星回日运，凤举龙骧。南游赤野，北洎幽乡，西经昧谷，东极浮桑。于是季秋之辰，微风起凉。聊回轩驾，左翔右昂。步马于畴阜，逍遥乎陵冈。顾见髑髅，委于路旁。下居淤壤，上有玄霜。

张平子怅然而问之曰："子将并粮椎命，以夭逝乎？本丧此土，流迁来乎？为是上智，为是下愚？为是女子，为是丈夫？"

于是肃然有灵，但闻神响，不见其形。答曰："吾宋人也，姓庄名周。游心方外，不能自修。寿命终极，来而玄幽。公子何以问之？"

对曰："我欲告之于五岳，祷之于神祇。

That your white bones may arise,
And your limbs be joined anew.
The God of the North shall give me back your ears;
I will scour the Southland for your eyes.
From the sunrise I will wrest your feet;
The West shall yield your heart.
I will set each several organ in its throne;
Each subtle-sense will I restore.
Would you not have it so?'
The dead man answered me:
'O Friend, how strange and unacceptable your words!
In death I rest and am at peace; in life, I toiled and strove.
Is the hardness of the winter stream
Better than the melting of spring?
All pride that the body knew
Was it not lighter than dust?
What Ch'ao and Hsü despised,
What Po-ch'êng fled,
Shall I desire, whom death
Already has hidden in the Eternal Way—
Where Li Chu cannot see me,
Nor Tzŭ Yeh hear me,
Where neither Yao nor Shun can reward me,
Nor the tyrants Chieh and Hsin condemn me,
Leopard nor tiger harm me,
Lance prick me nor sword wound me?
Of the Primal Spirit is my substance;
I am a wave
In the river of Darkness and Light.
The Maker of All Things is my Father and Mother,
Heaven is my bed and earth my cushion,
The thunder and lightning are my drum and fan,
The sun and moon my candle and my torch,
The Milky Way my moat, the stars my jewels.
With Nature my substance is joined;
I have no passion, no desire.
Wash me and I shall be no whiter,
Foul me and I shall yet be clean.
I come not, yet am here;
Hasten not, yet am swift.'
The voice stopped, there was silence.
A ghostly light
Faded and expired.
I gazed upon the dead, stared in sorrow and compassion.
Then I called upon my servant that was with me
To tie his silken scarf about those bones
And wrap them in a cloak of sombre dust;
While I, as offering to the soul of this dead man,
Poured my hot tears upon the margin of the road.

起子素骨，反之四支，取耳北坎，求目南离；使东震献足，西坤受腹；五内皆还，六神皆复；子欲之不乎？"

　　髑髅曰："公子言之殊难也。死为休息，生为役劳。冬冰之凝，何如春冰之消？荣位在身，不亦轻于尘毛？巢、许所耻，伯成所逃。况我已化，与道逍遥。离朱不能见，子野不能听。尧舜不能赏，桀纣不能刑。虎豹不能害，剑戟不能伤。与阴阳同其流，与元气合其朴。以造化为父母，天地为床蓐。雷电为鼓扇，日月为灯烛。云汉为川池，星宿为珠玉。合体自然，无情无欲。澄之不清，混之不浊。不行而至，不疾而速。"

　　于是言卒响绝，神光除灭。顾时发轸，乃命仆夫，假之以缟巾，袭之以玄尘，为之伤涕，酹于路滨。

《全汉赋校注》，第 752—753 页。

THE DANCERS OF HUAI-NAN

(A Fragment)

By CHANG HÊNG

I saw them dancing at Huai-nan and made this poem of praise:

THE instruments of music are made ready,
Strong wine is in our cups;
Flute-songs flutter, to a din of magic drums.
Sound scuds and scatters, surges free as a flood....
And now when the drinkers were all drunken,
And the sun had fallen to the west,
Up rose the fair ones to the dance,
Well painted and apparelled,
In veils of soft gossamer
All wound and meshed;
And ribbons they unravelled,
And scarfs to bind about their heads.
The wielder of the little stick
Whispers them to their places and the steady drums
Draw them through the mazes of the dance.
They have raised their long sleeves, they have covered their eyes;
Slowly their shrill voices
Swell the steady song.
And the song said:
As a frightened bird whose love
Has wandered away from the nest,
I flutter my desolate wings.
For the wind blows back to my home,
And I long for my father's house.

舞赋（并序）

〔汉〕张衡

　　昔客有观舞于淮南者，美而赋之，曰：

　　音乐陈兮旨酒施，击灵鼓兮吹参差。叛淫衍兮漫陆离。于是饮者皆醉，日亦既戾。美人兴而将舞，乃修容而改袭。服罗縠之杂错，申绸缪以自饰。拊者啾其齐列，盤鼓焕以骈罗。抗修袖以翳面兮，展清声而长歌。歌曰："惊雄逝兮孤雌翔，临归风兮思故乡。"

Subtly from slender hips they swing,
Swaying, slanting delicately up and down.
And like the crimson lotus flower
Glows their beauty, shedding flames afar.
They lift languid glances,
Peep distrustfully, till of a sudden
Ablaze with liquid light
Their soft eyes kindle. So dance to dance
Endlessly they weave, break off and dance again.
Now flutter their skirts like a great bird in flight,
Now toss their long white sleeves like whirling snow.
So the hours go by, till at last
The powder has blown from their cheeks, the black from their brows,
Flustered now are the fair faces, pins of pearl
Torn away, tangled the black tresses.
With combs they catch and gather in
The straying locks, put on the gossamer gown
That trailing winds about them, and in unison
Of body, song and dress, obedient
Each shadows each, as they glide softly to and fro.

搦纤腰而互折；嬛倾倚兮低昂。增芙蓉之红花兮，光的皪以发扬。腾矘目以顾眄，盼烂烂以流光。连翩骆驿，乍续乍绝。裾似飞燕，袖如回雪。徘徊相佪，提若霆震，闪若电灭。搴兮宕往，彳兮中辄。于是粉黛施兮玉质粲，珠簪挺兮缁发乱。然后整笄揽发，被纤垂紫。同服骈奏，合体齐声。进退无差，若影追形。

《全汉赋校注》，第 760 页。

THE LYCHEE-TREE

(Fragment)

By WANG I (*c.* A.D. 120)

SOMBRE as the heavens when morning clouds arise,

Bushy as a great broom held across the sky,

Vast as the spaces of a lofty house,

Deep fretted as a line of stony hills.

Long branches twining,

Green leaves clustering,

And all a-glimmer like a mist that lightly lies

Across the morning sun;

All spangled, darted with fire like a sky

Of populous stars.

Shell like a fisherman's red net;

Fruit white and lustrous as a pearl…

Lambent as the jewel of Ho, more strange

Than the saffron-stone of Hsia.

Now sigh we at the beauty of its show,

Now triumph in its taste.

Sweet juices lie in the mouth,

Soft scents invade the mind.

All flavours here are joined, yet none is master;

A hundred diverse tastes

Blend in such harmony no man can say

That one outstrips the rest. Sovereign of sweets,

Peerless, pre-eminent fruit, who dwellest apart

In noble solitude!

再
造
的
镜
像

荔支赋（节选）

〔汉〕王逸

　　暖若朝云之兴，森如横天之彗，湛若大厦之容，郁如峻岳之势。修干纷错，绿叶臻臻。灼灼若朝霞之映日，离离如繁星之着天。皮似丹罽，肤若明珰。润侔和璧，奇喻五黄。仰叹丽表，俯尝嘉味。口含甘液，心受芳气。兼五滋而无常主，不知百和之所出。卓绝类而无俦，超众果而独贵。

《全汉赋校注》，第 832 页。

THE WANGSUN[①]

By WANG YEN-SHOU, SON OF WANG I (*c.* A.D. 130)

SUBLIME was he, stupendous in invention,
Who planned the miracles of earth and sky.
Wondrous the power that charged
Small things with secret beauty, moving in them all.
See now the wangsun, crafty creature, mean of size,
Uncouth of form; the wrinkled face
Of an aged man; the body of a little child.
See how in turn he blinks and blenches with an air
Pathetically puzzled, dimly gazes
Under tired lids, through languid lashes
Looks tragic and hollow-eyed, rumples his brow,
Scatters this way and that
An insolent, astonished glare;
Sniffs and snorts, snuffs and sneezes,
Snicks and cocks his knowing little ears!
Now like a dotard mouths and chews
Or hoots and hisses through his pouted lips;
Shows gnashing teeth, grates and
grinds ill-temperedly,
Gobbles and puffs and scolds.
And every now and then,
Down to his belly, from the larder that he keeps
In either cheek, he sends
Little consignments lowered cautiously.
Sometimes he squats
Like a puppy on its haunches or hare-like humps
An arching back;
Smirks and wheedles with ingratiating sweetness;
Or suddenly takes to whining, surly snarling;
Then, like a ravening tiger roars.

He lives in thick forests, deep among the hills,
Or houses in the clefts of sharp, precipitous rocks;
Alert and agile is his nature, nimble are his wits;
Swift are his contortions,
Apt to every need,
Whether he climb tall tree-stems of a hundred feet,
Or sways on the shuddering shoulder of a long bough,
Before him, the dark gullies of unfathomable streams;
Behind, the silent hollows of the lonely hills.

---

① Kind of small, tailless ape (?).

王孙赋

〔汉〕王延寿

原天地之造化，实神伟之屈奇，道玄微以密妙，信无物而弗为。有王孙之狡兽，形陋观而丑仪。颜状类乎老公，躯体似乎小儿。眼眶睸以眈恤，视睉睫以映睞。突高目而曲额，眼瞑历而隳离。鼻魋齁以齁䶗，耳聿役以适知。口嗛呻以齫齚，唇皷嚼以形覒。齿崖崖以齹齹，嚼咗哧而嚥呪。储粮食于两颊，稍委输于胃脾。蹻菟蹲而狗踞，声历鹿而喔㖡。或喟喟而嗷嗷，又嘀嗅其若啼。姿僭傫而惚赣，豀盰阋以琐醯。眙睕腃而睍晹。眈睒恍而跛㾩。生深山之茂林，处崭岩之嵌崎。性獟猜之猵疾，态峰出而横施。缘百仞之高木，攀窈袤之长枝。背牢落之峻壑，临不测之幽溪。

Twigs and tendrils are his rocking-chairs,

On rungs of rotting wood he trips

Up perilous places; sometimes, leap after leap,

Like lightning flits through the woods.

Sometimes he saunters with a sad, forsaken air;

Then suddenly peeps round

Beaming with satisfaction. Up he springs,

Leaps and prances, whoops, and scampers on his way.

Up cliffs he scrambles, up pointed rocks,

Dances on shale that shifts or twigs that snap,

Suddenly swerves and lightly passes....

Oh, what tongue could unravel

The tale of all his tricks?

Alas, one trait

With the human tribe he shares; their sweet's his sweet,

Their bitter is his bitter. Off sugar from the vat

Or brewer's dregs he loves to sup.

So men put wine where he will pass.

How he races to the bowl!

How nimbly licks and swills!

Now he staggers, feels dazed and foolish,

Darkness falls upon his eyes....

He sleeps and knows no more.

Up steal the trappers, catch him by the mane,

Then to a string or ribbon tie him, lead him home;

Tether him in the stable or lock him into the yard;

Where faces all day long

Gaze, gape, gasp at him and will not go away.

寻柯条以宛转，或捉腐而登危。若将颓而复著，纷羸绌以陆离。或犀跳而电透，或瓜悬而瓠垂。上触手而拿攫，下对足而登跂，至攀揽以狂接，覆缩臂而电赴。时辽落以萧索，乍睥睨以容与。或蹂跌以践游，又咨嗷而攒聚。扶嶔岙以榺橼，蹑危桌而腾舞。忽涌逸而轻迅，羌难得而觊缕。同甘苦于人类，好哺糟而啜醨。乃设酒于其侧，竟争饮而踣驰。项陋酗以迷醉，曚眠睡而无知。暂拿鬃以缠缚，遂缨络以縻羁。归琐系于庭厩，观者吸咽而忘疲。

《全汉赋校注》，第 868 页。

再
造
的
镜
像

THE NIGHTMARE
By WANG YEN-SHOU

One night, about the time I came of age, I dreamt that demon creatures fought with me while I slept.... When I woke I told this vision in verse, that the dreamers of posterity might use my poem as a spell to drive off evil dreams. And so often has it proved its worth that I dare not any longer hide it from the world. The words are these:

ONCE, as in the darkness I lay asleep by night,
Strange things suddenly saw I in my dream;
All my dream was of monsters that came about me while I slept,
Devils and demons, four-horned, serpent-necked,
Fishes with bird-tails, three-legged bogies
From six eyes staring, dragons hideous,
Yet three-part human.
On rushed the foul flocks, grisly legions,
Stood round me, stretched out their arms,
Danced their hands about me, and sought to snatch me from my bed.
Then cried I (and in my dream
My voice was thick with anger and my words all awry),
'Ill-spawned elves, how dare you
Beset with your dire shapes Creation's cleanest
Shapeliest creature, Man?' Then straightway I struck out,
Flashed my fists like lightning among them, thumped like thunder,
Here slit Jack-o'-Lantern,
Here smashed fierce Hog-Face,
Battered wights and goblins,
Smote venturous vampires, pounded in the dust
Imps, gnomes and lobs,
Kobolds and kelpies;
Swiped bulge-eyed bogies, oafs and elves;
Clove Tough-head's triple skull, threw down
Clutching Night-hag, flogged the gawky Ear-wig Fiend
That floundered toward me on its tail.

梦赋（并序）

〔汉〕王延寿

　　臣弱冠尝夜寝，见鬼物与臣战；遂得东方朔与臣作骂鬼之书，臣遂作赋一篇叙梦。后人梦者读诵以却鬼，数数有验。臣不敢蔽。其词曰：

　　余夜寝息，乃有非恒之梦。其为梦也，悉睹鬼神之变怪，则蛇头而四角，鱼首而鸟身，三足而六眼，龙形而似人。群行而辈摇，忽来到吾前。申臂而舞手，意欲相引牵。于是梦中惊怒，膈臆纷纭，曰："吾含天地之纯和，何妖孽之敢臻！"乃挥手振拳，雷发电舒。戡游光，轩猛趹，狒毅，斫鬼魅，捎魍魉，荆诸渠，撞纵目，打三头，扑魖莫，扶夔魖，

I struck at staring eyes,
Stamped on upturned faces; through close ranks
Of hoofs I cut my way, buried my fingers deep
In half-formed flesh;
Ghouls tore at my touch; I slit sharp noses,
Trod on red tongues, seized shaggy manes,
Shook bald-heads by the beard.
Then was a scuffling. Arms and legs together
Chasing, crashing and sliding; a helter-skelter
Of feet lost and found in the tugging and toppling,
Cuffing, cudgelling, frenzied flogging....

So fought I, till terror and dismay
Shook those foul flocks; panic spread like a flame
Down mutinous ranks; they stand, they falter,
Those ghastly legions, but fleeing, suddenly turn
Glazed eyes upon me, to see how now I fare.
At last, to end their treachery
Again I rushed upon them, braved their slaver and snares,
Stood on a high place, and lashed down among them,
Shrieking and cursing as my blows crashed.
Then three by three and four by four
One after another hop-a-trot they fled,
Bellowing and bawling till the air was full of their breath—
Grumbling and snarling,
Those vanquished ogres, demons discomfited,
Some that would fain have run
Lolling and lurching, some that for cramped limbs
Could not stir from where they stood. Some over belly-wounds

博脾睨，蹴睢盰，剖列羼，制羯孽，劋尖鼻，踏赤舌，拿伦氊，挥犎鬆。于是手足俱中，捷猎摧拉。澎濞趹抗，揩倒批，笞强梁，捶挶列，捄撩予，揔攎黠，拖毇犢，抨橙轧。于是群邪众魅，骇扰遑遽，焕衍叛散，乍留乍去，变形瞪眲，顾望犹豫。吾于是更奋奇谲脉，捧獲喷，扼挠岘，挞咿嚘，批擅喷。尔乃三三四四，相随踉蹡而历僻。隆隆磕磕，精气充布。輷輷䝉䝉，鬼惊魅怖。或盘跚而欲走，或拘挛而不能步，或中创

Bent double; some in agony gasping and groaning.
Suddenly the clouds broke and (I knew not why)
A thin light filtered the darkness; then, while again
I sighed in wonder that those disastrous creatures,
Dire monstrosities, should dare assail
A clean and comely man, … there sounded in my ears
A twittering and crowing. And outdoors it was light.
The noisy cock, mindful that dawn was in the sky,
Had crowed his warning, and the startled ghosts,
Because they heard dawn heralded, had fled
In terror and tribulation from the rising day.

(In an epilogue the poet seeks consolation in the fact that many evil dreams and occurrences have in the past been omens of good. Duke Huan of Ch'i, while hunting in the marshes, saw in a vision an ogre 'as broad as a cartwheel and as long as a shaft, wearing a purple coat and red cap'. It was an omen that he would rise to the Pentarchy. Wu Ting, Emperor of the Shang dynasty, was haunted in a dream by the face of the man who afterwards became his wise counsellor and friend. Wên, Duke of Chin, dreamt that the Marquis of Ch'u held him prostrate and sucked out his brains; yet his kingdom defeated Ch'u. Lao Tzǔ made use of demons, and thereby became leader among the Spirits of Heaven. 'So evil turns to good.')

而婉转，或捧痛而号呼。奄雾消而光蔽，寂不知其何故。嗟妖邪之怪物，岂干真人之正度！耳聊嘈而外朗，忽屈申而觉寤。于是鸡知天曙而奋羽，忽嘈然而自鸣。鬼闻之以迸失，心慴怖而皆惊。

乱曰：齐桓梦物，而亦以霸。武丁夜感，而得贤佐。周梦九龄克百庆，晋文盬脑国以竞。老子役鬼为神将，传祸为福永无恙。

《全汉赋校注》，第 863—864 页。

TO HIS WIFE

Ch'in Chia (*c*. A. D. 147) was summoned to take up an appointment at the capital at a time when his wife was ill and staying with her parents. He was therefore unable to say goodbye to her, and sent her three poems instead. This is the last of the three.

SOLEMN, solemn the coachman gets ready to go;
'Chiang, chiang' the harness bells ring.
At break of dawn I must start on my long journey;
At cock-crow I must gird on my belt.
I turn back and look at the empty room;
For a moment I almost think I see you there.
One parting, but ten thousand regrets;
As I take my seat, my heart is unquiet.
What shall I do to tell you all my thoughts?
How can I let you know of all my love?
Precious hairpins make the head to shine
And bright mirrors can reflect beauty.
Fragrant herbs banish evil smells
And the scholar's lute has a clear note.
The man in the Book of Songs[①] who was given a quince
Wanted to pay it back with precious stones.
When I think of all the things you have done for me,
How ashamed I am to have done so little for you!
Although I know that it is a poor return,
All I can give you is this description of my feelings.

① See my *The Book of Songs*.

赠妇诗三首（其三）

〔东汉〕秦嘉

肃肃仆夫征。锵锵扬和铃。
清晨当引迈。束带待鸡鸣。
顾看空室中。仿佛想姿形。
一别怀万恨。起坐为不宁。
何用叙我心。遗思致款诚。
宝钗好耀首。明镜可鉴形。
芳香去垢秽。素琴有清声。
诗人感木瓜。乃欲答瑶琼。
愧彼赠我厚。惭此往物轻。
虽知未足报。贵用叙我情。

《先秦汉魏晋南北朝诗》（上），第 186—187 页。

CH'IN CHIA'S WIFE'S REPLY

MY poor body is alas unworthy;
I was ill when first you brought me home.
Limp and weary in the house—
Time passed and I got no better.
We could hardly ever see each other;
I could not serve you as I ought.
Then you received the Imperial Mandate;
You were ordered to go far away to the City.
Long, long must be our parting;
I was not destined to tell you thoughts.
I stood on tiptoe gazing into the distance,
Interminably gazing at the road that had taken you.
With thoughts of you my mind is obsessed;
In my dreams I see the light of your face.
Now you are started on your long journey
Each day brings you further from me.
Oh that I had a bird's wings
And high flying could follow you.
Long I sob and long I cry;
The tears fall down and wet my skirt.

答秦嘉诗

〔东汉〕徐淑

妾身兮不令。婴疾兮来归。
沉滞兮家门。历时兮不差。
旷废兮侍觐。情敬兮有违。
君今兮奉命。远适兮京师。
悠悠兮离别。无因兮叙怀。
瞻望兮踊跃。伫立兮徘徊。
思君兮感结。梦想兮容晖。
君发兮引迈。去我兮日乖。
恨无兮羽翼。高飞兮相追。
长吟兮永叹。泪下兮沾衣。

《先秦汉魏晋南北朝诗》（上），第 188 页。

ON THE DEATH OF HIS FATHER

By WEI WÊN-TI, son of Ts'ao Ts'ao, who founded the dynasty of Wei, and died in A.D. 220.

I LOOK up and see his curtains and bed;
I look down and examine his table and mat.
The things are there just as before;
But the man they belonged to is not there.
His spirit suddenly has taken flight
And left me behind far away.
To whom shall I look, on whom rely?
My tears flow in an endless stream.
'Yu, yu' cry the wandering deer
As they carry fodder to their young in the wood.
Flap, flap fly the birds
As they carry their little ones back to the nest.
I alone am desolate
Dreading the days of our long parting;
My grieving heart's settled pain
No one else can understand.
There is saying among people
'Sorrow makes us grow old.'
Alas, alas for my white hairs!
All too early they have come!
Long wailing, long sighing
My thoughts are fixed on my sage parent.
They say the good live long;
Then why was he not spared?

短歌行

〔魏〕曹丕

仰瞻帷幕。俯察几筵。
其物如故。其人不存。
神灵倏忽。弃我遐迁。
靡瞻靡恃。泣涕连连。
呦呦游鹿。衔草鸣麑。
翩翩飞鸟。挟子巢栖。
我独孤茕。怀此百离。
忧心孔疚。莫我能知。
人亦有言。忧令人老。
嗟我白发。生一何早。
长吟永叹。怀我圣考。
曰仁者寿。胡不是保。

《先秦汉魏晋南北朝诗》（上），第 389 页。

THE RUINS OF LO-YANG

By TS'AO CHIH (A.D. 192-232), third son of Ts'ao Ts'ao. He was a great favourite with his father till he made a mistake in a campaign. This is one of two poems of farewell to a friend who was going north. Lo-yang was sacked by rebels in A.D. 190.

I CLIMB to the ridge of the Pei-mang Hills

And look down on the city of Lo-yang.

In Lo-yang how still it is!

Palaces and houses all burnt to ashes.

Walls and fences all broken and gaping,

Thorns and brambles shooting up to the sky.

I do not see the old old-men;

I only see the new young men.

I turn aside, for the straight road is lost;

The fields are overgrown and will never be ploughed again.

I have been away such a long time

That I do not know which path is which.

How sad and ugly the empty moors are!

A thousand miles without the smoke of a chimney.

I think of our life together all those years;

My heart is tied with sorrow and I cannot speak.

送应氏诗二首（其一）

〔魏〕曹植

步登北邙阪。遥望洛阳山。
洛阳何寂寞。宫室尽烧焚。
垣墙皆顿擗。荆棘上参天。
不见旧耆老。但睹新少年。
侧足无行径。荒畴不复田。
游子久不归。不识陌与阡。
中野何萧条。千里无人烟。
念我平常居。气结不能言。

《先秦汉魏晋南北朝诗》（上），第 454 页。

THE COCK-FIGHT
By TS'AO CHIH

再
造
的
镜
像

OUR wandering eyes are sated with the dancer's skill,
Our ears are weary with the sound of 'kung' and 'shang'[①].
Our host is silent and sits doing nothing;
All the guests go on to places of amusement.

On long benches the sportsmen sit ranged
Round a cleared room, watching the fighting-cocks.
The gallant birds are all in battle-trim;
They raise their tails and flap defiantly.
Their beating wings stir the calm air;
Their angry eyes gleam with a red light.
Where their beaks have struck, the fine feathers are scattered;
With their strong talons they wound again and again.
Their long cries enter the blue clouds;
Their flapping wings tirelessly beat and throb.
'Pray God the lamp-oil lasts a little longer,
Then I shall not leave without winning the match!'

---

① Notes of the scale.

斗鸡诗

〔魏〕曹植

游目极妙伎。清听厌宫商。
主人寂无为。众宾进乐方。
长筵坐戏客。斗鸡间观房。
群雄正翕赫。双翘自飞扬。
挥羽激清风。悍目发朱光。
觜落轻毛散。严距往往伤。
长鸣入青云。扇翼独翱翔。
愿蒙狸膏助。常得擅此场。

《先秦汉魏晋南北朝诗》（上），第 450 页。

再造的镜像

A VISION

By TS'AO CHIH

IN the Nine Provinces there is not room enough;
I want to soar high among the clouds,
And, far beyond the Eight Limits of the compass,
Cast my gaze across the unmeasured void.
I will wear as my gown the red mists of sunrise
And as my skirt the white fringes of the clouds;
My canopy—the dim lustre of Space,
My chariot—six dragons mounting heavenward;
And before the light of Time has shifted a pace
Suddenly stand upon the World's blue rim.
The doors of Heaven swing open,
The double gates shine with a red light.
I roam and linger in the palace of Wên-ch'ang,
I climb up to the hall of T'ai-wei.
The Lord God lies at his western lattice;
And the lesser Spirits are together in the eastern gallery.
They wash me in a bath of rainbow-spray
And gird me with a belt of jasper and rubies.
I wander at my ease gathering divine herbs;
I bend down and touch the scented flowers.
Wang-tzŭ[①] gives me drugs of long-life
And Hsien-mên hands me strange potions.
By the partaking of food I evade the rites of Death;
My span is extended to the enjoyment of life everlasting.

---

① Names of Immortals.

五游咏

〔魏〕曹植

九州不足步。愿得凌云翔。
逍遥八纮外。游目历遐荒。
披我丹霞衣。袭我素霓裳。
华盖芬晻蔼。六龙仰天骧。
曜灵未移景。倏忽造昊苍。
阊阖启丹扉。双阙曜朱光。
徘徊文昌殿。登陟太微堂。
上帝休西棂。群后集东厢。
带我琼瑶佩。漱我沆瀣浆。
踟蹰玩灵芝。徙倚弄华芳。
王子奉仙药。羡门进奇方。
服食享遐纪。延寿保无疆。

《先秦汉魏晋南北朝诗》（上），第 433—434 页。

THE LIBERATOR
A Political Allegory
By TS'AO CHIH

IN the high trees—many doleful winds;
The ocean waters—lashed into waves.
If the sharp sword be not in your hand,
How can you hope your friends will remain many?
Do you not see that sparrow on the fence?
Seeing the hawk it casts itself into the snare.
The fowler to catch the sparrow is delighted;
The Young Man to see the sparrow is grieved.
He takes his sword and cuts through the netting;
The yellow sparrow flies away, away.
Away, away, up to the blue sky
And down again to thank the Young Man.

野田黄雀行

〔魏〕曹植

高树多悲风。海水扬其波。
利剑不在掌。结友何须多。
不见篱间雀。见鹞自投罗。
罗家得雀喜。少年见雀悲。
拔剑捎罗网。黄雀得飞飞。
飞飞摩苍天。来下谢少年。

《先秦汉魏晋南北朝诗》（上），第 425 页。

THE CURTAIN OF THE WEDDING BED
By LIU HSÜN'S WIFE (Third Century A.D.)

After she had been married to him for a long while, General Liu Hsün sent his wife back to her home, because he had fallen in love with a girl of the Ssu-ma family.

FLAP, flap, you curtain in front of our bed!
I hung you there to screen us from the light of day.
I brought you with me when I left my father's house;
Now I am taking you back with me again.
I will fold you up and lay you flat in your box.
Curtain—shall I ever take you out again?

代刘勋妻王氏杂诗

〔魏〕曹丕

　　王宋者。平虏将军刘勋妻也。入门二十余年。后勋悦山阳司马氏女。以宋无子出之。还于道中。作诗二首。

　　　　　　翩翩床前帐。张以蔽光辉。
　　　　　　昔将尔同去。今将尔共归。
　　　　　　缄藏箧笥里。当复何时披。

　　　　　　　　　《玉台新咏》，第 34—35 页。

BEARER'S SONG

By MIU HSI (A.D. 186-245). Cf. the *Han Burial Songs*, p.55

WHEN I was alive, I wandered in the streets of the Capital;

Now that I am dead, I am left to lie in the fields.

In the morning I drove out from the High Hall;

In the evening I lodged beneath the Yellow Springs[①].

When the white sun had sunk in the Western Chasm

I hung up my chariot and rested my four horses.

Now even the mighty Maker of All

Could not bring the life back to my limbs.

Shape and substance day by day will vanish:

Hair and teeth will gradually fall away.

For ever from of old men have been so:

And none born can escape this thing.

① Hades.

挽歌诗

〔魏〕缪袭

生时游国都，死没弃中野。
朝发高堂上，暮宿黄泉下。
白日入虞渊，悬车息驷马。
造化虽神明，安能复存我？
形容稍歇灭，齿发行当堕。
自古皆有然，谁能离此者。

《汉魏六朝诗鉴赏辞典》，第 236—237 页。

REGRET

By YÜAN CHI (A.D. 210-263)

WHEN I was young I learnt fencing
And was better at it than Ch'ü-ch'êng[①].
My spirit was high as the rolling clouds
And my fame resounded beyond the World.
I took my sword to the desert sands,
I watered my horse in the Nine Winds.
My flags and banners flapped in the wind,
And nothing was heard but the song of my drums.

War and its travels have made me sad,
And a fierce anger burns within me.
It's thinking of how I've wasted my time
That makes this fury tear my heart.

再
造
的
镜
像

① Famous swordsman, *c.* 112 B.C.

咏怀诗（六十一）

〔魏〕阮籍

少年学击刺。妙伎过曲城。
英风截云霓。超世发奇声。
挥剑临沙漠。饮马九野坰。
旗帜何翩翩。但闻金鼓鸣。
军旅令人悲。烈烈有哀情。
念我平常时。悔恨从此生。

《先秦汉魏晋南北朝诗》（上），第 507 页。

TAOIST SONG

By HSI K'ANG (A.D. 223-262)

I will cast out Wisdom and reject Learning,
My thoughts shall wander in the silent Void.
Always repenting of wrongs done
Will never bring my heart to rest.
I cast my hook in a single stream;
But my joy is as though I possessed a Kingdom.
I loose my hair and go singing;
To the four frontiers men join in my refrain.
This is the purport of my song:
'My thoughts shall wander in the Silent Void.'

再
造
的
镜
像

代秋胡歌诗（其五）

〔魏〕嵇康

绝智弃学。游心于玄默。
绝智弃学。游心于玄默。
遇过而悔。当不自得。
垂钓一壑。所乐一国。
被发行歌。和气四塞。
歌以言之。游心于玄默。

《先秦汉魏晋南北朝诗》（上），第 480 页。

A GENTLE WIND

By Fu HSÜAN (A.D. 217-278)

A GENTLE wind fans the calm night;
A bright moon shines on the high tower.
A voice whispers, but no one answers when I call;
A shadow stirs, but no one comes when I beckon.
The kitchen-man brings in a dish of bean-leaves;
Wine is there, but I do not fill my cup.
Contentment with poverty is Fortune's best gift;
Riches and Honour are the handmaids of Disaster.
Though gold and gems by the world are sought and prized,
To me they seem no more than weeds or chaff.

再
造
的
镜
像

杂诗二首（其一）

〔西晋〕傅玄

闲夜微风起。明月照高台。
清响呼不应。玄景招不来。
厨人进藿茹。有酒不盈杯。
安贫福所与。富贵为祸媒。
金玉虽高堂。于我贱蒿莱。

《先秦汉魏晋南北朝诗》（上），第 570 页。

WOMAN

By FU HSÜAN

How sad it is to be framed in woman's form!
Nothing on earth is held so cheap.
A boy that comes to a home
Drops to earth like a god that chooses to be born.
His bold heart braves the Four Oceans,
The wind and dust of a thousand miles.
No one is glad when a girl is born;
By *her* the family sets no store.
When she grows up, she hides in her room
Afraid to look a man in the face.
No one cries when she leaves her home—
Sudden as clouds when the rain stops.
She bows her head and composes her face,
Her teeth are pressed on her red lips.
She bows and kneels countless times,
She must humble herself even to the servants.
While his love lasts he is distant as the stars;
She is a sun-flower, looking up to the sun.
Soon their love will be severed more than water from fire;
A hundred evils will be heaped upon her.
Her face will follow the year's changes;
Her lord will find new pleasures.
They that were once like substance and shadow
Are now as far as Hu and Ch'in[①].
Yes, Hu and Ch'in shall sooner meet
Than they, whose parting is like Shên and Ch'ên[②].

---

① The land of the barbarians and China.
② Hesperus and Lucifer.

苦相篇

〔西晋〕傅玄

苦相身为女。卑陋难再陈。
男儿当门户。堕地自生神。
雄心志四海。万里望风尘。
女育无欣爱。不为家所珍。
长大逃深室。藏头羞见人。
垂泪适他乡。忽如雨绝云。
低头和颜色。素齿结朱唇。
跪拜无复数。婢妾如严宾。
情合同云汉。葵藿仰阳春。
心乖甚水火。百恶集其身。
玉颜随年变。丈夫多好新。
昔为形与影。今为胡与秦。
胡秦时相见。一绝逾参辰。

《先秦汉魏晋南北朝诗》（上），第 555—556 页。

SATIRE ON PAYING CALLS IN AUGUST
By CH'ÊNG HSIAO (*c.* A.D. 220-264)

WHEN I was young, throughout the hot season
There were no carriages driving about the roads.
People shut their doors and lay down in the cool;
Or if they went out, it was not to pay calls.
Nowadays—ill-bred, ignorant fellows,
When they feel the heat, make for a friend's house.
The unfortunate host when he hears someone coming
Scowls and frowns, but can think of no escape.
'There's nothing for it but to rise and go to the door,'
And in his comfortable seat he groans and sighs.
The conversation does not end quickly;
Prattling and babbling, what a lot he says!
Only when one is almost dead with fatigue
He asks at last if one isn't finding him tiring.
(One's arm is almost in half with continual fanning;
The sweat is pouring down one's neck in streams).
Do not say that this is a small matter;
I consider the practice a blot on our social life.
I therefore caution all wise men
That August visitors should not be admitted.

嘲热客诗

〔魏〕程晓

平生三伏时。道路无行车。
闭门避暑卧。出入不相过。
今世㺍㺍子。触热到人家。
主人闻客来。颦蹙奈此何。
谓当起行去。安坐正跘跨。
所说无一急。唶唶一何多。
疲瘅向之久。甫问君极那。
摇扇臂中疼。流汗正滂沱。
莫谓此小事。亦是人一瑕。
传戒诸高朋。热行宜见诃。

《先秦汉魏晋南北朝诗》（上），第 578 页。

HOT CAKE

Part of a Poem

By SHU HSI (*c.* A.D. 265-306)

再
造
的
镜
像

WINTER has come, fierce is the cold;

In the sharp morning air new-risen we meet.

Rheum freezes in the nose;

Frost hangs about the chin.

For hollow bellies, for chattering teeth and shivering knees

What better than hot cake?

Soft as the down of spring,

Whiter than autumn floss!

Dense and swift the steam

Rises, swells and spreads.

Fragrance flies through the air,

Is scattered far and wide,

Steals down along the winds and wets

The covetous mouth of passer-by.

Servants and grooms

Throw sidelong glances, munch the empty air.

They lick their lips who serve;

While lines of envious lackeys by the wall

Stand dryly swallowing.

饼赋①

〔西晋〕束皙

若夫三春之初，阴阳交际，寒气既除，温不至热。于时享宴，则馒头宜设。炎律方回，纯阳布畅，服绤饮冰，随阴而凉。此时为饼，莫若薄壮。商风既厉，大火西移；鸟兽毨毛，树木疏枝，肴馔尚温，则起溲可施。元冬猛寒，清晨之会，涕冻鼻中，霜凝口外，充虚解战，汤饼为最。然皆用之有时，所适者也。苟错其次，则不能斯善，其可以通冬达夏。终岁常施，四时从用，无所不宜，惟牢丸乎？尔乃重罗之面，尘飞白雪，胶黏筋韧，溎液濡泽。肉则羊膀豕胁，脂肤相半；臠如蜿首，珠连砾散。姜枝葱本，萃缕切判，辛桂剉末，椒兰是洒，和盐漉豉，揽和胶乱。于是火盛汤涌，猛气蒸作；振衣振裳，握搦拊搏。面迷离于指端，手萦回而交错；纷纷驳驳，星分霞落。笼无进肉，饼无流面；姝媮冽敕，薄而不绽。弱如春绵，白若秋练；气勃郁以扬布，香飞散而远遍。行人垂涎于下风，童仆空噍而斜盼；擎器者舐唇，立侍者干咽。

《历代赋汇》，第 592—593 页。

---

① 此为《饼赋》全诗，韦利只选部分翻译。

THE DESECRATION OF THE HAN TOMBS

By CHANG TSAI (*c.* A D. 289)

再
造
的
镜
像

AT Pei-mang how they rise to Heaven,

Those high mounds, four or five in the fields!

What men lie buried under these tombs?

All of them were Lords of the Han world.

'Kung' and 'Wên'[1] gaze across at each other;

The Yüan mound is all grown over with weeds.

When the dynasty was falling, tumult and disorder arose.

Thieves and robbers roamed like wild beasts.

Of earth[2] they have crumbled more than one handful,

They have gone into vaults and opened the secret doors.

Jewelled scabbards lie twisted and defaced;

The stones that were set in them, thieves have carried away;

The ancestral temples are hummocks in the ground;

The walls that went round them are all levelled flat.

Over everything the tangled thorns are growing;

A herd-boy pushes through them up the path.

Down in the thorns rabbits have made their burrows;

The weeds and thistles will never be cleared away.

Over the tombs the ploughshare will be driven

And peasants will have their fields and orchards there.

They that were once lords of ten thousand chariots

Are now become the dust of the hills and ridges.

I think of what Yung-mên[3] said

And am sorely grieved at the thought of 'then' and 'now'.

---

① Names of two tombs.

② In the early days of the Han dynasty a man who stole one handful of earth from the Imperial Tombs was put to death.

③ Yung-mên said to Mêng Ch'ang-chün (died 279 B.C.), 'Does it not grieve you to think that a hundred years hence this terrace will be cast down?' Ch'ang-chün wept.

七哀诗二首（其一）

〔西晋〕张载

北芒何垒垒。高陵有四五。
借问谁家坟。皆云汉世主。
恭文遥相望。原陵郁膴膴。
季世丧乱起。贼盗如豺虎。
毁壤过一抔。便房启幽户。
珠柙离玉体。珍宝见剽虏。
园寝化为墟。周墉无遗堵。
蒙茏荆棘生。蹊径登童竖。
狐兔窟其中。芜秽不复扫。
颓陇并垦发。萌隶营农圃。
昔为万乘君。今为丘中土。
感彼雍门言。凄怆哀今古。

《先秦汉魏晋南北朝诗》（上），第 740—741 页。

DAY DREAMS
By TSO SSŬ (died *c.* A.D. 306)

WHEN I was young, writing was my one sport,
And I read a prodigious quantity of books.
In prose I made *The Faults of Ch'in* my standard;
In verse I imitated *The Tale of Mr Nothing*.
But then the arrows began singing at the frontier
And a winged summons came flying from the City.
Although arms were not my profession
I had once read the war-book of Jang-chü.
I whooped aloud; my shouts rent the air;
I felt as though Eastern Wu were already annihilated.
The scholar's knife cuts best at its first use,
In day-dreams only are his glorious plans fulfilled;
By a glance to the left, I cleared the Yangtze and Hsiang,
By a glance to the right, I quelled the Tibetans and Hu.
When my task was done, I did not accept a barony,
But refusing with a bow retired to a cottage in the country.

咏史八首（其一）

〔西晋〕左思

弱冠弄柔翰，卓荦观群书。
著论准《过秦》，作赋拟《子虚》。
边城苦鸣镝，羽檄飞京都。
虽非甲胄士，畴昔览《穰苴》。
长啸激清风，志若无东吴。
铅刀贵一割，梦想骋良图。
左眄澄江湘，右盼定羌胡。
功成不受爵，长揖归田庐。

《左思诗集释》，第 23 页。

THE SCHOLAR IN THE NARROW STREET
By TSO SSŬ

FLAP, flap, the captive bird in the cage
Beating its wings against the four corners.
Sad and dreary, the scholar in the narrow street;
Clasping a shadow he dwells in an empty hut.
When he goes out, there is nowhere for him to go;
Thorns and brambles block his every path.
His plans are all discarded and come to nothing;
He is left stranded like a fish in a dry pond.
Without—he has not a single farthing of salary;
Within—there is not a peck of grain in his larder.
His relations all despise him for his lack of success;
Friends and companions grow daily more aloof.
Su Ch'in toured in triumph through the North,
Li Ssŭ rose to be Premier in the West;
With sudden splendour shone the flower of their fame,
With like swiftness it withered and decaycd.
Though one drinks at a river, one cannot drink more than a belly-full;
Enough is good, but there is no use in satiety.
The bird in a forest can perch but on one bough,
And this should be the wise man's pattern.

咏史诗八首（其八）

〔西晋〕左思

习习笼中鸟。举翮触四隅。
落落穷巷士。抱影守空庐。
出门无通路。枳棘塞中涂。
计策弃不收。块若枯池鱼。
外望无寸禄。内顾无斗储。
亲戚还相蔑。朋友日夜疏。
苏秦北游说。李斯西上书。
俯仰生荣华。咄嗟复凋枯。
饮河期满腹。贵足不愿余。
巢林栖一枝。可为达士模。

《先秦汉魏晋南北朝诗》（上），第 734 页。

THE VALLEY WIND
By LU YÜN (Fourth Century A.D.)

LIVING in retirement beyond the World,
Silently enjoying isolation,
I pull the rope of my door tighter
And bind firmly this cracked jar.
My spirit is tuned to the Spring-season;
At the fall of the year there is autumn in my heart
Thus imitating cosmic changes
My cottage becomes a Universe.

再
造
的
镜
像

失题（之五）

〔西晋〕陆云

闲居外物。静言乐幽。
绳枢增结。瓮牖绸缪。
和神当春。清节为秋。
天地则尔。户庭已悠。

《先秦汉魏晋南北朝诗》（上），第 715 页。

A PEACOCK FLEW
(Third to Fifth Century A.D.)

A peacock flew, far off to the south-east;
Flew for a mile, then always dallied in its flight.
'At thirteen I knew how to weave silk,
At fourteen I learnt to make clothes.
At fifteen I could play the small lute,
At sixteen I knew the Songs and Book.
At seventeen I was made your wife;
From care and sorrow my heart was never free,
For you already were a clerk in the great town
Diligent in your duties and caring for nothing else.
I was left alone in an empty bridal-room;
It was not often that we two could meet.
At cock-crow I went to the loom to weave;
Night after night I toiled and got no rest.
In three days I would finish five bits,
And yet the Great One① chid me for being slow.
Husband, it is not because I weave too slowly
That I find it hard to be a wife in your house.
It is not in my power to do the tasks I am set;
There is no use in staying for the sake of staying.

Go then quickly, speak to the lady my mistress
And while there is time let me go back to my home.'
The clerk her husband listened to her words;
Up to the Hall he went and 'Mother', he said,
'The signs of my birth marked me for a humble course;
Yet luck was with me when I took this girl to wife.
Our hair was plaited, we shared pillow and mat,
Swore friendship until the Yellow Springs of Death.
We have served you together two years or three,
Since the beginning only so little a while.
In nothing has the girl offended or done amiss;
What has happened to bring trouble between you?'
Then spoke the clerk's mother:
'Come, my son, such love is foolish doting;
This wife neglects all rules of behaviour,
And in all her ways follows her own whim.
Myself I have long been discontented with her;
You must not think only of what pleases you.

---

① The mother-in-law.

古诗为焦仲卿妻作

〔东汉〕佚名

孔雀东南飞，五里一徘徊。

十三能织素。十四学裁衣。十五弹箜篌。十六诵诗书。十七为君妇。心中常苦悲。君既为府吏。守节情不移。贱妾留空房。相见常日稀。鸡鸣入机织。夜夜不得息。三日断五匹。大人故嫌迟。非为织作迟。君家妇难为。妾不堪驱使。徒留无所施。便可白公姥。及时相遣归。

府吏得闻之。堂上启阿母。儿已薄禄相。幸复得此妇。结发同枕席。黄泉共为友。共事三二年。始尔未为久。女行无偏斜。何意致不厚。

Our neighbour to eastward has a
steadfast daughter;
She calls herself Lo-fu of the house
of Ch'in.
The loveliest limbs that ever yet you
saw!
Let mother get her for you to be your
wife,
And as soon as may be send the
other away;
Send her quickly, and do not let her
bide.'
Long her son knelt down before her
and pleaded:
'Bowing before you, mother, I make
my plea.
If now you send her away
I will live single all the days of my
life.'
And when his mother heard him
She banged the bed, flying into a
great rage,
And 'Little son', she said, 'are you
not afraid?
Dare you answer me in such a wife's
praise?
By this you have forfeited all my
love and kindness;
Do not dream that I will let you work
your will.'
He did not speak, he made no cry.
Twice he bowed, and went back to
his room;
He lifted up his voice to speak with
his young bride,
But his breath caught and the words
would not come.
'It is not *I* that would send you away,

It is my mother that has scolded and
harried me.
Do you live at your father's, just for
a little while,
For I must be going to take my
orders in the town—
Not for long; I shall soon be coming
home,
And when I am home, I will fetch
you back again.
Let this put down the doubts that rise
in your heart;
Turn it over in your thoughts and do
not disobey me.'
The young wife spoke to the
government clerk:
'Give me no more of this foolish
tangled talk.
Long ago, when the year was at its
spring,
I left my father and came to your
grand home.
I obeyed my mistress in every task I
plied;
Day and night I hurried on with my
tasks
In solitude, caught in endless toil.
Never in word or deed was I at fault;
In tender service I waited on
Madam's needs,
Yet even so she sought to send me
away.
It is no use to talk of coming back.
These things are mine: a broidered
waist-jacket,
Lovely and rare, shining with a light
of its own;

阿母谓府吏。何乃太区区。此妇无礼节。举动自专由。吾意久怀忿。汝岂得自由。

东家有贤女。自名秦罗敷。可怜体无比。阿母为汝求。便可速遣之。遣之慎莫留。

府吏长跪告。伏惟启阿母。今若遣此妇。终老不复取。

阿母得闻之。槌床便大怒。小子无所畏。何敢助妇语。吾已失恩义。会不相从许。

府吏默无声。再拜还入户。举言谓新妇。哽咽不能语。我自不驱卿。逼迫有阿母。卿但暂还家。吾今且报府。不久当归还。还必相迎取。以此下心意。慎勿违吾语。

新妇谓府吏。勿复重纷纭。往昔初阳岁。谢家来贵门。奉事循公姥。进止敢自专。昼夜勤作息。伶俜萦苦辛。谓言无罪过。供养卒大恩。仍更被驱遣。何言复来还。妾有绣腰襦。葳蕤自生光。

A canopy of red gauze
With scented bags hanging at the four corners;
And shuttered boxes, sixty, seventy,
With grey marbles strung on green threads—
So many boxes, and none is like the last;
And in the boxes, so many kinds of things!
If I am vile, my things must also be scorned.
They will not be worth keeping for the after-one[①];
Yet I leave them here; they may come in handy as presents.
From now onward we shall not meet again.
Once in a while let me have your news,
And let us never, never forget one another.'

A cock crowed; outside it was growing light.
The young wife rose and tidied herself.
She puts about her a broidered, lined gown,
Takes what she needs, four or five things,
And now on her feet she slips her silk shoes;
In her hair are shining combs of tortoise-shell.
Her waist is supple as the flow of rustling silk;
At her ear she dangles a bright crescent moon.
White her fingers as the slender onion stem;
She seems in her mouth to hold cinnabar and pearls.
Slender, slender she treads with small steps,
More fine, more lovely than any lady in the world.
She goes to the Hall, low she bows her head;
But the stubborn mother's anger did not cease.
'When I was a girl', the young wife said,
'I was brought up far from any town,
A wild thing, never schooled or taught,
And needs must shame a great man's house.
From you I have taken much money and silk,
Yet was not fit to do the tasks that you set.
Today I am going back to my father's home;
I am sorry to leave you burdened by household cares.'
From her little sister[②] it was worse work to part;
Her tears fell like a string of small pearls:
'When new-wed I first came to your home,
You had just learnt to lean on the bed and walk.
Today, when I run driven away,
Little sister, you have grown as tall as me.

---

① Her successor.

② Sister-in-law.

红罗复斗帐。四角垂香囊。箱帘六七十。绿碧青丝绳。物物各自异。种种在其中。人贱物亦鄙。不足迎后人。留待作遗施。于今无会因。时时为安慰。久久莫相忘。

鸡鸣外欲曙。新妇起严妆。著我绣夹裙。事事四五通。足下蹑丝履。头上玳瑁光。腰若流纨素。耳著明月珰。指如削葱根。口如含朱丹。纤纤作细步。精妙世无双。

上堂拜阿母。阿母怒不止。昔作女儿时。生小出野里。本自无教训。兼愧贵家子。受母钱帛多。不堪母驱使。今日还家去。念母劳家里。却与小姑别。泪落连珠子。新妇初来时。小姑如我长。

Work for Madam, cherish her with all your heart,
Strive to serve and help her as best you may.
Those seventh-days and last days but one[①]
Do not forget what nice romps we had!'
She left the gate, mounted her coach and went;
Of tears she dropt many hundred rows.
The clerk with his horse was riding on before;
The young wife rode in her carriage behind.
A pattering of hoofs, a thundering of wheels—
And they met each other at the mouth of the great road.

He left his horse and sat beside her in the coach,
He bowed his head and into her ear he spoke:
'I swear an oath that I will not give you up
If for a little while you go back to your home.
I for a little must go back to the town;
It will not be long before I am here again.
I swear by Heaven that I will not abandon you.'
'Dear husband', the young wife cried,
'Of your fond love I have not any doubt,
And since you have said you still accept me as your wife
It will not be long, I hope, before you are back.
You now must be like the great rock;
And I will be like the reed that grows by the stream.
The reed by the stream that bends but does not break;
The great rock, too mighty to move from its place.
I have a brother, my own father's son,
Whose nature and deeds are wild as a summer storm.
I fear he will not let me have my way,
And the thought of this fills my heart with dread.'
They raise their heads, bidding long farewell,
Her heart and his equally loath to part.

---

① Holidays.

勤心养公姥。好自相扶将。初七及下九。嬉戏莫相忘。出门登车去。涕落百余行。

府吏马在前。新妇车在后。隐隐何甸甸。俱会大道口。下马入车中。低头共耳语。誓不相隔卿。且暂还家去。吾今且赴府。不久当还归。誓天不相负。

新妇谓府吏。感君区区怀。君既若见录。不久望君来。君当作磐石。妾当作蒲苇。蒲苇纫如丝。磐石无转移。我有亲父兄。性行暴如雷。恐不任我意。逆以煎我怀。举手长劳劳。二情同依依。

She enters the gate, she mounts her father's Hall,
Languidly moves with no greeting in her face.
'Child', cries her mother, and loud she claps her hands,
'We little thought to see you home so soon.
For at thirteen I taught you to weave silk,
At fourteen you could cut clothes.
At fifteen you played on the small lute,
At sixteen you knew the customs and rites.
At seventeen I sent you to be a bride
And fully thought that nothing had gone amiss.
What is your fault, what wrong have you done
That uninvited you now come back to your home?'
Then Lan-chih, ashamed before her mother,
'Oh nothing, nothing, mother, have I done amiss;'
And a deep pity tore the mother's heart.

She had been at home ten days or more
When the local magistrate sends a go-between,
Saying: 'My master has a third son,
For grace and beauty none like him in the world;
He is eighteen or nineteen years old,
A lovely boy, gifted and of ready speech.'
Then said the mother to her daughter,
'Daughter, this offer cannot be refused.'
But the daughter weeping answered,
'When I left my husband's house,
He looked kindly upon me and an oath he swore
That come what might he would not abandon me.
And today, false and wicked should I be,
Were I untrue to this our great love.
It would surely be better to break off the parley;
There is no hurry; we can answer them later on.'
Then said her mother to that go-between:
'In our humble house there is indeed a daughter,
Was once married, but came back to us again.
If she was not fit to be a clerk's wife
How can she suit a magistrate's noble son?
Pray go further and seek a better match;
At the present moment we cannot give our consent.'
Not many days had the messenger been gone
When a deputy-prefect[1] came on like quest:
'They tell me that here is a lady called Lan-chih
Whose father's fathers long served the State.
My master would have you know that his fifth son
Is handsome, clever, and has not yet a wife.

---

[1] As messenger from the Prefect, who was much grander than a district magistrate.

入门上家堂。进退无颜仪。阿母大拊掌。不图子自归。十三教汝织。十四能裁衣。十五弹箜篌。十六知礼仪。十七遣汝嫁。谓言无誓违。汝今何罪过。不迎而自归。兰芝惭阿母。儿实无罪过。阿母大悲摧。

还家十余日。县令遣媒来。云有第三郎。窈窕世无双。年始十八九。便言多令才。

阿母谓阿女。汝可去应之。

阿女含泪答。兰芝初还时。府吏见丁宁。结誓不别离。今日违情义。恐此事非奇。自可断来信。徐徐更谓之。

阿母白媒人。贫贱有此女。始适还家门。不堪吏人妇。岂合令郎君。幸可广问讯。不得便相许。

媒人去数日。寻遣丞请还。说有兰家女。承籍有宦官。云有第五郎。娇逸未有婚。

His own deputy he sends as go-between
And his deputy-assistant to carry you his words.'
The assistant told them: 'In the Lord Prefect's house
Has grown up this fine young gentleman
Who now wishes to be bound with the Great Bond,
And therefore sends us with a message to your noble gate.'
The girl's mother sent word to the messengers:
'This daughter of mine is already bound by a vow;[①]
I cannot venture to speak of such a match.'
When news of this reached the brother's ear
His heart within him was much angered and vexed.
He raised his voice and thus to his sister he said:
'The plan you follow is not well considered.
Your former husband was only a Prefect's clerk;
Now you have the chance to marry a young lord!
Wide as earth from sky is the space between;
Here is a splendour that shall brighten all your days.
But if you will not be married to this fine lord,
What refuge have you, whither else shall you turn?'
Then Lan-chih raised her hand and answered:
'Brother, there is good sense in what you say.
I left my home to serve another man,
But in mid-road[①] returned to my brother's house,
And in his hands must all my fortunes rest;
I must not ask to follow my own desire.
Though to the clerk I am bound, yet now, I think,
To eternity we shall not meet again.
Let us now accept the offer of this match
And say that the wedding may take place at once.'
The messengers left their couch, their faces beaming,
With a bland 'yes, yes' and 'so, so'.
They went to their quarters and to the Prefect they spoke:
'We, your servants, have fulfilled your high command;
The words we have uttered were not without effect.'
When the Lord Prefect was told of all that had passed,
His heart was filled with great mirth and joy;
He read the Calendar, he opened the sacred book.
He found it written that in this very month
The Six Points were in fortunate harmony,
The Good Omen fell in the thirtieth day;
And now already the twenty-seventh was come.

---

①   In the mid-road of marriage.

遣丞为媒人。主簿通语言。直说太守家。有此令郎君。既欲结大义。故遣来贵门。

阿母谢媒人。女子先有誓。老姥岂敢言。

阿兄得闻之。怅然心中烦。举言谓阿妹。作计何不量。先嫁得府吏。后嫁得郎君。否泰如天地。足以荣汝身。不嫁义郎体。其住欲何云。

兰芝仰头答。理实如兄言。谢家事夫婿。中道还兄门。处分适兄意。那得自任专。虽与府吏要。渠会永无缘。登即相许和。便可作婚姻。

媒人下床去。诺诺复尔尔。还部白府君。下官奉使命。言谈大有缘。府君得闻之。心中大欢喜。视历复开书。便利此月内。六合正相应。良吉三十日。今已二十七。

'Go, my servants, and make this wedding for me.'
With urgent message they speed the marriage gear;
Hither and thither they whirl like clouds in the sky.
A green-sparrow[①] and white-swan boat;
At its four corners a dragon-child flag
Delicately curls in the wind; a golden coach
With jade-set wheels. And dappled courses prance
With tasselled manes and saddles fretted with gold.
The wedding gift, three million cash
Pierced in the middle and strung with green thread.
Of coloured stuffs three hundred bits,
And rare fish from the markets of Chiao and Kuang.
The bridegroom's friends, four or five hundred
In great array go up to the Prefect's gate.
Then said the mother:
'Daughter dear, this moment a letter has come,
Saying tomorrow my Lord will fetch you away.
How comes it, girl, that you are not making your dress?
Don't leave it so late that the wedding cannot start!'
She did not answer, she did not make a sound;
With her handkerchief she covered her face and wept,

Her tears flowed like water poured from a jar.
She shifts her stool that is bright with crystal beads
And close to the front window she sets it down.
With her left hand she wields ruler and knife;
In her right hand she holds the silk gauze.
In the morning she finishes her lined, broidered gown;
By evening she has finished her thin gauze robe.
The day was over, and she in the gathering gloom
With sorrowful heart walked sobbing to the gate.
When the clerk her husband heard of what had passed
He asked for leave to return for a little while.
He had still to ride two leagues or three
When his horse neighed, raising a doleful moan.
The young wife knew the horse's neigh;
She slipped on her shoes and set out to meet him.
Woefully they looked on each other from afar,
When each saw it was his dear one that had come.
She raised her hand, she struck the horse's saddle,
Wailing and sobbing as though her heart would break.

---

① Grosbeak.

卿可去成婚。交语速装束。络绎如浮云。青雀白鹄舫。四角龙子幡。婀娜随风转。金车玉作轮。踯躅青骢马。流苏金镂鞍。赍钱三百万。皆用青丝穿。杂彩三百匹。交用市鲑珍。从人四五百。郁郁登郡门。

　　阿母谓阿女。适得府君书。明日来迎汝。何不作衣裳。莫令事不举。

　　阿女默无声。手巾掩口啼。泪落便如泻。移我琉璃榻。出置前窗下。左手持刀尺。右手执绫罗。朝成绣夹裙。晚成单罗衫。晻晻日欲暝。愁思出门啼。

　　府吏闻此变。因求假暂归。未至二三里。摧藏马悲哀。新妇识马声。蹑履相逢迎。怅然遥相望。知是故人来。举手拍马鞍。嗟叹使心伤。

'Since you left me—' she said,
'Things happen to one that cannot be foreseen—
It is true that I have not done as I wished to do;
But I do not think that you fully understand.
Remember that I have an own father and mother
Who with my brother forced me to do this,
Made me give myself over to another man.
How could I hope that you would ever come again?'
Then said her husband the clerk to his young wife:
'Well done!' he cried, 'well done to have climbed so high!
The great rock that is so firm and square
Was strong enough to last a thousand years.
The river reed that once was thought so tough
Was a frail thing that broke between dawn and dusk.
From glory to glory will my fine lady stride,
While I go down to the Yellow Springs alone.'
Then answered the young wife and to the clerk she said:
'What do you mean, why do you speak to me so?
It was the same with both; each of us was forced;
You were, and so was I too.
In the land of death you shall not be alone;
Do not fail me in what to-day you have said.'

They held hands, they parted and went their ways,
He to his house and she back to hers.
That live men can make a death-parting
Is sorrowful more than words can tell;
To know they are leaving the world and all it holds,
Doing a thing that can never be undone!

When the young clerk had got back to his home
He went to the Hall and bowing to his mother he said:
'Mother, today the great wind is cold.
A cold wind shakes the bushes and trees.
A cruel frost has stiffened the orchids in the court.
Mother, mother, to-day I go to darkness
Leaving you to stay here alone.
For my mind is set on a very sad plan;
Let your grievance against me stop when I am dead.
May your life endure like a rock of the Southern Hills,
Your back be straight and your limbs ever strong!'
When the young clerk's mother heard this
Bitter tears at each word flowed.
'O woe, will you that are of good house,
Whose father's fathers were ministers at Court
Die for a woman? Little sense do you show

自君别我后。人事不可量。果不如先愿。又非君所详。我有亲父母。逼迫兼弟兄。以我应他人。君还何所望。

　　府吏谓新妇。贺卿得高迁。磐石方且厚。可以卒千年。蒲苇一时纫。便作旦夕间。卿当日胜贵。吾独向黄泉。

　　新妇谓府吏。何意出此言。同是被逼迫。君尔妾亦然。黄泉下相见。勿违今日言。执手分道去。各各还家门。生人作死别。恨恨那可论。念与世间辞。千万不复全。

　　府吏还家去。上堂拜阿母。今日大风寒。寒风摧树木。严霜结庭兰。儿今日冥冥。令母在后单。故作不良计。勿复怨鬼神。命如南山石。四体康且直。

　　阿母得闻之。零泪应声落。汝是大家子。仕宦于台阁。慎勿为妇死。

Of which things matter! Listen now
to my plan.
Our eastern neighbour has good girl,
Dainty and pretty, the fairest in the
town.
Let Mother get her to be your wife;
I'll be quick about it; you shall have
her between dawn and dusk.'
The clerk bowed twice, and turned to
go;
Deep he sighed in the empty bridal
room,
He was thinking of his plan and
therefore sighing stood.
He turned his head, he moved
towards the door,
Drawn by the grief that surged in his
boiling breast.

That day, while horses whinnied and
oxen lowed[1],
The bride went in to her tabernacle
green.
Swiftly the day closed and the dusk
grew black;
There was not a sound; the second
watch had begun.
'With the day that has ended my life
also ends,
My soul shall go and only my body
stay.'
She lifts her skirt, she takes off her
silk shoes,
She rises up and walks into the blue
lake.
When the young clerk heard what
had happened
And knew in his heart that they had
parted for ever,
He hovered a while under the
courtyard tree,
Then hanged himself from the
south-east bough.

The two families buried them in the
same grave,
Buried them together on the side of
the Hua Shan.
To east and west they planted cypress
and pine,
To left and right they sowed the
wu-t'ung.
The trees prospered; they roofed the
tomb with shade,
Bough with bough, leaf with leaf
entwined;
And on the boughs are two flying
birds
Who name themselves Birds of True
Love.
They lift their heads and face to face
they sing
Every night till the fifth watch is
done.
The passing traveller stays his foot to
hear,
The widowed wife rises and walks
her room.

This tale is a warning for the men of
the afterworld;
May they learn its moral and hold it
safe in their hearts.

---

[1] A bad omen.

贵贱情何薄。东家有贤女。窈窕艳城郭。阿母为汝求。便复在旦夕。

府吏再拜还。长叹空房中。作计乃尔立。转头向户里。渐见愁煎迫。

其日牛马嘶。新妇入青庐。奄奄黄昏后。寂寂人定初。我命绝今日。魂去尸长留。揽裙脱丝履。举身赴清池。

府吏闻此事。心知长别离。徘徊顾树下。自挂东南枝。

两家求合葬。合葬华山傍。东西植松柏。左右种梧桐。枝枝相覆盖。叶叶相交通。中有双飞鸟。自名为鸳鸯。仰头相向鸣。夜夜达五更。行人驻足听。寡妇起彷徨。多谢后世人。戒之慎勿忘。

《先秦汉魏晋南北朝诗》（上），第283—286页。

POEMS BY T'AO CH'IEN
(A.D. 372-427)

(1)

SHADY, shady the wood in front of
the Hall;
At midsummer full of calm shadows.
The south wind follows summer's
train;
With its eddying puffs it blows open
my coat.
I am free from ties and can live a life
of retirement.
When I rise from sleep, I play with
books and lute.
The lettuce in the garden still grows
moist;
Of last year's grain there is always
plenty left.
Self-support should maintain its
strict limits;
More than enough is not what I want.
I grind millet and make good wine;
When the wine is heated, I pour it
out for myself.
My little children are playing at my
side,
Learning to talk, they babble
unformed sounds.
These things have made me happy
again
And I forget my lost cap of office.
Distant, distant I gaze at the white
clouds;
With a deep yearning I think of the
Sages of Antiquity.

(2)

IN the quiet of the morning I heard a
knock at my door;
I threw on my clothes and opened it
myself.
I asked who it was who had come so
early to see me;
He said he was a peasant, coming
with good intent.
He brought with him a full flagon of
wine,
Believing my household had fallen
on evil days.
'You live in rags under a thatched
roof
And seem to have no desire for a
better lot.
The rest of mankind have all the
same ambitions;
You, too, must learn to wallow in
their mire.'
'Old man, I am impressed by what
you say,
But my soul is not fashioned like
other men's.
To drive in their rut I might perhaps
learn;
To be untrue to myself could only
lead to muddle.
Let us drink and enjoy together the
wine you have brought;
For my course is set and cannot now
be altered.'

和郭主簿诗二首（之一）

〔东晋〕陶渊明

蔼蔼堂前林。中夏贮清阴。
凯风因时来。回飙开我襟。
息交游闲业。卧起弄书琴。
园蔬有余滋。旧谷犹储今。
营己良有极。过足非所钦。
春秫作美酒。酒熟吾自斟。
弱子戏我侧。学语未成音。
此事真复乐。聊用忘华簪。
遥遥望白云。怀古一何深。

《先秦汉魏晋南北朝诗》（上），第 978—979 页。

饮酒（其九）

〔东晋〕陶渊明

清晨闻叩门。倒裳往自开。
问子为谁与。田父有好怀。
壶浆远见候。疑我与时乖。
褴褛茅檐下。未足为高栖。
一世皆尚同。愿君汩其泥。
深感父老言。禀气寡所谐。
纡辔诚可学。违己讵非迷。
且共欢此饮。吾驾不可回。

《先秦汉魏晋南北朝诗》（上），第 999 页。

(3)

A LONG time ago
I went on a journey,
Right to the corner
Of the Eastern Ocean.
The road there
Was long and winding,
And stormy waves
Barred my path.
What made me
Go this way?
Hunger drove me
Into the World.
I tried hard
To fill my belly,
And even a little
Seemed a lot.
But this was clearly
A bad bargain,
So I went home
And lived in idleness.

饮酒（其十）

〔东晋〕陶渊明

在昔曾远游，直至东海隅。
道路迥且长，风波阻中途。
此行谁使然，似为饥所驱。
倾身营一饱，少许便有余。
恐此非名计，息驾归闲居。

《陶渊明集》（上），第 92—93 页。

第二章　汉魏六朝诗

(4)

SUBSTANCE, SHADOW, AND SPIRIT

High and low, wise and simple, all busily hoard up the moments of life. How greatly they err! Therefore I have to the utterrmost exposed the bitterness both of Substance and Shadow, and have made Spirit show how, by following Nature, we may dissolve this bitterness.

Substance speaks to Shadow:

HEAVEN and Earth exist for ever;
Mountains and rivers never change.
But herbs and trees in perpetual rotation
Are renovated and withered by the dews and frosts;
And Man the wise, Man the divine—
Shall he alone escape this law?
Fortuitously appearing for a moment in the World
He suddenly departs, never to return.
Who will notice there is one person less?
His friends and relations will not give him a thought.
Only when they chance on the things he used
Day in day out, do their spirits sink for a while.
Me no magical arts can save;

Of that I am certain and cannot ever doubt.
I beg you listen to this advice—
When you get wine, be sure to drink it.

Shadow replies:

There is no way to preserve life;
Drugs of Immortality are instruments of folly.
I would gladly wander in Paradise,
But it is far away and there is no road.
Since the day that I was joined to you
We have shared all our joys and pains.
While you rested in the shade, I left you a while;
But till the end we shall be together.
Our joint existence is impermanent,
Sadly together we shall slip away.
That when the body decays Fame should also go
Is a thought unendurable, burning the heart.
Let us strive and labour while yet we may
To do some deed that men will praise.
Wine may in truth dispel our sorrow,
But how compare it with lasting Fame?

形影神诗三首

〔东晋〕陶渊明

贵贱贤愚。莫不营营以惜生。斯甚惑焉。故极陈形影之苦。言神辨自然以释之。好事君子。共取其心焉。

形赠影

天地长不没。山川无改时。
草木得常理。霜露荣悴之。
谓人最灵智。独复不如兹。
适见在世中。奄去靡归期。
奚觉无一人。亲识岂相思。
但余平生物。举目情凄洏。
我无腾化术。必尔不复疑。
愿君取吾言。得酒莫苟辞。

影答形

存生不可言。卫生每苦拙。
诚愿游昆华。邈然兹道绝。
与子相遇来。未尝异悲悦。
憩荫若暂乖。止日终不别。
此同既难常。黯尔俱时灭。
身没名亦尽。念之五情热。
立善有遗爱。胡为不自竭。
酒云能消忧。方此讵不劣。

Spirit expounds:

God can only set in motion;

He cannot control the things he has made.

Man, the second of the Three Orders,

Owes his precedence to Me.

Though I am different from you.

We were born involved in one another;

Nor by any means can we escape

The intimate sharing of good and ill.

The Three Emperors were saintly men,

Yet to-day—where are they?

P'êng[①] lived to a great age,

Yet he went at last, when he longed to stay.

And late or soon, all go;

Wise and simple have no reprieve.

Wine may bring forgetfulness,

But does it not hasten old-age?

If you set your heart on noble deeds,

How do you know that any will praise you?

By all this thinking you do Me injury;

You had better go where Fate leads

Drift on the Stream of Infinite Flux,

Without joy, without fear;

When you must go—then go,

And make as little fuss as you can.

---

① The Chinese Methuselah.

神释

大钧无私力。万物自森著。
人为三才中。岂不以我故。
与君虽异物。生而相依附。
结托既喜同。安得不相语。
三皇大圣人。今复在何处。
彭祖爱永年。欲留不得住。
老少同一死。贤遇无复数。
日醉或能忘。将非促龄具。
立善常所欣。谁当为汝誉。
甚念伤吾生。正宜委运去。
纵浪大化中。不喜亦不惧。
应尽便须尽。无复独多虑。

《先秦汉魏晋南北朝诗》（中），第 989—990 页。

(5)

CHILL and harsh the year draws to its close;
In my hempen dress I seek sunlight on the porch.
In the southern orchard all the leaves are gone;
In the north garden rotting boughs lie heaped.
I empty my cup and drink it down to the dregs;
I look towards the kitchen, but no smoke rises.
Poems and books lie piled beside my chair;
But the light is going and I shall not have time to read them.
My life here is not like the Agony in Ch'ên[①],
But often I have to bear bitter reproaches.
Let me then remember, to calm my heart's distress,
That the Sages of old were often in like case.

(6)

BLAMING SONS
(An apology for his own drunkenness, A.D. 406)

WHITE hairs cover my temples,
I am wrinkled and gnarled beyond repair,
And though I have got five sons,
They all hate paper and brush.
A-shu is eighteen:
For laziness there is none like him.
A-hsüan does his best,
But really loathes the Fine Arts.
Yung and Tuan are thirteen,
But do not know 'six' from 'seven'.
T'ung-tzu in his ninth year
Is only concerned with things to eat.
If Heaven treats me like this,
What can I do but fill my cup?

---

① Confucius was maltreated in Ch'ên.

咏贫士诗七首（其二）

凄厉岁云暮。拥褐曝前轩。
南圃无遗秀。枯条盈北园。
倾壶绝余沥。窥灶不见烟。
诗书塞座外。日昃不遑研。
闲居非陈厄。窃有愠见言。
何以慰我怀。赖古多此贤。

《先秦汉魏晋南北朝诗》（中），第 1008 页。

责子诗

白发被两鬓。肌肤不复实。
虽有五男儿。总不好纸笔。
阿舒已二八。懒惰故无匹。
阿宣行志学。而不爱文术。
雍端年十三。不识六与七。
通子垂九龄。但觅梨与栗。
天运苟如此。且进杯中物。

《先秦汉魏晋南北朝诗》（中），第 1002—1003 页。

(7)

I BUILT my hut in a zone of human habitation,
Yet near me there sounds no noise of horse or coach.
Would you know how that is possible?
A heart that is distant creates a wilderness round it.
I pluck chrysanthemums under the eastern hedge,
Then gaze long at the distant hills.
The mountain air is fresh at the dusk of day;
The flying birds two by two return.
In these things there lies a deep meaning;
Yet when we would express it, words suddenly fail us.

(8)
MOVING HOUSE

MY old desire to live in the Southern Village
Was not because I had taken a fancy to the house.
But I heard it was a place of simple-minded men
With whom it were a joy to spend the mornings and evenings.
Many years I had longed to settle here;
Now at last I have managed to move house.
I do not mind if my cottage is rather small
So long as there's room enough for bed and mat.
Often and often the neighbours come to see me
And with brave words discuss the things of old.
Rare writings we read together and praise;
Doubtful meanings we examine together and settle.

饮酒（其五）

结庐在人境。而无车马喧。
问君何能尔。心远地自偏。
采菊东篱下。悠然见南山。
山气日夕佳。飞鸟相与还。
此还有真意。欲辨已忘言。

《先秦汉魏晋南北朝诗》（中），第 998 页。

移居诗二首（其一）

昔欲居南村。非为卜其宅。
闻多素心人。乐与数晨夕。
怀此颇有年。今日从兹役。
敝庐何必广。取足蔽床席。
邻曲时时来。抗言谈在昔。
奇文共欣赏。疑义相与析。

《先秦汉魏晋南北朝诗》（中），第 993—994 页。

(9)
RETURNING TO THE FIELDS

WHEN I was young, I was out of tune with the herd;
My only love was for the hills and mountains.
Unwitting I fell into the Web of the World's dust
And was not free until my thirtieth year.
The migrant bird longs for the old wood;
The fish in the tank thinks of its native pool.
I had rescued from wildness a patch of the Southern Moor
And, still rustic, I returned to field and garden.
My ground covers no more than ten acres;
My thatchcd cottage has eight or nine rooms.
Elms and willows cluster by the eaves;
Peach trees and plum trees grow before the Hall.
Hazy, hazy the distant hamlets of men;
Steady the smoke that hangs over cottage roofs.
A dog barks somewhere in the deep lanes,
A cock crows at the top of the mulberry tree.
At gate and courtyard—no murmur of the World's dust;
In the empty rooms — leisure and deep stillness.
Long I lived checked by the bars of a cage;
Now I have turned again to Nature and Freedom.

(10)
READING THE BOOK OF HILLS AND SEAS

IN the month of June the grass grows high
And round my cottage thick-leaved branches sway.
There is not a bird but delights in the place where it rests;
And I too — love my thatched cottage.
I have done my ploughing;
I have sown my seed.
Again I have time to sit and read my books.
In the narrow lane there are no deep ruts;
Often my friends' carriages turn back.
In high spirits I pour out my spring wine
And pluck the lettuce growing in my garden.
A gentle rain comes stealing up from the east
And a sweet wind bears it company.
My thoughts float idly over the story of the king of Chou,
My eyes wander over the pictures of Hills and Seas.
At a single glance I survey the whole Universe.
He will never be happy, whom such pleasures fail to please!

归园田居诗五首（其一）

少无适俗韵。性本爱丘山。
误落尘网中。一去三十年。
羁鸟恋旧林。池鱼思故渊。
开荒南野际。守拙归园田。
方宅十余亩。草屋八九间。
榆柳荫后檐。桃李罗堂前。
暧暧远人村。依依墟里烟。
狗吠深巷中。鸡鸣桑树巅。
户庭无尘杂。虚室有余闲。
久在樊笼里。复得返自然。

《先秦汉魏晋南北朝诗》（中），第 991 页。

读山海经诗十三首（其一）

孟夏草木长。绕屋树扶疏。
众鸟欣有托。吾亦爱吾庐。
既耕亦已种。时还读我书。
穷巷隔深辙。颇回故人车。
欢然酌春酒。摘我园中蔬。
微雨从东来。好风与之俱。
泛览周王传。流观山海图。
俯仰终宇宙。不乐复何如。

《先秦汉魏晋南北朝诗》（中），第 1010 页。

第二章　汉魏六朝诗

(11)
FLOOD

THE lingering clouds, rolling, rolling,
And the settled rain, dripping, dripping,
In the Eight Directions—the same dusk.
The level lands—one great river.
Wine I have, wine I have;
Idly I drink at the eastern window.
Longingly—I think of my friends,
But neither boat nor carriage comes.

(12)
NEW CORN

SWIFTLY the years, beyond recall.
Solemn the stillness of this fair morning.
I will clothe myself in spring-clothing
And visit the slopes of the Eastern Hill.
By the mountain-stream a mist hovers,
Hovers a moment, then scatters.
There comes a wind blowing from the south
That brushes the fields of new corn.

停云（节选）

霭霭停云，濛濛时雨。
八表同昏，平路伊阻。
静寄东轩，春醪独抚。
良朋悠邈，搔首延伫。

《陶渊明集校笺》，第 1 页。

时运（节选）

迈迈时运。穆穆良朝。
袭我春服。薄言东郊。
山涤余霭。宇暧微霄。
有风自南。翼彼新苗。

《先秦汉魏晋南北朝诗》（上），第 968 页。

SAILING HOMEWARD

by CHAN FANG-SHÊNG

(*c.* A.D. 400)

CLIFFS that rise a thousand feet
Without a break,
Lake that stretches a hundred miles
Without a wave,
Sands that are white through all the year
Without a stain,
Pine-tree woods, winter and summer
Ever-green,
Streams that for ever flow and flow
Without a pause,
Trees that for twenty thousand years
Your vows have kept,
You have suddenly healed the pain of a traveller's heart,
And moved his brush to write a new song.

还都帆诗

〔东晋〕湛方生

高岳万丈峻。长湖千里清。
白沙穷年洁。林松冬夏青。
水无暂停流。木有千载贞。
寤言赋新诗。忽忘羁客情。

《先秦汉魏晋南北朝诗》（中），第 944 页。

FOLK-SONGS
(Fourth or Fifth Century A.D.)

I HAVE brought my pillow and am lying at the northern window,
So come to me and play with me a while.
With so much roughness and so little play
How long do you think our love can last?

I will gather up my skirt, but not put on my belt;
I will trim my eyebrows and stand at the front window.
My tiresome petticoat keeps on flapping about;
If it opens a little I shall say it was the spring wind.

I am steadfast as the star of the Northern Pole;
In a thousand years it never shifts from its place.
You have ways that are like the bright sun;
In the morning, east; in the evening again west.

When dusk gathered you came in over the hedge;
But when dawn was near you sallied out at the gate.
Alas that my dear one should care only for himself;
What happens to me he does not care at all.

At the fifth watch I rose and opened the door
Just in time to see my love go by.
'Where do you come from, where have you spent the night,
Dear love, that your clothes are covered with frost and dew?'

I heard my love was going to Yang-chow
And went with him as far as Ch'u Hill.
For amoment, when you held me fast in your outstretched arms
I thought the river stood still and did not flow.

子夜歌四十二首

（其十三）

揽枕北窗卧，郎来就侬嬉。
小喜多唐突，相怜能几时。

（其二十四）

揽裙未结带，约眉出前窗。
罗裳易飘飏，小开骂春风。

（其三十六）

侬作北辰星，千年无转移。
欢行白日心，朝东暮还西。

《乐府诗集》，第 642—643 页。

读曲歌八十九首

（其三十九）

合冥过藩来，向晓开门去。
欢取身上好，不为侬作虑。

（其四十）

五鼓起开门，正见欢子度。
何处宿行还，衣被有霜露。

《乐府诗集》，第 674 页。

莫愁乐（其二）

闻欢下扬州，相送楚山头。
探手抱腰看，江水断不流。

《乐府诗集》，第 698 页。

THE LITTLE LADY OF CH'ING-CH'I

A Children's Song

HER door opened on the white water
Close by the side of the timber bridge;
That's where the little lady lived
All alone without a lover.

再
造
的
镜
像

青溪小姑曲

开门白水。侧近桥梁。
小姑所居。独处无郎。

《先秦汉魏晋南北朝诗》(中),第 1059 页。

PLUCKING THE RUSHES

A boy and girl are sent to gather rushes for thatching.

Anon. (Fourth or Fifth Century)

GREEN rushes with red shoots,
Long leaves bending to the wind—
You and I in the same boat
Plucking rushes at the Five Lakes.

We started at dawn from the orchid-island;
We rested under the elms till noon.
You and I plucking rushes
Had not plucked a handful when night came!

拔蒲二曲

青蒲衔紫茸，长叶复从风。
与君同舟去，拔蒲五湖中。
朝发桂兰渚，昼息桑榆下。
与君同拔蒲，竟日不成把。

《乐府诗集》，第 718—719 页。

BALLAD OF THE WESTERN ISLAND IN THE NORTH COUNTRY

'SEEING the plum-tree I thought of the Western Island
And I plucked a branch to send to the North Country.
I put on my dress of apricot-yellow silk
And bound up my hair black as the crow's wing.
But which is the road that leads to the Western Island?
I'll ask the man at the ferry by the Bridge of Boats.
But the sun is sinking and the orioles flying home;
And the wind is blowing and sighing in the walnut-tree.
I'll stand under the tree just beside the gate;
I'll stand by the door and show off my enamelled hair-pins.'
She's opened the gate, but her lover has not come;
She's gone out at the gate to pluck red lotus.
As she plucks the lotus on the southern dyke in autumn,
The lotus flowers stand higher than a man's head.
She bends down—and plays with the lotus seeds,
The lotus seeds are green like the lake-water.
She gathers the flowers and puts them into her gown—
The lotus-bud that is red all through.
She thinks of her lover, her lover that does not come;
She looks up and sees the wild geese flying—
The Western Island is full of wild geese.
To look for her lover she climbs the Blue Tower.
The tower is high: she looks, but cannot see;
All day she leans on the balcony rails.
The rail is twisted into a twelve-fold pattern.
She lets fall her hand white like the colour of jade.
She rolls up the awning, she sees the wide sky,
And the sea-water waving its vacant blue.
'The sea shall carry my dreams far away,
So that you shall be sorry at last for my sorrow.
If the South wind only knew my thoughts
It would blow my dreams till they got to the Western Island.'

西洲曲

忆梅下西洲，折梅寄江北。
单衫杏子红，双鬓鸦雏色。
西洲在何处？两桨桥头渡。
日暮伯劳飞，风吹乌臼树。
树下即门前，门中露翠钿。
开门郎不至，出门采红莲。
采莲南塘秋，莲花过人头。
低头弄莲子，莲子青如水。
置莲怀袖中，莲心彻底红。
忆郎郎不至，仰首望飞鸿。
鸿飞满西洲，望郎上青楼。
楼高望不见，尽日栏杆头。
栏杆十二曲，垂手明如玉。
卷帘天自高，海水摇空绿。
海水梦悠悠，君愁我亦愁。
南风知我意，吹梦到西洲。

《古诗源》，第 289—290 页。

SONG OF THE MEN OF CHIN-LING

(Marching back into the Capital)

By HSIEH T'IAO (A.D. 464-499)

CHIANG-NAN[①] is a glorious and beautiful land
And Chin-ling[②] an exalted and kingly province!
The green canals of the city twist and coil
And its high towers stretch up and up.
Flying gables lean over the bridle-road;
Drooping willows cover the Royal Aqueduct.
Shrill flutes sing by the coach's awning,
And reiterated drums bang near its painted wheels.
The names of the deserving shall be presented at the Cloud Terrace;
For those who have done valiantly rich reward awaits.

---

① 'South of the River.'
② South-west of Nanking.

入朝曲

〔南齐〕谢朓

江南佳丽地。金陵帝王州。
逶迤带绿水。迢递起朱楼。
飞甍夹驰道。垂杨荫御沟。
凝笳翼高盖。叠鼓送华辀。
献纳云台表。功名良可收。

《先秦汉魏晋南北朝诗》（中），第 1414 页。

DREAMING OF A DEAD LADY
By SHÊN YO (A.D. 441-513)

'I HEARD at nights your long sighs
And knew that you were thinking of me.'
As she spoke, the doors of Heaven opened;
Our souls conversed and I saw her face.
She set me a pillow to rest on;
She brought me meat and drink.
I stood beside her where she lay,
But suddenly woke and she was not there.
And none knew how my soul was torn,
How the tears fell surging over my breast.

再
造
的
镜
像

梦见美人诗

〔梁〕沈约

夜闻长叹息。
知君心有忆。
果自阊阖开。
魂交睹颜色。
既荐巫山枕。
又奉齐眉食。
立望复横陈。
忽觉非在侧。
那知神伤者。
潺湲泪沾臆。

《先秦汉魏晋南北朝诗》（中），第 1640 页。

PEOPLE HIDE THEIR LOVE

By WU-TI, Emperor of the Liang Dynasty (A.D. 464-549)

再
造
的
镜
像

WHO says that it's by my desire,
This separation, this living so far from you?
My dress still smells of the perfume that you wore;
My hand still holds the letter that you sent.
Round my waist I wear a double sash;
I dream that it binds us both with a same-heart knot.
Did you know that people hide their love,
Like a flower that seems too precious to be picked?

有所思

（梁武帝）萧衍

谁言生离久。适意与君别。
衣上芳犹在。握里书未灭。
腰中双绮带。梦为同心结。
常恐所思露。瑶华未忍折。

《先秦汉魏晋南北朝诗》（中），第 1514 页。

SUMMER SONG
By WU TI

AT the time when blossoms fall from the cherry-tree,
On a day when orioles flitted from bough to bough,
You said you must stop, because your horse was tired;
I said I must go, because my silkworms were hungry.

再
造
的
镜
像

夏歌四首（其四）

（梁武帝）萧衍

含桃落花日。黄鸟莺飞时。
君住马已疲。妾去蚕欲饥。

《先秦汉魏晋南北朝诗》（中），第 1517 页。

LO-YANG
By the EMPEROR CHIEN WÊN-TI (A.D. 503-551)

A BEAUTIFUL place is the town of Lo-yang;
The big streets are full of spring light.
The lads go driving out with lutes in their hands;
The mulberry girls go out to the fields with their baskets.
Golden saddles glint at the horses' flanks,
Gauze sleeves brush the green boughs.
Racing dawn, the carriages come home—
And the girls with their high baskets full of fruit.

再
造
的
镜
像

洛阳道

（梁简文帝）萧纲

洛阳佳丽所。大道满春光。
游童初挟弹。蚕妾始提筐。
金鞍照龙马。罗袂拂春桑。
玉车争晚入。潘果溢高箱。

《先秦汉魏晋南北朝诗》（下），第 1911 页。

WINTER NIGHT
By CHIEN WÊN-TI

MY bed is so empty that I keep on waking up;
As the cold increases, the night-wind begins to blow.
It rustles the curtains, making a noise like the sea.
Oh that those were waves which could carry me back to you!

杂咏诗

（梁简文帝）萧纲

被空眠数觉。寒重夜风吹。
罗帷非海水。那得度前知。

《先秦汉魏晋南北朝诗》（下），第 1970 页。

THE WATERS OF LUNG-T'OU
(The North-West Frontier)
By HSÜ LING (A.D. 507-583)

再
造
的
镜
像

THE road that I came by mounts eight thousand feet;
The river that I crossed hangs a hundred fathoms.
The brambles so thick that in summer one cannot pass;
The snow so high that in winter one cannot climb!
With branches that interlace Lung Valley is dark;
Against cliffs that tower one's voice beats and echoes.
I turn my head, and it seems only a dream
That I ever lived in the streets of Hsien-yang.

陇头水

〔梁〕徐陵

别涂耸千仞。离川悬百丈。
攒荆夏不通。积雪冬难上。
枝交陇底暗。石碍波前响。
回首咸阳中。唯言梦时往。

《先秦汉魏晋南北朝诗》（下），第 2524 页。

TELEG SONG
(Sixth Century A.D.)

TELEG River
Lies under the Dark Mountains,
Where the sky is like the sides of a tent
Stretched down over the Great Steppe.
The sky is grey, grey
And the steppe wide, wide.
Over grass that the wind has battered low
Sheep and oxen roam.

敕勒歌

敕勒川，阴山下。
天似穹庐，笼盖四野。
天苍苍，野茫茫，风吹草低见牛羊。

《汉魏晋南北朝隋诗鉴赏词典》，第 1859—1860 页。

THE BALLAD OF MULAN
(Written in northern China during the
domination of the Wei Tartars, Sixth
Century A.D.)

CLICK, click, for ever click, click;
Mulan sits at the door and weaves.
Listen, and you will not hear the
shuttle's sound,
But only hear a girl's sobs and sighs.
'Oh, tell me, lady, are you thinking
of your love,
Oh tell me, lady, are you longing for
your dear?'
'Oh no, oh no, I am not thinking of
my love,
Oh no, oh no, I am not longing for
my dear.
But last night I read the battle-roll;
The Khan has ordered a great levy of
men.
The battle-roll was written in twelve
books,
And in each book stood my father's
name.
My father's sons are not grown men,
And of all my brothers, none is older
than me.
Oh let me to the market to buy
saddle and horse,
And ride with the soldiers to take my
father's place.'
In the eastern market she's bought a
gallant horse,
In the western market she's bought
saddle and cloth.
In the southern market she's bought
snaffle and reins,
In the northern market she's bought a
tall whip.
In the morning she stole from her
father's and mother's house;
At night she was camping by the
Yellow River's side.
She could not hear her father and
mother calling to her by her name,
But only the voice of the Yellow
River as its waters swirled through
the night.
At dawn they left the River and went
on their way;
At dusk they came to the Black
Water's side.
She could not hear her father and
mother calling to her by her name,
She could only hear the muffled
voices of foreign horsemen riding on
the hills of Yen.
A thousand leagues she tramped on
the errands of war,
Frontiers and hills she crossed like a
bird in flight.
Through the northern air echoed the
watchman's tap;
The wintry light gleamed on coats of
mail.
The captain had fought a hundred
fights, and died;
The warriors in ten years had won
their rest.
They went home, they saw the
Emperor's face;
The Son of Heaven was seated in the
Hall of Light.
The deeds of the brave were
recorded in twelve books;
In prizes he gave a hundred thousand
cash.

木兰诗

唧唧复唧唧。木兰当户织。

不闻机杼声。唯闻女叹息。

问女何所思。问女何所忆。

女亦无所思。女亦无所忆。

昨夜见军帖。可汗大点兵。

军书十二卷。卷卷有爷名。

阿爷无大儿。木兰无长兄。

愿为市鞍马。从此替爷征。

东市买骏马。西市买鞍鞯。

南市买辔头。北市买长鞭。

朝辞爷娘去。暮宿黄河边。

不闻爷娘唤女声。但闻黄河流水鸣溅溅。

旦辞黄河去。暮宿黑山头。

不闻爷娘唤女声。但闻燕山胡骑声啾啾。

万里赴戎机。关山度若飞。

朔气传金柝。寒光照铁衣。

将军百战死。壮士十年归。

归来见天子。天子坐明堂。

策勋十二转。赏赐百千强。

Then spoke the Khan and asked her what she would take.

'Oh, Mulan asks not to be made

A Counsellor at the Khan's court;

I only beg for a camel that can march

A thousand leagues a day,

To take me back to my home.'

When her father and mother heard that she had come,

They went out to the wall and led her back to the house.

When her little sister heard that she had come,

She went to the door and rouged her face afresh.

When her little brother heard that his sister had come,

He sharpened his knife and darted like a flash

Towards the pigs and sheep.

She opened the gate that leads to the eastern tower,

She sat on her bed that stood in the western tower.

She cast aside her heavy soldier's cloak,

And wore again her old-time dress.

She stood at the window and bound her cloudy hair;

She went to the mirror and fastened her yellow combs.

She left the house and met her messmates in the road;

Her messmates were startled out of their wits.

They had marched with her for twelve years of war

And never known that Mulan was a girl.

For the male hare sits with its legs tucked in,

And the female hare in known for her bleary eye;

But set them both scampering side by side,

And who so wise could tell you 'This is he?'

可汗问所欲。木兰不用尚书郎。

愿驰千里足。送儿还故乡。

爷娘闻女来。出郭相扶将。

阿姊闻妹来。当户理红妆。

小弟闻姊来。磨刀霍霍向猪羊。

开我东阁门。坐我西间床。

脱我战时袍。著我旧时裳。

当窗理云鬓。对镜帖花黄。

出门看火伴。火伴始惊惶。

同行十二年。不知木兰是女郎。

雄兔脚扑朔。雌兔眼迷离。

两兔傍地走。安能辨我是雄雌。

《汉魏晋南北朝隋诗鉴赏词典》，第 2160—2161 页。

第三章　隋唐诗选（附寒山诗）

导言

　　韦利编选他所译的隋唐诗，着重对寒山与白居易诗作的翻译，对其他隋唐诗作，只是蜻蜓点水，甚至完全忽略。他的理由是，翻译这些中国诗，并非作为学术研究来展示隋唐诗的全景，而是呈现个人喜好的诗作，译成赏心悦耳的英文。因此，本章的重点是寒山，下一章的重点是白居易，另外又零星选择了几首他满意的译作，如隋炀帝的《春江花月夜》，几首李白的诗作，以及王绩、陈子昂、元结、王建的诗作。对于完全不选杜甫的诗作，他的解释很简单，也很诚实，就是怎么尝试都不满意，译文难登大雅之堂，那就不必献丑。

　　关于韦利编选唐诗的问题，钱锺书早年出版的诗论《谈艺录》（1948）第五十九节说：“英人 Arthur Waley 以译汉诗得名。余见其 *170 Chinese Poems* 一书，有文弁首，论吾国风雅正变，上下千载，妄欲别裁，多暗中摸索语。”钱锺书批评韦利推崇白居易，是因为白居易“老妪都解”，诗艺的境界远不如陶渊明与杜甫，只是浅易而已。钱锺书眼高于顶，对白居易充满了不屑，言下之意，韦利推崇白居易，是因为白诗简明好懂，也不能体会中国诗的精髓。

　　钱锺书批评韦利译的中国诗不能展现中国诗的博大精深，不能呈现中国诗歌上下千载的浩瀚全貌。然而，这种批评似乎是无的放矢，因为韦利选译中国诗，说明了他译诗的意图，不是为了呈现中国诗史，而是随着他对诗情的感受，展示他个人译成优美英文诗篇的快意。

再
造
的
镜
像

古诗英汉对照

FLOWERS AND MOONLIGHT ON THE SPRING RIVER
By YANG-TI, Emperor of the Sui Dynasty from 604 till 618.

THE evening river is level and motionless—
The spring colours just open to their full.
Suddenly a wave carries the moon away
And the tidal water comes with its freight of stars.

春江花月夜二首（其一）（节选）

〔隋〕杨广

暮江平不动。春花满正开。
流波将月去。潮水带星来。

《汉魏晋南北朝隋诗鉴赏词典》，第 2663 页。

COCK-CROW SONG

Anon. (Sixth Century A.D.?)

IN the eastern quarter dawn breaks, the stars flicker pale;
The Morning Cock[①] from Ju-nan mounts his stand and calls.
The song is over, the clock[②] run down, the mats and screens are set;
The moon grows dim and the stars are few; morning has come to the world.
At a thousand gates and ten thousand doors the fish-shaped[③] bolts are drawn;
Round the Palace and up over the walls crows and magpies are flying.

---

① Fowls were not kept in the Palace, so a watchman woke the Court by singing this song. These watchmen came from Ju-nan in Honan.

② A water-clock.

③ The fish, which never sleeps, is a symbol of watchfulness.

鸡鸣歌

〔隋〕佚名

东方欲明星烂烂，汝南晨鸡登坛唤。
曲终漏尽严具陈，月没星稀天下旦。
千门万户递鱼钥，宫中城上飞乌鹊。

《御定佩文斋咏物诗选》，第 608 页。

TELL ME NOW
By WANG CHI (A.D. 584-644)

再
造
的
镜
像

'TELL me now, what should a man want
But to sit alone, sipping his cup of wine?'
I should like to have visitors come and discuss philosophy
And not to have the tax-collector coming to collect taxes;
My three sons married into good families
And my five daughters wedded to steady husbands.
Then I could jog through a happy five-score years
And, at the end, need no Paradise.

独坐

〔唐〕王绩

问君樽酒外。独坐更何须。
有客谈名理。无人索地租。
三男婚令族。五女嫁贤夫。
百年随分了。未羡陟方壶。

《全唐诗》（第 2 册），第 482 页。

BUSINESS MEN

By CH'ÊN TZǓ-ANG (A.D. 656-698)

BUSINESS men boast of their skill and cunning
But in philosophy they are like little children.
Bragging to each other of successful depredations
They neglect to consider the ultimate fate of the body.
What should they know of the Master of Dark Truth
Who saw the wide world in a jade cup,
By illumined conception got clear of Heaven and Earth,
On the chariot of Mutation entered the Gate of Immutability?

再
造
的
镜
像

感遇（其五）

〔唐〕陈子昂

市人矜巧智。于道若童蒙。
倾夺相夸侈。不知身所终。
曷见玄真子。观世玉壶中。
窅然遗天地。乘化入无穷。

《全唐诗》（第 3 册），第 890 页。

IN THE MOUNTAINS ON A SUMMER DAY

By LI PO (A.D. 701-762)

GENTLY I stir a white feather fan,

With open shirt sitting in a green wood.

I take off my cap and hang it on a jutting stone;

A wind from the pine-tree trickles on my bare head.

夏日山中

〔唐〕李白

懒摇白羽扇，裸袒青林中。
脱巾挂石壁，露顶洒松风。

《李白集校注》，第 1347 页。

SELF-ABANDONMENT

By LI PO

I SAT drinking and did not notice the dusk,
Till falling petals fllled the folds of my dress.
Drunken I rose and walked to the moonlit stream;
The birds were gone, and men also few.

自遣

〔唐〕李白

对酒不觉暝，落花盈我衣。
醉起步溪月，鸟还人亦稀。

《李白集校注》，第 1354 页。

TO TAN-CH'IU

By LI PO

再
造
的
镜
像

MY friend is lodging high in the Eastern Range,
Dearly loving the beauty of valleys and hills.
At green Spring he lies in the empty woods,
And is still asleep when the sun shines on high.
A pine-tree wind dusts his sleeves and coat;
A pebbly stream cleans his heart and ears.
I envy you, who far from strife and talk
Are high-propped on a pillow of blue cloud.

题元丹丘山居

〔唐〕李白

故人栖东山，自爱丘壑美。
青春卧空林，白日犹不起。
松风清襟袖，石潭洗心耳。
羡君无纷喧，高枕碧霞里。

《李白集校注》，第 1438 页。

CLEARING AT DAWN
By LI PO

THE fields are chill, the sparse rain has stopped;
The colours of Spring teem on every side.
With leaping fish the blue pond is full;
With singing thrushes the green boughs droop.
The flowers of the field have dabbled their powdered cheeks;
The mountain grasses are bent level at the waist.
By the bamboo stream the last fragment of cloud
Blown by the wind slowly scatters away.

再
造
的
镜
像

晓晴

〔唐〕李白

野凉疏雨歇，春色遍萋萋。
鱼跃青池满，莺吟绿树低。
野花妆面湿，山草纽斜齐。
零落残云片，风吹挂竹溪。

《李白集校注》，第 1704 页。

STONE FISH LAKE
By YÜAN CHIEH (A.D. 719-772)

I LOVED you dearly, Stone Fish Lake,
With your rock-island shaped like a swimming fish!
On the fish's back is the Wine-cup Hollow
And round the fish—the flowing waters of the Lake.
The boys on the shore sent little wooden ships,
Each made to carry a single cup of wine.
The island-drinkers emptied the liquor boats
And set their sails and sent them back for more.
On the shores of the Lake were jutting slabs of rock
And under the rocks there flowed an icy stream.
Heated with wine, to rinse our mouths and hands
In those cold waters was a joy beyond compare!
Of gold and jewels I have not any need;
For Caps and Coaches I do not care at all.
But I wish I could sit on the rocky banks of the Lake
For ever and ever staring at the Stone Fish.

再
造
的
镜
像

石鱼湖上作

〔唐〕元结

吾爱石鱼湖，石鱼在湖里。
鱼背有酒樽，绕鱼是湖水。
儿童作小舫，载酒胜一杯。
座中令酒舫，空去复满来。
湖岸多欹石，石下流寒泉。
醉中一盥漱，快意无比焉。
金玉吾不须，轩冕吾不爱。
且欲坐湖畔，石鱼长相对。

《全唐诗》（上），第 610 页。

CIVILIZATION
By YÜAN CHIEH

To the south-east—three thousand leagues—
The Yüan and Hsiang form into a mighty lake.
Above the lake are deep mountain valleys,
And men dwelling whose hearts are without guile.
Gay like children, they swarm to the tops of the trees;
And run to the water to catch bream and trout.
Their pleasures are the same as those of beasts and birds;
They put no restraint either on body or mind.
Far I have wandered throughout the Nine Lands;
Wherever I went such manners had disappeared.
I find myself standing and wondering, perplexed,
Whether Saints and Sages have really done us good.

再
造
的
镜
像

思太古

〔唐〕元结

东南三千里，沅湘为太湖。
湖上山谷深，有人多似愚。
婴孩寄树颠，就水捕鯿鲈。
所欢同鸟兽，身意复何拘。
吾行遍九州，此风皆已无。
吁嗟圣贤教，不觉久踌躇。

《全唐诗》（上），第 606 页。

HEARING THAT HIS FRIEND WAS
COMING BACK FROM THE WAR
By WANG CHIEN

IN old days those who went to fight

In three years had one year's leave.

But in *this* war the soldiers are never changed;

They must go on fighting till they die on the battlefield.

I thought of you, so weak and indolent,

Hopelessly trying to learn to march and drill.

That a young man should ever come home again

Seemed about as likely as that the sky should fall.

Since I got the news that you were coming back,

Twice I have mounted to the high wall of your home.

I found your brother mending your horse's stall;

I found your mother sewing your new clothes.

I am half afraid; perhaps it is not true;

Yet I never weary of watching for you on the road.

Each day I go out at the City Gate

With a flask of wine, lest you should come thirsty.

Oh that I could shrink the surface of the World,

So that suddenly I might find you standing at my side!

闻故人自征戍回

〔唐〕王建

昔闻著征戍，三年一还乡。
今来不换兵，须死在战场。
念子无气力，徒学事戎行。
少年得生还，有同堕穹苍。
自去报尔家，再行上高堂。
尔弟修废枥，尔母缝新裳。
恍恍恐不真，犹未苦承望。
每日空出城，畏渴携壶浆。
安得缩地经，忽使在我傍。
亦知远行劳，人悴马玄黄。
慎莫多停留，苦我居者肠。①

《全唐诗》（上），第 745 页。

---

① 韦利未译此四句："亦知远行劳，人悴马玄黄。慎莫多停留，苦我居者肠。"

THE SOUTH
By WANG CHIEN

IN the southern land many birds sing;
Of towns and cities half are unwalled.
The country markets are thronged by wild tribes;
The mountain-villages bear river-names.
Poisonous mists rise from the damp sands;
Strange fires gleam through the night-rain.
And none passes but the lonely seeker of pearls
Year by year on his way to the South Sea.

南中

〔唐〕王建

天南多鸟声，州县半无城。
野市依蛮姓，山村逐水名。
瘴烟沙上起，阴火雨中生。
独有求珠客，年年入海行。

《全唐诗》（上），第 751 页。

POEMS BY HAN-SHAN

The Chinese poet Han-shan lived in the 8th and 9th centuries. He and his brothers worked a farm that they had inherited; but he fell out with them, parted from his wife and family, and wandered from place to place, reading many books and looking in vain for a patron. He finally settled as a recluse on the Cold Mountain (Han-shan) and is always known as 'Han-shan.' This retreat was about twenty-five miles from T'ien-t'ai, famous for its many monasteries, both Buddhist and Taoist, which Han-shan visited from time to time. In one poem he speaks of himself as being over a hundred. This may be an exaggeration; but it is certain that he lived to a great age.

In his poems the Cold Mountain is often the name of a state of mind rather than of a locality. It is on this conception, as well as on that of the 'hidden treasure,' the Buddha who is to be sought not somewhere outside us, but 'at home' in the heart, that the mysticism of the poems is based.

The poems, of which just over three hundred survive, have no titles.

FROM my father and mother I inherited land enough
And need not envy others' orchards and fields.
Creak, creak goes the sound of my wife's loom;
Back and forth my children prattle at their play.
They clap their hands to make the flowers dance;
Then chin on palm listen to the birds' song.
Does anyone ever come to pay his respects?
Yes, there is a woodcutter who often comes this way.

I have thatched my rafters and made a peasant hut;
Horse and carriage seldom come to my gate—
Deep in the woods, where birds love to forgather,
By a broad stream, the home of many fish.
The mountain fruits child in hand I pluck;
My paddy field along with my wife I hoe.
And what have I got inside my house?
Nothing at all but one stand of books.

When I was young I weeded book in hand,
Sharing at first a home with my elder brothers.
Something happened, and they put the blame on me;
Even my own wife turned against me.
So I left the red dust of the world and wandered
Hither and thither, reading book after book
And looking for some one who would spare a drop of water
To keep alive the gudgeon in the carriage rut.

寒山诗

寒山子，不知何许人。居天台唐兴县寒岩，时往还国清寺。以桦皮为冠，布裘弊履。或长廊唱咏，或村墅歌啸，人莫识之。闾丘胤宦丹丘，临行，遇丰干师，言从天台来。闾丘问彼地有何贤堪师，师曰："寒山文殊，拾得普贤。在国清寺库院厨中著火。"闾丘到官三日，亲往寺中。见二人，便礼拜。二人大笑曰："丰干饶舌，饶舌。阿弥不识，礼我何为？"即走出寺，归寒岩。寒山子入穴而去，其穴自合。尝于竹木石壁书诗，并村墅屋壁所写文句三百余首。今编诗一卷。

　　　　　父母续经多，田园不羡他。
　　　　　妇摇机轧轧，儿弄口喝喝。
　　　　　拍手摧花舞，支颐听鸟歌。
　　　　　谁当来叹赏，樵客屡经过。

　　　　　茅栋野人居，门前车马疏。
　　　　　林幽偏聚鸟，溪阔本藏鱼。
　　　　　山果携儿摘，皋田共妇锄。
　　　　　家中何所有，唯有一床书。

　　　　　少小带经锄，本将兄共居。
　　　　　缘遭他辈责，剩被自妻疏。
　　　　　抛绝红尘境，常游好阅书。
　　　　　谁能借斗水，活取辙中鱼。

Wretched indeed is the scholar without money
Who else knows such hunger and cold?
Having nothing to do he takes to writing poems,
He grinds them out till his thoughts refuse to work.
For a starveling's words no one has any use;
Accept the fact and cease your doleful sighs.
Even if you wrote your verses on a macaroon
And gave them to the dog, the dog would refuse to eat.

Wise men, you have forsaken me;
Foolish men, I have forsaken you.
Being not foolish and also not wise
Henceforward I shall hear from you no more.
When night falls I sing to the bright moon,
At break of dawn I dance among the white clouds.
Would you have me with closed lips and folded hands
Sit up straight, waiting for my hair to go grey?

I am sometimes asked the way to the Cold Mountain;
There is no path that goes all the way.
Even in summer the ice never melts;
Far into the morning the mists gather thick.
How, you may ask, did I manage to get here?
My heart is not like your heart.
If only your heart were like mine
You too would be living where I live now.

Long, long the way to the Cold Mountain;
Stony, stony the banks of the chill stream.
Twitter, twitter—always there are birds;
Lorn and lone—no human but oneself.
Slip, slap the wind blows in one's face;
Flake by flake the snow piles on one's clothes.
Day after day one never sees the sun;
Year after year knows no spring.

I make my way up the Cold Mountain path;
The way up seems never to end.
The valley so long and the ground so stony;
The stream so broad and the brush so tangled and thick.
The moss is slippery, rain or no rain;
The pine-trees sing even when no wind blows.
Who can bring himself to transcend the bonds of the world
And sit with me among the white clouds?

蹭蹬诸贫士，饥寒成至极。
闲居好作诗，札札用心力。
贱他言孰采，劝君休叹息。
题安糊饼上，乞狗也不吃。

智者君抛我，愚者我抛君。
非愚亦非智，从此断相闻。
入夜歌明月，侵晨舞白云。
焉能拱口手，端坐鬓纷纷。

人问寒山道，寒山路不通。
夏天冰未释，日出雾朦胧。
似我何由届，与君心不同。
君心若似我，还得到其中。

杳杳寒山道，落落冷涧滨。
啾啾常有鸟，寂寂更无人。
碛碛风吹面，纷纷雪积身。
朝朝不见日，岁岁不知春。

登陟寒山道，寒山路不穷。
谿长石磊磊，涧阔草濛濛。
苔滑非关雨，松鸣不假风。
谁能超世累，共坐白云中。

Pile on pile, the glories of hill and
stream;
Sunset mists enclose flanks of blue.
Brushed by the storm my gauze cap
is wet;
The dew damps my straw-plaited
coat.
My feet shod with stout pilgrim-
shoes,
My hand grasping my old holly staff
Looking again beyond the dusty
world
What use have I for a land of empty
dreams?

I went off quietly to visit a wise
monk,
Where misty mountains rose in
myriad piles.
The Master himself showed me my
way back,
Pointing to where the moon, that
round lamp, hung.

In old days, when I was very poor,
Night by night I counted another's
treasures.
There came a time when I thought
things over
And decided to set up in business on
my own.
So I dug at home and came upon a
buried treasure;

A ball of saphire—that and nothing
less!
There came a crowd of blue-eyed
traders from the west
Who had planned together to bid for
it and take it away.
But I straightway answered those
merchants, saying
'This is a jewel that no price could
buy.'

Leisurely I wandered to the top of
the Flowery Peak;
The day was calm and the morning
sun flashed.
I looked into the clear sky on every
side.
A white cloud was winging its
crane's flight.

I have for dwelling the shelter of a
green cliff;
For garden, a thicket that knife has
never trimmed.
Over it the fresh creepers hang their
coils;
Ancient rocks stand straight and tall.
The mountain fruits I leave for the
monkeys to pick;
The fish of the pool vanish into the
heron's beak.
Taoist writings, one volume or two,
Under the trees I read—*nam, nam.*

层层山水秀，烟霞锁翠微。
岚拂纱巾湿，露沾蓑草衣。
足蹑游方履，手执古藤枝。
更观尘世外，梦境复何为。

闲自访高僧，烟山万万层。
师亲指归路，月挂一轮灯。

昔日极贫苦，夜夜数他宝。
今日审思量，自家须营造。
掘得一宝藏，纯是水精珠。
大有碧眼胡，密拟买将去。
余即报渠言，此珠无价数。

闲游华顶上，日朗昼光辉。
四顾晴空里，白云同鹤飞。

家住绿岩下，庭芜更不芟。
新藤垂缭绕，古石竖巉岩。
山果猕猴摘，池鱼白鹭衔。
仙书一两卷，树下读喃喃。

The season's change has ended a dismal year

Spring has come and the colours of things are fresh.

Mountain flowers laugh into the green pools,

The trees on the rock dance in the blue mist.

Bees and butterflies pursue their own pleasure;

Birds and fishes are there for my delight.

Thrilled with feelings of endless comradeship

From dusk to dawn I could not close my eyes.

A place to prize is this Cold Mountain,

Whose white clouds for ever idle on their own,

Where the cry of monkeys spreads among the paths,

Where the tiger's roar transcends the world of men.

Walking alone I step from stone to stone,

Singing to myself I clutch at the creepers for support.

The wind in the pine-trees makes its shrill note;

The chatter of the birds mingles its harmony.

The people of the world when they see Han-shan

All regard him as not in his right mind.

His appearance, they say, is far from being attractive,

Tied up as he is in bits of tattered cloth.

'What we say, he cannot understand;
What he says, we do not say.'

You who spend all your time in coming and going,

Why not try for once coming to the Han-shan?

Ever since the time when I hid in the Cold Mountain

I have kept alive by eating the mountain fruits.

From day to day what is there to trouble me?

This my life follows a destined course.

The days and months flow ceaseless as a stream;

Our time is brief as the flash struck on a stone.

If Heaven and Earth shift, then let them shift;

I shall still be sitting happy among the rocks.

When the men of the world look for this path amid the clouds

It vanishes, with not a trace where it lay.

The high peaks have many precipices;

On the widest gulleys hardly a gleam falls.

Green walls close behind and before;
White clouds gather east and west.

Do you want to know where the cloud-path lies?

The cloud-path leads from sky to sky.

岁去换愁年，春来物色鲜。
山花笑渌水，岩岫舞青烟。
蜂蝶自云乐，禽鱼更可怜。
朋游情未已，彻晓不能眠。

可重是寒山，白云常自闲。
猿啼畅道内，虎啸出人间。
独步石可履，孤吟藤好攀。
松风清飒飒，鸟语声喧喧。

时人见寒山，各谓是风颠。
貌不起人目，身唯布裘缠。
我语他不会，他语我不言。
为报往来者，可来向寒山。

一自遁寒山，养命餐山果。
平生何所忧，此世随缘过。
日月如逝川，光阴石中火。
任你天地移，我畅岩中坐。

时人寻云路，云路杳无踪。
山高多险峻，涧阔少玲珑。
碧嶂前兼后，白云西复东。
欲知云路处，云路在虚空。

Since first I meant to explore the
eastern cliff
And have not done so, countless
years have passed.
Yesterday I pulled myself up by the
creepers,
But half way, was baffled by storm
and fog.
The cleft so narrow that my clothing
got caught fast;
The moss so sticky that I could not
free my shoes.
So I stopped here under this red
cinnamon,
To sleep for a while on a pillow of
white clouds.

Sitting alone I am sometimes
overcome
By vague feelings of sadness and
unrest.
Round the waist of the hill the clouds
stretch and stretch;
At the mouth of the valley the winds
sough and sigh.
A monkey comes; the trees bend and
sway;
A bird goes into the wood with a
shrill cry.
Time hastens the grey that wilts on
my brow;
The year is over, and age is
comfortless.

Last year when the spring birds were
singing
At this time I thought about my
brothers.
This year when chrysanthemums are
fading
At this time the same thought comes
back.

Green waters sob in a thousand
streams,
Dark clouds lie flat on every side.
Till life ends, though I live a hundred
years,
It will rend my heart to think of
Ch'ang-an.

In the third month when the
silkworms were still small
The girls had time to go and gather
flowers,
Along the wall they played with the
butterflies,
Down by the water they pelted the
old frog.
Into gauze sleeves they poured the
ripe plums;
With their gold hairpins they dug up
bamboo-sprouts.
With all that glitter of outward
loveliness
How can the Cold Mountain hope to
compete?

Last night I dreamt that I was back in
my home
And saw my wife weaving at her
loom.
She stayed her shuttle as though
thinking of something;
When she lifted it again it was as
though she had no strength.
I called to her and she turned her
head and looked;
She stared blankly, she did not know
who I was.
Small wonder, for we parted years
ago
When the hair on my temples was
still its old colour.

欲向东岩去，于今无量年。
昨来攀葛上，半路困风烟。
径窄衣难进，苔粘履不全。
住兹丹桂下，且枕白云眠。

独坐常忽忽，情怀何悠悠。
山腰云缦缦，谷口风飕飕。
猿来树袅袅，鸟入林啾啾。
时催鬓飒飒，岁尽老惆惆。

去年春鸟鸣，此时思弟兄。
今年秋菊烂，此时思发生。
绿水千肠咽，黄云四面平。
哀哉百年内，肠断忆咸京。

三月蚕犹小，女人来采花。
隈墙弄蝴蝶，临水掷虾蟆。
罗袖盛梅子，金錍挑笋芽。
斗论多物色，此地胜余家。

昨夜梦还家，见妇机中织。
驻梭如有思，擎梭似无力。
呼之回面视，况复不相识。
应是别多年，鬓毛非旧色。

I have sat here facing the Cold Mountain
Without budging for twenty-nine years.
Yesterday I went to visit friends and relations;
A good half had gone to the Springs of Death.
Life like a guttering candle wears away—
A stream whose waters forever flow and flow.
Today, with only my shadow for company,
Astonished I find two tear-drops hang.

In old days (how long ago it was!)
I remember a house that was lovelier than all the rest.
Peach and plum lined the little paths;
Orchid and iris grew by the stream below.
There walked beside it girls in satins and silks;
Within there glinted a robe of kingfisher-green.
That was how we met; I tried to call her to me,
But my tongue stuck and the words would not come.

I sit and gaze on this highest peak of all;
Wherever I look there is distance without end.
I am all alone and no one knows I am here,
A lonely moon is mirrored in the cold pool.
Down in the pool there is not really a moon;
The only moon is in the sky above.
I sing to you this one piece of song;
But in the song there is not any Zen.

Should you look for a parable of life and death
Ice and water are the true comparisons.
Water binds and turns into ice;
Ice melts and again becomes water.
Whatever has died will certainly be born,
Whatever has come to life must needs die.
Ice and water do each other no harm;
Life and death too are both good.

一向寒山坐，淹留三十年。
昨来访亲友，太半入黄泉。
渐减如残烛，长流似逝川。
今朝对孤影，不觉泪双悬。

昨日何悠悠，场中可怜许。
上为桃李径，下作兰荪渚。
复有绮罗人，舍中翠毛羽。
相逢欲相唤，脉脉不能语。

高高峰顶上，四顾极无边。
独坐无人知，孤月照寒泉。
泉中且无月，月自在青天。
吟此一曲歌，歌终不是禅。

欲识生死譬，且将冰水比。
水结即成冰，冰消返成水。
已死必应生，出生还复死。
冰水不相伤，生死还双美。

《全唐诗》（下），第 1975—1982 页。

第四章　唐白居易诗

导言

韦利的"中隐"：最爱白居易

韦利在 1918 年正式出版《中国诗歌一百七十首》，1919 年出版了《续译中国文学》，他因译笔流畅，声名鹊起。接着他又选译了日本古典文学的《万叶集》及《古今和歌集》，出版了《日本诗》（1919）。在 20 世纪 20 年代，他翻译出版了《日本能剧》、紫式部的《源氏物语》、清少纳言的《枕草子》；在 20 世纪 30 年代，翻译出版了《道德经》《诗经》《论语》《长春真人西游记》，以及介绍道家（庄子）、儒家（孟子）及法家（韩非）的《古中国的三种思想》。他后来还译介了《白居易生平及时代》《李白生平及诗作》《玄奘西游记》《中国人眼中的鸦片战争》。对于英文读众而言，韦利英译的中日古典文学作品，几乎包罗了东方文化的精髓，时间跨度大，选材精审，译笔细腻，几乎可以臻于"信、达、雅"的境界。

韦利在 1946 年选编了一本《中国诗》（*Chinese Poems*），这本译诗集的出版，目的是介绍中国古典诗词歌赋之美，让一般英国读者，特别是从未接触过中国古诗的人感受中国诗情的优雅。这本译诗集收录了《诗经》以来的中国古典诗，有汉晋六朝诗，有唐宋诗，一直到晚明的冯梦龙与陈子龙，但其中五分之二的篇幅，呈现的都是白居易的作品，实在不同寻常。对于这个奇特的安排，韦利总要说个缘由，他在《中国诗》的序中说："我翻译白居易的诗，数量十倍于其他诗人的作品，并不是我认为白居易的诗，比其他诗人好过十倍，只是我觉得他在中国大诗人中最为出色。我并非不熟悉其他唐宋诗人的作品，其实我尝试译过李白、杜甫、苏轼，可是结果都不让我满意。"换句话说，韦利面临的是译成英文的审美效果问题，不是中国文学评介与鉴赏的问题。他要呈现给英文读者的译诗，是让他自己满意的英译，是优美流畅的英文诗，要让不懂中文的读者读起来赏心悦目。至于是否妥善介绍了中国诗的全貌，则不是他考虑的问题。

韦利以翻译家闻名于世，其实他内心深处是个诗人，对翻译的文字是否能够表达诗感与诗情，最为关注。他的个性腼腆含蓄，绝不张扬，对跻身学术界成为权威的烦琐行规，视若浮云。他属于伦敦文化精英的圈内人，是布鲁斯伯里文会（Bloomsbury Group）的一分子，与当时文坛的翘楚来往密切，如雷纳德与弗吉尼亚·伍尔夫、福斯特、斯特拉奇、艾略特等，都是他经常会面的朋友。有趣的是，这些朋友对韦利的印象是，沉静安闲，有如隐士。或许这种隐于市廛的性格，让他感到，自己与白居易的隐逸心境可以相通。

白居易有一首《中隐》，作于公元 829 年，是他在洛阳担任太子宾客时所作。这首诗的前半段是："大隐住朝市，小隐入丘樊。丘樊太冷落，朝市太嚣喧。不如作中隐，隐在留司官。似出复似处，非忙亦非闲。不劳心与力，又免饥与寒。终岁无公事，随月有俸钱。"在网上查一查，有人把"中隐"译作"middle-hermit thought"，是以"中隐"作为"大"与"小"中间的隐居方式或态度，虽然意思没错，但这样表达出来的感觉却相当笨拙。韦利译成"half-recluse"，以"half"（半）来移译"中隐"的"中"字，含蓄蕴藉，深得诗题意蕴。这前半首诗，韦利的译文如下：

'THE great recluse lives in market and court;/ The small recluse hides in thickets and hills.'/ Thickets and hills are too lonely and cold;/ Market and court are too unrestful and thronged./ Far better to be a half-recluse,/ And hermitize in a liaison job./ It is like office, yet like being at large;/ One is not busy, but also not bored./ It makes no demand either on hand or brain,/ Yet still prevents one being hungry or cold./ All the year one has no official work,/ Yet every month one draws rations and pay.

在大英博物馆工作时，韦利虽然生活在大英帝国的政治中心伦敦，却与红尘世事无牟，心境大概近乎白居易说的"中隐"，既非隐居山林，也不参与政治与商界的纷扰，留在政府机构当小公务员，不忙又不闲，每月领着薪水，一头钻进中国与日本的古典世界，整理敦煌经卷，做着别人以为枯燥无味的工作，自己却感到顺适满意。辞职之后专心译作，依然住在伦敦，心存隐逸之念，靠译著的版税过起闲适的生活，仿佛大英帝国的白居易。

白居易诗作的特色是平易近人，流畅易懂，有"老妪能懂"之说。韦利喜欢白居易，翻译了大量的白居易诗歌。白诗固然是易懂易译，但主要还是因为他与白居易性情相近，白居易的诗句触及了他内心的诗情。此外，白居易在日本古典世界备受赞誉，其诗在日本也广泛流传，如《源氏物语》中经常对其进行征引，清少纳言在《枕草子》中也表达了对白居易的无限仰慕之情，这些都间接引发了韦利对白居易的亲切观感。韦利译白居易的诗，保留了诗句清新流畅的特色，选用的英文词语也尽量清晰简明，既有散文的平实易读之感，又有诗歌有余不尽的含蓄之美。如白居易的《村居卧病三首》中有句："戚戚抱羸病，悠悠度朝暮。夏木才结阴，秋兰已含露。"韦利译作："Sad, sad—lean with long illness;/ Monotonous, monotonous—days and nights pass./ The summer trees have clad themselves in shade;/ The autumn 'lan' already houses the dew.""戚戚"与"悠悠"都是单音叠字，韦利直接沿用中文句式，译成"sad, sad"与"monotonous, monotonous"。对译中文的一音节字，韦利前面用了一音节字，后面用了四音节字，乍看好像不能对称，然而整句读下来却流利顺口。尤其是接着的"抱羸病"译成"lean with long illness"，"度朝暮"译成"days and nights pass"，让你觉得长久抱病十分凄惨，的确是"sad, sad"，而朝朝暮暮如此无聊度日，也实在是"monotonous, monotonous"。最有趣的是，不把"秋兰"译成"autumn orchid"，而是译作"The autumn 'lan'"，给英文读者完全朦胧恍惚的感觉，只能想象到底是秋天的什么可以结露呢？翻译白居易，在流利明畅之中，带出谜语一般的"花非花，雾非雾"的诗境，也真难为了韦利。

类似的叠字处理方式，韦利在翻译白居易《寄行简》一诗的开头时，也如法炮制。"郁郁眉多敛，默默口寡言"，译成："Sullen, sullen, my brows are ever knit;/ Silent, silent, my lips will not move."原来的两句是押韵的，韦利转成自由诗体，表面是散文化了，但读起来却没有松散的感觉，那是因为他同时使用了中国诗叠字与英文诗头韵（alliteration）的技巧，让两音节的"sullen, sullen"与"silent, silent"在两句诗中回旋激荡，产生了很好的音律效果。

白居易生平

LIFE OF PO CHÜ-I

772   Born on 20th of first month.

800   Passes his Examinations.

806   Receives a minor post at Chou-chih, near the capital.

807   Made Scholar of the Han Lin Academy.

811   Retires to Wei River, being in mourning for his mother.

812   Returns to Court.

814   Banished to Hsün-yang.

818   Removed to Chung-chou.

820   Reprieved and returns to Court.

822   Governor of Hangchow.

825   Governor of Soochow.

826   Retires owing to illness.

827   Returns to Ch'ang-an.

829   Settles permanently at Lo-yang.

831   Governor of Ho-nan, the province of which Lo-yang was capital.

833   Retires owing to illness.

839   Has paralytic stroke in tenth month.

846   Dies in the eighth month.

古诗英汉对照

AFTER PASSING THE EXAMINATION
(A.D. 800)

FOR ten years I never left my books;
I went up... and won unmerited praise.
My high place I do not much prize;
The joy of my parents will first make me proud.
Fellow students, six or seven men,
See me off as I leave the City gate.
My covered coach is ready to drive away;
Flutes and strings blend their parting tune.
Hopes achieved dull the pains of parting;
Fumes of wine shorten the long road...
Shod with wings is the horse of him who rides
On a Spring day the road that leads to home.

及第后归觐，留别诸同年

十年常苦学，一上谬成名，
擢第未为贵，贺亲方始荣。
时辈六七人，送我出帝城；
轩车动行色，丝管举离声。
得意减别恨，半酣轻远程。
翩翩马蹄疾，春日归乡情。

《白居易集》，第 103 页。

ESCORTING CANDIDATES TO THE EXAMINATION HALL
(A.D. 805)

AT dawn I rode to escort the Doctors of Art;
In the eastern quarter the sky was still grey.
I said to myself: 'You have started far too soon,'
But horses and coaches already thronged the road.
High and low the riders' torches bobbed;
Muffled or loud, the watchman's drum beat.
Riders, when I see you trot, so pleased with yourselves
To your early levee, pity fill my heart.
When the sun rises and the hot dust flies
And the creatures of earth resume their great strife,
You, with your striving, what shall you each seek?
Profit and fame, for that is all your care.
But I, you courtiers, rise from my bed at noon
And live idly in the city of Ch'ang-an.
Spring is deep and my term of office spent;
Day by day my thoughts go back to the hills.

早送举人入试

夙驾送举人，东方犹未明；
自谓出太早，已有车马行。
骑火高低影，街鼓参差声。
可怜早朝者，相看意气生。
日出尘埃飞，群动互营营。
营营各何求？无非利与名。
而我常晏起，虚住长安城。
春深官又满，日有归山情。

《白居易集》，第 93 页。

IN EARLY SUMMER LODGING IN A TEMPLE TO ENJOY THE MOONLIGHT

(A.D. 805)

IN early summer, with two or three more
That were seeking fame in the city of Ch'ang-an,
Whose low employ gave them less business
Than ever they had since first they left their homes—
With these I wandered deep into the shrine of Tao,
For the joy we sought was promised in this place.
When we reached the gate, we sent our coaches back;
We entered the yard with only cap and stick.
Still and clear, the first weeks of May,
When trees are green and bushes soft and wet;
When the wind freshens the shadows of new leaves
And birds linger on the last boughs that bloom.
Towards evening when the sky grew clearer yet
And the South-east was still clothed in red,
To the western cloister we carried our jar of wine;
We waited for the moon before starting to drink.
Soon, how soon her golden ghost was born,
Swiftly, as though she had waited for us to come.
The beams of her light shone in every place,
On towers and halls dancing to and fro.
Till day broke we sat in her clear light
Laughing and singing, and yet never grew tired.
In Ch'ang-an, the place of profit and fame,
Such moods as this, how many men know?

首夏同诸校正游开元观，因宿玩月

我与二三子，策名在京师：
官小无职事，闲于为客时。
沉沉道观中，心赏期在兹。
到门车马回，入院巾杖随。
清和四月初，树木正华滋。
风清新叶影，鸟思残花枝。
向夕天又晴，东南余霞披。
置酒西廊下，待月杯行迟。
须臾金魄生，若与吾徒期：
光华一照耀，楼殿相参差。
终夜清景前，笑歌不知疲。
长安名利地，此兴几人知？

《白居易集》，第 92 页。

BEING ON DUTY ALL NIGHT IN THE PALACE AND DREAMIING OF THE
HSIEN-YU TEMPLE

AT the western window I paused from writing rescripts;
The pines and bamboos were all buried in stillness.
The moon rose and a calm wind came;
Suddenly, it was like an evening in the hills.
And so, as I dozed, I dreamed of the South West
And thought I was staying at the Hsien-yu Temple.
When I woke and heard the dripping of the Palace clock
I still thought it the trickle of a mountain stream.

再
造
的
镜
像

禁中寓直，梦游仙游寺

西轩草诏暇，松竹深寂寂。
月出清风来，忽似山中夕。
因成西南梦，梦作游仙客；
觉闻宫漏声，犹谓山泉滴。

《白居易集》，第 101 页。

WATCHING THE REAPERS
(A.D. 806)

再
造
的
镜
像

TILLERS of the earth have few idle months;
In the fifth month their toil is double-fold.
A south wind visits the fields at night;
Suddenly the ridges are covered with yellow corn.
Wives and daughters shoulder baskets of rice,
Youths and boys carry flasks of wine,
In a long train, to feed the workers in the field—
The strong reapers toiling on the southern hill,
Whose feet are burned by the hot earth they tread,
Whose backs are scorched by the flames of the shining sky
Tired they toil, caring nothing for the heat,
Grudging the shortness of the long summer day.
A poor woman with a young child at her side
Follows behind, to glean the unwanted grain.
In her right hand she holds the fallen ears,
On her left arm a broken basket hangs.
Listening to what they said as they worked together
I heard something that made me very sad:
They lost in grain-tax the whole of their own crop;
What they glean here is all they will have to eat.
And I today—in virtue of what desert
Have I never once tended field or tree?
My government-pay is three hundred 'stones';
At the year's end I have still grain in hand.
Thinking of this, secretly I grew ashamed
And all day the thought lingered in my head.

观刈麦

田家少闲月，五月人倍忙。
夜来南风起，小麦覆陇黄。
妇姑荷箪食，童稚携壶浆。
相随饷田去，丁壮在南冈。
足蒸暑土气，背灼炎天光：
力尽不知热，但惜夏日长。
复有贫妇人，抱子在其傍：
右手秉遗穗，左臂悬敝筐。
听其相顾言，闻者为悲伤。
家田输税尽，拾此充饥肠。
今我何功德？曾不事农桑；
吏禄三百石，岁晏有余粮。
念此私自愧，尽日不能忘！

《白居易集》，第 4—5 页。

SICK LEAVE

(While Chief Clerk to the sub-prefecture of Chou-chih, near Ch'ang-an, in A.D. 806)

PROPPED on pillows, not attending to business;
For two days I've lain behind locked doors.
I begin to think that those who hold office
Get no rest, except by falling ill!
For restful thoughts one does not need space;
The room where I lie is ten foot square.
By the western eaves, above the bamboo-twigs,
From my couch I see the White Mountain rise.
But the clouds that hover on its far-distant peak
Bring shame to a face that is buried in the World's dust.

再
造
的
镜
像

病假中南亭闲望

敧枕不视事，两日门掩关；
始知吏役身，不病不得闲。
闲意不在远，小亭方丈间。
西檐竹梢上，坐见太白山。
遥愧峰上云，对此尘中颜！

《白居易集》，第 94—95 页。

GOING ALONE TO SPEND A NIGHT AT THE HSIEN-YU TEMPLE
(A.D. 806)

THE crane from the shore standing at the top of the steps
The moon on the pool seen at the open door;
Where these are, I made my lodging-place
And for two nights could not turn away.
I am glad I chanced on a place so lonely and still
With no companion to drag me early home.
Now that I have tasted the joy of being alone,
I will never again come with a friend at my side.

仙游寺独宿

沙鹤上阶立，潭月当户开。
此中留我宿，两夜不能回。
幸与静境遇，喜无归侣催。
从今独游后，不拟共人来。

《白居易集》，第 95 页。

PLANTING BAMBOOS
(A.D. 806?)

I AM not suited for service in a country town;
At my closed door autumn grasses grow.
What could I do to ease a rustic heart?
I planted bamboos, more than a hundred shoots.
When I see their beauty, as they grow by the stream-side,
I feel again as though I lived in the hills,
And many a time when I have not much work
Round their railing I walk till night comes.
Do not say that their roots are still weak,
Do not say that their shade is still small;
Already I feel that both in courtyard and house
Day by day a fresher air moves.
But most I love, lying near the window-side,
To hear in their branches the sound of the autumn wind.

再
造
的
镜
像

新栽竹

佐邑意不适，闭门秋草生。
何以娱野性？种竹百余茎。
见此溪上色，忆得山中情。
有时公事暇，尽日绕栏行。
勿言根未固，勿言阴未成。
已觉庭宇内，稍稍有余清。
最爱近窗卧，秋风枝有声。

《白居易集》，第 168 页。

PASSING T'IEN-MEN STREET IN CH'ANG-AN AND SEEING A DISTANT VIEW OF CHUNG-NAN MOUNTAINS

再
造
的
镜
像

THE snow has gone from Chung-nan; spring is almost come.

Lovely in the distance its blue colours, against the brown of the streets.

A thousand coaches, ten thousand horsemen pass down the Nine Roads;

Turns his head and looks at the mountains—not one man!

过天门街

雪尽终南又欲春，遥怜翠色对红尘。
千车万马九衢上，回首看山无一人。

《白居易集》，第 257 页。

TO LI CHIEN

Part of a Poem

(A.D. 810)

再
造
的
镜
像

WORLDLY matters again draw my body;

Worldly things again seduce my heart.

Whenever for long I part from Li Chien

Gradually my thoughts grow narrow and covetous.

I remember how once I used to visit you;

I stopped my horse and tapped at the garden-gate.

Often when I came you were still lying in bed;

Your little children were sent to let me in.

And you, laughing, ran to the front-door

With coat-tails flying and cap all awry.

On the swept terrace, green patterns of moss;

On the dusted bench the shade of the creepers was cool.

To gaze at the hills we sat in the eastern lodge;

To wait for the noon we walked to the southern moor.

At your quiet gate only birds spoke;

In your distant street few drums were heard.

Opposite each other all day we talked,

And never once spoke of profit or fame.

Since we parted hands, how long has passed?

Thrice and again the full moon has shone.

For when we parted the last flowers were falling,

And today I hear new cicadas sing.

The scented year suddenly draws to its close,

Yet the sorrow of parting is still unsubdued.

寄李十一建（节选）

外事牵我形，外物诱我情；
李君别来久，褊吝从中生。
忆昨访君时，立马扣柴荆。
有时君未起，稚子喜先迎。
连步笑出门，衣翻冠或倾。
扫阶苔文绿，拂榻藤阴清。
家醅及春熟，园葵乘露烹。
看山东亭坐，待月南原行。
门静唯鸟语，坊远少鼓声。
相对尽日言，不及利与名。
分手来几时？明月三四盈。
别时残花落，及此新蝉鸣。
芳岁忽已晚，离抱怅未平。

《白居易集》，第 100 页。

THE OLD LUTE

再
造
的
镜
像

OF cord and cassia-wood is the lute compounded;
Within it lie ancient melodies.
Ancient melodies—weak and savourless,
Not appealing to present men's taste.
Light and colour are faded from the jade stops;
Dust has covered the rose-red strings.
Decay and ruin came to it long ago,
But the sound that is left is still cold and clear.
I do not refuse to play it, if you want me to;
But even if I play, people will not listen.

How did it come to be neglected so?
Because of the Ch'iang flute and the zithern of Ch'in[①].

---

① Non-classical instruments.

废琴

丝桐合为琴，中有太古声。
古声淡无味，不称今人情。
玉徽光彩灭，朱弦尘土生。
废弃来已久，遗音尚泠泠。
不辞为君弹，纵弹人不听。
何物使之然？羌笛与秦筝。

《白居易集》，第 6 页。

THE PRISONER

(Written *c.* A.D. 809)

TARTARS led in chains,

Tartars led in chains!

Their ears pierced, their faces bruised—they are driven into the land of Ch'in.

The Son of Heaven took pity on them and would not have them slain.

He sent them away to the south-east, to the lands of Wu and Yüeh.

A petty officer in a yellow coat took down their names and surnames;

They were led from the city of Ch'ang-an by relays of armed guards.

Their bodies were covered with the wounds of arrows, their bones stood out from their cheeks.

They had grown so weak they could only march a single stage a day.

In the morning they must satisfy hunger and thirst with neither plate nor cup;

At night they must lie in their dirt and rags on beds that stank with filth.

Suddenly they came to the Yangtze River and remembered the waters of Chiao[1].

With lowered hands and levelled voices they sobbed a muffled song.

Then one Tartar lifted up his voice and spoke to the other Tartars,

'Your sorrows are none at all compared with my sorrows.'

Those that were with him in the same band asked to hear his tale;

As he tried to speak the words were choked by anger.

He told them 'I was born and bred in the plain of Liang-chou[2];

In the frontier wars of Ta-li[3] I fell into the Tartars' hands.

Since the days the Tartars took me alive, forty years ago,

I have had to wear a coat of skins tied with a fur belt.

Only on the first of the first month might I wear my Chinese dress.

As I put on my coat and arranged my cap, how fast the tears flowed!

I made in my heart a secret vow I would find a way home;

I hid my plan from my Tartar wife and the children she had borne me in the land.

---

① In Turkestan.

② In Kansu.

③ A.D. 766-780.

缚戎人

缚戎人，缚戎人，耳穿面破驱入秦。
天子矜怜不忍杀，诏徙东南吴与越。
黄衣小使录姓名，领出长安乘递行。
身被金创面多瘠，扶病徒行日一驿；
朝餐饥渴费杯盘，夜卧腥臊污床席。
忽逢江水忆交河，垂手齐声呜咽歌。
其中一虏语诸虏：尔苦非多我苦多。
同伴行人因借问，欲说喉中气愤愤。
自云乡管本凉原，大历年中没落蕃。
一落蕃中四十载，遣著皮裘系毛带。
唯许正朝服汉仪，敛衣整巾潜泪垂；
誓心密定归乡计，不使蕃中妻子知。

I thought to myself, "It is well for me that my limbs are still strong,"
And yet, being old, in my heart I feared I should never live to return.
The Tartar chieftains shoot so well that the birds are afraid to fly;
From the risk of their arrows I escaped alive and fled swiftly home.
Hiding all day and walking all night, I crossed the Great Desert[①],
Where clouds are dark and the moon black and the sands eddy in the wind.
Frightened, I sheltered at the Green Grave[②], where the frozen grasses are few;
Stealthily I crossed the Yellow River, at night, on the thin ice,
Suddenly I heard Han[③] drums and the sound of soldiers coming;
I went to meet them at the road-side, bowing to them as they came.
But the moving horsemen did not hear that I spoke the Han tongue;
Their Captain took me for a Tartar born and had me bound in chains.
They are sending me away to the south-east, to a low and swampy land
Provided with hardly any kit and no protective drugs.
Thinking of this my voice chokes and I ask of Heaven above,
Was I spared from death only to spend the rest of my years in sorrow?
My native village in Liang plain I shall not see again;
My wife and children in the Tartars' land I have fruitlessly deserted.
When I fell among Tartars and was taken prisoner, I pined for the land of Han;
Now that I am back in the land of Han, they have turned me into a Tartar.
Had I but known what my fate would be, I would not have started home!
For the two lands, so wide apart, are alike in the sorrow they bring.
Tartar prisoners in chains!
Of all the sorrows of all the prisoners mine is the hardest to bear!
Never in the world has so great a wrong fallen to the lot of man—
A Han heart and a Han tongue set in the body of a Turk.'

---

① The Gobi Desert.

② The grave of Chao-chün, a Chinese girl who in 33 B.C. was 'bestowed upon the Khan of the Hsiung-nu as a mark of Imperial regard' (Giles). Hers was the only grave in this desolate district on which grass would grow.

③ i.e. Chinese.

暗思幸有残筋力，更恐年衰归不得。
蕃候严兵鸟不飞，脱身冒死奔逃归。
昼伏宵行经大漠，云阴月黑风沙恶；
惊藏青冢寒草疏，偷渡黄河夜冰薄。
忽闻汉军鼙鼓声，路傍走出再拜迎；
游骑不听能汉语，将军遂缚作蕃生。
配向江南卑湿地，定无存恤空防备。
念此吞声仰诉天，若为辛苦度残年！
凉原乡井不得见，胡地妻儿虚弃捐！
没蕃被囚思汉土，归汉被劫为蕃虏：
早知如此悔归来，两地宁如一处苦？
缚戎人，戎人之中我苦辛。
自古此冤应未有，汉心汉语吐蕃身！

《白居易集》，第 71—72 页。

THE OLD MAN WITH THE BROKEN ARM

(A Satire on Militarism)

(*c.* A.D. 809)

AT Hsin-fêng an old man—four-score and eight;

The hair on his head and the hair of his eyebrows—white as the new snow.

Leaning on the shoulders of his great-grandchildren, he walks in front of the Inn;

With his left arm he leans on their shoulders; his right arm is broken.

I asked the old man how many years had passed since he broke his arm;

I also asked the cause of the injury, how and why it happened?

The old man said he was born and reared in the District of Hsin-fêng;

At the time of his birth—a wise reign; no wars or discords.

'Often I listened in the Pear-Tree Garden to the sound of flute and song;

Naught I knew of banner and lance; nothing of arrow or bow.

Then came the wars of T'ien-pao[①] and the great levy of men;

Of three men in each house—one man was taken.

And those to whom the lot fell, where were they taken to?

Five months' journey, a thousand miles—away to Yün-nan.

We heard it said that in Yün-nan there flows the Lu River;

As the flowers fall from the pepper-trees, poisonous vapours rise.

When the great army waded across, the water seethed like a cauldron;

When barely ten had entered the water, two or three were dead.

To the north of my village, to the south of my village the sound of weeping and wailing,

Children parting from fathers and mothers; husbands parting from wives.

Everyone says that in expeditions against the Man tribes

Of a million men who are sent out, not one returns.

I, that am old, was then twenty-four;

My name and fore-name were written down in the rolls of the Board of War.

---

① A. D. 742-756.

新丰折臂翁

新丰老翁八十八，头鬓眉须皆似雪；
玄孙扶向店前行，左臂凭肩右臂折。
问翁臂折来几年？兼问致折何因缘？
翁云贯属新丰县，生逢圣代无征战；
惯听梨园歌管声，不识旗枪与弓箭。
无何天宝大征兵，户有三丁点一丁。
点得驱将何处去？五月万里云南行。
闻道云南有泸水，椒花落时瘴烟起；
大军徒涉水如汤，未过十人二三死。
村南村北哭声哀，儿别爷娘夫别妻。
皆云前后征蛮者，千万人行无一回。
是时翁年二十四，兵部牒中有名字。

In the depth of the night not daring to let anyone know

I secretly took a huge stone and dashed it against my arm.

For drawing the bow and waving the banner now wholly unfit

I knew henceforward I should not be sent to fight in Yün-nan.

Bones broken and sinews wounded could not fail to hurt;

My plan was to be rejected and sent back to my home.

My arm—broken ever since; it was sixty years ago.

One limb, although destroyed—whole body safe!

But even now on winter nights when the wind and rain blow

From evening on till day's dawn I cannot sleep for pain.

Not sleeping for pain

Is a small thing to bear,

Compared with the joy of being alive when all the rest are dead.

For otherwise, years ago, at the ford of Lu River

My body would have died and my soul hovered by the bones that no one gathered.

A ghost, I'd have wandered in Yün-nan, always looking for home.

Over the graves of ten thousand soldiers, mournfully hovering,'

So the old man spoke,

And I bid you listen to his words.

Have you not heard

That the Prime Minister of K'ai-yüan[1], His Excellency Sung[2],

Did not reward frontier exploits, lest a spirit of aggrssion should prevail?

And have you not heard

That the Prime Minister of T'ien-pao, Yang Kuo-chung[3],

Desiring to win imperial favour, started a frontier war,

But long before he could win the war, people had lost their temper?

Ask the man with the broken arm in the village of Hsin-fêng.

---

[1] A. D. 713-741.

[2] Sung Ying; died in 737.

[3] Cousin of the notorious mistress of Ming-huang, Yang Kuei-fei.

夜深不敢使人知，偷将大石捶折臂。
张弓簸旗俱不堪，从兹始免征云南。
骨碎筋伤非不苦，且图拣退归乡土。
臂折来来六十年，一肢虽废一身全。
至今风雨阴寒夜，直到天明痛不眠。
痛不眠，终不悔，且喜老身今独在。
不然当时泸水头，身死魂飞骨不收；
应作云南望乡鬼，万人冢上哭呦呦。
老人言，君听取。
君不闻：
开元宰相宋开府，不赏边功防黩武？
又不闻：
天宝宰相杨国忠，欲求恩幸立边功？
边功未立生人怨，请问新丰折臂翁。

《白居易集》，第 62 页。

THE FIVE-STRING[①]

THE singers have hushed their notes of shrill song;
The red sleeves of the dancers are motionless.
Old Chao[②] hugs his five-stringed lute;
Then his fingers dart, as he holds it close to his breast.
The loud notes swell and scatter abroad;
'Sa, sa', like wind blowing the rain.
The soft notes dying almost to nothing;
'Ch'ieh, ch'ieh', like the voice of ghosts talking.
Now as glad as the magpie's lucky song;
Again bitter as the gibbon's ominous cry.
His ten fingers have no fixed note;
Up and down—*kung, chih,* and *yü*[③].
And those who sit and listen to the tune he plays
Of soul and body lose the mastery.
And those who pass that way as he plays the tune
Suddenly stop and cannot raise their feet.

Alas, alas that the ears of common men
Should love the modern and not love the old.
Thus it is that the lute in the green window
Day by day is covered deeper with dust.

---

① A kind of guitar imported from Bukhara.
② Chao Pi, a famous player of this instrument.
③ Tonic, dominant and sixth of the pentatonic scale.

秦中吟十首·五弦

清歌且罢唱，红袂亦停舞。
赵叟抱五弦，宛转当胸抚。
大声粗若散，飒飒风和雨。
小声细欲绝，切切鬼神语。
又如鹊报喜，转作猿啼苦。
十指无定音，颠倒宫徵羽。
坐客闻此声，形神若无主。
行客闻此声，驻足不能举。
嗟嗟俗人耳，好今不好古；
所以绿窗琴，日日生尘土。

《白居易集》，第 34 页。

THE FLOWER MARKET

IN the Royal City spring is almost over;
Tinkle, tinkle—the coaches and horsemen pass.
We tell each other 'This is the peony season';
And follow with the crowd that goes to the Flower Market.
'Cheap and dear—no uniform price;
The cost of the plant depends on the number of blossoms.
The flaming reds, a hundred on one stalk;
The humble white with only five flowers.
Above is spread an awning to protect them;
Around is woven a wattle-fence to screen them.
If you sprinkle water and cover the roots with mud,
When they are transplanted, they will not lose their beauty.'
Each household thoughtlessly follows the custom,
Man by man, no one realizing:
There happened to be an old farm labourer
Who came by chance that way.
He bowed his head and sighed a deep sigh;
But this sigh nobody understood.
He was thinking, 'A cluster of deep-red flowers
Would pay the taxes of ten poor houses.'

秦中吟十首·买花

帝城春欲暮，喧喧车马度。
共道牡丹时，相随买花去。
贵贱无常价，酬直看花数：
灼灼百朵红，戋戋五束素。
上张幄幕庇，旁织笆篱护。
水洒复泥封，移来色如故。
家家习为俗，人人迷不悟。
有一田舍翁，偶来买花处：
低头独长叹，此叹无人谕。
一丛深色花，十户中人赋！

《白居易集》，第 34—35 页。

AT THE END OF SPRING
To Yüan Chên[①]
(A.D. 810)

THE flower of the pear-tree gathers and turns to fruit;
The swallows' eggs have hatched into young birds.
When the Seasons' changes thus confront the mind
What comfort can the Doctrine of Tao give?
It will teach me to watch the days and months fly
Without grieving that Youth slips away;
If the Fleeting World is but a long dream,
It does not matter whether one is young or old.
But ever since the day that my friend left my side
And has lived an exile in the City of Chiang-ling,
There is one wish I cannot quite destroy:
That from time to time we may chance to meet again.

---

① Po Chü-i's great friend.

春暮寄元九

梨花结成实，燕卵花为雏。
时物又若此，道情复何如？
但觉日月促，不嗟年岁徂。
浮生都是梦，老小亦何殊？
唯与故人别，江陵初谪居。
时时一相见，此意未全除。

《白居易集》，第 172 页。

THE POEM ON THE WALL
(A.D. 810)

再
造
的
镜
像

Yüan Chên wrote that on his way to exile he had discovered a poem inscribed by
Po Chü-i on the wall of the Lo-k'ou Inn.

MY clumsy poem on the inn-wall none cared to see;
With bird-droppings and moss's growth the letters were blotched away.
There came a guest with heart so full, that though a page to the Throne,
He did not grudge with his broidered coat to wipe off the dust, and read.

酬和元九东川路诗十二首·骆口驿旧题诗

拙诗在壁无人爱，鸟污苔侵文字残。
唯有多情元侍御，绣衣不惜拂尘看。

《白居易集》，第 282—283 页。

AN EARLY LEVÉE

Addressed to Ch'ên, the Hermit

AT Ch'ang-an—a full foot of snow;
A levée at dawn—to bestow congratulations on the Emperor.
Just as I was nearing the Gate of the Silver Terrace,
After I had left the ward of Hsin-ch'ang
On the high causeway my horse's foot slipped;
In the middle of the journey my lantern suddenly went out.
Ten leagues riding, always facing to the North;
The cold wind almost blew off my ears.
I waited for the bell outside the Five Gates;
I waited for the summons within the Triple Hall.
My hair and beard were frozen and covered with icicles;
My coat and robe—chilly like water.
Suddenly I thought of Hsien-yu Valley
And secretly envied Ch'ên Chü-shih,
In warm bed-socks dozing beneath the rugs
And not getting up till the sun has mounted the sky.

再造的镜像

340

早朝贺雪，寄陈山人

长安盈尺雪，早朝贺君喜。
将赴银台门，始出新昌里。
上堤马蹄滑，中路蜡烛死。
十里向北行，寒风吹破耳。
待漏五门外，候对三殿里；
须鬓冻生冰，衣裳冷如水。
忽思仙游谷，暗谢陈居士：
暖覆褐裘眠，日高应未起。

《白居易集》，第 175 页。

THE LETTER
(A.D. 810)

Preface—After I parted with Yüan Chên, I suddenly dreamt one night that I saw him. When I awoke, I found that a letter from him had just arrived and, enclosed in it, a poem on the *paulovnia* flower.

WE talked together in the Yung-shou Temple;
We parted to the north of the Hsin-ch'ang ward.
Going home—I shed a few tears,
Grieving about things—not sorry for you.
Long, long the Lan-t'ien road;
You said yourself you would not be able to write.
Reckoning up your halts for eating and sleeping—
By this time you've crossed the Shang mountains.
Last night the clouds scattered away;
A thousand leagues, the same moonlight scene.
When dawn came, I dreamt I saw your face;
It must have been that you were thinking of me.
In my dream, I thought I held your hand
And asked you to tell me what your thoughts were.
And *you* said: 'I miss you bitterly,
But there's no one here to send to you with a letter.'
When I awoke, before I had time to speak,
A knocking on the door sounded 'Doong, doong!'
They came and told me a messenger from Shang-chou
Had brought a letter—a single scroll from you!
Up from my pillow I suddenly sprang out of bed,
And threw on my clothes, all topsy-turvy.
I undid the knot and saw the letter within,
A single sheet with thirteen lines of writing.
At the top it told the sorrows of an exile's heart;
At the bottom it described the pains of separation.
The sorrows and pains took up so much space
There was no room left to talk about the weather!
But you said that when you wrote
You were staying for the night to the east of Shang-chou;
Sitting alone, lighted by a solitary candle
Lodging in the mountain hostel of Yang-ch'êng.
Night was late when you finished writing,
The mountain moon was slanting towards the west.

再
造
的
镜
像

342

初与元九别后，忽梦见之。及寤，而书适至，兼寄《桐花诗》。怅然感怀，因以此寄

永寿寺中语，新昌坊北分。
归来数行泪，悲事不悲君。
悠悠蓝田路，自去无消息。
计君食宿程，已过商山北。
昨夜云四散，千里同月色。
晓来梦见君，应是君相忆。
梦中握君手，问君意何如？
君言苦相忆，无人可寄书。
觉来未及说，叩门声冬冬；
言是商州使，送君书一封。
枕上忽惊起，颠倒著衣裳。
开缄见手札，一纸十三行。
上论迁谪心，下说离别肠。
心肠都未尽，不暇叙炎凉。
云作此书夜，夜宿商州东；
独对孤灯坐，阳城山馆中。
夜深作书毕，山月向西斜。

What is it lies aslant across the moon?

A single tree of purple paulovnia flowers—

Paulovnia flowers just on the point of falling

Are a symbol to express 'thinking of an absent friend'.

Lovingly—you wrote on the back side,

To send in the letter, your 'Poem of the Paulovnia Flower'

The Poem of the Paulovnia Flower has eight rhymes;

Yet these eight couples have cast a spell on my heart.

They have taken hold of this morning's thoughts

And carried them to yours, the night you wrote your letter.

The whole poem I read three times;

Each verse ten times I recite.

So precious to me are the fourscore words

That each letter changes into a bar of gold!

月前何所有？一树紫桐花。
桐花半落时，复道正相思；
殷勤书背后，兼寄《桐花诗》。
《桐花诗》八韵，思绪一何深！
以我今朝意，忆君此夜心。
一章三遍读，一句十回吟。
珍重八十字，字字化为金！

《白居易集》，第 175—176 页。

GOLDEN BELLS

WHEN I was almost forty
I had a daughter whose name was Golden Bells.
Now it is just a year since she was born;
She is learning to sit and cannot yet talk.
Ashamed—to find that I have not a sage's heart;
I cannot resist vulgar thoughts and feelings.
Henceforward I am tied to things outside myself;
My only reward—the pleasure I am getting now.
If I am spared the grief of her dying young,
Then I shall have the trouble of getting her married.
My plan for retiring and going back to the hills
Must now be postponed for fifteen years!

金銮子晬日

行年欲四十，有女曰金銮。
生来始周岁，学坐未能言。
惭非达者怀，未免俗情怜。
从此累身外，徒云慰目前。
若无夭折患，则有婚嫁牵。
使我归山计，应迟十五年。

《白居易集》，第 173 页。

CHU CH'ÊN VILLAGE
(In north-west Kiangsu)
(A.D. 811)

IN Hsü-chou, in the District of Ku-fêng
There lies a village whose name is Chu-ch'ên—
A hundred miles away from the county town,
Amid fields of hemp and green of mulberry-trees.
Click, click, the sound of the spinning-wheel;
Donkeys and oxen pack the village streets.
The girls go drawing the water from the brook;
The men go gathering fire-wood on the hill.
So far from the town Government affairs are few;
So deep in the hills, men's way are simple.
Though they have wealth, they do not traffic with it;
Though they reach the age, they do not enter the Army.
Each family keeps to its village trade;
Grey-headed, they have never left the gates.
Alive, they are the people of Ch'ên Village;
Dead, they become the dust of Ch' ên Village.
Out in the fields old men and young
Gaze gladly, each in the other's face.
In the whole village there are only two clans;
Age after age Chus have married Ch'êns.
Near or distant, they live in one clan;
Young or old, they move as one flock.
On white wine and brown fowl they fare
At joyful meetings more than 'once a week'.
While they are alive, they have no distant partings;
For marriage takes them no further than the next village.
When they are dead—no distant burial;
Round the village graves lie thick.
They are not troubled either about life or death;
They have no anguish either of body or soul.
And so it happens that they live to a ripe age
And great-great-grandsons are often seen.
I was born in the Realms of Etiquette;
In early years, unprotected and poor.
In vain I learnt to distinguish between Evil and Good;
Bringing myself only labour and toil.

朱陈村

徐州古丰县，有村曰朱陈。
去县百余里，桑麻青氛氲。
机梭声札札，牛驴走纭纭。
女汲涧中水，男采山上薪。
县远官事少，山深人俗淳。
有财不行商，有丁不入军。
家家守村业，头白不出门。
生为陈村民，死为陈村尘。
田中老与幼，相见何欣欣！
一村唯两姓，世世为婚姻。
亲疏居有族，少长游有群。
黄鸡与白酒，欢会不隔旬。
生者不远别，嫁娶先近邻。
死者不远葬，坟墓多绕村。
既安生与死，不苦形与神。
所以多寿考，往往见玄孙。
我生礼义乡，少小孤且贫；
徒学辨是非，只自取辛勤。

The age we live in honours the Doctrine of Names^①;
Scholars prize marriages and rank.
With these fetters I gyved my own hands;
Truly I became a much-deceived man.
At ten years old I learnt to read books;
At fifteen, I knew how to write prose.
At twenty I was made a Bachelor of Arts;
At thirty I became a Censor at the Court.
Above, the duty I owe to Prince and parents;
Below, the ties that bind me to wife and child.
The support of my family, the service of my country—
For these tasks my nature is not apt.
I reckon the time that I first left my home;
From then till now—fifteen Springs!
My lonely boat has twice sailed to Ch'u;
Four times through Ch'in my lean horse has passed.
I have walked in the morning with hunger in my face;
I have lain at night with a soul that could not rest.
East and West I have wandered without pause,
Hither and thither like a cloud adrift in the sky.
In the civil-war my old home was destroyed;
Of my flesh and blood many are scattered and parted.
North of the River, yes, and South of the River—
In both lands are the friends of all my life;
Life-friends whom I never see at all—
Whose deaths I hear of only after the lapse of years.
Sad at morning, I lie on my bed till dusk;
Weeping at night, I sit and wait for dawn.
The fire of sorrow has burnt my heart's core;
The frost of trouble has seized my hair's roots.
In such anguish my whole life has passed;
Long I have envied the people of Ch'ên Village.

---

① Confucianism.

世法贵名教，士人重官婚；
以此自桎梏，信为大谬人。
十岁解读书，十五能属文。
二十举秀才，三十为谏臣。
下有妻子累，上有君亲恩。
承家与事国，望此不肖身。
忆昨旅游初，迨今十五春。
孤舟三适楚，羸马四经秦。
昼行有饥色，夜寝无安魂。
东西不暂住，来往若浮云。
离乱失故乡，骨肉多散分；
江南与江北，各有平生亲。
平生终日别，逝者隔年闻；
朝忧卧至暮，夕哭坐达晨。
悲火烧心曲，愁霜侵鬓根。
一生苦如此，长羡陈村民！

《白居易集》，第 184—185 页。

FISHING IN THE WEI RIVER

(A.D. 811)

IN waters still as a burnished mirror's face,

In the depths of Wei, carp and grayling swim.

Idly I come with my bamboo fishing-rod

And hang my hook by the banks of Wei stream.

A gentle wind blows on my fishing-gear

Softly shaking my ten feet of line.

Though my body sits waiting for fish to come,

My heart has wandered to the Land of Nothingness.[1]

Long ago a white-headed man

Also fished at the same river's side;

A hooker of men, not a hooker of fish,

At seventy years, he caught Wên Wang. [2]

But *I*, when I come to cast my hook in the stream,

Have no thought either of fish or men.

Lacking the skill to capture either prey,

I can only bask in the autumn water's light.

When I tire of this, my fishing also stops;

I go to my home and drink my cup of wine.

---

[1] See *Chuang Tzŭ*, ch. I end.

[2] The Sage T'ai-kung sat till he was seventy, apparently fishing, but really waiting for a prince who would employ him. At last Wên Wang, king of Chou, happened to come that way and at once made him his counsellor.

渭上偶钓

渭水如镜色，中有鲤与鲂。
偶持一竿竹，悬钓至其傍。
微风吹钓丝，袅袅十尺长。
谁知对鱼坐，心在无何乡。
昔有白头人，亦钓此渭阳：
钓人不钓鱼，七十得文王。
况我垂钓意，人鱼又兼忘。
无机两不得，但弄秋水光。
兴尽钓亦罢，归来饮我觞。

《白居易集》，第 110 页。

LAZY MAN'S SONG
(A.D. 811)

I COULD have a job, but am too lazy to choose it;
I have got land, but am too lazy to farm it.
My house leaks; I am too lazy to mend it.
My clothes are torn; I am too lazy to darn them.
I have got wine, but I am too lazy to drink;
So it's just the same as if my cup were empty.
I have got a lute, but am too lazy to play;
So it's just the same as if it had no strings.
My family tells me there is no more steamed rice;
I want to cook, but am too lazy to grind.
My friends and relatives write me long letters;
I should like to read them, but they're such a bother to open.
I have always been told that Hsi Shu-yeh[1]
Passed his whole life in absolute idleness.
But he played his lute and sometimes worked at his forge;
So even *he* was not so lazy as I.

再
造
的
镜
像

---

[1] Hsi K'ang.

咏慵

有官慵不选，有田慵不农。
屋穿慵不葺，衣裂慵不缝。
有酒慵不酌，无异樽长空。
有琴慵不弹，亦与无弦同。
家人告饭尽，欲炊慵不舂。
亲朋寄书至，欲读慵开封。
尝闻嵇叔夜，一生在慵中。
弹琴复锻铁，比我未为慵。

《白居易集》，第 119 页。

WINTER NIGHT
Written during his retirement in 812

MY house is poor; those that I love have left me.
My body is sick; I cannot join the feast.
There is not a living soul before my eyes
As I lie alone locked in my cottage room.
My broken lamp burns with a feeble flame;
My tattered curtains are crooked and do not meet.
'Tsek, tsek' on the door-step and window-sill
Again I hear the new snow fall.
As I grow older, gradually I sleep less;
I wake at midnight and sit up straight in bed.
If I had not learned the 'art of sitting and forgetting'[1],
How could I bear this utter loneliness?
Stiff and stark my body cleaves to the earth;
Unimpeded my soul yields to Change[2].
So has it been for four tedious years,
Through one thousand and three hundred nights!

再
造
的
镜
像

---

[1] Yen Hui told Confucius that he had acquired the 'art of sitting and forgetting'. Asked what that meant, Yen Hui replied: 'I have learnt to discard my body and obliterate my intelligence; to abandon matter and be impervious to sense-perception. By this method I become one with the All-pervading.'—*Chuang Tzŭ*, chap. vi.

[2] 'Change' is the principle of endless mutation which governs the Universe.

冬夜

家贫亲爱散，身病交游罢：
眼前无一人，独掩村斋卧。
冷落灯火暗，离披帘幕破。
策策窗户前，又闻新雪下。
长年渐省睡，夜半起端坐；
不学坐忘心，寂寞安可过？
兀然身寄世，浩然心委化：
如此来四年，一千三百夜。

《白居易集》，第 120 页。

THE CHRYSANTHEMUMS IN THE EASTERN GARDEN
(A.D. 812)

THE days of my youth left me long ago;
And now in their turn dwindle my years of prime.
With what thoughts of sadness and loneliness
I walk again in this cold, deserted place!
In the midst of the garden long I stand alone;
The sunshine, faint; the wind and dew chill.
The autumn lettuce is tangled and turned to seed;
The fair trees are blighted and withered away.
All that is left are a few chrysanthemum-flowers
That have newly opened beneath the wattled fence.
I had brought wine and meant to fill my cup,
When the sight of these made me stay my hand.
I remember, when I was young,
How quickly my mood changed from sad to gay.
If I saw wine, no matter at what season,
Before I drank it, my heart was already glad.
But now that age comes
A moment of joy is harder and harder to get.
And always I fear that when I am quite old
The strongest liquor will leave me comfortless.
Therefore I ask you, late chrysanthemum-flower,
At this sad season why do you bloom alone?
Though well I know that it was not for my sake,
Taught by you, for a while I will smooth my frown.

东园玩菊

少年昨已去，芳岁今又阑；
如何寂寞意？复此荒凉园！
园中独立久，日淡风露寒；
秋蔬尽芜没，好树亦凋残。
唯有数丛菊，新开篱落间。
携觞聊就酌，为尔一留连。
忆我少小日，易为兴所牵：
见酒无时节，未饮已欣然。
近从年长来，渐觉取乐难；
常恐更衰老，强饮亦无欢。
顾谓尔菊花，后时何独鲜？
诚知不为我，借尔暂开颜。

《白居易集》，第 116 页。

THE TEMPLE

AUTUMN: the ninth year of Yüan Ho[①];
The eighth month, and the moon swelling her arc.
It was then I travelled to the Temple of Wu-chên,
A temple terraced on Wang Shun's Hill.
While still the mountain was many leagues away,
Of scurrying waters we heard the plash and fret.
From here the traveller, leaving carriage and horse,
Begins to wade through the shallows of the Blue Stream,
His hand pillared on a green holly-staff,
His feet treading the torrent's white stones.
A strange quiet stole on ears and eyes,
That knew no longer the blare of the human world.
From mountain-foot gazing at mountain-top,
Now we doubted if indeed it could be climbed;
Who had guessed that a path deep hidden there
Twisting and bending crept to the topmost brow?
Under the flagstaff we made our first halt;
Next we rested in the shadow of the Stone Shrine[②].

The shrine-room was scarce a cubit long,
With doors and windows unshuttered and unbarred.
I peered down, but could not see the dead;
Stalactites hung like a woman's hair.
Waked from sleep, a pair of white bats
Fled from the coffin with a whirr of snowy wings.
I turned away, and saw the Temple gate—
Scarlet eaves flanked by steeps of green;
'Twas as though a hand had ripped the mountain-side
And filled the cleft with a temple's walls and towers.
Within the gate, no level ground;
Little ground, but much empty sky.
Cells and cloisters, terraces and spires
High and low, followed the jut of the hill.
On rocky plateaux with no earth to hold
Were trees and shrubs, gnarled and very lean.
Roots and stems stretched to grip the stone;
Humped and bent, they writhed like a coiling snake.

---

① A.D. 814.

② Where the mummified bodies of priests were kept, in miniature temples.

游悟真寺诗一百三十韵

元和九年秋，八月月上弦。
我游悟真寺，寺在王顺山。
去山四五里，先闻水潺湲。
自兹舍车马，始涉蓝溪湾。
手拄青竹杖，足踏白石滩。
渐怪耳目旷，不闻人世喧。
山下望山上，初疑不可攀；
谁知中有路，盘折通岩巅。
一息幡竿下，再休石龛边。
龛间长丈余，门户无扃关；
俯窥不见人，石发垂若鬟。
惊出白蝙蝠，双飞如雪翻。
回首寺门望，青崖夹朱轩；
如擘山腹开，置寺于其间。
入门无平地，地窄虚空宽；
房廊与台殿，高下随峰峦。
岩崿无撮土，树木多瘦坚。
根株抱石长，屈曲虫蛇蟠。

In broken ranks pine and cassia
stood,
Through the four seasons forever
shady-green.
On tender twigs and delicate
branches breathing
A quiet music played like strings in
the wind.
Never pierced by the light of sun or
moon,
Green locked with green, shade
clasping shade.
A hidden bird sometimes softly
sings;
Like a cricket's chirp sounds its
muffled song.

At the Strangers' Arbour a while we
stayed our steps;
We sat down, but had no mind to
rest.
In a little while we had opened the
northern door.
Ten thousand leagues suddenly
stretched at our feet!
Brushing the eaves, shredded
rainbows swept;
Circling the beams, clouds spun and
whirled.
Through red sunlight white rain fell;
Azure and storm swam in a blended
stream.
In a wild green clustered grasses and
trees,
The eye's orbit swallowed the plain
of Ch'in.
Wei River was too small to see;

The Mounds of Han[①], littler than a
clenched fist.
I looked back; a line of red fence.
Broken and twisting, marked the way
we had trod.
Far below, toiling one by one
Later climbers straggled on the face of
the hill.

Straight before me were many
Treasure Towers,
Whose wind-bells at the four corners
sang.
At door and window, cornice and
architrave
A thick cluster of gold and green-jade.
Some say that here the Buddha
Kāśyapa[②]
Long ago quitted Life and Death.
Still they keep his iron begging-bowl,
With the furrow of his fingers
chiselled deep at the base.
To the east there opens the jade Image
Hall,
Where white Buddhas sit like serried
trees.
We shook from our garments the
journey's grime and dust,
And bowing worshipped those faces
of frozen snow
Whose white cassocks like folded
hoar-frost hung,
Whose beaded crowns glittered like a
shower of hail.

---

① The tombs of the Han Emperors.
② Lived about 600,000,000,000 years ago and achieved Buddhahood at the age of 20,000.

松桂乱无行，四时郁芊芊。
枝梢袅清吹，韵若风中弦。
日月光不透，绿阴相交延。
幽鸟时一声，闻之似寒蝉。
首憩宾位亭，就坐未及安；
须臾开北户，万里明豁然。
拂檐虹霏微，绕栋云回旋。
赤日间白雨，阴晴同一川。
野绿簇草树，眼界吞秦原。
渭水细不见，汉陵小于拳。
却顾来时路，萦纡映朱栏；
历历上山人，一一遥可观。
前对多宝塔，风铎鸣四端；
栾栌与户牖，袷恰金碧繁。
云昔迦叶佛，此地坐涅槃；
至今铁钵在，当底手迹穿。
西开玉像殿，白佛森比肩：
抖擞尘埃衣，礼拜冰雪颜。
叠霜为袈裟，贯雹为华鬘；

We looked closer; surely Spirits willed
This handicraft, never chisel carved!
Next we climbed to the Chamber of Kuan-yin[①];
From afar we sniffed its odours of sandal-wood.
At the top of the steps each doffed his shoes;
With bated stride we crossed the Jasper Hall.
The Jewelled Mirror on six pillars propped,
The Four Seats cased in hammered gold
Through the black night glowed with beams of their own,
Nor had we need to light candle or lamp.
These many treasures in concert nodded and swayed—
Banners of coral, pendants of cornaline.
When the wind came jewels chimed and sang
Softly, softly like the music of Paradise.
White pearls like frozen dewdrops hanging;
Dark rubies spilt like clots of blood,

Spangled and sown on the Buddha's twisted hair,
Together fashioned his Sevenfold Jewel-crown.
In twin vases of pallid tourmaline
(Their colour colder than the waters of an autumn stream)
The calcined relics of Buddha's Body rest—
Rounded pebbles, smooth as the Specular Stone.
A jade flute, by angels long ago
Borne as a gift to the Garden of Jetavan![②]
It blows a music sweet as the crane's song
That Spirits of Heaven earthward well might draw.

It was at autumn's height,
The fifteenth day and the moon's orbit full.
Wide I flung the three eastern gates;
A golden spectra walked at the chapel-door!
And now with moonbeams jewel-beams strove,
In freshness and beauty darting a crystal light
That cooled the spirit and limbs of all it touched,
Nor night-long needed they to rest.

---

① One of the self-denying Bodhisattvas who abstain from entering Buddhahood in order better to assist erring humanity. In Sanskrit, Avalokitesvara.

② Near Benares; here Buddha preached most of his Sūtras and the first monastery was founded.

逼观疑鬼功，其迹非雕镌。
次登观音堂，未到闻栴檀：
上阶脱双履，敛足升净筵。
六楹排玉镜，四座敷金钿；
黑夜自光明，不待灯烛燃。
众宝互低昂，碧珮珊瑚幡；
风来似天乐，相触声珊珊。
白珠垂露凝，赤珠滴血殷；
点缀佛髻上，合为七宝冠。
双瓶白琉璃，色若秋水寒；
隔瓶见舍利，圆转如金丹。
玉笛何代物？天人施祇园：
吹如秋鹤声，可以降灵仙。
是时秋方中，三五月正圆：
宝堂豁三门，金魄当其前。
月与宝相射，晶光争鲜妍。
照人心骨冷，竟夕不欲眠。

At dawn I sought the road to the Southern Tope,
Where wild bamboos nodded in clustered grace.
In the lonely forest no one crossed my path;
Beside me faltered a cold butterfly.
Mountain fruits whose names I did not know
With their prodigal bushes hedged the pathway in;
The hungry here copious food had found;
Idly I plucked, to test sour and sweet.

South of the road, the Spirit of the Blue Dell[①],
With his green umbrella and white paper pence!
When the year is closing, the people are ordered to grow,
As herbs of offering, marsil and motherwort;
So sacred the place, that never yet was stained
Its pure earth with sacrificial blood.

In a high cairn four or five rocks
Dangerously heaped, deep-scarred and heeling—
With what purpose did he that made the World
Pile them here at the eastern corner of the cliff!
Their slippery flank no foot has marked,

But mosses stipple like a flowered writing-scroll.
I came to the cairn, I climbed it right to the top;
Beneath my feet a measureless chasm dropped.
My eyes were dizzy, hand and knee quaked—
I did not dare bend my head and look.
A boisterous wind rose from under the rocks,
Seized me with it and tore the ground from my feet.
My shirt and robe fanned like mighty wings,
And wide-spreading bore me like a bird to the sky.
High about me, triangular and sharp,
Like a cluster of sword-points many summits rose.
The white mist that struck them in its airy course
They tore asunder, and carved a patch of blue.

And now the sun was sinking in the north-west;
His evening beams from a crimson globe he shed,
Till far beyond the great fields of green
His sulphurous disk suddenly down he drove.

---

① A native, non-Buddhist deity.

晓寻南塔路，乱竹低婵娟；
林幽不逢人，寒蝶飞翾翾。
山果不识名，离离夹道蕃；
足以疗饥乏，摘尝味甘酸。
道南蓝谷神，紫伞白纸钱：
若岁有水旱，诏使修蘋蘩；
以地清净故，献奠无荤膻。
危石叠四五，垒嵬欹且刓；
造物者何意，堆在岩东偏；
冷滑无人迹，苔点如花笺。
我来登上头，下临不测渊；
目眩手足掉，不敢低头看。
风从石下生，薄人而上抟：
衣服似羽翮，开张欲飞搴。
岌岌三面峰，峰尖刀剑攒；
往往白云过，决开露青天。
西北日落时，夕晖红团团；
千里翠屏外，走下丹砂丸。

And now the moon was rising in the south-east;
In waves of coolness the night air flowed.
From the grey bottom of the hundred-fathom pool
Shines out the image of the moon's golden disk!
Blue as its name, the Lan River flows
Singing and plashing forever day and night.
I gazed down; like a green finger-ring
In winding circuits it follows the curves of the hill,
Sometimes spreading to a wide, lazy stream,
Sometimes striding to a foamy cataract.
Out from the deepest and clearest pool of all,
In a strange froth the Dragon's-spittle[1] flows.

I bent down; a dangerous ladder of stones
Paved beneath me a sheer and dizzy path.
I gripped the ivy, I walked on fallen trees,
Tracking the monkeys who came to drink at the stream.
Like a whirl of snowflakes the startled herons rose,
In damask dances the red sturgeon leapt.
For a while I rested, then plunging in the cool stream,
From my weary body I washed the stains away.
Deep or shallow, all was crystal clear;
I watched through the water my own thighs and feet.
Content I gazed at the stream's clear bed;
Wondered, but knew not, whence its waters flowed.

The eastern bank with rare stones is rife;
In serried courses the azure malachite,
That outward turns a smooth, glossy face;
In its deep core secret diamonds[2] lie,
Pien of Ch'u[3] died long ago,
And rare gems are often cast aside.
Sometimes a radiance leaks from the hill by night
To link its beams with the brightness of moon and stars.

---

① Ambergris.

② The stone mentioned (*yü-fan*), though praised by Confucius and used in the ceremonies of his native state, cannot be identified. Its name evokes vague ideas of rarity and beauty.

③ Suffered mutilation because he had offered to his prince a gem which experts rejected. Afterwards it turned out to be genuine.

东南月上时，夜气青漫漫；
百丈碧潭底，写出黄金盘。
蓝水色似蓝，日夜长潺潺；
周回绕山转，下视如青环。
或铺为慢流，或激为奔湍；
泓澄最深处，浮出蛟龙涎。
侧身入其中，悬磴尤险难。
扪萝踏樛木，下逐饮涧猿。
雪迸起白鹭，锦跳惊红鳣。
歇定方盥漱，濯去支体烦；
浅深皆洞澈，可照脑与肝。
但爱清见底，欲寻不知源。
东崖饶怪石，积甃苍琅玕；
温润发于外，其间韫玙璠。
卞和死已久，良玉多弃捐；
或时泄光彩，夜与星月连。

At the central dome, where the hills highest rise,
The sky is pillared on a column of green jade;
Where even the spotty lizard cannot climb
Can I, a man, foothold hope to find?
In the top is hollowed the White-lotus lake;
With purple cusps the clear waves are crowned.
The name I heard, but the place I could not reach;
Beyond the region of mortal things it lies.
And standing here, a flat rock I saw,
Cubit-square, like a great paving-stone,
Midway up fastened in the cliff-wall;
And down below it, a thousand-foot drop.
Here they say that a Master in ancient days
Sat till he conquered the concepts of Life and Death.
The place is called the Settled Heart Stone;
By aged men the tale is still told.

I turned back to the Shrine of Fairies' Tryst;
Thick creepers covered its old walls.
Here it was that a mortal[①] long ago
On new-grown wings flew to the dark sky;
Westward a garden of agaric and rue
Faces the terrace where his magic herbs were dried.
And sometimes still on clear moonlit nights
In the sky is heard a yellow-crane's voice.

I turned and sought the Painted Dragon Hall,
Where the bearded figures of two ancient men
By the Holy Lectern at sermon-time are seen
In gleeful worship to nod their hoary heads;
Who, going home to their cave beneath the river,
Of weather-dragons the writhing shapes assume
When rain is coming they puff a white smoke
In front of the steps, from a round hole in the stone.

---

① The wizard Wang Shun after whom the hill is named?

中顶最高峰，拄天青玉竿；
嗣嶺上不得，岂我能攀援？
上有白莲池，素葩覆清澜。
闻名不可到，处所非人寰。
又有一片石，大如方尺砖；
插在半壁上，其下万仞悬。
云有过去师，坐得无生禅；
号为定心石，长老世相传。
却上谒仙祠，蔓草生绵绵：
昔闻王氏子，羽化升上玄。
其西晒药台，犹对芝术田；
时复明月夜，上闻黄鹤言。
回寻画龙堂，二叟鬓发斑：
想见听法时，欢喜礼印坛；
复归泉窟下，化作龙蜿蜒。
阶前石孔在，欲雨生白烟。

Once a priest[①] who copied the Holy Books
(Of purpose dauntless and body undefiled)
Loved yonder pigeons, that far beyond the clouds
Fly in flocks beating a thousand wings.
They came and dropped him water in his writing-bowl;
Then sipped afresh in the river under the rocks.
Each day thrice they went and came,
Nor ever once missed their wonted time.
When the Book was finished they sent for a holy priest,
A disciple of his, named Yang-nan.
He sang the hymns of the Lotus Blossom Book[②],
Again and again, a thousand, a million times.
His body perished, but his mouth still spoke,
The tongue resembling a red lotus-flower.
Today this relic is no longer shown;
But they still treasure the pyx in which it lies.

On a plastered wall are frescoes from the hand of Wu[③],
Whose pencil-colours never-fading glow.
On a white screen is writing by the master Ch'u[④],
The tones subtle as the day it first dried.

Magical prospects, monuments divine—
Now all were visited.
Here we had tarried five nights and days;
Yet homeward now with loitering footsteps trod.
I, that a man of the wild hills was born,
Floundering fell into the web of the World's net.
Caught in its trammels, they forced me to study books;
Twitched and tore me down the path of public life.
Soon I rose to be Bachelor of Arts;
In the Record Office, in the Censorate I sat.
My simple bluntness did not suit the times;
A profitless servant, I drew the royal pay.

---

① Fa-ch'èng, A.D. 563-640.

② The verses of the Saddharmapundarika Sūtra, *Sacred Books of the East,* vol. 21.

③ The great eighth-century painter, Wu Tao-tzǔ.

④ The calligrapher, Ch'u Sui-liang, A.D. 596-658.

往有写经僧，身静心精专。
感彼云外鸽，群飞千翩翩；
来添砚中水，去吸岩底泉；
一日三往复，时节长不愆。
经成号圣僧，弟子名杨难；
诵此莲花偈，数满百亿千；
身坏口不坏，舌根如红莲。
颅骨今不见，石函尚存焉。
粉壁有吴画，笔彩依旧鲜。
素屏有褚书，墨色如新干。
灵境与异迹，周览无不殚。
一游五昼夜，欲返仍盘桓。
我本山中人，误为时网牵：
牵率使读书，推挽令劾官。
既登文字科，又忝谏诤员；
拙直不合时，无益同素餐。

The sense of this made me always ashamed,
And every pleasure a deep brooding dimmed.
To little purpose I sapped my heart's strength,
Till seeming age shrank my youthful frame.
From the very hour I doffed belt and cap
I marked how with them sorrow slank away.
But now that I wander in the freedom of streams and hills
My heart to its folly comfortably yields.
Like a wild deer that has torn the hunter's net
I range abroad by no halters barred.
Like a captive fish loosed into the Great Sea
To my marble basin I shall not ever return.
My body girt in the hermit's single dress,
My hands holding the Book of Chuang Chou[①],
On these hills at last I am come to dwell,
Loosed forever from the shackles of a trim world,
I have lived in labour forty years and more;
If Life's remnant vacantly I spend,
Seventy being our span, then thirty years
Of idleness are still left to live.

---

① The great Taoist philosopher, see my *Three ways of Thought Ancient China*, 1939.

以此自惭惕，戚戚常寡欢；
无成心力尽，未老形骸残。
今来脱簪组，始觉离忧患；
及为山水游，弥得纵疏顽。
野麋断羁绊，行走无拘挛；
池鱼放入海，一往何时还！
身著居士衣，手把南华篇；
终来此山住，永谢区中缘。
我今四十余，从此终身闲；
若以七十期，犹得三十年。

《白居易集》，第 120—123 页。

ILLNESS AND IDLENESS
(A.D. 812)

ILLNESS and idleness give me much leisure.
What do I do with my leisure, when it comes?
I cannot bring myself to discard inkstone and brush;
Now and then I make a new poem.
When the poem is made, it is slight and flavourless,
A thing of derision to almost every one.
Superior people will be pained at the flatness of the metre;
Common people will hate the plainness of the words.
I sing it to myself, then stop and think about it...

The Prefects of Soochow and P'êng-tsē[①]
Would perhaps have praised it, but they died long ago.
Who else would care to hear it?
No one to-day except Yüan Chên,
And *he* is banished to the City of Chiang-ling,
For three years a Clerk of Public Works.
Parted from me by three thousand leagues,
He will never know even that the poem was made.

---

① Wei Ying-wu, eighth century A.D., and T'ao Ch'ien, A.D., 365-427.

自吟拙什，因有所怀

懒病每多暇，暇来何所为？
未能抛笔砚，时作一篇诗。
诗成淡无味，多被众人嗤：
上怪落声韵，下嫌拙言词。
时时自吟咏，吟罢有所思：
苏州及彭泽，与我不同时。
此外复谁爱？唯有元微之：
趁向江陵府，三年作判司。
相去二千里，诗成远不知。

《白居易集》，第 118 页。

POEMS IN DEPRESSION, AT WEI VILLAGE
(A.D. 812)

再
造
的
镜
像

I

I HUG my pillow and do not speak a word;
In my empty room no sound stirs.
Who knows that, all day a-bed,
I am not ill and am not even asleep?

II

TURNED to jade are the boy's rosy cheeks;
To his sick temples the frost of winter clings...
Do not wonder that my body sinks to decay;
Though my limbs are old, my heart is older yet.

昼卧

抱枕无言语，空房独悄然。
谁知尽日卧，非病亦非眠。

答友问

似玉童颜尽，如霜病鬓新。
莫惊身顿老，心更老于身！

《白居易集》，第 289 页。

ILLNESS

SAD, sad—lean with long illness;
Monotonous, monotonous—days and nights pass.
The summer trees have clad themselves in shade;
The autumn 'lan' already houses the dew.
The eggs that lay in the nest when I took to bed
Have changed into little birds and flown away.
The worm that then lay hidden in its hole
Has hatched into a cricket sitting on the tree.
The Four Seasons go on for ever and ever;
In all Nature nothing stops to rest
Even for a moment. Only the sick man's heart
Deep down still aches as of old!

村居卧病三首（其一）

戚戚抱羸病，悠悠度朝暮。
夏木才结阴，秋兰已含露。
前日巢中卵，化作雏飞去。
昨日穴中虫，蜕为蝉上树。
四时未常歇，一物不暂住。
唯有病客心，沉然独如故。

《白居易集》，第 193 页。

HERMIT AND POLITICIAN

'I WAS going to the City to sell the herbs I had plucked;
On the way I rested by some trees at the Blue Gate.
Along the road there came a horseman riding,
Whose face was pale with a strange look of dread.
Friends and relations, waiting to say good-bye,
Pressed at his side, but he did not dare to pause.
I, in wonder, asked the people about me
Who he was and what had happened to him.
They told me this was a Privy Councillor
Whose grave duties were like the pivot of State.
His food allowance was ten thousand cash;
Three times a day the Emperor came to his house.
Yesterday his counsel was sought by the Throne;
Today he is banished to the country of Yai-chou[1].
So always, the Counsellors of Kings;
Favour and ruin changed between dawn and dusk!'

Green, green—the grass of the Eastern Suburb;
And amid the grass, a road that leads to the hills.
Resting in peace among the white clouds,
Can the hermit doubt that he chose the better part?

---

[1] In the south of the island of Hainan, off Kwangtung.

寄隐者

卖药向都城，行憩青门树。
道逢驰驿者，色有非常惧。
亲族走相送，欲别不敢住。
私怪问道旁，何人复何故？
云是右丞相，当国握枢务。
禄厚食万钱，恩深日三顾。
昨日延英对，今日崖州去。
由来君臣间，宠辱在朝暮。
青青东郊草，中有归山路；
归去卧云人，谋身计非误。

《白居易集》，第 25 页。

REJOICING AT THE ARRIVAL OF CH'ÊN HSIUNG
(A.D. 814)

WHEN the yellow bird's note was almost stopped,
And half formed the green plum's fruit—
Sitting and grieving that spring things were over,
I rose and entered the Eastern Garden's gate.
I carried my cup and was dully drinking alone;
Suddenly I heard a knocking sound at the door.
Dwelling secluded, I was glad that someone had come;
How much the more, when I saw it was Ch'ên Hsiung!
At ease and leisure—all day we talked;
Crowding and jostling—the feelings of many years.
How great a thing is a single cup of wine!
For it makes us tell the story of our whole lives.

喜陈兄至

黄鸟啼欲歇，青梅结半成：
坐怜春物尽，起入东园行。
携觞懒独酌，忽闻叩门声。
闲人犹喜至，何况是陈兄？
从容尽日语，稠叠长年情。
勿轻一盏酒，可以话平生。

《白居易集》，第 125 页。

REMEMBERING GOLDEN BELLS

再
造
的
镜
像

RUINED and ill—a man of two score;
Pretty and guileless—a girl of three.
Not a boy—but still better than nothing:
To soothe one's feeling—from time to time a kiss!
There came a day—they suddenly took her from me;
Her soul's shadow wandered I know not where.
And when I remember how just at the time she died
She lisped strange sounds, beginning to learn to talk,
Then I know that the ties of flesh and blood
Only bind us to a load of grief and sorrow.
At last, by thinking of the time before she was born,
By thought and reason I drove the pain away.
Since my heart forgot her, many days have passed
And three times winter has changed to spring.
This morning, for a little, the old grief came back,
Because, in the road, I met her foster-nurse.

念金銮子二首（其一）

衰病四十身，娇痴三岁女；
非男犹胜无，慰情时一抚。
一朝舍我去，魂影无处所！
况念夭化时，呕哑初学语。
始知骨肉爱，乃是忧悲聚。
唯思未有前，以理遣伤苦。
忘怀日已久，三度移寒暑。
今日一伤心，因逢旧乳母。

《白居易集》，第 191 页。

KEPT WAITING IN THE BOAT AT CHIU-K'OU TEN DAYS BY AN ADVERSE WIND
(A.D. 815)

WHITE billows and huge waves block the river crossing;
Wherever I go, danger and difficulty; whatever I do, failure.
Just as in my worldly career I wander and lose the road,
So when I come to the river crossing, I am stopped by contrary winds.
Of fishes and prawns sodden in the rain the smell fills my nostrils;
With the stings of insects that come with the fog my whole body is sore.
I am growing old, time flies, and my short span runs out,
While I sit in a boat at Chiu-k'ou[①], wasting ten days!

再
造
的
镜
像

臼口阻风十日

洪涛白浪塞江津，处处邅回事事迍。
世上方为失途客，江头又作阻风人。
鱼虾遇雨腥盈鼻，蚊蚋和烟痒满身。
老大光阴能几日？等闲臼口坐经旬。

《白居易集》，第 315 页。

ON BOARD SHIP: READING YÜAN CHÊN'S POEMS

再
造
的
镜
像

I TAKE your poems in my hand and read them beside the candle;
The poems are finished, the candle is low, dawn not yet come.
My eyes smart; I put out the lamp and go on sitting in the dark,
Listening to waves that, driven by the wind, strike the prow of the ship.

舟中读元九诗

把君诗卷灯前读，诗尽灯残天未明。
眼痛灭灯犹暗坐，逆风吹浪打船声。

《白居易集》，第 316 页。

STARTING EARLY FROM THE CH'U-CH'ÊNG INN
(A.D. 815)

WASHED by the rain, dust and grime are laid;

Skirting the river, the road's course is flat.

The moon has risen on the last remnants of night;

The travellers' speed profits by the early cold.

In the great silence I whisper a faint song;

In the black darkness are bred sombre thoughts.

On the lotus-bank hovers a dewy breeze;

Through the rice furrows trickles a singing stream.

At the noise of our bells a sleeping dog stirs;

At the sight of our torches a roosting bird wakes.

Dawn glimmers through the shapes of misty trees…

For ten miles, till day at last breaks.

再
造
的
镜
像

早发楚城驿

雨过尘埃灭，沿江道径平。
月乘残夜出，人趁早凉行。
寂历闲吟动，冥濛暗思生。
荷塘翻露气，稻垄泻泉声。
宿犬闻铃起，栖禽见火惊。
昽昽烟树色，十里始天明。

《白居易集》，第 341 页。

ARRIVING AT HSÜN-YANG

(Two Poems)

I

A BEND of the river brings into view two triumphal arches;
That is the gate in the western wall of the suburbs of Hsün-yang.
I have still to travel in my solitary boat three or four leagues—
By misty waters and rainy sands, while the yellow dusk thickens.

II

We are almost come to Hsün-yang; how my thoughts are stirred
As we pass to the south of Yü Liang's tower and the east of P'ên Port.
The forest trees are leafless and withered—after the mountain rain;
The roofs of the houses are hidden low among the river mists.
The horses, fed on water grass, are too weak to carry their load;
The cottage walls of wattle and thatch let the wind blow on one's bed.
In the distance I see red-wheeled coaches driving from the towngate;
They have taken the trouble, these civil people, to meet their new Prefect!

再
造
的
镜
像

望江州

江回望见双华表，知是浔阳西郭门。
犹去孤舟三四里，水烟沙雨欲黄昏。

初到江州

浔阳欲到思无穷，庾亮楼南溢口东。
树木凋疏山雨后，人家低湿水烟中。
菰蒋喂马行无力，芦荻编房卧有风。
遥见朱轮来出郭，相迎劳动使君公。

《白居易集》，第 320—321 页。

TO HIS BROTHER HSING-CHIEN, WHO WAS SERVING IN TUNG-CH'UAN

(Eastern Ssechuan)

(A.D. 815)

SULLEN, sullen, my brows are ever knit;

Silent, silent, my lips will not move.

It is not indeed that I choose to sorrow thus;

If I lift my eyes, who would share my joy?

Last Spring *you* were called to the West

To carry arms in the lands of Pa and Shu;

And this Spring *I* was banished to the South

To nurse my sickness on the River's oozy banks.

You are parted from me by six thousand leagues;

In another world, under another sky.

Of ten letters, nine do not reach;

What can I do to open my sad face?

Thirsty men often dream of drink;

Hungry men often dream of food.

Since Spring came where do my dreams lodge?

Ere my eyes are closed, I have travelled to Tung-ch'uan.

寄行简

郁郁眉多敛，默默口寡言。
岂是愿如此，举目谁与欢！
去春尔西征，从事巴蜀间。
今春我南谪，抱疾江海壖。
相去六千里，地绝天邈然。
十书九不达，何以开忧颜？
渴人多梦饮，饥人多梦餐。
春来梦何处？合眼到东川。

《白居易集》，第 202 页。

RAIN

(A.D. 815)

SINCE I lived a stranger in the City of Hsün-yang
Hour by hour bitter rain has poured.
On few days has the dark sky cleared;
In listless sleep I have spent much time.
The lake has widened till it almost joins the sky;
The clouds sink till they touch the water's face.
Beyond my hedge I hear the boatman's talk;
At the street-end I hear the fisher's song.
Misty birds are lost in yellow air;
Windy sails kick the white waves.
In front of my gate the horse and carriage-way
In a single night has turned into a river-bed.

霖雨苦多，江湖暴涨，块然独望，因题北亭

自作浔阳客，无如苦雨何！
阴昏晴日少，闲闷睡时多。
湖阔将天合，云低与水和。
篱根舟子语，巷口钓人歌。
雾鸟沉黄气，风帆蹙白波。
门前车马道，一宿变江河。

《白居易集》，第 332 页。

RELEASING A MIGRANT 'YEN'
(WILD GOOSE)

AT Nine Rivers[1], in the tenth year[2], in winter—heavy snow;

The river-water covered with ice and the forests broken with their load[3].

The birds of the air, hungry and cold, went flying east and west;

And with them flew a migrant 'yen', loudly clamouring for food.

Among the snow it pecked for grass, and rested on the surface of the ice;

It tried with its wings to scale the sky, but its tired flight was slow.

The boys of the river spread a net and caught the bird as it flew;

They took it in their hands to the city-market and sold it there alive.

I that was once a man of the North am now an exile here;

Bird and man, in their different kind, are each strangers in the south.

And because the sight of an exiled bird wounded an exile's heart,

I paid your ransom and set you free, and you flew away to the clouds.

Yen, Yen, flying to the clouds, tell me, whither shall you go?

Of all things I bid you, do not fly to the land of the north-west.

In Huai-hsi there are rebel bands[4] that have not been subdued;

And a thousand thousand armoured men have long been camped in war.

The official army and the rebel army have grown old in their opposite trenches;

The soldier's rations have grown so small, they'll be glad of even you.

The brave boys, in their hungry plight, will shoot you and eat your flesh;

They will pluck from your body those long feathers and make them into
arrow-wings!

---

[1] Kiukiang, the poet's place of exile.

[2] A.D. 815. His first winter at Kiukiang.

[3] By the weight of snow.

[4] The revolt of Wu Yüan-chi, put down in A.D. 817.

放旅雁（元和十年冬作）

九江十年冬大雪，江水生冰树枝折。
百鸟无食东西飞，中有旅雁声最饥；
雪中啄草冰上宿，翅冷腾空飞动迟。
江童持网捕将去，手携入市生卖之。
我本北人今谴谪，人鸟虽殊同是客。
见此客鸟伤客人，赎汝放汝飞入云。
雁雁汝飞向何处？第一莫飞西北去。
淮西有贼讨未平，百万甲兵久屯聚。
官军贼军相守老，食尽兵穷将及汝。
健儿饥饿射汝吃，拔汝翅翎为箭羽。

《白居易集》，第 232—233 页。

THE BEGINNING OF SUMMER
(A.D. 815)

AT the rise of summer a hundred beasts and trees
Join in gladness that the Season bids them thrive.
Stags and does frolic in the deep woods;
Snakes and insects are pleased by the rank grass.
Winged birds love the thick leaves;
Scaly fish enjoy the fresh weeds.
But to one place Summer forgot to come;
I alone am left like a withered straw…
In solitude, banished to the world's end;
Flesh and bone all in distant ways.
From my native place no tidings come;
Rebel troops flood the land with war.
Sullen grief in the end, what will it bring?
I am only wearing my own heart away.
Better far to let both body and mind
Blindly yield to the fate that Heaven made.
Hsün-yang abounds in good wine;
I will fill my cup and never let it be dry.
On P'ên River fish are cheap as mud;
Early and late I will eat them, boiled and fried.
With morning rice at the temple under the hill,
And evening wine at the island in the lake…
Why should my thoughts turn to my native land?
For in this place one could well end one's age.

首夏

孟夏百物滋，动植一时好。
麋鹿乐深林，虫蛇喜丰草。
翔禽爱密叶，游鳞悦新藻。
天和遗漏处，而我独枯槁。
一身在天末，骨肉皆远道。
旧国无来人，寇戎尘浩浩。
沉忧竟何益？只自劳怀抱。
不如放身心，冥然任天造。
浔阳多美酒，可使杯不燥。
溢鱼贱如泥，烹炙无昏早。
朝饭山下寺，暮醉湖中岛。
何必归故乡？兹焉可终老！

《白居易集》，第 202 页。

HEARING THE EARLY ORIOLE

(*c*.A.D. 816)

再
造
的
镜
像

WHEN the sun rose I was still lying in bed;

An early oriole sang on the roof of my house.

For a moment I thought of the Royal Park at dawn

When the birds of Spring greeted their Lord from his trees.

I remembered the days when I served before the Throne

Pencil in hand, on duty at the Ch'êng-ming;

At the height of spring, when I paused from drafting papers,

Morning and evening, was *this* the voice I heard?

Now in my exile the oriole sings again

In the dreary stillness of Hsün-yang town...

The bird's note cannot really have changed;

All the difference lies in the listener's heart.

If he could but forget that he lives at the world's end,

The bird would sing as it sang in the Palace of old.

闻早莺

日出眠未起，屋头闻早莺；
忽如上林晓，万年枝上鸣。
忆为近臣时，秉笔直承明：
春深视草暇，旦暮闻此声。
今闻在何处？寂寞浔阳城！
鸟声信如一，分别在人情；
不作天涯意，岂殊禁中听？

《白居易集》，第 134 页。

DREAMING THAT I WENT WITH LI AND YÜ TO VISIT YÜAN CHÊN
(Written in exile)

AT night I dreamt I was back in Ch'ang-an;

I saw again the faces of old friends.

And in my dreams, under an April sky,

They led me by the hand to wander in the spring winds.

Together we came to the ward of Peace and Quiet;

We stopped our horses at the gate of Yüan Chên.

Yüan Chên was sitting all alone;

When he saw me coming, a smile came to his face.

He pointed back at the flowers in the western court;

Then opened wine in the northern summer-house.

He seemed to be saying that neither of us had changed;

He seemed to be regretting that joy will not stay;

That our souls had met only for a little while,

To part again with hardly time for greeting.

I woke up and thought him still at my side;

I put out my hand; there was nothing there at all.

再
造
的
镜
像

梦与李七、庚三十二同访元九（节选）

夜梦归长安，见我故亲友：
损之在我左，顺之在我右。
云是二月天，春风出携手；
同过靖安里，下马寻元九。
元九正独坐，见我笑开口。
还指西院花，仍开北亭酒。
如言各有故，似惜欢难久。
神合俄顷间，神离欠申后；
觉来疑在侧，求索无所有。

《白居易集笺校》，第 571 页。

MADLY SINGING IN THE MOUNTAINS

再
造
的
镜
像

THERE is no one among men that has not a special failing;
And my failing consists in writing verses.
I have broken away from the thousand ties of life;
But this infirmity still remains behind.
Each time that I look at a fine landscape,
Each time that I meet a loved friend,
I raise my voice and recite a stanza of poetry
And marvel as though a God had crossed my path.
Ever since the day I was banished to Hsün-yang
Half my time I have lived among the hills.
And often, when I have finished a new poem,
Alone I climb the road to the Eastern Rock.
I lean my body on the banks of white Stone;
I pull down with my hands a green cassia branch.
My mad singing startles the valleys and hills;
The apes and birds all come to peep.
Fearing to become a laughing-stock to the world,
I choose a place that is unfrequented by men.

山中独吟

人各有一癖，我癖在章句；
万缘皆已销，此病独未去。
每逢美风景，或对好亲故：
高声咏一篇，恍若与神遇。
自为江上客，半在山中住。
有时新诗成，独上东岩路。
身倚白石崖，手攀青桂树；
狂吟惊林壑，猿鸟皆窥觑。
恐为世所嗤，故就无人处。

《白居易集》，第 146 页。

AFTER LUNCH

AFTER lunch—one short nap;
On waking up—two cups of tea.
Raising my head, I see the sun's light
Once again slanting to the south-west.
Those who are happy regret the shortness of the day;
Those who are sad tire of the year's sloth.
But those whose hearts are devoid of joy or sadness
Just go on living, regardless of 'short' or 'long'.

再
造
的
镜
像

食后

食罢一觉睡，起来两瓯茶。
举头看日影，已复西南斜。
乐人惜日促，忧人厌年赊。
无忧无乐者，长短任生涯。

《白居易集》，第 143 页。

VISITING THE HSI-LIN TEMPLE
(A.D. 817)

I DISMOUNT from my horse at the Hsi-lin Temple;
I hurry forward, speeding with light cane.
In the morning I work at a Govemment office-desk;
In the evening I become a dweller in the Sacred Hills.
In the second month to the north of K'uang-lu
The ice breaks and the snow begins to melt.
On the southern plantation the tea-plant thrusts its sprouts;
Through the northern crevice the veins of the spring ooze.

This year there is war in An-hui,
In every place soldiers are rushing to arms.
Men of learning have been summoned to the Council Board;
Men of action are marching to the battle-line.
Only I, who have no talents at all,
Am left in the mountains to play with the pebbles of the stream.

再
造
的
镜
像

| 412

春游西林寺①（节选）

下马西林寺，翛然进轻策；
朝为公府吏，暮是灵山客。
二月匡庐北，冰雪始消释：
阳丛抽茗芽，阴窦泄泉脉。
······
是年淮寇起，处处兴兵革。
智士劳思谋，戎臣苦征役。
独有不才者，山中弄泉石！

《白居易集》，第 133 页。

---

① 诗题亦作"春游二林寺"。

EATING BAMBOO-SHOOTS

MY new Province is a land of bamboo-groves:

Their shoots in spring fill the valleys and hills.

The mountain woodman cuts an armful of them

And brings them down to sell at the early market.

Things are cheap in proportion as they are common;

For two farthings I buy a whole bundle.

I put the shoots in a great earthen pot

And heat them up along with boiling rice.

The purple skins broken—like an old brocade;

The white skin opened—like new pearls.

Now every day I eat them recklessly;

For a long time I have not touched meat.

All the time I was living at Lo-yang

They could not give me enough to suit my taste.

Now I can have as many shoots as I please;

For each breath of the south-wind makes a new bamboo!

食笋

此州乃竹乡，春笋满山谷；
山夫折盈抱，抱来早市鬻。
物以多为贱，双钱易一束。
置之炊甑中，与饭同时熟。
紫箨坼故锦，素肌擘新玉。
每日遂加餐，经时不思肉。
久为京洛客，此味常不足。
且食勿踟蹰，南风吹作竹。

《白居易集》，第 135—136 页。

TO A PORTRAIT PAINTER WHO DESIRED HIM TO SIT

再
造
的
镜
像

YOU, so bravely plying reds and blues
Just when I am getting wrinkled and old!
Why should you waste the moments of inspiration
Tracing the withered limbs of a sick man?
Tall, tall is the Palace of the Unicorn[①];
But my deeds have not been frescoed on its walls.
Minutely limned on a foot of painting silk—
What can I do with a portrait such as that?

---

① A sort of National Portraint Gallery.

赠写真者

子骋丹青日，予当丑老时：
无劳役神思，更画病容仪。
迢递麒麟阁，图功未有期。
区区尺素上，焉用写真为？

《白居易集》，第 359 页。

SEPARATION

再
造
的
镜
像

YESTERDAY I heard that such-a-one was gone,
This morning they tell me that so-and-so is dead.
Of friends and acquaintances more than two-thirds
Have suffered change and passed to the Land of Ghosts.
Those that are gone I shall not see again;
They, alas, are for ever finished and done.
Those that are left—where are they now?
They are all scattered—a thousand miles away.
Those I have known and loved through all my life,
On the fingers of my hand—how many do I count?
Only the prefects of T'ung, Kuo and Li
And Fêng Province—just those four.[①]
Longing for each other we are all grown grey;
Through the Fleeting World rolled like a wave in the stream.
Alas that the feasts and frolics of old days
Have withered and vanished, bringing us to this!
When shall we meet and drink a cup of wine
And laughing gaze into each other's eyes?

---

① The Prefect of T'ung was Yüan Chên; the Prefect of Li was Li Chien (died A.D. 821).

感逝寄远

昨日闻甲死，今朝闻乙死。
知识三分中，二分化为鬼。
逝者不复见，悲哉长已矣！
存者今如何？去我皆万里。
平生知心者，屈指能有几？
通果澧凤州，眇然四君子。
相思俱老大，浮世如流水。
应叹旧交游，凋零日如此。
何当一杯酒？开眼笑相视！

《白居易集》，第 183 页。

HAVING CLIMBED TO THE TOPMOST PEAK OF THE INCENSE-BURNER MOUNTAIN

UP and up, the Incense-burner Peak!
In my heart is stored what my eyes and ears perceived.
All the year—detained by official business;
Today at last I got a chance to go.
Grasping the creepers, I clung to dangerous rocks;
My hands and feet—weary with groping for hold.
There came with me three or four friends,
But two friends dared not go further.
At last we reached the topmost crest of the Peak;
My eyes were blinded, my soul rocked and reeled.
The chasm beneath me—ten thousand feet;
The ground I stood on, only a foot wide.
If you have not exhausted the scope of seeing and hearing,
How can you realize the wideness of the world?
The waters of the River looked narrow as a ribbon,
P'ên Castle smaller than a man's fist.
How it clings, the dust of the world's halter!
It chokes my limbs; I cannot shake it away.
Coming home I thought this over and sighed;
Then, with lowered head, came back to the Ants' Nest.

登香炉峰顶

迢迢香炉峰，心存耳目想；
终年牵物役，今日方一往。
攀萝蹋危石，手足劳俯仰。
同游三四人，两人不敢上。
上到峰之顶，目眩神恍恍。
高低有万寻，阔狭无数丈。
不穷视听界，焉识宇宙广？
江水细如绳，湓城小于掌。
纷吾何屑屑？未能脱尘鞅。
归去思自嗟，低头入蚁壤！

《白居易集》，第 138 页。

THE FIFTEENTH VOLUME

(Having completed the fifteenth volume of his works, the poet sends it to his friends, Yüan Chên and Li Shên, with a jesting poem.)

(Written in 818)

MY long poem, the 'Eternal Grief',[1] is a beautiful and moving work;
My ten 'Songs of Shensi' are models of tunefulness.
I cannot prevent Old Yüan from stealing my best rhymes;
But Little Li by a bitter lesson has learnt respect for my songs.
While I am alive, riches and honour will never fall to my lot;
But well I know that after I am dead the fame of my books will live.
This random talk and foolish boasting forgive me, for today
I have added Volume Fifteen to the row that stands to my name.

---

[1] See Giles, *Chinese Literature*, p.169.

编集拙诗，成一十五卷，因题卷末，戏赠元九、李二十

一篇长恨有风情，十首秦吟近正声。
每被老元偷格律，苦教短李伏歌行。
世间富贵应无分，身后文章合有名。
莫怪气粗言语大，新排十五卷诗成。

《白居易集》，第 349 页。

ALARM AT FIRST ENTERING THE YANG-TZE GORGES

(Written in A.D. 819, when he was being towed up the rapids to Chung-chou, in Ssechwan)

ABOVE, a mountain ten thousand feet high;
Below, a river a thousand fathoms deep.
A strip of sky, walled by cliffs of stone;
Wide enough for the passage of a single reed.[1]
At Chü-t'ang a straight cleft yawns;
At Yen-yü islands block the stream.
Long before night the walls are black with dusk;
Without wind white waves rise.
The big rocks are like a flat sword;
The little rocks resemble ivory tusks.

We are stuck fast and cannot move a step.
How much the less, three hundred miles[2]?
Frail and slender, the twisted-bamboo rope;
Weak, the treacherous hold of the punters' feet.
A single slip—the whole convoy lost;
And *my* life hangs on *this* thread!
I have heard a saying 'He that has an upright heart
Shall walk scatheless through the lands of Man and Mo[3].'
How can I believe that since the world began
In every shipwreck none have drowned but rogues?
And how can I, born in evil days
And fresh from failure, ask a kindness of Fate?
Often I fear that these un-talented limbs
Will be laid at last in an un-named grave!

---

① See *The Book of Songs*, p. 48.
② The distance to Chung-chou.
③ Dangerous savages.

再
造
的
镜
像

初入峡有感

上有万仞山，下有千丈水；
苍苍两崖间，阔狭容一苇。
瞿唐呀直泻，滟滪屹中峙。
未夜黑岩昏，无风白浪起。
大石如刀剑，小石如牙齿。
一步不可行，况千三百里！
苒蒻竹蔑稔，欹危楫师趾；
一跌无完舟，吾生系于此。
常闻仗忠信，蛮貊可行矣。
自古漂沉人，岂尽非君子？
况吾时与命，蹇舛不足恃；
常恐不才身，复作无名死！

《白居易集》，第 208 页。

ON BEING REMOVED FROM HSÜN-YANG AND SENT TO CHUNG-CHOU

再
造
的
镜
像

BEFORE this, when I was stationed at Hsün-yang,
Already I regretted the fewness of friends and guests.
Suddenly, suddenly—bearing a stricken heart
I left the gates, with nothing to comfort me.
Henceforward—relegated to deep seclusion
In a bottomless gorge, flanked by precipitous mountains.
Five months on end the passage of boats is stopped
By the piled billows that toss and leap like colts.
The inhabitants of Pa resemble wild apes;
Fierce and lusty, they fill the mountains and prairies.
Among such as these I cannot hope for friends
And am pleased with anyone who is even remotely human.

自江州至忠州

前在浔阳日，已叹宾朋寡。
忽忽抱忧怀，出门无处写。
今来转深僻，穷峡巅山下。
五月断行舟，滟堆正如马。
巴人类猿狄，蛮铄满山野。
敢望见交亲？喜逢似人者。

《白居易集》，第 209 页。

PLANTING FLOWERS ON THE EASTERN EMBANKMENT

(Written when Governor of Chung-chou)

(A.D. 819)

I TOOK money and brought flowering trees
And planted them out on the bank to the east of the Keep.
I simply bought whatever had most blooms,
Not caring whether peach, apricot, or plum.
A hundred fruits, all mixed up together;
A thousand branches, flowering in due rotation.
Each has its season coming early or late;
But to all alike the fertile soil is kind.
The red flowers hang like a heavy mist;
The white flowers gleam like a fall of snow.
The wandering bees cannot bear to leave them;
The sweet birds also come there to roost.
In front there flows an ever-running stream;
Beneath there is built a little flat terrace.
Sometimes I sweep the flagstones of the terrace;
Sometimes, in the wind, I raise my cup and drink.
The flower-branches screen my head from the sun;
The flower-buds fall down into my lap.
Alone drinking, alone singing my songs
I do not notice that the moon is level with the steps.
The people of Pa do not care for flowers;
All the spring no one has come to look.
But their Governor General, alone with his cup of wine,
Sits till evening and will not move from the place!

东坡种花二首（其一）

持钱买花树，城东坡上栽。
但购有花者，不限桃杏梅。
百果参杂种，千枝次第开。
天时有早晚，地力无高低。
红者霞艳艳，白者雪皑皑。
游蜂遂不去，好鸟亦栖来。
前有长流水，下有小平台。
时拂台上石，一举风前杯。
花枝荫我头，花蕊落我怀。
独酌复独咏，不觉月平西。
巴俗不爱花，竟春无人来。
唯此醉太守，尽日不能回。

《白居易集》，第 215—216 页。

INVITATION TO HSIAO CH'U-SHIH
(Written when Governor of Chung-chou)

WITHIN the Gorges there is no lack of men;
They are people one meets, not people one cares for.
At my front door guests also arrive;
They are people one sits with, not people one knows.
When I look up, there are only clouds and trees;
When I look down—only my wife and child.
I sleep, eat, get up or sit still;
Apart from that, nothing happens at all.
But beyond the city Hsiao the hermit dwells,
And with *him* at least I find myself at ease.
For *he* can drink a full flagon of wine
And is good at reciting long-line poems.
Some afternoon, when the clerks have gone home,
At a season when the path by the river bank is dry,
I beg you, take up your staff of bamboo-wood
And find your way to the parlour of Government House.

再
造
的
镜
像

招萧处士

峡内岂无人？所逢非所思；
门前亦有客，相对不相知。
仰望但云树，俯顾惟妻儿。
寝食起居外，端然无所为。
东郊萧处士，聊可与开眉。
能饮满杯酒，善吟长句诗。
庭前吏散后，江畔路乾时。
请君携竹杖，一赴郡斋期。

《白居易集》，第 211 页。

TO LI CHIEN

(A.D. 819)

THE province I govern is humble and remote;
Yet our festivals follow the Courtly Calendar.
At rise of day we sacrificed to the Wind God,
When darkly, darkly, dawn glimmered in the sky.
Officers followed, horsemen led the way;
They brought us out to the wastes beyond the town,
Where river mists fall heavier than rain,
And the fires on the hill leap higher than the stars
Suddenly I remembered the early levees at Court
When you and I galloped to the Purple Yard.
As we walked our horses up Dragon Tail Way
We turned and gazed at the green of the Southern Hills.
Since we parted, both of us have been growing old;
And our minds have been vexed by many anxious cares;
Yet even now I fancy my ears are full
Of the sound of jade tinkling on your bridle-straps.

早祭风伯，因怀李十一舍人

远郡虽褊陋，时祀奉朝经；
夙兴祭风伯，天气晓冥冥。
导骑与从吏，引我出东垌。
水雾重如雨，山火高于星。
忽忆早朝日，与君趋紫庭；
步登龙尾道，却望终南青。
一别身向老，所思心未宁。
至今想在耳，玉音尚玲玲。

《白居易集》，第 213 页。

THE RED COCKATOO
(A.D. 820)

SENT as a present from Annam—
A red cockatoo.
Coloured like the peach-tree blossom,
Speaking with the speech of men.
And they did to it what is always done
To the learned and eloquent.
They took a cage with stout bars
And shut it up inside.

红鹦鹉

安南远进红鹦鹉，色似桃花语似人。
文章辩慧皆如此，笼槛何年出得身？

《白居易集》，第 313 页。

THE SPRING RIVER

HEAT and cold, dusk and dawn have crowded one upon the other;

Suddenly I find it is two years since I came to Chung-chou.

Through my closed doors I hear nothing but the morning and evening drum;

From my upper windows all I see is the ships that come and go.

In vain the orioles tempt me with their song to stray beneath the flowering trees;

In vain the grasses lure me by their colour to sit beside the pond.

There is one thing and one alone I never tire of watching—

The spring river as it trickles over the stones and babbles past the rocks.

春江

炎凉昏晓苦推迁，不觉忠州已二年。
闭阁只听朝暮鼓，上楼空望往来船。
莺声诱引来花下，草色勾留坐水边。
唯有春江看未厌，萦砂绕石渌潺湲。

《白居易集》，第 390—391 页。

AFTER COLLECTING THE AUTUMN TAXES

FROM these high walls I look at the town below
Where the natives of Pa cluster like a swarm of flies.
How can I govern these people and lead them aright?
I cannot even understand what they say.
But at least I am glad, now that the taxes are in,
To learn that in my province there is no discontent.
I fear its prosperity is not due to me
And was only caused by the year's abundant crops.
The papers I have to deal with are simple and few;
My arbour by the lake is leisurely and still.
In the autumn rain the berries fall from the eaves;
At the evening bell the birds return to the wood.
A broken sunlight quavers over the southern porch
Where I lie on my couch abandoned to idleness.

征秋税毕，题郡南亭

高城直下视，蠢蠢见巴蛮。
安可施政教？尚不通语言！
且喜赋敛毕，幸闻闾井安。
岂伊循良化？赖此丰登年。
案牍既简少，池馆亦清闲。
秋雨檐果落，夕钟林鸟还。
南亭日潇洒，偃卧恣疏顽。

《白居易集》，第 219 页。

LODGING WITH THE OLD MAN OF THE STREAM

(A.D. 820)

MEN'S hearts love gold and jade;

Men's mouths covet wine and flesh.

Not so the old man of the stream;

He drinks from his gourd and asks nothing more.

South of the stream he cuts firewood and grass;

North of the stream he has built wall and roof.

Yearly he sows a single acre of land;

In spring he drives two yellow calves.

In these things he finds great repose;

Beyond these he has no wish or care.

By chance I met him walking by the water-side;

He took me home and lodged me in his thatched hut.

When I parted from him, to seek market and Court,

This old man asked my rank and pay.

Doubting my tale, he laughed loud and long:

'Privy Counsellors do not sleep in barns.'

宿溪翁

众心爱金玉，众口贪酒肉。
何此溪上翁，饮瓢亦自足？
溪南刈薪草，溪北修墙屋。
岁种一顷田，春驱两黄犊。
于中甚安适，此外无营欲。
溪畔偶相逢，庵中遂同宿。
辞翁向朝市，问我何官禄？
虚言笑杀翁，郎官应列宿！

《白居易集》，第 221 页。

TO HIS BROTHER HSING-CHIEN

(A.D. 820)

再
造
的
镜
像

CAN the single cup of wine
We drank this morning have made my heart so glad?
This is a joy that comes only from within,
Which those who witness will never understand.
I have but two brothers
And bitterly grieved that both were far away;
This spring, back through the Gorges of Pa,
I have come to them safely, ten thousand leagues.
Two cousins I had
Who had put up their hair, but not twined the sash[①];
Yesterday both were married and taken away
By good husbands in whom I may well trust.
I am freed at last from the thoughts that made me grieve,
As though a sword had cut a rope from my neck.
And limbs grow light when the heart sheds its care;
Suddenly I seem to be flying up to the sky!

Hsing-chien, drink your cup of wine,
Then set it down and listen to what I say.
Do not sigh that your home is far away;
Do not mind if your salary is small.
Only pray that as long as life lasts
You and I may never be forced to part.

---

① i.e. got married.

对酒示行简（节选）

今旦一樽酒，欢畅何怡怡！
此乐从中来，他人安得知？
兄弟唯二人，远别恒苦悲。
今春自巴峡，万里平安归。
复有双幼妹，笄年未结襦。
昨日嫁娶毕，良人皆可依。
忧念两消释，如刀断羁縻。
身轻心无系，忽欲凌空飞。
······
行简劝尔酒，停杯听我辞：
不叹乡国远，不嫌官禄微；
但愿我与尔，终老不相离！

《白居易集》，第 144—145 页。

CHILDREN

(*c.* A.D. 820)

MY nephew, who is six years old, is called 'Tortoise';

My daughter of three—little 'Summer Dress'.

One is beginning to learn to joke and talk;

The other can already recite poems and songs.

At morning they play clinging about my feet;

At night they sleep pillowed against my dress.

Why, children, did you reach the world so late,

Coming to me just when my years are spent?

Young things draw our feelings to them;

Old people easily give their hearts.

The sweetest vintage at last turns sour;

The full moon in the end begins to wane.

And so with men the bonds of love and affection

Soon may change to a load of sorrow and care.

But all the world is bound by love's ties;

Why did I think that I alone should escape?

弄龟、罗

有侄始六岁，字之为阿龟。
有女生三年，其名曰罗儿。
一始学笑语，一能诵歌诗。
朝戏抱我足，夜眠枕我衣。
汝生何其晚？我年行已衰。
物情小可念，人意老多慈。
酒美竟须坏，月圆终有亏。
亦如恩爱缘，乃是忧恼资。
举世同此累，吾安能去之！

《白居易集》，第 140 页。

PRUNING TREES

TREES growing—right in front of my window;
The trees are high and the leaves grow thick.
Sad alas! the distant mountain view,
Obscured by this, dimly shows between.
One morning I took knife and axe;
With my own hand I lopped the branches off.
Ten thousand leaves fell about my head;
A thousand hills came before my eyes.
Suddenly, as when clouds or mists break
And straight through, the blue sky appears.
Again, like the face of a friend one has loved
Seen at last after an age of parting.
First there came a gentle wind blowing;
One by one the birds flew back to the tree.
To ease my mind I gazed to the South-East;
As my eyes wandered, my thoughts went far away.
Of men there is none that has not some preference;
Of things there is none but mixes good with ill.
It was not that I did not love the tender branches;
But better still—to see the green hills!

截树

种树当前轩，树高柯叶繁。
惜哉远山色，隐此蒙笼间！
一朝持斧斤，手自截其端。
万叶落头上，千峰来面前。
忽似决云雾，豁达睹青天。
又如所念人，久别一款颜。
始有清风至，稍见飞鸟还。
开怀东南望，目远心辽然。
人各有偏好，物莫能两全；
岂不爱柔条？不如见青山！

《白居易集》，第 140 页。

BEING VISITED BY A FRIEND DURING ILLNESS

I HAVE been ill so long that I do not count the days;
At the southern window, evening—and again evening.
Sadly chirping in the grasses under my eaves
The winter sparrows morning and evening sing.
By an effort I rise and lean heavily on my bed;
Tottering I step towards the door of the courtyard.
By chance I meet a friend who is coming to see me;
Just as if I had gone specially to meet him.
They took my couch and placed it in the setting sun;
They spread my rug and I leaned on the balcony-pillar.
Tranquil talk was better than any medicine;
Gradually the feelings came back to my numbed heart.

病中友人相访

卧久不记日，南窗昏复昏。
萧条草檐下，寒雀朝夕闻。
强扶床前杖，起向庭中行。
偶逢故人至，便当一逢迎。
移榻就斜日，披裘倚前楹。
闲谈胜服药，稍觉有心情。

《白居易集》，第 194—195 页。

THE PINE-TREES IN THE COURTYARD
(A.D. 821)

BELOW the Hall what meets my eyes?
Ten pine-trees growing near to the steps.
Irregularly scattered, not in ordered line;
In height also strangely unassorted.
The highest of them is thirty feet tall;
The lowest scarcely measures ten feet.
They have the air of things growing wild;
Who first planted them, no one now knows.
They touch the walls of my blue-tiled house;
Their roots are sunk in the terrace of white sand.
Morning and evening they are visited by the wind and moon;
Rain or fine—they are free from dust and mud.
In the gales of autumn they whisper a vague tune;
From the suns of summer they yield a cool shade.
At the height of spring the fine evening rain
Fills their leaves with a load of hanging pearls.
At the year's end the time of great snow
Stamps their branches with a fret of glittering jade.
At each season they have their varying mood;
Vying in this with any tree that grows.
Last year, when they heard I had bought this house,
Neighbours mocked and the World called me mad—
That a whole family of twice ten souls
Should move house for the sake of a few pines!
Now that I have come to them, what have they given me?
They have only loosened the shackles that bind my heart.
But even so, they are 'profitable friends'[①],
And fill my need of 'converse with wise men'.
Yet when I consider how, still a man of the world,
In belt and cap I scurry through dirt and dust,
From time to time my heart twinges with shame
That I am not fit to be master of my pines!

---

① See my *Analects of Confucius*, p.205, where three kinds of 'profitable friends' and three kinds of 'profitable pleasures' are described; the third of the latter being 'plenty of intelligent companions'.

庭松

堂下何所有？十松当我阶。
乱立无行次，高下亦不齐。
高者三丈长，下者十尺低。
有如野生物，不知何人栽。
接以青瓦屋，承之白沙台。
朝昏有风月，燥湿无尘泥。
疏韵秋械械，凉阴夏凄凄。
春深微雨夕，满叶珠蓑蓑。
岁暮大雪天，压枝玉皑皑。
四时各有趣，万木非其侪。
去年买此宅，多为人所咍。
一家二十口，移转就松来。
移来有何得？但得烦襟开。
即此是益友，岂必交贤才？
顾我犹俗士，冠带走尘埃。
未称为松主，时时一愧怀！

《白居易集》，第 222 页。

ON THE WAY TO HANGCHOW: ANCHORED ON THE RIVER AT NIGHT

再
造
的
镜
像

LITTLE sleeping and much grieving—the traveller
Rises at midnight and looks back towards home.
The sands are bright with moonlight that joins the shores;
The sail is white with dew that has covered the boat.
Nearing the sea, the river grows broader and broader
Approaching autumn—the nights longer and longer.
Thirty times we have slept amid mists and waves,
And still we have not reached Hangchow!

夜泊旅望

少睡多愁客，中宵起望乡。
沙明连浦月，帆白满船霜。
近海江弥阔，迎秋夜更长。
烟波三十宿，犹未到钱塘。

《白居易集》，第 433 页。

SLEEPING ON HORSEBACK
(A.D. 822)

WE had ridden long and were still far from the inn;
My eyes grew dim; for a moment I fell asleep.
Under my right arm the whip still dangled;
In my left hand the reins for an instant slackened.
Suddenly I woke and turned to question my groom.
'We have gone a hundred paces since you fell asleep.'
Body and spirit for a while had changed place;
Swift and slow had turned to their contraries.
For these few steps that my horse had carried me
Had taken in my dream countless aeons of time!
True indeed is that saying of Wise Men
'A hundred years are but a moment of sleep.'

再
造
的
镜
像

自望秦赴五松驿，马上偶睡，睡觉成吟

长途发已久，前馆行未至：
体倦目已昏，瞌然遂成睡。
右袂尚垂鞭，左手暂委辔；
忽觉问仆夫，才行百步地。
形神分处所，迟速相乖异：
马上几多时，梦中无限事。
诚哉达人语：百龄同一寐！

《白居易集》，第 150 页。

PARTING FROM THE WINTER STOVE
(A.D. 822)

ON the fifth day after the rise of Spring,
Everywhere the season's gracious attitudes!
The white sun gradually lengthening its course,
The blue-grey clouds hanging as though they would fall;
The last icicle breaking into splinters of jade:
The new stems marshalling red sprouts.
The things I meet are all full of gladness;
It is not only I who love the Spring.
To welcome the flowers I stand in the back garden;
To enjoy the sunlight I sit under the front eaves.
Yet still in my heart there lingers one regret;
Soon I shall part with the flame of my red stove!

立春后五日

立春后五日，春态纷婀娜。
白日斜渐长，碧云低欲堕。
残冰坼玉片，新萼排红颗。
遇物尽欣欣，爱春非独我。
迎芳后园立，就暖前檐坐。
还有惆怅心，欲别红炉火！

《白居易集》，第 156 页。

THE SILVER SPOON

(While on the road to his new province, Hangchow, in 822, he sent a silver spoon
to his nephew A-kuei, whom he had been obliged to leave behind with his nurse,
old Mrs Tsou.)

To distant service my heart is well accustomed;
When I left home, it wasn't that which was difficult
But because I had to leave Kuei at home—
For this it was that tears filled my eyes.
Little boys ought to be daintily fed:
Mrs Tsou, please see to this!
That's why I've packed and sent a silver spoon;
You will think of me and eat up your food nicely!

路上寄银匙与阿龟

谛宦心都惯，辞乡去不难；
缘留龟子住，涕泪一阑干。
小子须娇养，邹婆为好看。
银匙封寄汝，忆我即加餐。

《白居易集》，第 430 页。

THE HAT GIVEN TO THE POET BY LI CHIEN
(Died, A.D. 821)

LONG ago to a white-haired gentleman
You made the present of a black gauze hat.
The gauze hat still sits on my head;
But you already are gone to the Nether Springs.
The thing is old, but still fit to wear;
The man is gone and will never be seen again.
Out on the hill the moon is shining tonight
And the trees on your tomb are swayed by the autumn wind.

再
造
的
镜
像

感旧纱帽（帽即故李侍郎所赠）

昔君乌纱帽，赠我白头翁。
帽今在顶上，君已归泉中。
物故犹堪用，人亡不可逢。
岐山今夜月，坟树正秋风！

《白居易集》，第 151 页。

GOOD-BYE TO THE PEOPLE OF HANGCHOW
(A.D. 824)

ELDERS and officers line the returning road;
Flagons of wine load the parting table.
I have not ruled you with the wisdom of Shao Kung[①];
What is the reason your tears should fall so fast?
My taxes were heavy, though many of the people were poor;
The farmers were hungry, for often their fields were dry.
All I did was to dam the water of the Lake[②]
And help a little in a year when things were bad.

---

① A legendary ruler who dispensed justice sitting under a wild pear-tree.
② Po Chü-i built the dam on the Western Lake which is still known as 'Po's dam'.

462

别州民

耆老遮归路，壶浆满别筵。
甘棠无一树，那得泪潸然？
税重多贫户，农饥足旱田。
唯留一湖水，与汝救凶年。

《白居易集》，第 513 页。

AFTER GETTING DRUNK, BECOMING SOBER IN THE NIGHT

再
造
的
镜
像

OUR party scattered at yellow dusk and I came home to bed;

I woke at midnight and went for a walk, leaning heavily on a friend.

As I lay on my pillow my vinous complexion, soothed by sleep, grew sober:

In front of the tower the ocean moon, accompanying the tide, had risen.

The swallows, about to return to the beams, went back to roost again;

The candle at my window, just going out, suddenly revived its light.

All the time till dawn came, still my thoughts were muddled;

And in my ears something sounded like the music of flutes and strings.

饮后夜醒

黄昏饮散归来卧，夜半人扶强起行。
枕上酒容和睡醒，楼前海月伴潮生。
将归梁燕还重宿，欲灭窗灯复却明。
直至晓来犹妄想，耳中如有管弦声。

《白居易集》，第 447 页。

WRITTEN WHEN GOVERNOR OF SOOCHOW

(A.D. 825)

A GOVERNMENT building, not my own home.

A Government garden, not my own trees.

But at Lo-yang I have a small house,

And on Wei River I have built a thatched hut.

I am free from the ties of marriage and giving in marriage;

If I choose to retire, I have somewhere to end my days.

And though I have lingered long beyond my time,

To retire now would be better than not at all!

再
造
的
镜
像

自咏五首之五

官舍非我庐，官园非我树。
洛中有小宅，渭上有别墅。
既无婚嫁累，幸有归休处。
归去诚已迟，犹胜不归去。

《白居易集》，第 464 页。

GETTING UP EARLY ON A SPRING MORNING

(Part of a poem written when Governor of Soochow in 825)

THE early light of the rising sun shines on the beams of my house;
The first banging of opened doors echoes like the roll of a drum.
The dog lies curled on the stone step, for the earth is wet with dew;
The birds come near to the window and chatter, telling that the day is fine.
With the lingering fumes of yesterday's wine my head is still heavy;
With new doffing of winter clothes my body has grown light.
I woke up with heart empty and mind utterly extinct;
Lately, for many nights on end, I have not dreamt of home.

再
造
的
镜
像

早兴

晨光出照屋梁明，初打开门鼓一声。
犬上阶眠知地湿，鸟临窗语报天晴。
半销宿酒头仍重，新脱冬衣体乍轻。
睡觉心空思想尽，近来乡梦不多成。

《白居易集》，第 452 页。

STOPPING THE NIGHT AT JUNG-YANG

I GREW up near the town of Jung-yang.[①]

I was still young when I left my village home.

On and on—forty years passed

Till again I stayed for the night at Jung-yang.

When I went away, I was only eleven or twelve;

This year I am turned fifty-six.

Yet thinking back to the times of my childish games,

Whole and undimmed, still they rise before me.

The old houses have all disappeared;

Down in the village none of my people are left.

It is not only that streets and buildings have changed;

But steep is level and level changed to steep!

Alone unchanged, the waters of Chên and Wei

Passionless—flow in their old course.[②]

---

① In Honan near K'ai-fêng.

② Ever since the far-off days of the *Book of Songs*.

宿荥阳

生长在荥阳，少小辞乡曲；
迢迢四十载，复到荥阳宿。
去时十一二，今年五十六；
追思儿戏时，宛然犹在目。
旧居失处所，故里无宗族。
岂唯变市朝，兼亦迁陵谷。
独有溱洧水，无情依旧绿。

《白居易集》，第 469 页。

RESIGNATION
Part of a Poem
(A.D. 826)

KEEP off your thoughts from things that are past and done;
For thinking of the past wakes regret and pain.
Keep off your thoughts from thinking what will happen;
To think of the future fills one with dismay.
Better by day to sit like a sack in your chair;
Better by night to lie like a stone in your bed.
When food comes, then open your mouth;
When sleep comes, then close your eyes.

有感三首之三（节选）

往事勿追思，追思多悲怆；
来事勿相迎，相迎亦惆怅。
不如兀然坐，不如塌然卧。
食来即开口，睡来即合眼；

《白居易集》，第 469 页。

CLIMBING THE TERRACE OF KUAN-YIN AND LOOKING AT THE CITY
OF CH'ANG-AN
(A.D. 827)

HUNDREDS of houses, thousands of houses—like a great chess-board.
The twelve streets like a huge field planted with rows of cabbage.
In the distance I see faint and small the torches of riders to Court,
Like a single row of stars lying to the west of the Five Gates.

登观音台望城

百千家似围棋局，十二街如种菜畦。
遥认微微入朝火，一条星宿五门西。

《白居易集》，第 560 页。

CLIMBING THE LING-YING TERRACE AND LOOKING NORTH

再
造
的
镜
像

MOUNTING on high I begin to realize the smallness of Man's Domain;
Gazing into distance I begin to know the vanity of the Carnal World.
I turn my head and hurry home—back to the Court and Market,
A single grain of rice falling—into the Great Barn.

登灵应台北望

临高始见人寰小，对远方知色界空。
回首却归朝市去，一稊米落太仓中。

《白居易集》，第 561 页。

REALIZING THE FUTILITY OF LIFE
(Written on the wall of a priest's cell, *circa* 828)

EVER since the time when I was a lusty boy

Down till now when I am ill and old,

The things I have cared for have been different at different times,

But my being busy, *that* has never changed.

Then on the shore—building sand-pagodas.

Now, at Court, covered with tinkling jade.

This and that—equally childish games,

Things whose substance passes in a moment of time!

While the hands are busy, the heart cannot understand;

When there is no Attachment, Doctrine is sound.

Even should one zealously strive to learn the Way,

That very striving will make one's error more.

感悟妄缘，题如上人壁

自从为騃童，直至作衰翁；
所好随年异，为忙终日同。
弄沙成佛塔，锵玉谒王宫；
彼此皆儿戏，须臾即色空。
有营非了义，无著是真宗；
兼恐勤修道，犹应在妄中。

《白居易集》，第 555 页。

THE GRAND HOUSES AT LO-YANG
(*c.* A.D. 829)

BY woods and water, whose houses are these
With high gates and wide-stretching lands?
From their blue gables gilded fishes hang;
By their red pillars carven coursers run.
Their spring arbours, warm with caged mist;
Their autumn yards with locked moonlight cold.
To the stem of the nine-tree amber beads cling;
The bamboo-branches ooze ruby-drops.
Of lake and terrace who may the masters be?
High officers, Councillors-of-State.
All their lives they have never come to see,
But know their houses only from the bailiff's map!

题洛中第宅

水木谁家宅？门高占地宽。
悬鱼挂青甃，行马护朱栏。
春榭笼烟暖，秋庭锁月寒。
松胶粘琥珀，筠粉扑琅玕。
试问池台主，多为将相官。
终身不曾到，唯展宅图看！

《白居易集》，第 568 页。

THE HALF-RECLUSE
(A.D. 829)

再
造
的
镜
像

'THE great recluse lives in market and court;
The small recluse hides in thickets and hills.'
Thickets and hills are too lonely and cold;
Market and court are too unrestful and thronged.
Far better to be a half-recluse,
And hermitize in a liaison job.
It is like office, yet like being at large;
One is not busy, but also not bored.
It makes no demand either on hand or brain,
Yet still prevents one being hungry or cold.
All the year one has no official work,
Yet every month one draws rations and pay.
For one who likes to take a strenuous climb
To the South of the city there are pleasant autumn hills;
For one who loves to take an idle stroll
To the East of the city are orchards lovely in spring.
If once in a while you want to get drunk
You can always accept an invitation to dine.
In Lo-yang there are many delightful people
Always ready for endless pleasant talk.
But if you would rather lie quietly at home
All you need do is to bar your outer door;
There is no fear that official coaches or chairs
Will press for admittance, crowding in front of your gate
It is well known that life being what it is
To have things both ways is always very hard.
The lot of the humble is embittered by hunger and cold;
The great are compassed by many worries and cares.
Only the half-hermit of whom I speak
Achieves a life that is fortunate and secure.
Failure, success, affluence and want—
At an equal distance from all these four.

(Written when he was Lo-yang *liaison* to the Crown Prince's Social Secrctary.)

中隐

大隐住朝市，小隐入丘樊；
丘樊太冷落，朝市太嚣喧。
不如作中隐，隐在留司官。
似出复似处，非忙亦非闲。
不劳心与力，又免饥与寒。
终岁无公事，随月有俸钱。
君若好登临，城南有秋山。
君若爱游荡，城东有春园。
君若欲一醉，时出赴宾筵。
洛中多君子，可以恣欢言。
君若欲高卧，但自深掩关。
亦无车马客，造次到门前。
人生处一世，其道难两全：
贱即苦冻馁，贵则多忧患。
唯此中隐士，致身吉且安；
穷通与丰约，正在四者间。

《白居易集》，第 490 页。

THE CRANES

(A.D. 830)

THE western wind has blown but a few days;

Yet the first leaf already flies from the bough.

On the drying paths I walk in my thin shoes;

In the first cold I have donned my quilted coat.

Through shallow ditches the floods are clearing away;

Through sparse bamboos trickles a slanting light.

In the early dusk, down an alley of green moss,

The garden-boy is leading the cranes home.

西风

西风来几日，一叶已先飞。
新霁乘轻屐，初凉换熟衣。
浅渠销慢水，疏竹漏斜晖。
薄暮青苔巷，家僮引鹤归。

《白居易集》，第 637—638 页。

RISING LATE, AND PLAYING WITH A-TS'UI, AGED TWO

(Written in 831)

ALL the morning I have lain snugly in bed;

Now at dusk I rise with many yawns.

My warm stove is quick to get ablaze;

At the cold mirror I am slow in doing my hair.

With melted snow I boil fragrant tea;

Seasoned with curds I cook a milk-pudding.

At my sloth and greed there is no one but me to laugh;

My cheerful vigour none but myself knows.

The taste of my wine is mild and works no poison;

The notes of my lute are soft and bring no sadness.

To the Three Joys in the book of Mencius

I have added the fourth of playing with my baby-boy.

晚起

烂熳朝眠后，频伸晚起时。
暖炉生火早，寒镜裹头迟。
融雪煎香茗，调酥煮乳糜。
慵馋还自哂，快活亦谁知？
酒性温无毒，琴声淡不悲。
荣公三乐外，仍弄小男儿。

《白居易集》，第 639—640 页。

ON BEING SIXTY

再
造
的
镜
像

BETWEEN thirty and forty one is distracted by the Five Lusts;

Between seventy and eighty one is prey to a hundred diseases.

But from fifty to sixty one is free from all ills;

Calm and still—the heart enjoys rest.

I have put behind me Love and Greed, I have done with Profit and Fame;

I am still short of illness and decay, and far from decrepit age.

Strength of limb I still possess to seek the rivers and hills;

Still my heart has spirit enough to listen to flutes and strings.

At leisure I open new wine and taste several cups;

Drunken I recall old poems and chant a stray verse.

To Tun-shih and Mêng-tê[1] I offer this advice:

Do not complain of three-score, 'the time of obedient ears.'[2]

---

[1] Ts'ui Ch'ün and Liu Yü-hsi, who were the same age as Po Chü-i.

[2] Confucius said that not till sixty did 'his ears obey him'.

耳顺吟寄敦诗、梦得

三十四十五欲牵，七十八十百病缠；
五十六十却不恶，恬淡清净心安然。
已过爱贪声利后，犹在病羸昏耄前。
未无筋力寻山水，尚有心情听管弦。
闲开新酒尝数盏，醉忆旧诗吟一篇。
敦诗梦得且相劝，不用嫌他耳顺年。

《白居易集》，第 473 页。

ON HIS BALDNESS

(A.D. 832)

AT dawn I sighed to see my hairs fall;
At dusk I sighed to see my hairs fall.
For I dreaded the time when the last lock should go...
They are all gone and I do not mind at all!
I have done with that cumbrous washing and getting dry;
My tiresome comb for ever is laid aside.
Best of all, when the weather is hot and wet,
To have no top-knot weighing down on one's head!
I put aside my messy cloth wrap;
I have got rid of my dusty tasselled fringe.
In a silver jar I have stored a cold stream,
On my bald pate I trickle a ladle full.
Like one baptized with the Water of Buddha's Law,
I sit and receive this cool, cleansing joy.
Now I know why the priest who seeks Repose
Frees his heart by first shaving his head.

嗟发落

朝亦嗟发落，暮亦嗟发落；
落尽诚可嗟，尽来亦不恶。
既不劳洗沐，又不烦梳掠。
最宜湿暑天，头轻无髻缚。
脱置垢巾帻，解去尘缨络。
银瓶贮寒泉，当顶倾一勺。
有如醍醐灌，坐受清凉乐。
因悟自在僧，亦资于剃削。

《白居易集》，第 496 页。

LOSING A SLAVE-GIRL
(A.D. 832)

AROUND my courtyard the little wall is low;
At the street door her loss was posted late.
I am ashamed to think we were not always kind;
I regret your labours, that will never be repaid.
The caged bird owes no allegiance;
The wind-tossed flower does not cling to the tree.

Where tonight she lies none can give us news;
Nor any knows, save the bright watching moon.

失婢

宅院小墙库，坊门帖榜迟。
旧恩惭自薄，前事悔难追。
笼鸟无常主，风花不恋枝。
今宵在何处？唯有月明知！

《白居易集笺校》，第 1863 页。

THINKING OF THE PAST
(A.D. 833)

IN an idle hour I thought of former days
And former friends seemed to be standing in the room.
And then I wondered 'Where are they now?'
Like fallen leaves they have tumbled to the Nether Springs.
Han Yü[①] swallowed his sulphur pills,
Yet a single illness carried him straight to the grave.
Yüan Chên smelted autumn stone[②],
But before he was old, his strength crumbled away.
Master Tu possessed a cinnabar receipt;
All day long he fasted from strong meats.
The Lord Ts'ui, trusting in the power of drugs,
Through the whole winter wore his summer coat.
Yet some by illness and some by sudden death...
All vanished ere their middle years were passed.

Only I, who never dieted myself,
Have succeeded in living to a ripe old age.
I who in young days
Yielded lightly to every lust and greed;
Whose palate craved only for the richest meat
When hunger came, I gulped steaming food;
When thirst came, I drank from the frozen stream.
With verse I laboured the spirits of my Five Guts[③];
With wine I deluged the three Vital Spots.
Yet day by day joining fissures and breaks
I have lived till now almost sound and whole.
There is no gap in my two rows of teeth;
Limbs and body still serve me well.
Already I have opened my seventh set of years;
Yet I eat my fill and sleep quietly.
I drink, while I may, the wine that lies in my cup,
And all else commit to Heaven's care.

---

① The famous poet, died A.D. 824.

② Carbamide crystals.

③ Heart, liver, stomach, lungs, and kidneys.

思旧

闲日一思旧，旧游如目前；
再思今何在？零落归下泉！
退之服流黄，一病讫不痊。
微之炼秋石，未老身溘然。
杜子得丹诀，终日断腥膻。
崔君夸药力，经冬不衣绵。
或疾或暴夭，悉不过中年。
唯予不服食，老命反迟延。
况在少壮时，亦为嗜欲牵。
但耽荤与血，不识汞与铅。
饥来吞热物，渴来饮寒泉。
诗役五藏神，酒汩三丹田。
随日合破坏，至今粗完全。
齿牙未缺落，支体尚轻便。
已开第七秩，饱食仍安眠。
且进杯中物，其余皆付天。

《白居易集》，第 664 页。

ON A BOX CONTAINING HIS OWN WORKS
(A.D. 835)

I BREAK up cypress and make a book-box;
The box well-made—and the cypress-wood tough.
In it shall be kept what author's works?
The inscription says PO LO-T'IEN.
All my life has been spent in writing books,
From when I was young till now that I am old.
First and last—seventy whole volumes;
Big and little—three thousand themes.
Well I know in the end they'll be scattered and lost;
But I cannot bear to see them thrown away.
With my own hand I open and shut the locks,
And put it carefully in front of the book-curtain.
I am like Têng Pai-tao[①];
But to-day there is not any Wang Ts'an[②].
All I can do is to divide them among my daughters
To be left by them to give to my grandchildren.

---

① Who died childless in A.D. 326.
② To whom Ts'ai Y'ung (died A.D. 192) bequeathed his writings.

题文集柜

破柏作书柜，柜牢柏复坚。
收贮谁家集？题云白乐天。
我生业文字，自幼及老年；
前后七十卷，小大三千篇。
诚知终散失，未忍遽弃捐。
自开自锁闭，置在书帷前。
身是邓伯道，世无王仲宣；
只应分付女，留与外孙传。

《白居易集》，第 682 页。

A MAD POEM ADDRESSED TO MY NEPHEWS AND NIECES
(A.D. 835)

再
造
的
镜
像

THE World cheats those who cannot read;
I, happily, have mastered script and pen.
The World cheats those who hold no office;
I am blessed with high official rank.
Often the old have much sickness and pain;
With me, luckily, there is not much wrong.
People when they are old are often burdened with ties;
But *I* have finished with marriage and giving in marriage.
No changes happen to jar the quiet of my mind;
No business comes to impair the vigour of my limbs.
Hence it is that now for ten years
Body and soul have rested in hermit peace.
And all the more, in the last lingering years
What I shall need are very few things.
A single rug to warm me through the winter;
One meal to last me the whole day.
It does not matter that my house is rather small;
One cannot sleep in more than one room!
It does not matter that I have not many horses;
One cannot ride on two horses at once!
As fortunate as me among the people of the world
Possibly one would find seven out of ten.
As contented as me among a hundred men
Look as you may, you will not find one.
In the affairs of others even fools are wise;
In their own business even sages err.
To no one else would I dare to speak my heart,
So my wild words are addressed to my nephews and nieces.

狂言示诸侄

世欺不识字，我忝攻文章。
世欺不得官，我忝居班秩。
人老多病苦，我今幸无疾。
人老多忧累，我今婚嫁毕。
心安不移转，身泰无牵率：
所以十年来，形神闲且逸。
况当垂老岁，所要无多物：
一裘暖过冬，一饭饱终日。
勿言舍宅小，不过寝一室。
何用鞍马多？不能骑两匹。
如我优幸身，人中十有七；
如我知足心，人中百无一。
傍观愚亦见，当己贤多失。
不敢论他人，狂言示诸侄。

《白居易集》，第 689—690 页。

OLD AGE

(Addressed to Liu Yü-hsi, who was born in the same year)

(A.D. 835)

WE are growing old together, you and I;

Let us ask ourselves, what is age like?

The dull eye is closed ere night comes;

The idle head, still uncombed at noon.

Propped on a staff, sometimes a walk abroad;

Or all day sitting with closed doors.

One dares not look in the mirror's polished face;

One cannot read small-letter books.

Deeper and deeper, one's love of old friends;

Fewer and fewer, one's dealings with young men.

One thing only, the pleasure of idle talk,

Is great as ever, when you and I meet.

咏老，赠梦得

与君俱老也，自问老何如？
眼涩夜先卧，头慵朝未梳。
有时扶杖出，尽日闭门居。
懒照新磨镜，休看小字书。
情于故人重，迹共少年疏。
唯是闲谈兴，相逢尚有余。

《白居易集》，第 735 页。

EASE

(Congratulating himself on the comforts of his life during a temporary retirement from office. A.D. 835)

LINED coat, warm cap and easy felt slippers,
In the little tower, at the low window, sitting over the sunken brazier.
Body at rest, heart at peace; no need to rise early.
I wonder if the courtiers at the Western Capital know of these things, or not?

即事重题

重裘暖帽宽毡履，小阁低窗深地炉。
身稳心安眠未起，西京朝士得知无？

《白居易集》，第 734 页。

TO A TALKATIVE GUEST
(A.D. 836)

再
造
的
镜
像

THE town visitor's easy talk flows in an endless stream;
The country host's quiet thoughts ramble timidly on.
'I beg you, Sir, do not tell me about things at Ch'ang-an;
For you entered just when my lute was tuned and lying balanced on my knees.'

赠谈客

上客清谈何亹亹？幽人闲思自寥寥。
请君休说长安事，膝上风清琴正调。

《白居易集》，第 746 页。

GOING TO THE MOUNTAINS WITH A LITTLE DANCING GIRL, AGED FIFTEEN

(Written when the poet was about sixty-five)

TWO top-knots not yet plaited into one.
Of thirty years—just beyond half.
You who are really a lady of silks and satins
Are now become my hill and stream companion!
At the spring fountains together we splash and play;
On the lovely trees together we climb and sport.

Her cheeks grow rosy, as she quickens her sleeve-dancing:
Her brows grow sad, as she slows her song's tune.
Don't go singing the Song of the Willow Branches,①
When there's no one here with a heart for you to break!

___

① A plaintive love-song, to which Po Chü-i had himself written words.

山游示小妓

双鬟垂未合。三十才过半。
本是绮罗人。今为山水伴。
春泉共挥弄。好树同攀玩。
笑容花底迷。酒思风前乱。
红凝舞袖急。黛惨歌声缓。
莫唱杨柳枝。无肠与君断。

《全唐诗》（第 14 册），第 5112—5113 页。

TO LIU YU-HSI

(A.D. 838)

IN length of days and soundness of limb you and I are one;
Our eyes are not wholly blind, nor our ears quite deaf.
Deep drinking we lie together, fellows of a spring day;
Or gay-hearted boldly break into gatherings of young men.
When, seeking flowers, we borrowed his horse, the Governor[①] was vexed;
When, to play on the water, we stole his boat, the Duke of Chin[②] was sore.
I hear it said that in Lo-yang people are all shocked,
And call us by the name of 'Liu and Po, those two mad old men.'

① The Governor of Lo-yang.
② Po's friend and patron P'ei Tu (A.D. 765-837).

再
造
的
镜
像

赠梦得

年颜老少与君同，眼未全昏耳未聋。
放醉卧为春日伴，趁欢行入少年丛。
寻花借马烦川守，弄水偷船恼令公。
闻道洛城人尽怪，呼为刘白二狂翁。

《白居易集》，第 756 页。

DREAMING OF YÜAN CHÊN

(A.D. 839)

AT night you came and took my hand and we wandered together in my dream;

When I woke in the morning there was no one to stop the tears that fell on my handkerchief.

At the Chang Inlet[①] your aged body three times passed through sickness;

At Hsien-yang[②] to the grasses on your grave eight autumns have come.

You—buried beneath the Springs, your bones mingled with clay;

I—lodging in the world of men, my hair white as snow.

A-wei and Han-lang[③] both followed in their turn;

Among the shadows of the Terrace of Night did you know them or not?

---

① Near Tang-yang, central Hupeh.

② Near Ch'ang-an, the capital.

③ Familiar names of Yüan Chên's son and son-in-law.

梦微之

夜来携手梦同游，晨起盈巾泪莫收。
漳浦老身三度病，咸阳宿草八回秋。
君埋泉下泥销骨，我寄人间雪满头。
阿卫韩郎相次去，夜台茫昧得知不？

《白居易集》，第 801 页。

MY SERVANT WAKES ME

(A.D. 839)

MY servant wakes me: 'Master, it is broad day.
Rise from bed; I bring you bowl and comb.
Winter comes and the morning air is chill;
Today your Honour must not venture abroad.'
When I stay at home, no one comes to call;
What must I do with the long, idle hours?
Setting my chair where a faint sunshine falls
I have warmed wine and opened my poetry books.

懒放二首，呈刘梦得、吴方之（其一）（节选）

青衣报平旦，呼我起盥栉：
今早天气寒，郎君应不出。
又无宾客至，何以销闲日？
已向微阳前，暖酒开诗帙。

《白居易集》，第 671 页。

SINCE I LAY ILL
(A.D. 840)

SINCE I lay ill, how long has passed?
Almost a hundred heavy-hanging days.
The maids have learnt to gather my medicine-herbs;
The dog no longer barks when the doctor comes.
The jars in my cellar are plastered deep with mould;
My singers' mats are half crumbled to dust.
How can I bear, when the Earth renews her light,
To watch from a pillow the beauty of Spring unfold?

卧疾来早晚

卧疾来早晚，悬悬将十旬。
婢能寻本草，犬不吠医人。
酒瓮全生醭，歌筵半委尘。
风光还欲好，争向枕前春。

《白居易集》，第 794—795 页。

ON HEARING SOMEONE SING A POEM BY YÜAN CHÊN

(Written long after Chên's death, *c.* A.D. 840)

NO new poems his brush will trace;

Even his fame is dead.

His old poems are deep in dust

At the bottom of boxes and cupboards.

Once lately, when someone was singing,

Suddenly I heard a verse—

Before I had time to catch the words

A pain had stabbed my heart.

再
造
的
镜
像

闻歌者唱微之诗

新诗绝笔声名歇，旧卷生尘箧笥深。
时向歌中闻一句，未容倾耳已伤心。

《白居易集》，第 701 页。

A DREAM OF MOUNTAINEERING

(Written when he was seventy)

AT night, in my dream, I stoutly climbed a mountain

Going out alone with my staff of holly-wood.

A thousand crags, a hundred hundred valleys—

In my dream-journey none were unexplored

And all the while my feet never grew tired

And my step was as strong as in my young days.

Can it be that when the mind travels backward

The body also returns to its old state?

And can it be, as between body and soul,

That the body may languish, while the soul is still strong?

Soul and body—both are vanities;

Dreaming and waking—both alike unreal.

In the day my feet are palsied and tottering;

In the night my steps go striding over the hills.

As day and night are divided in equal parts—

Between the two, I *get* as much as I *lose*.

梦上山

夜梦上嵩山，独携藜杖出；
千岩与万壑，游览皆周毕。
梦中足不病，健似少年日。
既悟神返初，依然旧形质。
始知形神内，形病神无疾。
形神两是幻，梦寐俱非实。
昼行虽蹇涩，夜步颇安逸。
昼夜既平分，其间何得失？

《白居易集》，第 823 页。

ILLNESS

(Written *c*. A.D. 842, when he was paralysed)

DEAR friends, there is no cause for so much sympathy.

I shall certainly manage from time to time to take my walks abroad.

All that matters is an active mind, what is the use of feet?

By land one can ride in a carrying-chair; by water, be rowed in a boat.

再
造
的
镜
像

病中五绝（其五）（节选）

交亲不要苦相忧，亦拟时时强出游。
但有心情何用脚？陆乘肩舆水乘舟。

《白居易集》，第 788—789 页。

THE PHILOSOPHERS
LAO TZŬ

再
造
的
镜
像

'THOSE who speak know nothing;
Those who know are silent.'
Those words, I am told,
Were spoken by Lao-tzŭ.
If we are to believe that Lao-tzŭ
Was himself one who knew,
How comes it that he wrote a book
Of five thousand words?

读《老子》

言者不知知者默，此语吾闻于老君。
若道老君是知者，缘何自著五千文？

《白居易集》，第 716 页。

CHUANG TZU, THE MONIST

CHUANG-TZU levels all things
And reduces them to the same Monad.
But I say that even in their sameness
Difference may be found.
Although in following the promptings of their nature
They display the same tendency,
Yet it seems to me that in some ways
A phoenix is superior to a reptile!

读《庄子》

庄生齐物同归一，我道同中有不同。
遂性逍遥虽一致，鸾凰终校胜蛇虫。

《白居易集》，第 716 页。

TAOISM AND BUDDHISM

(Written shortly before his death)

A TRAVELLER came from across the seas
Telling of strange sights.
'In a deep fold of the sea-hills
I saw a terrace and tower.
In the midst there stood a Fairy Temple
With one niche empty.
They all told me this was waiting
For Lo-t'ien to come.'

Traveller, I have studied the Empty Gate;[1]
I am no disciple of Fairies.
The story you have just told
Is nothing but an idle tale.
The hills of ocean shall never be
Lo-t'ien's home.
When I leave the earth it will be to go
To the Heaven of Bliss Fulfilled.[2]

---

[1] Buddhism. The poem is quite frivolous, as is shown by his claim to Bodhisattva-hood.

[2] The 'Tushita' Heaven, where Bodhisattvas wait till it is time for them to appear on earth as Buddhas.

客有说

近有人从海上回，海山深处见楼台：
中有仙龛虚一室，多传此待乐天来。

答客说

吾学空门非学仙，恐君此说是虚传。
海山不是吾归处，归即应归兜率天。

《白居易集》，第 840 页。

LAST POEM^①

THEY have put my bed beside the unpainted screen;
They have shifted my stove in front of the blue curtain.
I listen to my grandchildren reading me a book;
I watch the servants heating up my soup.
With rapid pencil I answer the poems of friends,
I feel in my pockets and pull out medicine-money.
When this superintendence of trifling affairs is done,
I lie back on my pillows and sleep with my face to the South.

---

① 韦利仅译了后八句。

自咏老身，示诸家属（节选）

寿及七十五，俸沾五十千。
夫妻偕老日，甥侄聚居年。
粥美尝新米，袍温换故绵。
家居虽濩落，眷属幸团圆。
置榻素屏下，移炉青帐前。
书听孙子读，汤看侍儿煎。
走笔还诗债，抽衣当药钱。
支分闲事了，把背向阳眠。

《白居易集》，第 855 页。

第五章　唐宋明诗词

导言

　　韦利在本书中，选编自己的唐诗译文，跳过王维、杜甫，点缀性地选了几首李白的诗，而以寒山、白居易的诗为主，是十分率性的选择。他毫不讳言，自己选入本书的标准，是译文的艺术成就，而非原诗的艺术成就，关心的是，他个人的翻译作品作为"英诗"，是否已经达到英诗的审美要求，是否可以立足于英文诗歌之林。他翻译中国诗，是诗人译诗，并不考虑如何呈现中国诗歌的全貌，随意性很大。在相当程度上，是"借他人酒杯，浇自己块垒"，企图通过翻译，展现自己蕴藏在心底的诗情。

　　本书选取唐宋明诗歌作品，基本上循着 1941 年美国插图版《中国文学译丛》（*Translations from the Chinese*，此书扉页有"译自中国文"五个汉字）的最后部分，不过，删去了不属于诗词的元稹《莺莺传》与白行简《李娃传》。有趣的是，韦利还删了一首苏轼的《洗儿戏作》，不知道是否因为此诗充满了自我调侃的黑色幽默，又有一种海阔天空的豪气，与自己译诗的性格不合，难以掌握原诗的谐趣，干脆摒弃了苏轼，却补上一首冯梦龙的情歌。这一部分选录了他译的元稹、欧阳修、陆游、陈子龙等人的作品，显得零零星星，像蜻蜓点水轻飘飘地掠过唐宋明诗歌的水面。

　　不过，韦利对自己的翻译作品，还是十分自豪的。他在 1941 年插图版《中国文学译丛》的序文中说："或许会有专家来挑刺，不过，我希望，不会有太多误导一般读者之处。想要毫无瑕疵地理解千多年来的作品，不是件容易的事，然而，我的中国友人向我保证，我的翻译十分贴近原文。他们有时还很客气地说，比所有其他译者都贴切。"又过了二十年，在编选本书时，韦利还做了少许更动与润色，想来在他自己心目中，应该更贴近原作的诗情了。

古诗英汉对照

THE PITCHER[1]
By YÜAN CHÊN
(A.D. 779-831)

I DREAMT I climbed to a high, high plain;
And on the plain I found a deep well.
My throat was dry with climbing and I longed to drink,
And my eyes were eager to look into the cool shaft.
I walked round it, I looked right down;
I saw my image mirrored on the face of the pool.
An earthen pitcher was sinking into the black depths;
There was no rope to pull it to the well-head.
I was strangely troubled lest the pitcher should be lost,
And started wildly running to look for help.
From village to village I scoured that high plain;
The men were gone; fierce dogs snarled.
I came back and walked weeping round the well;
Faster and faster the blinding tears flowed—
Till my own sobbing suddenly woke me up;
My room was silent, no one in the house stirred.
The flame of my candle flickered with a green smoke;
The tears I had shed glittered in the candle-light.
A bell sounded; I knew it was the midnight-chime;
I sat up in bed and tried to arrange my thoughts:
The plain in my dream was the graveyard at Ch'ang-an,
Those hundred acres of untilled land.
The soil heavy and the mounds heaped high;
And the dead below them laid in deep troughs.
Deep are the troughs, yet sometimes dead men
Find their way to the world above the grave.
And to-night my love who died long ago
Came into my dream as the pitcher sunk in the well.
That was why the tears suddenly streamed from my eyes,
Streamed from my eyes and fell on the collar of my dress.

---

① 韦利未译最后十句。

梦井

〔唐〕元稹

梦上高高原，原上有深井。
登高意枯渴，愿见深泉冷。
裴回绕井顾，自照泉中影。
沉浮落井瓶，井上无悬绠。
念此瓶欲沉，荒忙为求请。
遍入原上村，村空犬仍猛。
还来绕井哭，哭声通复哽。
哽噎梦忽惊，觉来房舍静。
灯焰碧胧胧，泪光凝炯炯。
钟声夜方半，坐卧心难整。
忽忆咸阳原，荒田万余顷。
土厚圹亦深，埋魂在深埂。
埂深安可越？魂通有时逞。
今宵泉下人，化作瓶相警。
感此涕汍澜，汍澜涕沾领。
所伤觉梦间，便隔死生境。
岂无同穴期，生期谅绵永。
又恐前后魂，安能两知省？
寻环意无极，坐见天将晒。
吟此《梦井》诗，春朝好光景。

《元稹集》，第 100—101 页。

THE LADY AND THE MAGPIE

(Anon. Ninth Century A.D., written on the back of a Buddhist scripture)

'LUCKY magpie, holy bird, what hateful lies you tell!
Prove, if you can, that ever once your coming brought good luck.
Once too often you have come, and this time I have caught you
And shut you up in a golden cage, and will not let you talk.'
'Lady, I came with kind intent and truly bring you joy;
Little did I think you would hold me fast and lock me in a golden cage.
If you really want that far-off man to come quickly home,
Set me free; I will bear him word, flying through the grey clouds.'

雀踏枝

　　叵耐灵鹊多满语，送喜何曾有凭据？几度飞来活捉取，锁上金笼休共语。

　　比拟好心来送喜，谁知锁我在金笼里。欲他征夫早归来，腾身却放我向青云里。

《敦煌拾零》，第 16 页。

A PROTEST IN THE SIXTH YEAR OF CH'IEN FU (A.D. 879)

By TS'AO SUNG

(*c.* A.D. 830-910)

THE hills and rivers of the lowland country
You have made your battle-ground,
How do you suppose the people who live there
Will procure 'firewood and hay'[①]?
Do not let me hear you talking together
About titles and promotions;
For a single general's reputation
Is made out of ten thousand corpses.

---

① The necessities of life.

己亥岁二首·僖宗广明元年（其一）

〔唐〕曹松

泽国江山入战图，生民何计乐樵苏。
凭君莫话封侯事，一将功成万骨枯。

《全唐诗》（第 21 册），第 8237 页。

IMMEASURABLE PAIN

By Li HOU-CHU, last Emperor of the Southern T'ang Dynasty
(deposed in A.D. 975)

IMMEASURABLE pain!
My dreaming soul last night was king again.
As in past days
I wandered through the Palace of Delight,
And in my dream
Down grassy garden-ways
Glided my chariot, smoother than a summer stream;
There was moonlight,
The trees were blossoming,
And a faint wind softened the air of night,
For it was spring.

再
造
的
镜
像

望江南

〔南唐〕李煜

多少恨，昨夜梦魂中。还似旧时游上苑，车如流水马如龙。花月正春风。

《全唐五代词》，第 746 页。

THE CICADA
By OU-YANG HSIU
(A.D. 1007-1072)

In the summer of the first year of Chia-yu (A.D. 1056), there was a great flood. By order of the Emperor I went to the Wine Spring Temple to pray for fine weather, when I heard a cicada singing. Upon which subject I wrote this poem:

HUSHED was the courtyard of the temple;
Solemn stood I, gazing
At the bright roofs and gables,
The glorious summits of that towering shrine.
Untroubled were my thoughts, intently prayed
My fasting soul, for every wandering sense
Was gathered to its home.
Unmoved I watched the motions of the world,
Saw deep into the nature of ten thousand things.
Suddenly the rain was over, no wind stirred
The morning-calm; round all the sky
Was cloudless blue, and the last thunder rolled.
Then we, to strew sweet-scented herbs upon the floor,
Drew near the coloured cloister, by whose side
Some old trees grew amid the grass
Of the deserted court. Here was a thing that cried
Upon a tree-top, sucking the shrill wind
To wail it back in a long whistling note—
That clasping in its arms
A tapering twig perpetually sighed,
Now shrill as flute, now soft as mandolin,
Sometimes a piercing cry
Choked at its very uttering, sometimes a cold tune
Dwindled to silence, then suddenly flowed again,
A single note, wandering in strange keys,
An air, yet fraught
With undertone of hidden harmony.
'What creature can this be?' 'Cicada is its name.'
'Are you not he, cicada,
Of whom I have heard told you can transform
Your body, magically moulding it
To new estate? Are you not he who, born
Upon the dung-heap, coveted the sky,
The clean and open air;
Found wings to mount the wind, yet skyward sailing

鸣蝉赋并序

〔北宋〕欧阳修

嘉祐元年夏。大雨水。奉诏祈晴于醴泉宫。闻鸣蝉有感而赋云。

肃祠庭以祗事兮。瞻玉宇之峥嵘。收视听以清虑兮。斋予心以荐诚。因以静而求动兮。见乎万物之情。于时朝雨骤止。微风不兴。四无云以青天。雷曳曳其余声。乃席芳药。临华轩。古木数株。空庭草间。爰有一物。鸣于树颠。引清风以长啸。抱纤柯而永叹。嘒嘒非管。泠泠若弦。裂方号而复咽。凄欲断而还连。吐孤韵以难律。含五音之自然。吾不知其何物。其名曰蝉。岂非因物造形能变化者邪。出自粪壤慕清虚者邪。凌风高飞知所止者邪。

Upon a leafy tree-top checked your flight,
Pleased with its trim retreat? Are you not he
Who with the dew for drink, the wind for food,
Grows never old nor languid; who with looped locks
Frames womanish beauty;
Again your voice, cicada!
Not grave; not gay; part Lydian,
Part Dorian your tune that, suddenly begun,
Suddenly ceases.
Long since have I marvelled
How of ten thousand creatures there is not one
But has its tune; how, as each season takes its turn,
A hundred new birds sing, each weather wakes
A hundred insects from their sleep.
Now lisp the mango-birds
Like pretty children, prattling at their play.
As shuttle at the sounding loom
The tireless cricket creaks. Beautiful the flexions
Of tongue and trilling throat, how valiantly
They spend themselves to do it!
And even the croakers of the pond,
When they get rain to fill
Their miry, parching puddles, while they sip
New rivulets and browse the soppy earth,
Sing through the live-long night. And like enough
May frogs be passionate; but oh, what seeks
The silent worm in song?[①]
These and a thousand others, little and great,
Too many to name them all,
Myriads of creatures—each after its own shape and kin,
Hold at their season ceaseless tournament of song;
But swiftly, swiftly
Their days run out, time transmutes them, and there is silence,
Desert-silence where they sang.

---

① All through the winter and spring the worm lives underground. On the first night of summer it issues and, in the thrill of its second birth, begins to sing in a shrill, woman's voice. It sings all night, and then is silent for ever.

嘉木茂树喜清阴者邪。呼吸风露能尸解者邪。绰约双鬟修婵娟者邪。其为声也。不乐不哀。非宫非徵。胡然而鸣。亦胡然而止。吾尝悲夫万物莫不好鸣。若乃四时代谢。百鸟嘤兮。一气候至。百虫惊兮。娇儿姹女。语鹂庚兮。鸣机络纬。响蟋蟀兮。转喉哳舌。诚可爱兮。引腹动股。岂勉强而为之兮。至于污池浊水。得雨而聒兮。饮泉食土。长夜而歌兮。彼虾蟆固若有欲。而蚯蚓又何求兮。其余大小万状。不可悉名。各有气类。随其物形。不知自止。有若争能。忽时变以物改。咸漠然而无声。

Alas, philosophy has taught

That the transcending mind in its strange, level world

Sees not kinds, contraries, classes or degrees.

And if of living things

Man once seemed best, what has he but a knack

Of facile speech, what but a plausible scheme

Of signs and ciphers that perpetuate

His thoughts and phrases? And on these expends

His brooding wits, consumes his vital breath—

One droning out the extremity of his woe,

Another to the wide world publishing

His nobleness of heart!

Thus, though he shares

The brief span of all creatures, yet his song

A hundred ages echoes after him.

But you, cicada,

What know you of this! Only for yourself

You make your music...'

So was I pondering, comparing,

Setting difference by difference, gain by gain,

When suddenly the clouds came back and overhead

The storm blazed and crashed, spilling huge drops

Out of the rumbling sky...

And silent now

Was the cicada's voice.

呜呼。达士所齐。万物一类。人于其间。所以为贵。盖已巧其语言。又能传于文字。是以穷彼思虑。耗其血气。或吟哦其穷愁。或发扬其志意。虽共尽于万物。乃长鸣于百世。予亦安知其然哉。聊为乐以自喜。方将考得失。较同异。俄而阴云复兴。雷电俱击。大雨既作。蝉声遂息。

《欧阳修全集》（上），第 110—111 页。

THE PEDLAR OF SPELLS

By LU YU

(A.D. 1125-1210)

AN old man selling charms in a cranny of the town wall;
He writes out spells to bless the silkworms and spells to protect the corn.
With the money he gets each day he only buys wine;
But he does not worry when his legs get wobbly, for he has a boy to lean on.

初夏

〔南宋〕陆游

老翁卖卜古城隅。兼写宜蚕保麦符。
日日得钱惟买酒。不愁醉倒有儿扶。

《陆放翁全集》，第 505 页。

BOATING IN AUTUMN

By LU YU

AWAY and away I sail in my light boat;

My heart leaps with a great gust of joy.

Through the leafless branches I see the temple in the wood,

Over the dwindling stream the stone bridge towers.

Down the grassy lanes sheep and oxen pass;

In the misty village cranes and magpies cry.

Back in my home I drink a cup of wine

And need not fear the greed① of the evening wind.

---

① Which 'eats' men.

泛舟

〔南宋〕陆游

去去泛轻舠。飘然兴自豪。
叶凋山寺出。溪瘦石桥高。
草径牛羊下。烟村鹳鹤号。
还家一杯酒。未畏暮风饕。

《陆放翁全集》，第 423 页。

THE HERD-BOY

By LU YU

IN the southern village the boy who minds the ox
With his naked feet stands on the ox's back.
Through the hole in his coat the river wind blows;
Through his broken hat the mountain rain pours.
On the long dyke he seemed to be far away;
In the narrow lane suddenly we were face to face.

———

The boy is home and the ox is back in its stall;
And a dark smoke oozes through the thatched roof.

牧牛儿

〔南宋〕陆游

南村牧牛儿。赤脚踏牛立。
衣穿江风冷。笠败山雨急。
长陂望若远。隘巷忽相及。
儿归牛入栏。烟火茆檐湿。

《陆放翁全集》，第 433 页。

HOW I SAILED ON THE LAKE TILL I CAME TO THE EASTERN STREAM
By LU YU

再
造
的
镜
像

OF Spring water—thirty or forty miles;
In the evening sunlight—three or four houses.
Youths and boys minding geese and ducks;
Women and girls tending mulberries and hemp.
The place—remote, their coats and scarves old;
The year—fruitful, their talk and laughter gay.
The old wanderer moors his flat boat
And staggers up the bank to pluck wistaria flowers.[1]

---

① To make a rustic wine.

泛湖至东泾

〔南宋〕陆游

春水六七里。夕阳三四家。
儿童牧鹅鸭。妇女治桑麻。
地僻衣巾古。年丰笑语哗。
老夫维小艇。半醉摘藤花。

《陆放翁全集》，第 378 页。

LOVE-POEM

By FÊNG MÊNG-LUNG

(*c.* 1590-1646)

DON'T set sail!

The wind is rising and the weather none too good.

Far better come back to my house.

If there is anything you want, just tell me.

If you are cold, my body is warm.

Let us be happy together this one night.

Tomorrow the wind will have dropped;

Then you can go, and I shan't worry about you.

江儿水

〔明〕冯梦龙

　　郎莫开船者！西风又大了些！不如依旧还奴舍。郎要东西和奴说。郎身若冷奴身热，且受用而今这一夜。明日风和，便去也奴心安帖。

《中国韵文史》，第 138—139 页。

THE LITTLE CART
By CH'ÊN TZŬ-LUNG
(A.D. 1608-1647)

再
造
的
镜
像

THE little cart jolting and banging through the yellow haze of dusk;

The man pushing behind, the woman pulling in front.

They have left the city and do not know where to go.

'Green, green, those elm-tree leaves; *they* will cure my hunger,

If only we could find some quiet place and sup on them together.'

The wind has flattened the yellow mother-wort;

Above it in the distance they see the walls of a house.

'There surely must be people living who'll give you something to eat.'

They tap at the door, but no one comes; they look in, but the kitchen is empty.

They stand hesitating in the lonely road and their tears fall like rain.

小车行

〔明〕陈子龙

　　小车斑斑黄尘晚，夫为推，妇为挽。出门何所之？青青者榆疗吾饥，愿得乐土共哺糜。风吹黄蒿，望见墙宇，中有主人当饲汝。叩门无人室无釜，踯躅空巷泪如雨。

《明诗选》，第 217 页。

作者情况资料

郑培凯

　　台湾大学外文系毕业，耶鲁大学历史学博士，哈佛大学费正清研究中心博士后。曾任教于纽约州立大学、耶鲁大学、佩斯大学、台湾大学、新竹清华大学等校，1998 年到香港城市大学创立中国文化中心，任中心主任，推展多元互动的中国文化通识教育。历任香港非物质文化遗产咨询委员会主席、香港集古学社社长、浙江大学客座教授、台湾逢甲大学特约讲座教授、香港康乐及文化事务署专家顾问、港台文化合作委员会委员、复旦大学文史研究院学术委员会委员等。2016 年获颁香港政府荣誉勋章。

　　著作所涉学术范围甚广，以文化意识史、文化审美、经典翻译及文化变迁与交流为主。近年出版的著作有：《汤显祖：戏梦人生与文化求索》《多元文化与审美情趣》《历史人物与文化变迁》《文化审美与艺术鉴赏》《妙笔缘来》《在乎山水之间》《游于艺：跨文化美食》《遨游于艺》《高尚的快乐》《谁共我醉明月》等。策划并主编"青青子衿"名家学术系列、史景迁作品（12 种）、近代海外汉学名著丛刊（百种）等。

　　其他已出版著作有：《汤显祖与晚明文化》《出土的愉悦》《真理愈辩愈昏》《树倒猢狲散之后》《在纽约看电影：电影与中国文化变迁》《吹笛到天明》《流觞曲水的感怀》《茶香与美食的记忆》《跳舞的螃蟹，明前的茶》《茶余酒后金瓶梅》《行脚八方》《迷死人的故事》《雅言与俗语》《品味的记忆》等。主编文化遗产与非文化遗产的著作，以昆曲、外销陶瓷、茶文化为主，有《口传心授与文化传承——非物质文化遗产：文献、现状与讨论》《文苑奇葩汤显祖》《袅晴丝吹来闲庭院》《陶瓷下西洋研究索引：十二至十五世纪中国陶瓷与中外贸易》《陶瓷下西洋：十二至十五世纪中国外销瓷》《逐波泛海：十六至十七世纪中国陶瓷外销与物质文明扩散》《陶瓷下西洋研究索引：十六至十七世纪中国陶瓷与中外贸易》《茶饮天地宽：茶文化与茶具的审美境界》《茶与中国文化：茶文化、茶科学、茶产业》《茶道的开始——茶经》等十余种。另主编《九州岛学林》季刊、《中国历代茶书汇编（校注本）》（合编）、*The Search for Modern China: A Documentary Collection*（《现代中国寻踪：文献汇编》，合编）、《中国文化导读》（合编）等。

鄢秀

上海外国语大学英语系毕业，得克萨斯大学（奥斯汀）博士。现任教于香港城市大学翻译及语言学系，翻译硕士科目主任，博士生导师。其他任职有：香港高等教育妇女协会会长、香港语常委（SCOLAR）项目评审委员会委员，并为多个出版社及国际期刊担任评审与编辑。致力建设共融教室，开发视障人士语言学习的教材，2021 年获日内瓦国际发明展银奖。

长期致力于翻译、语言教学的实证研究以及经典翻译的研究。曾获科研经费资助，主持大量研究计划；在多种国际学术刊物发表论文。著作及译著包括《论语英译及诠释》（译著）、*Research on Translator and Interpreter Training: A Collective Volume of Bibliometric Reviews and Empirical Studies on Learners*（《口笔译训练：文献计量分析及习者实证研究》），主编《文化认同与语言焦虑》，史景迁中国系列英译《前朝梦忆：张岱的浮华与苍凉》《康熙：重构一位皇帝的内心世界》《雍正王朝之大义觉迷》《太平天国》《大汗之国：西方眼中的中国》《王氏之死：大历史背后的小人物命运》《胡若望的疑问》《利玛窦的记忆宫殿》《曹寅与康熙：一个皇帝宠臣的生涯揭秘》《改变中国：在中国的西方顾问》《中国纵横：一个汉学家的学术探索之旅》等。

再造的镜像